ELEANOR

By the same author

Morning
A Letter
Memoir in the Middle of the Journey
Gabriel Young
Tug-of-War
Hounds of Spring
Happy Endings
Revolution Island
Gentleman's Gentleman
Memories of my Mother
Rules of Life
Cautionary Tales for Women
Hope Cottage
Best Friends
Small Change

ELEANOR

by

JULIAN FANE

CONSTABLE · LONDON

First published in Great Britain 1993
by Constable & Company Limited
3 The Lanchesters, 162 Fulham Palace Road
London W6 9ER
Copyright © Julian Fane 1993
The right of Julian Fane to be
identified as the author of this work
has been asserted by him in accordance
with the Copyright, Designs and Patents Act 1988
ISBN 0 09 472710 4
Set in Monophoto Poliphilus 12pt by
Servis Filmsetting Ltd, Manchester
Printed in Great Britain by
St Edmundsbury Press Limited
Bury St Edmunds, Suffolk

A CIP catalogue record for this book
is available from the British Library

1905 . . .

ON a sunny morning in November a hansom cab drew up outside a house in a northern suburb of London, and a middle-aged woman carrying a baby and a suitcase emerged from it and hurried indoors.

The hansom had conveyed the woman and child from a smart residence in Chelsea to 14 Summer Drive, Willesden, a smaller humbler dwelling. The cabbie turned his horse, which was sweating and obviously tired, and let it walk back towards central London between the autumnal lines of Summer Drive's young plane trees.

Meanwhile the front door with stained glass panels of number 14 was closed by the same hand, invisible from the street, that had opened it.

In the hall of the house another middle-aged woman, wearing an apron over her dress, embraced the one in outdoor clothes and exclaimed: 'Oh I am glad to have you home!'

Then she asked in a less anxious tone of voice, smiling with tender impatience: 'Well – can I see her?'

The two women were sisters, called Louisa and Helen Carty, Lou and Nell for short. Lou was the elder by three years, physically spare, and a competent sort of person. Nell was plump, with rosy cheeks and an excitable manner.

Lou, in answer to Nell's question, rearranged the fine white shawl enveloping the sleeping baby and so revealed her face.

Nell studied it for a moment and remarked wonderingly: 'She's beautiful.'

Lou said: 'She's good too. She's a lovely good little girl. But has she got a will of her own! And a voice to go with it! You hold her while I take these things off.'

The baby was transferred into Nell's open arms, and Lou removed her respectable old-fashioned blue bonnet and lightweight loose blue overcoat. Her dress was severely grey in colour, but had a pretty white collar and white cuffs.

The sound of children's voices was audible.

Lou inquired, gesturing with her head towards the back parts of the house: 'Are they all right?'

'Oh yes. But they did miss you. They can't have heard you arrive – they're longing to see you – they're in the garden with Donald.' Nell interrupted her contemplation of the baby's beauty, raised her guileless blue eyes and added: 'You must be tired. Would you like a cup of tea?'

'I'd rather just sit down before meeting the multitude,' Lou replied, leading the way into the parlour, the front room on the right-hand side of the hall. It had a lace-curtained bow window, an aspidistra, an upright piano and smelt of furniture polish.

Nell stood in front of the unlit fir-cone fire and asked, rocking the baby: 'Did you have a hard time?'

'Not specially. But it's always sad in the end.'

'What was Mrs B. like?'

'Very pretty.'

'Was she unhappy?'

'More worried – she was afraid baby would be late.'

'Where was Mr Beck?'

'Abroad – he's been abroad for a month – he gets back tomorrow.'

'No sign of the other interested party?'

'No, nothing.'

'But you were paid properly?'

'Yes. I'll have to take the cash to the bank tomorrow. About upstairs, Nell: I've been thinking that Jane and Matilda are old enough to move up in the world. They didn't disturb you while you were sleeping in my bed, did they? If they were to move in with you in the attic, our new little visitor could spread herself in my bedroom.'

[6]

Inconsequently Nell whispered: 'She's opening her eyes now.'

'In that case I'd better find her something to eat, or there'll be trouble. Shall we introduce her to the others?'

'What a pet! Hullo, dearie,' Nell was cooing at the baby.

Lou had risen to her feet and was making for the door.

'What's her Christian name?' Nell, following her sister, asked.

'First name, because she hasn't much chance of being christened,' Lou said correctively, and then: 'Mrs B. wouldn't call her anything. The name for her in my mind is Eleanor.'

'Oh but won't she become another Nell, like me?'

'I don't believe she will.'

The 'multitude' that Louisa Carty was not immediately ready to meet, those 'others' in the garden of 14 Summer Drive to whom the baby would be introduced, were Donald Wilson aged eleven, Michael Janes aged eight, April Studbrook aged six, Willy Hopkins aged five, and the twins Matilda and Jane Lovejoy aged three and a half.

The Carty sisters employed, and had rendered almost traditional, certain figures of speech: for instance 'multitude' to describe the children they looked after, and 'moving up in the world' as a description of a child's removal from a bedroom on the first to a bedroom on the top floor of the house. Lou with her dry ironic humour had probably invented such phrases; but Nell laughed at them in the first place and had recourse to them thereafter.

The house occupied by the two women and the six children, seven including baby Eleanor, was some twenty years old. It was one of the seventy-five homes with Summer Drive addresses, built in the last years of the reign of Queen Victoria when the completed rail link brought thousands of new residents to the village of Willesden.

The exterior of number 14 was mainly yellow brick, but red bricks in fancy patterns round the doorway and windows gave it a touch of distinction. A picket fence, originally painted white, enclosed the front garden, where lavender grew alongside the crazy-paved path to the door with the stained glass panels, and tea-roses in the beds edging the patch of lawn. The gate in the fence had rusty sprung hinges which closed it automatically, and a patent safety latch.

The larger garden behind the house was walled and to all intents and purposes child-proof. The fact that there was no tradesman's entrance or access to the back door suited the Carty sisters, who were always afraid a charge of theirs would escape into the road and be lost. Part of this garden was bricked; grass was either downtrodden or tussocky, and had a discouraging tendency to turn into mud; and the part at the bottom, beyond the sandpit and the privet hedge, was devoted to the cultivation of vegetables and fruit. The more architectural features were a potting-shed, a corrugated iron lean-to or so-called summer house, a rabbit hutch, several posts to which washing lines could be attached, a double swing made of iron, and a see-saw.

Every Tuesday morning Mr Bees pedalled his bicycle along Summer Drive, stopped at number 14, opened the picket gate and let it slam shut after he had wheeled his bike through, leant the bike against the fence, removed his trouser-clips and his cap, knocked on the door and shouted in the face of one Carty sister or the other: 'All present and correct!'

Mr Bees was an old soldier and the local jobbing gardener and handy-man. Lou and Nell would scold him for doing his best to deafen them and destroy their gate, but he took no notice. His egoism amused them, he was useful to the point of indispensability, and good with the children. He supervised the deliveries of coal through the manhole in the pavement and the sloping chute into the cellar. He filled hods with coal for the kitchen range. He painted and plumbed and tilled the garden. He carried his gardening equipment – a trowel, shears and string – in his knapsack with his sandwiches and bottle of cold tea. He had served in the Indian army, and he treated the children like his native troops. He would drill them in the garden for a treat, and his unintelligible curses provoked happy laughter.

He looked a bit Indian himself with his brown sun-dried complexion and white moustaches. Although he seemed to listen to nothing that was said to him, sooner or later he would get round to answering questions and doing whatever he was asked to do: it was as if he needed time in which to stand on his dignity.

[8]

Other callers at 14 Summer Drive were Ken the milkman, Sid the butcher's boy, Mr Skate the baker, and Henry Menny the postman. The children were extremely interested in the activities of the members of this quartet, possibly because they were the bearers of desirable items, food and mail, or possibly and simply because of their sex.

Henry Menny was welcomed not only by the children. Lou or Nell would sometimes ask him in for a cup of tea and a slice of cake, for instance after he had delivered one of those registered letters they had been waiting for. They were also pleased with him for minding his own business: he never pried into the whys and wherefores of the letters and parcels addressed to the young people with different names in the care of the Miss Cartys. In the month of December he would knock on the front door with a sackful of parcels over his shoulder and then be almost hauled indoors: each child was eager to know if this lovable version of Father Christmas had brought him or her anything, and the Carty sisters were equally determined not to give the neighbours grounds for still more gossip.

Throughout the year on Mondays, Wednesdays and Fridays Miss Elmes clocked in at 9 a.m. to teach the younger residents at 14 Summer Drive their three Rs. On Tuesday afternoons and evenings Mrs Cruse taught piano and singing, and on Saturdays Mr Svenson, who was a superannuated Swede, but frightfully fit, came to give a PT lesson and occasionally to take the boys to play football or cricket in the Recreation Ground.

The toys that arrived in parcels for the children were played with in the room opposite the parlour, that is to the left of the front door as you entered the house. The passage beside the staircase led to the kitchen, larder, pantry, scullery, and out past the 'men's' W.C. and through the backdoor into the garden. On the first floor were Lou's bedroom, another bedroom in which April Studbrook and Willy Hopkins presently slept, and a bathroom with lavatory. Nell had one of the two attic bedrooms, and Donald Wilson and Michael Janes the other.

Louisa Carty walked briskly ahead of her sister through the house and opened the backdoor. She called out in a light encouraging enthusiastic voice.

Donald Wilson in the garden meant that the other children were unlikely to have come to harm. He had been nicknamed 'the father of the family' by his Aunty Lou. From the earliest age he was paternalistic and protective of everyone at 14 Summer Drive, grown-ups included. He was a big boy for his eleven years with close-cropped spiky hair, a round face, a solemn expression and a sweetly transforming smile. He attended Dr Mackenzie's Day School down by Willesden Green and was meant to be going to a boarding school in due course.

It was typical of Donald that, in response to Aunty Lou's greeting, he waved and then rendered assistance to the twins, Jane and Matilda, who were shrieking excitedly and stumbling out of the sandpit.

April Studbrook and Willy Hopkins abandoned their beloved see-saw and ran towards Aunty Lou, and Michael Janes strode in her direction, declaring plaintively that no one had told him she had arrived.

She bent over with arms outstretched to embrace April and Willy and the twins, and finished on her knees on the bricks outside the backdoor. She was laughing, they were all laughing, and she was saying: 'Hullo, my dears! Oh what a hug! Oh what a great big hug! How nice to be with you again!' She stood up, reached out a hand to pat the cheek of Michael, and laid her other hand on Donald's shoulder and said to him: 'Thank you for helping Aunty Nell,' at which the boy grinned with sheepish pleasure.

Nell, meanwhile, had emerged through the back door into the sunshine.

The twin Matilda, who was noted for her inability to control the volume of her voice, yelled: 'Look at the baby!'

The children crowded round, were told not to touch, let alone tug, but were allowed to peep at the baby's face, and began to ask questions.

'Is it a boy?'

'Not "it" – she's a girl.'

'What's her name?'

'Eleanor.'

'Where did you get her?'

'I found her under a gooseberry bush.'

'What's her other name?'

The sisters exchanged a perplexed glance, and Nell said: 'Her surname's

[10]

the same as ours, though we're not related – she's Eleanor Carty, and proud of it.'

'Can I hold her?'

'In a minute, dear, when she's been fed.'

Now voices chorused: 'She's waking up – yawning – she's going to cry – what a racket!'

The baby was carried indoors. Half an hour later Nell admitted the other children into the kitchen. Eleanor's response to their curious overtures was to grip and squeeze the fingers of various sizes she was offered. Eventually she was taken upstairs by Lou to the first-floor bedroom they would share, and put to rest in the double-cot which had been the preserve of Jane and Matilda.

So Eleanor's sojourn in her first home began.

Before she knew much about it or anything else, some eighteen months after she swapped the gooseberry bush for her cosy billet, fortune smiled on April Studbrook, and consequently reminded her young companions that they were still frowned upon.

April's story differed from those frequently enacted at 14 Summer Drive – it had a happy ending. Most began with Henry Menny, the postman, bringing a written communication to a child, or to his or her Aunty Lou. The next act of the little drama, as observed by neighbours, was the arrival of a lady more richly dressed than the average housewife of Willesden. She was apt to be youngish and evincing signs of agitation. On rare occasions she would be accompanied by a gentleman, but usually she was on her own. She – or they – might have travelled by train, and either walked or come in a cab from the station, carrying shopping bags; sometimes they had driven all the way from central London in a grand equipage. Then the front door of the Carty house would open, a child white-faced with excitement would run into the lady's arms, and be taken out for a meal, a jaunt, a day, finishing up with more or less tearful kisses goodbye on the doorstep.

There were variations on the theme of such events. Ladies often wanted to speak to a Carty sister. Some ladies removed children for too long, others for too short a time. But the situations created indoors, in the hearts of the inhabitants of number 14, were mainly distressing before and after such visits. The anticipatory joys of the child to be visited were outweighed by the envious sorrows of the rest. The child who had again been abandoned was seldom completely consoled by the contents of those shopping bags, and his or her melancholy was infectious.

Lou and Nell dreaded the wretched rigmarole of interviews in their parlour with ladies anguished or angry, pleading poverty, apportioning blame, and then the task of – as it were – clearing up the latest emotional messes they had made and left behind them.

If the Cartys had been less compassionate and self-denying, they would have wished such ladies to keep well away from their charges, natural feelings notwithstanding.

But once in a blue moon an exception, that is to say a visit doing more good than harm, proved the rule.

April Studbrook was an almost albino, shy, gentle, lisping slip of a six-year-old girl. She had white eyelashes and straight waist-length hair. Despite the loving efforts of Aunty Lou and Aunty Nell, and although she was the object of the affections of Willy Hopkins, who shared her bedroom and spent hours sitting on the other end of the see-saw for her sake, she had never really settled down at number 14. She spent every fourth Wednesday, from eleven o'clock in the morning until early afternoon, driving round, having lunch, receiving presents and caresses, with and from a certain Mrs Wale.

Catherine Wale was a pale and thin young woman in her mid-twenties, well-to-do, emotional, not to say hysterical, and the mother of April. The unintended consequence of her maternal attentions was that her daughter's frail psyche was torn to shreds between hope and despair, misunderstanding and doubt. Every other fortnight of April's life was to some extent wasted in looking forward to the red-letter day of reunion, the next fortnight was likewise a waste of homesickness of a special kind, and all the time she wondered why she was not allowed to live with her mother, and vice versa, what were the secrets she was too young to be told, and who and where was her father.

On a particular Wednesday morning Mrs Wale arrived at Summer Drive in an array of widow's weeds. She was in mourning for a dear friend, she told April, who did not know what she was talking about, but was especially glad to see the sparkle in her mother's eyes.

Mrs Wale wore black for three months, while she put on weight, roses bloomed upon her cheeks, she shed no more tears when she said goodbye to April, and on a couple of occasions returned her to the care of the Cartys an hour earlier than usual.

Then, on the day on which fortune doled out its rough justice or injustice, April was subjected to a grooming unusually rigorous even by the high standards of Aunty Lou, who explained: 'Your mother wants you to be looking your nicest.'

Then April was detained in the kitchen by Aunty Nell while Aunty Lou went to answer the knock on the front door – another break with custom.

By the time April was summoned into the parlour she was in an apprehensive state, and was dismayed still further by the sight of a strange fair-complexioned man standing beside her mother.

She stopped in the doorway and her lower lip began to tremble.

Her mother crossed over, knelt down, embraced her and said: 'Oh please be happy, my darling. This is George Studbrook, this is your father. He's asked me to be his wife. We'll be married soon, and then you can come and live with us. And we're emigrating, darling, we'll all be Americans, we're going to start again in America – isn't it exciting? Please kiss your father, April – he's the best man in the whole world, the most patient and the truest. In just a little while we'll be able to be together – think of it – and we'll live happily ever after!'

Whereupon the three members of the future family unit cried and mingled their tears, George Studbrook having also sunk onto his knees in order to be kissed by and to kiss his new-found daughter.

Six weeks later Mr and Mrs Studbrook drove out to Willesden to fetch April, who was waiting impatiently in her best clothes in the parlour. As soon as she heard the sound of horse's hooves, she called Aunty Lou and Aunty Nell, embraced them, thanked them, begged them to open the front door, and ran down the garden path carrying her worldly goods in a small suitcase – she had already said farewell to her former playmates. Her parents and the Carty sisters bade one another goodbye by the garden gate, and the Studbrooks departed, laughing and briefly waving.

The reverse side of the medal of this merry scene showed Willy Hopkins sitting on the grounded end of the see-saw in the garden and blubbing with a red face, the twins boo-hooing in sympathy, and Michael Janes refusing to be cheered up by Donald Wilson's unselfish offer of a game of catch.

Louisa Carty was a trained nurse and midwife.

She had begun her career on the basis of recommendations from doctors, who had come across her in hospital before she was fully qualified: they would tell their better-off pregnant patients that she could be relied upon to see them through their lying-in and first weeks of motherhood.

Thanks to her charm, efficiency and loving kindness, she was soon working throughout the year in one house after another for the conventional period of a month. She made friends with her ladies. She returned to some of them at approximately annual intervals as each new baby was born. She had hardly any time to spend at home in Kilburn with her parents and her only sibling and younger sister Nell.

She was under considerable pressure to work and earn money. Her father John Carty, ex-bank clerk, had married late and was now dying of some mysterious creeping paralysis, and her mother Marian was a nervous wreck. Nell had to look after them, and Lou had to provide most of the necessary.

Personal experience of romance entered into neither sister's existence. Perhaps they were too busy from too early an age to think of it, or always thought more about helping others than helping themselves, or were just put off. After a few years of so-called monthly nursing, late at night and on rare occasions in the attic bedroom the sisters had shared since they were children, Lou told cautionary tales. Love and marriage, at any rate marriage for women and maternity, seemed to be two very different things, she would whisper in disillusioned accents. And Nell would sigh and whisper back, so as not to disturb their sick parents in the bedroom below: 'Wouldn't it be nice if we could just be together one day, and not here, not in our sad old home?'

An unlikely concatenation of events provided a positive and practical answer to this question.

It happened that Lou received the following note from her former client Lady Feltrim: 'In awful trouble – meet me at Grand Hotel 9 a.m. next Friday

– please! Don't write – just come. If you can't I'll suggest another time and place.'

Lou was between jobs, and therefore able to keep the appointment.

She bussed down from Kilburn to Mayfair, and in the Grand Hotel was escorted to Lady Feltrim's suite on the first floor.

Milly Feltrim was a society beauty, thirtyish, married to Sir Andrew Feltrim of Feltrim Court in Northamptonshire, who was about a quarter of a century older than she was. Lady Feltrim had borne her husband two sons with assistance from Lou, in whom she had eventually confided that she was far from happy with her husband and determined not to run the risk of having any more of his children.

But now, two years after her last confinement, as soon as the door was closed by the pageboy, she said without ado: 'I'm pregnant.'

She had big brown eyes, and some people, or rather some men, admired her all the more for her friendly slightly sticking-out teeth. She was wearing a pink satin lace-edged negligee over her nightdress.

Lou smiled in a congratulatory manner, then hedged her bets by asking: 'When are you expecting the baby, milady?'

'I can't have it,' Lady Feltrim returned, slumping down on a settee and beginning to whimper. 'At least I can't keep it, my husband won't let me. He's threatening to divorce me if there's a breath of scandal. He's so angry – you're lucky not to be married, Lou! Please help me – and don't stand there, sit on this chair and take off your hat!'

'Yes, milady.'

'That's better.'

'What had you in mind, milady?'

'I've got money of my own. I'll buy you a house, where I could live for the final month or two, and you could bring up my child. I won't have anything to do with those horrible doctors, I won't! And I don't want to go abroad, and then have my child adopted and lose track of it. I'd pay for everything, Lou.'

'That's a lot for me to think over, milady. I'm wondering about my other ladies.'

'You could go and look after them. You'd have to have servants to keep an eye on things in your absence.'

[15]

'When would you be wanting an answer, milady?'

'I was hoping you'd give me your answer now. I thought my offer would be advantageous for you as well as me.'

'Oh I do appreciate your confidence. And indeed I would help you if I could, and I'd love to have a baby to see to for more than just the month. But, as I say, you've given me so much to think of. When is the latest I could let you have my answer? Pardon me for asking, milady: how far gone are you?'

'Four months nearly.'

'It scarcely shows.'

'Thank God! But listen, Lou, I've got to make my arrangements. Come back here at the same time on the same day next week – can you? Or you could write to me at this address – no details – only yes or no. You know every single word we've spoken is a complete and absolute secret?'

'I do, milady. And I'll either be here next week, or shall have written. If I feel I can't help you I'll be extremely sorry, though I'm sure you'll soon find somebody else to take my place.'

Lady Feltrim wailed: 'I don't want somebody else. I'm frightened, Lou. I've been such a fool.'

'Poor milady.'

The interview ended. On the return journey to Kilburn Lou made up her mind to say no to Lady Feltrim. She was not willing to devote herself exclusively and for the foreseeable future to one child. She would certainly not entrust any child for which she was responsible to servants. She could imagine trouble over money and her legal position, and more trouble of one sort and another with fathers. She was neither especially shocked, nor influenced, by moral considerations: several of her ladies had confessed that their babies, which she was about to deliver or had delivered, bore no blood relationship to their husbands.

Half a dozen neighbours stood by the front door of the Carty house. They murmured words of sympathy and offered assistance as she hurried indoors, where her sister was washing the paintwork of the steep staircase.

An extraordinary accident had occurred. In the three hours that Lou had been absent her father and her mother had both died, been certified dead by a doctor, and laid out on the marital bed in their bedroom. In fact they had died in the course of the quarter of an hour of Nell's customary morning trot to the shop on the corner. Marian Carty must have been helping John Carty downstairs, when he burst a blood vessel, had a fatal hemorrhage, collapsed on top of her and caused her to fall and break her neck. Nell had discovered her father and mother spreadeagled on the stairs and in the hallway respectively, and blood everywhere.

The inference that Lou was soon to draw from this tragedy or happy release was that Nell, aged thirty and without any professional qualification, was going to be out of a job.

Seven days later, following the funerals and much sisterly discussion, Lou informed Lady Feltrim that she and Nell between them might be able to bring up the outcast babe; and was informed by her ladyship, who was determined to settle the matter at all costs and not to get involved in too many traceable financial transactions, that she intended to make an outright gift of premises of her choosing to the guardians of her child.

Agreement was reached; the rented house in Kilburn vacated; 14 Summer Drive bought; and Lady Feltrim lived there in seclusion, served by the Carty sisters, for the eight weeks before her confinement. She duly produced a baby boy and christened him with a tear or two Anthony Fitzpatrick; and in time she returned, as if from foreign travel, to Sir Andrew at Feltrim Court.

Within twelve months two more infants had joined Anthony, and thus it had gone on for the next seventeen years – that is, until Eleanor made her entrance upon the scene of life.

Anthony Fitzpatrick departed, actually at the age of four, because Sir Andrew Feltrim relented and introduced the child into the Feltrim family circle as a nephew of his wife; other children arrived.

Those not brought home by Lou were delivered in a different sense – like parcels to the stained glass door – by miserable mothers, or relieved grandparents, or penitent real or irate putative fathers, or doctors or gynaecologists. The sisters personified discretion, they kept themselves to themselves locally and would merely admit under cross-examination that they fostered the children of friends – in their description children who had lost their

[17]

mothers, or whose parents had gone to unhealthy outposts of empire, or orphans.

Their services were exclusive, confined to some of Lou's clients and to persons vouched for by respected intermediaries. They might wish to care for every illegitimate child in the whole wide world: they were too charitable to try to stretch their charity further than their strength would allow. Besides, they had to think about money. All their children suffered if one was not paid for. The two infants who kept Anthony Fitzpatrick company were accepted partly because Lady Feltrim posted registered letters containing cash and apologies only if and when she remembered. And other ladies in worse situations than hers, having no private means and depending either on shocked fathers or possessive husbands, were able to provide even less – or less regular – financial support of their love-children.

A secondary qualification of the parentage of potential residents of 14 Summer Drive, as well as financial dependability, had to be taken into consideration. Could a mother keep a secret, or at least her own counsel? Could her lover, could her relations? Careless talk had the power to disturb the peace of mind of many people, and wreck marriages and even lives.

Lou and Nell always therefore promoted the safety measure of a child's surname that differed from the surname of the members of his or her family: whence Fitzpatrick, Lovejoy, and so on. Even if this difference confused some children, it could protect them later on from gossip, and shield their relations from embarrassing discoveries and revelations.

Again, Lou and Nell did their best to persuade parents visiting Willesden not to attract too much attention, and they were against one child's parent meeting or at any rate being introduced formally to other children.

They could not completely hide the conspiratorial and mysterious elements of life at Summer Drive from their older charges, especially the ones that graduated from the private tuition of Miss Elmes and began to consort with boys and girls from normal homes at public scholastic establishments. The Cartys' answers to the questions, 'Why can't I be with my mother? Who is my father? Why am I here? Why won't anybody tell me the truth?' – were bound to be unsatisfactory. Partial understanding combined with much jumping to disagreeable conclusions spread a certain gloom from the top to the bottom of the young community. Laughter was closer to tears than it should have been, and smiles had a wistful quality. After the first intrusion of full-blown tragedy, when Walter Simms aged eight was deposited on the doorstep by the furious man he had mistaken for his father, and amidst a chorus of curses and shrieks Mrs Simms was dragged by her hair down the garden path and away from her child for ever, Nell remarked to Lou that their home should be called Heartbreak House.

Yet the place, the community, had a redeeming feature. When all was said, it – and what no doubt some called the vice behind it – was redeemed by virtue.

Nell Carty cooked the food that the children loved to eat, not only wholesome fare, but treats like ice cream and eclairs, and birthday teas to order. Moreover a hungry child could usually plead successfully for a compassionate slice of bread and jam between meals. In the mornings she dealt with tradesmen, the butcher, baker, milkman, the fishmonger who also sold ice in the summer, the Frenchmen selling onions in autumn, and then, as she would say, 'fried herself' over the kitchen range. She provided a substantial breakfast with porridge and eggs, elevenses, lunch and, as a rule, high tea. In the afternoons she might take some children for a walk, or play indoor games with them; or everyone might go on an expedition to see a sight or visit a museum. In the evenings she would help to put the younger children to bed, and read to them, kiss and cuddle them good night, sit with some who were afraid of the dark until they slept; and when at last the house was quiet, she would return to the kitchen to mend and darn clothes and chat to her sister uninterruptedly.

Lou was the leader of the band. She was the treasurer, the organiser, within her gentle limits the disciplinarian, and the setter of standards. She tended the babies; nursed the sick; comforted and cheered. She arranged things with the teaching staff, she did the washing and ironing, she spring-cleaned throughout the year, she supervised, and was judge and jury and ultimate authority. How could she be so powerful, so forceful, when she was so unassuming, approachable, tender-hearted, humorous? Effort did not enter into her air of command: she was simply forthright. Perhaps, still more simply, her goodness, her selflessness, made it difficult to argue with her commonsense, while her charm removed the sting from doing as she said.

[19]

Sometimes, particularly in the depth of winter when night fell early, she would suggest or agree to a suggestion of a game of charades in the playroom opposite the parlour. Each sister captained a team of resident children, plus any trustworthy young guests invited to join in. The fun became the more furious as Aunty Lou and Aunty Nell acted the roles traditionally assigned to them by their charges, for instance of a worm or an elephant, or a baby or the oldest inhabitant of the earth. If the original motive of such casting had been mischievous, and its intention to ridicule the sisters, in action it produced the reverse effect. The children laughed with their Auntys rather than at them, they all laughed together, and equally enjoyably. Nell, scarlet in the face, her greying brown hair frizzy on her shiny forehead, laughed so much after wriggling like a worm across the playroom floor that she said she would split her sides. Lou pretending to be a bawling babe on the lap of Donald Wilson emitted peal after peal of her rare contagious laughter. And the children screamed with approval, and giggled to an almost uncontrollable degree.

The characteristics of Lou and Nell that probably explained the close links they established with children were twofold. First, each had a childish streak, witness their attitude to charades – the knack of self-forgetfulness and of becoming in an instant, if temporarily, happy-go-lucky: thus they met youth halfway. Secondly, their predilection for the young was either all-embracing or indiscriminate, depending on how you looked at it: in other words they inspired confidence by their even-handedness – they made a favourite of every child.

However, during the sisters' sessions in the kitchen before retiring, Nell seated in one of their pair of old Windsor chairs beside the range, plying her needle and holding it up to the light to re-thread it, Lou in the other chair, invariably knitting something for somebody, and the door open so that they would hear any cry or summons, a new topic was discussed in their lowered voices.

The topic was Eleanor, and the implication of their discussion was that they must try not to get too fond of her.

The problem came into the open two years and a bit after Eleanor's arrival at 14 Summer Drive. Mrs Studbrook, formerly Mrs Catherine Wale, the mother of April, fixed an appointment and called on the Cartys on behalf of a friend of hers in familiar trouble. Lou and Nell really had room for another baby: it could sleep in the cot still occupied by Eleanor – she was old enough to move upstairs into Nell's bedroom while the twins Jane and Matilda could move down and share with Willy Hopkins. But Lou said they were full up. She told Mrs Studbrook she would be pleased to attend her friend for the confinement and for a few weeks following it, but that unfortunately there was no possibility of accommodating the child.

The lie was white inasmuch as seven children in the house were always a crush. Besides, the sisters could and did plead that they were beginning to feel their years, also the strain of coping with their multitude. Yet the truth was that neither wanted a new baby to supplant Eleanor in any sense, to rob them of some of the pleasure of concentrating on her development, or to upset her. Nell did not wish for another youngest to reserve titbits for, Lou did not wish to replace the companion of her nights. And after all they had no need of extra money: although some parents might pay irregularly, most paid more than was requested, and extra contributions were often the price of guilt.

So the two Cartys broke their rule of doing whatever they could for any poor illegitimate child in order to favour a third Carty, their namesake Eleanor.

They were quite agreed about it.

'I wouldn't be able to give her the same attention if I had a baby to see to,' Lou argued in the quieter nocturnal hours beside the kitchen range.

'She's got to have every chance,' Nell echoed.

Reasons existed for such rather specious reasoning. Six months of Eleanor's existence seemed to prove that she was out of the ordinary. Lou would tell Nell that in her experience she had not come across an infant so responsive or so determined. Nell, for her part, was surprised by the power of Eleanor's miniature affections. She would say to Lou with a smile and a grateful sigh: 'What a ball of love she is!'

But the child's more obvious qualities and talents counted for less with the sisters than her ability somehow to pluck at their heartstrings, or, as they were soon to worry, to establish herself in their hearts in an almost cuckoo-like manner.

Questions were asked beside the kitchen range, such as: 'Are we spoiling her? Are the others getting jealous?'

A further question was: 'What if Mrs Beck were to take her away?' It betrayed an unwonted trace of self-interest, although it referred to Eleanor's happiness as well as their own.

Her hypothetical removal from Summer Drive also preyed on the mind of Willy Hopkins, who, despite his five years of seniority, became even more slavishly dependent on the exuberant toddler than he had been on April Studbrook. He trailed after her, laughing at her antics, he begged to be allowed to dandle her on his knees, he let her clamber all over him and repeatedly appealed to one Aunty or the other: 'She isn't going anywhere, is she?'

Eleanor as she grew into a dark-haired vivid-looking little girl established a sort of ascendancy over everyone at number 14, pets included. Hefty and benevolent Donald Wilson was especially protective of her even by his standards. Michael Janes deigned to admit she was interesting, and the twins, for all their exclusive obsessions with each other, were apt unexpectedly to find her funny.

She went in for a sweet sort of teasing. She nicknamed Mr Bees Buzzer, and Henry Menny Henny-penny as if he had been a chicken, and won their allegiance. She changed the name of the sleek black and white cat, Puss of yesteryear: after listening to one of the stories read aloud by Aunty Nell she called it Fauntleroy. When she was five, some wellwisher replaced the late inhabitant of the rabbit hutch with a young white pink-eyed buck. He became her own Peter, who hopped up and down stairs in her wake and nibbled out of her hand a slice of bread and butter and marmalade for breakfast.

She had both energy and vitality – she lived life with unusual intensity. Her spirits were so high as to seem, and indeed occasionally to prove to be, precarious. Her enthusiasm presaged disappointment. She bore physical injury bravely, stoically, but her nerves were highly strung. She was responsive because she was sensitive, and temperamental because responsive. She could sizzle with anger briefly, and was respected by Michael Janes all the more because once in a fit of rage she slapped his large face with her small hand.

Her health, her innate vigour mostly expressed itself in confidence and optimism: she was still too young to be affected by the blight on the house and its inmates. She played and laughed and sang and ran about and fell over and hardly cried. She frightened Aunty Nell by jumping out and saying boo to her, then would hug her knees. On affectionate impulses she flung herself at Aunty Lou, sure that she would be caught in caring arms.

She idealised her mother. She certainly worshipped from afar in that Mrs Beck stayed well away from Willesden, except for a couple of brief visits a year, on Eleanor's birthdays or thereabouts, and before Christmas.

Poppy Beck had acquired a roofless automobile and a French chauffeur, and she promised Eleanor a ride the next time she came down. But on the day in question she arrived even later than usual and in bad weather. Indoors, having removed her motoring gear, she sat in the parlour with Aunty Lou, whom she called Louisa, and her daughter. She was a beautiful person with lustrous brown hair, a luminous complexion, a disarming smile and an irresistible tinkling laugh, and she wore elegant, colourful, soft and sweetly scented clothes. Eleanor was once again overcome with shyness and struck dumb, and reduced to peeping at her mother from behind Aunty Lou's skirt. Eventually she was persuaded to kiss Mrs Beck; but then her embrace was too heartfelt and violent to please. Moreover the loudness of her laughter, which she emitted only because her mother was laughing, and by way of a tribute, caused the latter to cover her ears. After three quarters of an hour of the grown-ups' stilted conversation, the sky cleared and the sun shone through the parlour window, reminding Mrs Beck that she had better hurry home: Eleanor would not want her to get soaked to the skin, would she? Aunty Lou had to help the lady into her overcoat and pretty veiled hat, and in the motor Adolphe wrapped a fur rug round her knees. She drove off with a gay wave and in a cloud of smoke. Eleanor, on the doorstep, said: 'She forgot my ride,' gripping Aunty Lou's hand as hard as she could and biting back her tears.

For a few days after this fairly typical visit the child was not her sunny self. But, typically again, she exculpated and forgave her mother.

'It was too rainy for me to have a drive,' she explained to the other children. 'My mother's going to take me soon.'

She badgered Aunty Lou to agree with her romantic idea of her mother: 'Isn't she lovely? She's smart, isn't she? Isn't she?'

[23]

Such questions put the Carty sisters in a quandary. They were loth to undermine Eleanor's faith in her mother, while at the same time distrusting Mrs Beck, who was irresponsible financially as well as maternally, and wishing to prepare the girl for the likely loss of her illusions. They had long been acquainted with the difficulty of helping children to continue to love and not to begin to hate their parents.

They warned Eleanor that her mother's motor might break down or be sold, and therefore should not be counted on. They repeated that Mrs Beck was a busy person and could not possibly come to Willesden as often as her daughter wished her to. But they were inhibited by more fears than those connected with Eleanor's welfare: that they were being disloyal to an employer, or proprietorial.

Late at night by the kitchen range they regretted the fact that Eleanor failed to see through her mother.

'She's such a sharp little thing as a rule,' they said. 'But then she will have things her own way.'

An incident illustrated both this last reading of Eleanor's character, and her still more basic capacity to be guided by the goodness of her heart.

Out shopping one day with Aunty Nell, in a stationer's shop, she saw and instantly fell in love with a box of pencils painted different bright colours. They were called the Harlequin Set; fifty or so boxes were piled up on a table in the centre of the shopfloor. She touched a pencil: it had six sides, its paint was seductively smooth, it was irresistibly blue, and had a darling green rubber at one end. Could she have a box? Aunty Nell said no. Could she buy it with her own money? Aunty Nell said it would be too expensive.

So she took a box off the table and stuffed it into her knickers.

Nobody noticed. She thought she was clever. She had got what she wanted. And why not? The shop had more Harlequin Sets than it could ever need.

At home she ran upstairs and hid the box under her pillow on the bed in which she now slept in Aunty Lou's bedroom. Intermittently throughout the day she sneaked up to write and rub out with her beloved pencils. But in the evening, while she was having a bath, she forgot about them, and in due course Aunty Lou came into the bathroom, wrapped her in a hot towel, sat her on her lap and began to cry.

'How could you?' she cried, turning down her lower lip strangely and shedding great teardrops.

Eleanor had never before seen Aunty Lou in tears or looking like that, was shocked, frightened, sorry, and soon crying too.

'How could you steal those pencils?'

Eleanor remembered that she had forgotten them and wished she had hidden them somewhere else, but boo-hooed defiantly: 'I didn't!'

'What do you mean? Aunty Nell's told me they weren't paid for. They were stolen. You weren't given them by a stranger, were you?'

'No.'

'Don't you understand how wrong it is to steal?'

'I only took them.'

'But that was a crime. You might have been arrested by the police. You still might be. You'll go straight back to the shop tomorrow and pay for them with your savings and apologise to the poor shopkeeper who trusted you.'

Eleanor, who was growing more and more frightened and unhappy, retorted: 'I won't! I can't!'

'Oh you obstinate child, why do you hurt me so?'

In military terms, Eleanor was defeated by this changed tactic.

She bawled, 'No, no!' – and threw her arms round Aunty Lou's neck and kissed her salty cheeks.

'But it does hurt to think you're a thief, and that other people are going to think it and blame Aunty Nell and me. Haven't you learned anything from us? We've put honesty first – haven't we taught you that? We've had such high hopes of our dear girl, and you've disgraced us all.'

'Oh Aunty Lou, I love you.'

'Do you? I wonder.'

'Oh I do, I do! And I'll never steal anything ever again.'

'There there, my dear. I believe you. We'll see the shopkeeper tomorrow and put things straight.'

'Yes, Aunty Lou.'

'Shall we be friends again, and dry our eyes?'

'Oh yes, yes, please!'

*

The Carty sisters entertained high hopes of Eleanor not only because they were afraid they loved her more than any of their other children, present and past, nor because she was attractive, affectionate and bright.

Her precocity caught their attention early on. Then she was so keen and so quick to learn. Miss Elmes marvelled at her aptitude for reading and her interest in the written word.

Yet the Cartys had fostered intelligent children before. They were inclined to take the intelligence of the very young with a pinch of salt – that is to say, with a resolution to wait and see. Michael Janes, for example, was intelligent, and even better at acting in charades than Eleanor turned out to be, if less engaging; but his Auntys privately took the view that his showy and feeble character would always hold him back.

The objective assessments on which they based their recognition of Eleanor's promise referred to a rare sort of refinement she had, a delicate air, a strange effortless superior quality that set her apart, and, secondly, to a more describable gift.

She had sung nursery rhymes sweetly and in tune. Later, and soon in order to make people laugh, she would accurately mimic the calls of birds and, in particular, noises. Aged four she could perfectly imitate the regular squeak of Mr Bees' bicycle. Her comical accomplishment was drawn to the attention of the music teacher Mrs Cruse, who opined excitedly that the girl probably possessed the aid to musicianship known as perfect pitch.

Eleanor there and then began to have piano lessons and to show startling aptitude.

Polly Cruse, a plump middle-aged woman with blond plaits of hair pinned into buns over each of her ears, communicated her enthusiasm to her potentially best pupil, who was also pleased to impress her contemporaries, to be told by Aunty Lou and Aunty Nell that they had always known she was special, and to interest her mother.

The last pleasure was by no means the least that Eleanor owed to music. She had neither seen nor heard from her mother for nearly a year when she received the following gratifying note: 'Darling, I'm so glad you're learning to play the piano. You should be talented, and your talent will stand you in good stead always. I promise to come and listen to you before too long.'

The reasons why Mrs Beck had steered clear of Willesden, apart from indolence and fecklessness, were the ever more searching questions which Eleanor was putting to her. The inquisitive sequence ran: 'Where have you come from . . . Do you live at home with my father . . . Why not . . . Are your other children my brother and sister . . . Can I meet them . . . Can I live with you . . . Can I post my letters to you instead of giving them to Aunty Lou . . . Where are you going?'

Poppy Beck's absence or absenteeism, which spared her the trouble of answering, had only made Eleanor grow fonder.

The promised visit was delayed until her seventh birthday party on 12 November 1912. Mrs Beck had instructed Aunty Lou to arrange Eleanor's performance for the quarter of an hour between four and four-fifteen o'clock, no longer, and to invite the other children and available friends to form an audience and partake of the subsequent tea: she was clearly determined not, as usual, to be left alone with her daughter. She arrived at four-forty-five, by which time the pianist was in a highly nervous state. Mrs Beck expressed the deepest regret for her tardiness, charmed Mrs Cruse with her grace and gratitude, hurried to assume the seat of honour in the parlour, where the young and older people were already assembled, and having listened intently to the music clapped and called out bravo in her silvery voice. Although Eleanor had started shakily, she was reassured by the proximity of Mrs Cruse, sitting on a chair beside her and turning pages, and managed to play her final Mozart minuet with a flourish. The picture of the pretty child on the piano stool, unable to reach the pedals, palely concentrating, compensated for the odd wrong note. And she took her bow in a delightfully droll way, exaggerating it as if professionally and laughing at herself, then ran straight into her mother's arms.

The prize and the present of a string of seed pearls and coral beads which she received from her mother after it, and the congratulations of Mrs Cruse, Miss Elmes and Buzzer Bees, not to mention Aunty Lou's and Aunty Nell's, were happier experiences for Eleanor than subsequent events.

For one thing she was mortified by the attentions of Willy Hopkins, who kept on trying to hug her to death in front of everyone. For another, when she frowned at Willy and shook him off, her mother rebuked her for being unkind. Eleanor was increasingly upset in the playroom, where the company was to sit at the long table, now covered with a white cloth and plates of hot buttered crumpets and savoury sandwiches. Mrs Beck decreed that she ought to have a gentleman on either side of her and proceeded to cast Willy and Michael Janes in these unsuitable roles. Her disappointed daughter was therefore forced to take the place between Michael, whom she despised, and Buzzer Bees, who talked to her so much that she could not hear what her mother was saying. Nor could she eat much, and she was infuriated by Aunty Nell's public reproach: 'What's wrong, dearie? I made it all specially for you.' The last straw was Mrs Beck looking at her watch even before the birthday cake had been carried into the playroom, throwing up her hands in mock horror, exclaiming that it was far later than she imagined, and rising and insisting that she be allowed to leave the room with the minimum disturbance of the party. Eleanor received a mere kiss goodbye on the top of her head. The receding chug of her mother's motor reduced her to tears.

But the successful aspect of this occasion, namely her exhibition of her musical skill, combining with the worship that obviously irked the heroine – Poppy Beck – and the cross-questioning that embarrassed, led to a situation and a scene infinitely more distressing.

A fortnight after Eleanor's seventh birthday Poppy Beck surprised everyone by returning to Summer Drive and taking the child out to tea in a smart teashop in Hampstead. They did not talk in the car – could not because of the noise – and anyway Eleanor, having only her second car-ride, was enjoying herself too much to do so. The relevant conversation took place over the teacups and cream cakes.

Mrs Beck began it.

'Darling, are you happy with the Cartys?'

'Oh yes.'

'Quite happy?'

Eleanor hesitated. Her loyalty to Aunty Lou and Aunty Nell battled with her hope of getting closer to her mother.

'Yes,' she replied. 'Why?'

'No reason – I just wondered. They're good women, and I don't think you could have been in a nicer establishment. And you've done so well there – everybody speaks well of you – and now you're on your way to becoming a famous pianist. No, you are, darling! You must work hard at your music. What's the name of your teacher – that's it, Mrs Cruse – do you like her?'

'Yes. Don't you, Mother?'

'I scarcely know her. But I can see there's a lot to her.'

'Do you mean she's fat?'

'Well – not a featherweight.'

'She's called Polly, like a parrot.'

'She ought to be called Piggy, like a pig.'

The resemblance between mother and daughter was more marked as they laughed at these pleasantries.

Mrs Beck continued: 'At your concert you two looked funny, sitting together at the piano. You reminded me of a baby piglet in danger of getting squashed by a great clumsy sow. You were lucky she didn't topple over and squash you. Seriously, I told Mrs Cruse how grateful we both were for her help and guidance. But I suppose the time's coming when you'll need a more advanced sort of teacher.'

'I probably will.'

'You might have to go far afield to get the right teaching. But you wouldn't mind that, would you?'

Eleanor, intoxicated after a fashion by all this flattering attention and the scrumptious food, claimed wildly: 'No!'

'You wouldn't miss your friends at Summer Drive?'

Eleanor thought of Michael Janes, and repeated with feeling: 'No!'

'Willesden really isn't the hub of the universe. Whatever happens, you won't be able to spend the rest of your life in Willesden.'

Eleanor again said no in a scornful tone of voice, then consequentially, as it seemed to her, asked: 'Couldn't I come to you, Mother?'

'If you were more settled, when you're settled, I don't see why you shouldn't meet your half-brother and your half-sister.'

'Oh could I? I write to them sometimes, but they don't write back. And I often write to you, Mother. But I don't believe Aunty Lou remembers to address my letters. Do Vivian and Winnie know about me?'

'Letters are difficult, my pet. Everything's difficult for us. One day you'll understand why. In the meanwhile you'll have to be patient and trust me. You do realise I want the best for you? Promise not to forget that.'

'I promise, Mother.'

'Have you nearly finished your tea?'

'Yes, but ...' Eleanor tried to prolong it with her wistful inquiries: 'Is Vivian very handsome?'

'Vivian's the apple of my eye.'

'What does that mean?'

'Oh – never mind.'

'Is Winnie beautiful?'

'Yes, darling.'

'She's thirteen, isn't she?'

'Yes.'

'And blond and tall?'

'Yes. Come along dear.'

'I wish we were staying here longer.'

'Well, we can't. Buck up, dear.'

On the return journey to Willesden Eleanor felt slightly sick, owing to the motion of the car, the cakes she had consumed, over-excitement and especially a sense of guilt, because she had sacrificed her Auntys and Mrs Cruse on the altar of her eagerness to agree with her mother.

At number 14, in the next few days, she suffered from an individualistic form of homesickness: she pined for the home she had never set eyes on, where, in her imagination, beauty and joy held undisputed sway.

She also waited for Henny-penny, in case he brought the letter from her mother offering her a future more romantic, luxurious and normal than her present; but in vain.

Then, a month after the outing to Hampstead, two letters from her mother did arrive, one for herself and the other for Aunty Lou. Hers, even if better than nothing, made no direct reference to removing her from Willesden or uniting her with the rest of her family. However, it was at least full of praise, saying that she was growing up and becoming much more realistic, and that her mother was sure she would now see sense and behave properly. And it added that she would again be coming to Willesden in a short while, bringing two very great friends of hers who were dying to meet Eleanor and hear her play the piano: 'So do practice for all you are worth, darling, and when the time comes try your hardest to shine.'

After a second reading and on second thoughts, Eleanor jumped to the conclusion that the couple in question must be Vivian and Winifred, her half-siblings. In a vague way she decided that she was about to be subjected to a rite of initiation, a trial or test, her passing of which would lead to inclusion in her family circle. She determined to succeed, and was seized by a mood of almost manic anticipatory optimism, thus failing to pay sufficient attention to Aunty Lou's letter.

Absently-mindedly she queried: 'What did Mother write to you?'

The repressive reply was: 'Nothing.'

Eleanor, equally, did not disclose the contents of her letter. Intuition restrained her from broadcasting the news that she wished not to stay at 14 Summer Drive: at the back of her young mind lurked the idea that it would hurt the feelings of Aunty Lou and Aunty Nell. Affection and innate tact got together to silence her. Besides, the Carty sisters must have been aware of the yearnings of all their children for their families – there was no need to state the obvious; and Eleanor liked to keep her secret, and to reserve for her very own the glorious daydream about to come true.

Again in the subliminal manner of childhood, and through the haze of excitement and extra work on her piano pieces, she registered changes in her Auntys' behaviour not conducive to confiding in either of them. Aunty Lou veered between being unusually impatient and unusually, almost fiercely, demonstrative, while Aunty Nell was particularly flustered, and shed tears when Eleanor jokingly complained that the shell of her boiled egg was overcooked.

One morning Aunty Lou announced: 'We'll be going shopping this afternoon. Your mother wants me to buy you a party dress.'

'Oh does she?' Eleanor exclaimed spontaneously and with undisguised delight.

Aunty Lou looked pale and grim.

Later, together, they walked to the dress shop in the village, Audrey's by name, which had a children's department. Eleanor, having deduced that the dress would be worn for the meeting with her mother's very great friends, kept on voicing opinions at once nervous and uncooperative.

At length, in the curtained cubicle, as Eleanor found fault with yet another of the dresses she had wanted to try on, Aunty Lou lost patience and, giving her a shake, hissed in her ear: 'Stop it – don't turn the knife – don't!' She then gathered up a white dress in sailor style with pale blue outlining and a blue silk sash, handed it to the salesgirl and told her to wrap it.

Eleanor was perturbed by whatever had been said and meant, and outside in the street she broke the ominous silence by asking in a conciliatory tone: 'It is pretty, isn't it – our dress?'

'Yes, child,' Aunty Lou replied with reassuring gentleness.

Impulsively Eleanor apologised: it had struck her that she had been naughty in the shop and not exactly good in her thoughts to the two women who had always been good to her.

'Sorry, Aunty Lou.'

'I'm sure we're all sorry. But it's not your fault, Eleanor.'

'Whose fault is it?'

'I often wonder.'

'What did you say about a knife?'

Aunty Lou had to laugh as she answered: 'Perhaps I was speaking about someone who's so sharp she must be careful not to cut herself.'

Eleanor laughed too. She knew the idiom, which had been applied to her on previous occasions, and was amused by it. Moreover she was relieved to have cheered up Aunty Lou for the time being. She skipped back to 14 Summer Drive the more happily for expecting to be living elsewhere soon. The unaccustomed moodiness of the Cartys must point to the parting of their ways and to her imminent relocation in a bigger and better home, she reflected; and her heart swelled with love of the person able to pay for a dress in which the riddles of her existence would soon be satisfactorily solved.

*

One hour late, at four-thirty on a mild spring afternoon, Mrs Beck's chauffeur Adolphe turned her car into Summer Drive, and Eleanor, watching through the parlour window of number 14, saw her mother sitting between a middle-aged dark-haired woman and a bespectacled man wearing a grey bowler hat.

She cried out to Aunty Lou: 'But they're not there!'

She had been getting more and more worked up in recent days and especially in the last sixty minutes. Her febrile high spirits, her inability to stay still, had added to the cares of her Auntys.

The anguished cry called forth the startled question: 'Who, child?'

Eleanor turned her crumpling face towards Aunty Lou.

'My sister and brother!'

'Who told you they were coming here?'

'I know they were.'

'No, dear. It was always Mr and Mrs Adamson who were coming.'

Eleanor, to stop herself crying, visibly bit her lip.

Aunty Lou said: 'We'll have to put our best foot forward now. Come and open the front door for your mother.'

Eleanor took the outstretched hand, muttering: 'I can't play to them – I won't!' And then: 'Don't leave me, Aunty Lou!'

Mrs Beck in her stylish motoring overcoat with the fur collar permitted her daughter's somewhat desperate embrace, then said with her silvery laugh: 'Oh don't cling, darling,' and effected introductions by explaining to the strangers, 'This is my darling little girl,' and by telling Eleanor to shake hands.

Mrs Adamson, who had dark eyes and a soft voice, said: 'What a becoming white dress!'

Mr Adamson's eyes moved – flickered – oddly behind his glasses and his smiling lips glistened.

He doffed his bowler and said: 'How do you do? We've been looking forward to meeting you.'

Aunty Lou helped to remove outdoor attire, and Mrs Beck remembered to introduce her by speaking her name: 'Louisa Carty.'

As the Adamsons were ushered into the parlour and Eleanor was given a motherly push in after them, Aunty Lou said in an undertone to Mrs Beck: 'Could I have a word, madam?'

[33]

'Some other time,' Mrs Beck returned, entering the room and closing the door behind her.

The grown-ups sat down.

Poppy Beck drew Eleanor towards her, kept an arm round her waist and asked: 'What's happened to your pretty smile? Don't be shy. Don't hide your light, dear. I'm sure you can call Mrs Adamson Aunt Mona, and Mr Adamson Uncle Jake.'

Eleanor interrupted: 'Where's Aunty Lou?'

Her mother dismissed the question with a wave of her small hand.

Mrs Adamson remarked softly: 'Your new aunt and uncle would very much like to hear you play the piano, Eleanor.'

Mr Adamson added with a flickering smile: 'We'd be honoured.'

But Eleanor hid her face amongst her mother's frills and ruffles.

'What is the matter?' the latter demanded. 'Don't be silly – please do as your Aunt Mona asks.'

With reluctance and awkwardly Eleanor went and seated herself on the piano stool, launched into the Mozart piece she had played at her birthday party, but made a mistake, got in a muddle, stopped and ran back to her mother.

The Adamsons clapped, which sounded ironical in the circumstances.

Eleanor moaned: 'Sorry!'

Her mother laughed and scolded: 'So you should be, my darling. You haven't done either of us justice. You really haven't.'

'Come come, Poppy, isn't that a bit hard?' Mr Adamson inquired.

'But she can play nicely, Jake, I promise you.'

'Music's not such an important consideration in my humble opinion,' Mrs Adamson cooed.

'Well, she'll play better when she's used to you, I hope and pray.'

At this point in the conversation, which increased Eleanor's bewilderment as well as her misery, Aunty Lou knocked on the door, entered without being asked to come in, and said determinedly, if with red patches on her white cheeks: 'Excuse me, madam, but I feel I should have an urgent word.'

Mrs Beck grimaced in a rather attractive manner in the direction of the Adamsons, shook off her daughter, rose to her feet and followed Aunty Lou out of the room, complaining: 'What is it? I can't spare more than a minute.'

Mrs Adamson said to Eleanor who not only must have felt trapped but looked it: 'Don't run away from us.'

Eleanor rejected the charge of cowardice in a trembling voice: 'I wouldn't run away.'

'And please don't be sad. Your music's not so important.'

'It isn't that,' Eleanor retorted the more vehemently for having to contradict herself: 'And it is − it is important!'

Mr Adamson weighed in pacifically: 'Would you like me to tell you about our homes?'

He proceeded to describe their house in the West End and their country seat in Hampshire, in the middle of which recital the door opened again and Aunty Lou summoned Eleanor.

In the hall lit by beams of sun through stained glass the child grabbed hold of the woman and asked: 'What's happening, Aunty Lou?'

'Your mother's in the playroom waiting for you.'

'But what's happening?'

'I can't say.'

Eleanor stood in the doorway of the playroom. Her eyes brimmed with tears, and she did not approach her mother, who was striding to and fro in front of the fireplace and looking as black as her pretty face permitted.

'Where on earth did you get the idea I'd bring Vivian and Winifred down here?' she rapped out.

Eleanor started to cry in a precociously adult fashion, shielding her eyes with a hand and bending over, doubling up, because of her pain and passion.

'Oh for heaven's sake − this is impossible − for heaven's sake shut that door!' Mrs Beck strode across and shut it herself. 'Please stop crying − you will meet Vivian and Winifred one day − but I can't get them involved at this stage − and I can't do more for you than I have done and am doing − I can't! Listen to me! Try to understand! The man I'm married to isn't your father and doesn't want to know you. My husband's the father of Winnie and Vivian and he's set on keeping you apart. Listen! You told me you weren't happy here − not all that happy. We agreed you couldn't stay put in the back of beyond for ever. There are things about your upbringing that don't please me − you shouldn't

[35]

have been called Carty, it isn't fitting, and I wasn't consulted. Besides, you'll need a better piano teacher, and a better start in life if it comes to that. I've been thinking of your future, and so should you, instead of crying over nothing. No, you've had nothing to cry about, and what's on offer ought to make you grin from ear to ear. Eleanor, listen – can you hear me? Mr and Mrs Adamson, your Aunt Mona and Uncle Jake, are extremely kind wealthy people, in one respect they're like your father although they don't know it, and they're prepared to give you their name and adopt you. They've got no other children and they want you to be theirs. What's wrong now?'

Eleanor, sobbing no more, but hiccuping, and staring, glaring at her mother, said: 'You're giving me away.'

'Of course not!'

'You are!'

'No, darling.'

Mrs Beck approached her daughter with a fond smile and proffered hand.

Eleanor took evasive action and said: 'I won't go. I hate them!'

'Ssh – lower your voice! And don't be absurd. It's silly to say you hate people who are only trying to help you. The Adamsons are offering you the sort of life that I can't give. I really can't even afford to keep you here. And there's nowhere else for you, darling – for good reasons, which you may not understand at present, I'm not at liberty to take you home with me. I would if I could – you must give me credit for having your best interests at heart. Come and talk to Uncle Jake and Aunt Mona, please. Please, Eleanor?'

'No.'

'But you must – it's so rude. What do you think you're going to do if you won't seize this chance, which may be your last? You'll starve.'

'Aunty Lou wouldn't let me.'

'How do you think the Cartys could feed you if I didn't pay them for your food? No – I'll tell you what's in store for you, my girl. You'll end up as a waif and stray in an institution, or in a police cell. Well, you will! You must learn to do as you're told. Now I've had enough of this nonsense. Come with me!'

Mrs Beck lunged at her daughter, who was backed up against the door, and caught her by the arm.

Eleanor shook her off, freed herself, and summoning further reserves of

[36]

energy, never tapped before, which seemed to flash fire from her eyes, cried out: 'I hate you!' – opened the door, ran through the hall and into the arms of Aunty Lou in the kitchen.

A storm of sobbing ensued, and torrents of tears were shed. Aunty Lou carried the child upstairs, out of harm's way, and eventually got her into bed.

Aunty Nell coped with and saw off the visitors.

That night and on succeeding nights beside the kitchen range the sisters discussed their narrow escape from the realisation of their worst fears, and the culmination of the drama, which had begun for them with Mrs Beck's confidential letter saying that Eleanor would be removed from Summer Drive and adopted by the Adamsons.

Apparently, in the playroom where Aunty Nell had found the lady also in tears, though only momentarily, Mrs Beck said she had received a look from her daughter that would haunt her to her dying day; that she had been spoken to cruelly; that the Cartys had alienated Eleanor's natural affections; and that she would neither forgive them nor pay them another penny ever. Then she had extricated the Adamsons from the parlour and hustled them out of the house.

Aunty Lou's reaction to the monetary threat was to say: 'We'll manage somehow.'

'Oh yes,' Aunty Nell agreed philosophically. 'After all, she's become our child, hasn't she?'

They pitied Eleanor and tended her. Aunty Lou sat for hours in her darkened bedroom holding the small hot hand, Aunty Nell made chicken broth.

Their feelings for Eleanor were deepened, if possible, by her rejection of the rich Adamsons in favour of their poor selves, by her fidelity and remembrance of their tried and tested devotion, and by a certain admiring awe of the strength of her character.

'How could she at her age stand up to those grown-ups?' Aunty Nell asked rhetorically. 'It beats me. She just wasn't going to be twisted round anyone's little finger, not even by that mother of hers.'

1913 . . .

ELEANOR was confined to her bed, or anyway to the bedroom she shared with Aunty Lou, for a fortnight following Poppy Beck's attempt to have her adopted by Jake and Mona Adamson.

When her Auntys tried to convince her that things were less bad than she seemed to think they were, she would contradict them thus: 'My family doesn't want me – I'll starve unless I go into an institution – or the police'll put me in a cell.' She rejected reassurance, and upset them as well as herself still further by her bitter comment on the claim that everyone at Summer Drive was doing and would do their best for her: 'That's what Mother said.'

The sisters had never come across a child so stubbornly miserable. At last exhaustion, if nothing else, turned her catnaps into nights and indeed days of proper sleep. But she was again shattered by nightmares, either terrifying or tragically happy. She would dream of a door studded with nails and of being dragged through it by her hair and thrown into a dark and damp confined space by pseudo-nurses or warders. The alternative was a heavenly vision of her godlike brother and angelic sister, and of herself being caressed by them and made much of.

Despite the confusion of her emotions she vowed single-mindedly never to speak to her mother again. Her Auntys appreciated her feelings, and shared some of them; but their professional principles and kindly natures compelled them to remonstrate. One night Aunty Lou, having been woken by Eleanor's cries, and after comforting her, urged her not to be too hard on her mother, whose predicament was beyond her comprehension.

Eleanor retorted: 'I wish she was dead.'

Time and the robustness of the girl's constitution began a healing process, perhaps a part of which was that she no longer mentioned her mother's name.

The other children asked vaguely where had she been, and why had she been there?

'I wasn't well,' she replied.

What had happened on the day her people came to visit her?

'Curiosity killed the cat,' she said, averting her face and talking to someone else.

The Carty sisters were able to resume their sewing and knitting in the late evenings beside the kitchen range: Lou was no longer worn out by Eleanor's insomnia, she did not drowse as soon as she sat down, and their confabulations were not interrupted by frantic summonses from upstairs.

Lou remarked: 'I'm afraid our girl may be sweeping the whole business under the carpet.'

'It was the giving away that did the damage. How could Mrs Beck have thought she could just palm her off in an afternoon?' Nell chimed in.

'What worries me is whether the damage will ever be properly repaired.'

'Oh, I expect it will,' Nell countered. 'She's got everything to live for.'

It became clear little by little that Eleanor had decided to commit her life rather to 14 Summer Drive than to some utopia inhabited by her relations. She wrote no more 'letters home', as she had been pleased to call them – thus sparing Aunty Lou the necessity of breaking her promise to deal with postage. She provided innumerable small proofs of being less like a child at school than a daughter of the house. She would want to embrace one Aunty or the other suddenly and speechlessly, and to be embraced by them with equal force.

She also took her piano-playing more seriously. At least she spent longer hours in the parlour by herself and voluntarily, practising, and derived apparent satisfaction from doing so.

Yet notwithstanding the recovery of her health and cheerfulness, the sensitive antennae of Aunty Lou, attuned to the moods of children, detected a change in Eleanor's attitude to the outside world. The shadow of a doubt, the scar of a wound, sullied the area behind her violet eyes; and she seemed to be trying to remember to check her spontaneity.

Time had also rung, and was ringing, changes in the rest of the multitude of 14 Summer Drive.

Donald Wilson was now nineteen and a student at a technical college in the north of England. His real father had produced the funds to enable him to pursue his study of engineering and to travel and gain experience in his vacations. When passing through London he would either call on his Auntys or spend a night or two, sleeping on the sofa in the playroom. He had grown tall and burly; but his hair was as spiky and his character as reliable as ever.

His Auntys would re-introduce him proudly to the others: 'Look who's come to see us!'

Eleanor, who loved Donald, would hang round his neck with her feet off the ground while he asked her in his man's voice: 'Hullo there – how's the piano going?'

Michael Janes, aged sixteen, still lived at Summer Drive. He attended a day school, but, again thanks to his unknown father, reputedly an actor of note, was soon moving to Brighton to study at an academy of dramatic art. He had grown into a lanky narcissistic youth, who might have looked as poetic as he wished to if he had not treated the spots on his face with peroxide – it dyed the nice brown hair over his forehead and round his temples bright orange. He was not altogether averse from the public interest aroused by his pied appearance, and scorned the mockery that it and his other affectations inspired.

That Willy Hopkins could peacefully share a bedroom with Michael was an achievement of a rather negative sort. Willy was too dense to see the condescending, testy, critical or spiteful points which the other was inclined to make.

Willy at thirteen continued to be the educational cross that Miss Elmes carried through life: she could drum almost no learning into his head. He would sit beside Eleanor at the big table in the playroom during lessons, inattentively and undeservedly smiling, and rousing himself only to congratulate his alert and accomplished nextdoor neighbour. Sometimes Aunty Nell felt she had to put in a good word for him: she would refer to his capacity for devotion to his female contemporaries and say that at any rate he would be a nice husband one day.

Aunty Nell was not alone in wishing to comfort Willy Hopkins: Miss Elmes did her best to grin and bear him, and Eleanor suffered his foolishness and his fawning more gladly than might well have been the case. There was general awareness of the fact, not least because he moaned about it, that he was to all intents and purposes an orphan. Neither of his parents had ever, as it were, owned up to him: following representations by a third party acquainted with Aunty Lou, the baby he once had been was delivered to 14 Summer Drive by a middle-aged and clearly uninvolved servant woman, and since then money for his upkeep had arrived from a solicitor's office. Adult opinion therefore pitied Willy, and most of the children were agreed that he was a bit worse off than they were.

Matilda Lovejoy, the loud-mouthed twin, and her sister Jane, eleven and a half by now, enjoyed an enviable advantage in the parental context: they were the only members of the multitude to be visited by their father.

Fathers were a rare species at number 14; for most of the children they had the charm of mystery; and frustrated filial yearnings got the better of sorrow and resentment whenever a representative of the breed hove into view.

Perhaps it was the power of a man to sire and to reject his issue that lent him extra value in the children's eyes. And perhaps their over-estimation of such men accounted for their eager interest in the male sex, including familiar examples of it like Buzzer Bees, Henny-penny, and the tradesmen Ken, Sid and Mr Skate.

The twins' father was not called Lovejoy: someone had discovered that for misunderstandable reasons his name was Robin Brook. Fatherless faces would if possible watch his comings and goings through the playroom or parlour net curtains. He was a dark lithe youngish man, who wore smart clothes and trousers with knife-edge creases. Eleanor thought he was beautiful, Michael Janes allowed that he was well-bred, and Willy said he was a regular toff; while the twins, basking in the reflected glory of these compliments, supplied information about Mr Brook in their respective bellows and whispers.

So far as the twins themselves were concerned, Eleanor was not especially drawn to them: like everybody else she was discouraged by their preoccupations with each other. Her great friend was Flavia Simmons, her senior by a few months and the only child of Willesden neighbours.

Flavia was another musical pupil of Polly Cruse, who had invited her to Eleanor's first concert at 14 Summer Drive. The girls met; they found they shared an interest in acting as well as music; Flavia asked Eleanor round to her home; and they began to spend time together.

They giggled a lot. They pretended even more: 'Let's pretend . . .' might have been the refrain of their friendship. They were always acting impromptu scenes from invented melodramas. Flavia, overgrown and heavily built, was apt to become a fearsome headmistress, Miss Itemard, and Eleanor one of her squeaky little schoolgirl victims, begging in vain for mercy and then in private having to bare her bottom so that Miss Itemard could live up to her surname.

This chastisement with the back of a hairbrush or by hand was daring and naughty, the girls realised, and all the more fun for having to be a secret: why it was naughty, they neither knew nor cared.

About the irregularities of Eleanor's birth and upbringing Flavia had a little knowledge; but it was more discouraging than dangerous. Having asked her friend: 'What are your parents like?' – and been told: 'I've never met my father' – she merely commented: 'Mine's boring.' She had been warned by her parents that the children in the care of the Miss Cartys were somehow disadvantaged; but she was given no details, guessed that explanations might become embarrassing, and let the matter drop.

Flavia and Eleanor were no less intrigued by the procreative process than children always have been and are. The younger members of the Summer Drive multitude could hardly fail to notice the physical differences between boys and girls, notwithstanding their Auntys' efforts to separate the sexes and insist upon observation of the proprieties. They even had a vocabulary of their own to describe such differences: Eleanor was pleased to use it to respond to Flavia's confession that she had never set eyes on the masculine physique, 'Well – boys have these tiny tails, and girls grow buffers.'

Yet their ignorance could establish no linkage between tails and buffers and their own presence upon the earth and exchange of confidences. The facts of life were a book not only closed, but put out of their reach by elders and betters – by the prudery of Mr and Mrs Simmons, and by a combination of the

[42]

sensibilities and the protectiveness of the Cartys, who instilled principles of chastity and good behaviour into adolescence and would not allow it to corrupt childhood.

Therefore Eleanor's mounting interest in fathers was purely sentimental, at least so far as she was aware. It helped to fill the vacuum created by her other parent. While she paid lip-service to the verdict that Mr Simmons was boring, in her heart she respected him for doing his paternal duty. He was a shop assistant, in charge of Soft Furnishings in a department store in the West End. If she mocked his shiny bald head and mimicked his obsequious manner to entertain Michael Janes or Willy Hopkins, she was merely having her revenge for the pangs of envy of Flavia that he was responsible for.

Once, on a Christmas Day which brought her neither a present nor a written communication from her mother, let alone a sign of life from her father, after a tea party at number 14 she watched the Simmons family walking home through the snow. Mr Simmons in a balaclava helmet and additional ear-muffs, and Mrs Simmons who was twice his size and looked gigantic in her furs, had come to fetch Flavia. The scene of the hopping child holding the hands of the two adults, the three dark figures in the white world of the snowy street illuminated by gas lamps and the warm glow from windows, and the inexpressible idea of their inter-dependence and emotional security, caused Eleanor to shed the tears of deprivation pent up throughout the festivities.

Her feelings for fathers, for her own and for the potential sort, were reinforced in her tenth year. The motivating episode occurred after the Great War had started and as a side-effect of it.

International events meant not much more to her than that Donald Wilson enlisted in the navy and turned up in Summer Drive in bell-bottomed trousers, and that her Auntys were more perturbed than usual by reading newspapers. She resented being roped in to roll bandages in the Town Hall, and the possibility that a bomb was going to fall on her head. Of course she was sorry for the casualties, too, when she was told about them. But Aunty Lou's announcement that she was taking her younger charges to Ireland, where they could have a holiday in safety, formed Eleanor's more positive view of the conflict.

Matilda and Jane Lovejoy were included in the treat. They were all going to stay in a boarding house beside the sea in County Waterford. Aunty Nell would remain at Summer Drive to look after Michael and Willy, Fauntleroy the cat and Peter Rabbit.

They travelled by bus to Paddington Station and for hours and hours by train to Fishguard. The season was autumn, the nights were already closing in, and by the time they arrived at Fishguard Harbour it was no longer light, also drizzling steadily. The weather, the crowd, the commotion and noise had a bewildering effect; and Aunty Lou, who was carrying a suitcase and a large basket of provisions, shepherded Matilda and Jane on to the steeply sloping gangplank from quay to ferry, and was forced by the press of other travellers to follow them. Since Eleanor was not behind her, as she should have been, Aunty Lou could neither see her, nor get an answer to her call, nor turn against the traffic, nor abandon the twins.

Meanwhile Eleanor began to realise she was lost, and to fear that the boat would steam away without her. She did not like to push into the queue of people shuffling towards the gangplank, and was not even sure where her friends were or how on earth to find them. She stood disconsolately amongst the hustle and bustle on the quayside, holding the paper bag full of most of her belongings in one hand and clutching the purse containing her nearly three pounds of savings in the other. The rain dripped on her new red beret, which she had been so proud of, and she grew ever more panicky.

'Are you Eleanor?'

It was like the voice of God, deep and strong and coming from somewhere above her.

She looked up into the smiling eyes of a tall male stranger wearing a tweed cap and tweed suit with a belted Norfolk-style jacket.

She smiled back at him and replied in the affirmative.

'Your aunt's on board – I volunteered to come and fetch you – we'd better hurry, before she has high strikes.'

Eleanor could not help laughing at his jolly conspiratorial way of talking to her.

He was bending down, and now he reached out confidently, lifted her in his great strong arms, and gained a place in the queue for the gangplank.

Eleanor was swept off her feet in every sense, literally, and by surprise, and because she had never before been so close to a man.

He said: 'Hang on to your bag – and we'll try not to knock anyone overboard!'

She gazed into his twinkling eyes with the crinkly corners, and heard herself laughing again. She felt the warmth of his sweet breath, and inhaled his lovely smell of mingled tweed, tobacco, hair oil and masculinity. They were already on the gangplank, mounting it with powerful purposeful steps. She was overcome with relief and pleasure, a new rippling sort of pleasure and excitement. Putting her trust in the hard arms clasping her to his bosom, she laid her head in its damp red beret against the tweedy lapel of his jacket.

Eleanor saw no more of her rescuer after he had deposited her on the deck of the Irish ferry and received heartfelt thanks.

She was glad to be reunited with Aunty Lou, despite the scolding she got for having strayed. She apologised for causing anxiety, she said how sorry she was though not exactly why; and she could not forget the man who figured in her dreams fraught with yearning and more often than not with disappointment, since he was apt to turn into her father and vanish.

Time passed, and back in Willesden she tackled Aunty Lou on the most vexed of the various vexed topics of conversation at 14 Summer Drive.

'But who was my father?'

'I'll repeat myself just this once more, child – I don't know.'

'You never met him with my mother?'

'No, dear.'

'Who do you think he might be?'

'Well, I'm sure he's clever, and probably handsome too.'

'Why do you say that?'

'A little bird tells me.'

'What do you mean, Aunty Lou?'

'Nothing, Eleanor. I can't answer your questions.'

'Please – why isn't he married to my mother – why didn't he marry her – and why is she married to Mr Beck?'

'Well, he couldn't – oh dear! – you'll soon understand.'

[45]

'Everybody says that! I think he's horrid not to want to know me.'

'I don't believe he can be horrid. But leave me in peace, I do beg you.'

One day Aunty Lou let slip the information that she had known Eleanor from the very moment she was born.

Eleanor pounced on it: 'How? Where was I born? Where?'

'At home – in your mother's home.'

'But where was that?'

'In London – not too far away – don't ask, child – I'm not at liberty to say.'

'Was it nice – a nice house, I mean?'

'Oh yes.'

'And big?'

'Yes, quite big.'

'Why couldn't I have stayed there?'

'It wasn't possible, dear.'

'Mr Beck wouldn't have me, would he?'

'No, but he didn't mean you any harm.'

'Do you know him?'

'No, dear, we've never met.'

'Where was he when I was being born?'

'I expect he'd gone to see a man about a dog.'

'No, seriously, Aunty Lou?'

'I believe he was abroad.'

'Did you meet my brother Vivian and my sister Winnie?'

'No – they were with their father – abroad with Mr Beck while you were screaming their house down.'

This personal remark charmed the self-centredness of Eleanor's youth.

She smiled tenderly at the image of her babyhood and inquired: 'Did I scream an awful lot?'

'And laughed – it was always sunshine or showers with you, and always will be, I expect – and now you've asked me an awful lot of questions.'

'Will you answer one more, please, Aunty Lou?'

'What's that?'

'But will you?'

'We'll see.'

'How are babies born?'

'Wait and see – you'll find out soon enough – now be off with you, my girl!'

Eleanor's juvenile curiosity was satisfied temporarily by such scraps of information, and her juvenile attention distracted by red herrings. The questions she omitted to ask were perhaps the most relevant: for instance, what was the meaning of the word bastard sometimes shouted at her and the other young inmates of 14 Summer Drive by the local street urchins. And for one reason or another she never concentrated on extracting the address of the Beck home from Aunty Lou, so that she herself could post her letters to her relations, should she decide to write to them again.

Moreover, like other good children of obscurantist periods of history, she obeyed grown-ups who responded to her interest in the reproduction of the species by telling her to be off. She did not prosecute her inquiries: Flavia's idea that babies formed inside their mothers was too preposterous, and Michael Janes' fairly accurate version of how they came into the world was too disgusting, to try out on Aunty Lou.

Her other interests intervened. After all she was quite happy to postpone consideration of a problem that still seemed academic, in order to practise on the piano in the parlour, do her lessons and homework, fool around with Flavia, beg titbits to eat from Aunty Nell, read, act in homemade plays, and so on.

She had always been keen on the written word, and she read the books in the playroom shelves with greater understanding as a result of her experience on the gangplank at Fishguard. The majority of these books were the romantic fiction Aunty Nell had a weakness for; and Eleanor, having retired out of range of interruption with – say – *Paradise Nextdoor* by Aurora Macy, was now able to identify closely with a heroine in distress who in the end found peace and joy in the arms of a gallant hero.

Fishguard, books, the theatrical inclinations of Flavia and Michael and their influence, and games of charades, and unhappier sources of inspiration, combined together to give Eleanor the idea of writing some of the plays acted at number 14.

She would scribble them out at high speed and rush to show them page by page to one of her Auntys.

'What do you think? Is it all right?'

'Yes, dear – very clever.'

'Really?'

'Yes.'

Adult approval was secretly qualified because the plays were so dismal and often so violent. Their central character was invariably a young female person: in one play she was a child maltreated by parents, in another a girl who murders her mother. In a third an orphaned seventeen-year-old falls in love with a paragon of a man who deserts her; in a fourth the ghost of a waif haunts her neglectful father.

The psychological implications betrayed by Eleanor's dramas were disturbing. On the other hand the playwright and her actors seemed to derive inhuman glee from introducing death and destruction into their Auntys' parlour.

The roles of female infant and little girl were played by a new member of the company of children. Her name was Unity Hart. Economically speaking, she brought into the house the fees that had gone out with Donald Wilson. But naturally, in the first place, the Carty sisters were persuaded by pity and nothing else to take care of her.

Unity was four years old when she arrived. She was a casualty of the war, born out of wedlock, the child of a soldier who had been killed. Her maternal grandparents had reared her, somehow explaining her existence discreetly; but then one grandparent died, the other felt unequal to the task, and the mother, a Miss Clare Williams, became engaged to an American soldier. Miss Williams did not dare tell her fiancé about Unity. She was going to start a new life in America, therefore she took the heart-breaking decision probably to sever her connection with her daughter for ever, having appointed a legal guardian and made full financial provision.

The paradoxical aspect of these sad developments was that Unity was the jolliest little creature imaginable. She had tight blond curls all over her head, rosy cheeks, a stout figure and a foolproof sense of humour. She ragged with the older children indefatigably, and laughed at life.

Considering that Unity was determined to act in Eleanor's plays, and that she was the baby of the multitude, she had to take the parts that allowed Flavia,

[48]

Michael, Willy and Eleanor herself to impersonate parental types. The twins Matilda and Jane were awkward customers when it came to casting, since they insisted on doing everything together. They usually ended up as a couple passing by or two dustmen.

After a few days of rehearsal, the Auntys and a few regulars like Mr and Mrs Simmons, Miss Elmes and Mrs Cruse were invited to attend the performance. When they were seated, Eleanor would enter, curtsey and – on an exemplary occasion – announce: 'The Fate of Amelia-Anne,' and the action would proceed as follows.

Flavia with a cushion stuffed into the front of her dress, and Michael made to look sinister with burnt-cork eyebrows and moustache, wheel in the old push-chair containing Unity, who is too big for it. Flavia – Mrs Blackwitch – and Michael – Mr Wilfred Blackwitch – complain about and frown upon Unity – their grinning child Amelia-Anne. Mrs B. says A.-A. is too fat, Mr B. says she is too wicked, and they threaten to box her ears, at which A.-A. giggles, but remembers to scream, the cue for Matilda and Jane, disguised as Police Constables, to enter and chorus loud and soft that the peace must be kept. The scene of the second and last act is the Blackwitch home. Mr and Mrs B. accuse A.-A. of her multiple faults: she is not only too fat and wicked, but untidy, unwilling, unpleasant, ungrateful, and deserves to be taught a sharp lesson. A.-A. pipes up hopefully, 'Are you going to beat me again?' – and, receiving a fierce answer in the affirmative, runs to bend over a chair and be held in position by Mrs B. while Mr B. administers six of the best with a stick supplied by Buzzer Bees. Neighbours in the form of Eleanor and Willy Hopkins – Mr and Mrs Goodbody – have overheard A.-A.'s squeals of pain, not intentionally of laughter, and force an entry and demand explanations. Mr and Mrs B. convince them by silencing A.-A. with kisses and cuddles that nothing is wrong. But as soon as the Goodbodys have departed they turn on their daughter once more, berate her for embarrassing them, manhandle her out of the house and lock the door. This bitter end of the play, with Amelia-Anne's knocking on the door growing fainter thanks to cold and hunger, and her parents commenting that it served her right, was sweetened to some extent when the actors took their bows and Unity punched Flavia in her false bosom for a joke.

Unity's intentional and unintentional jokes relieved the gloom for spectators, and even made the playwright laugh although they were apt to mangle her best effects. In the matricidal whodunit, since Flavia wanted to act the mother and die dramatically, and Eleanor and Michael the detectives, and Willy the judge and the hangman, Unity was bound to be the daughter and murderess. The first climax was the murder: Unity was meant to steal up behind Flavia, gesture with a blunt kitchen knife as if cutting her throat, and pour tomato juice out of a concealed jug over her neck and chest. Instead, she sloshed the tomato juice in her face. Flavia was coughing and sneezing tomato juice, and blundering about and falling over the furniture, momentarily blinded. The consequences were that the detectives could not stop giggling, and then the hooded figure on the scaffold was laughing so immoderately that she had a little accident.

Later that evening, after the general mirth had ceased to ring through the house, a coincidental conversation took place in Aunty Lou's bedroom. Eleanor now had to share the honour of sleeping there with Unity; but at present Unity was far away in the land of Nod. Aunty Lou sat on the edge of the narrow bed in which Eleanor lay back on the pillow, clinging to her hand and beseeching her not to go just yet.

'You'd have me sitting with you until tomorrow morning if you had your way, I do believe,' Aunty Lou remarked.

'But I'm not sleepy – I won't be able to sleep because of my play – please stay a bit longer – won't you – please?'

'What a persuasive girl it is! And what shining eyes! Very good! Since we're here together I might as well tell you something which ought to give you pleasant dreams.'

'Oh yes – do – please!'

'I heard from your mother again this morning.'

'Oh?'

'She's coming to see you next Saturday.'

'Is she?'

'I think she's hoping to patch things up, Eleanor.'

'What else was in her letter?'

'Nothing else. I promise you. I'll show you if you like. You don't need to be suspicious. And you should be glad to get back to being friends with your mother. Oh dear, I never guessed you'd take my news like this, I imagined you'd be pleased. But would you rather I hadn't told you?'

'No.'

'What can I do? What could I do?'

'You won't leave me alone with her, Aunty Lou?'

'I'll try not to.'

'Promise me that!'

'I'll do my level best, but it might be difficult.'

Eleanor sat up in bed and hugged her Aunty rather desperately and said: 'Don't leave me, don't — I'll be so afraid!'

'What — you — afraid? That doesn't sound likely. There there, dear! What have you got to be afraid of? Your mother didn't manage to take you away from us last time. I don't believe she ever could or would. You keep calm! We'll be all right, the two of us, or the three with my sister. And remember, Eleanor, you've always got to keep on top of life — never let it frighten you. There — is that better?'

'Thank you, Aunty Lou.'

'Night-night, dear.'

'Let me kiss you good night.'

'What a one for kisses you are!'

Mrs Beck had stated that her time of arrival at Summer Drive would be three-thirty on the Saturday afternoon in question.

Eleanor, having neither seen nor heard from her mother for eighteen months, dreaded their reunion. Her feelings were the opposite of what they used to be: she wished her mother would stay away. Doubt, distrust, and other rebellious ideas were exacerbated by the fact that the PT teacher Mr Svenson was giving Michael, Willy and the twins a swimming lesson at four-thirty on the same Saturday. She would miss it — her afternoon, when she might have realised her ambition to learn the side-stroke, was more than likely to end in tears, determined though she was not to be made to cry again.

She put on her best dress under protest, and in the parlour she kept on nearly quarrelling with Aunty Lou for saying she had duties to attend to elsewhere. She absolutely refused to be abandoned: she said she would lock herself in the lavatory, or jump out of an upstairs window, rather than face her mother on her own.

Aunty Lou besought her not to agitate herself and certainly not to issue such awful threats. But as the black marble clock on the mantelpiece ticked on to four o'clock she pleaded the cause of Mrs Beck with less and less conviction. She could not help remembering the ill-effects of Mrs Beck's previous visits, particularly the last disastrous one, since when nothing had been contributed towards her daughter's upkeep.

At twenty past four Eleanor declared decisively, if in a tearful tone of voice: 'I'm not waiting any longer. Why should I always have to wait for her? I bet she's forgotten. Aunty Lou, I'm going to go swimming.'

'Very well,' Aunty Lou allowed.

Eleanor changed her clothes in a rush and was ready to join the other members of the multitude and be escorted to the swimming baths by Mr Svenson.

In the pool she expressed her sense of release by means of daredevil jumps from the highest diving board. She splashed water at the boys in between practising her side-stroke. The lesson finished at five, and the children dried themselves and dressed and were ushered out of the building by Mr Svenson.

In the nice summer weather Mrs Beck sat in her new saloon car parked in the roadway by the exit.

She wound down the window and called out to Eleanor. To Mr Svenson she explained who she was and said she would drop her daughter back at Summer Drive in about an hour. Adolphe held the rear door open; when Eleanor had got into the car he received instructions to drive to the teashop in Hampstead.

Mrs Beck said: 'How you've grown, my darling, since I saw you last! Aren't you going to kiss me? I know I was late, I was born late – don't hold it against me. I would have arrived at the swimming baths sooner if I hadn't had to settle your account with the Cartys. Thank you – not a very loving kiss, but "owt's better than nowt", I suppose. Well – have you missed me? I've missed you. No, Eleanor, of course I have – and I don't approve of that disbelieving look of yours. Actually I've missed you very much indeed – I just haven't been able to get down here – I've had such a vile time – my Vivian, your brother, chose to join the army, he's been involved in the fighting in France, and I've been half off my head with worry. You wouldn't understand – why should you? – but I haven't had a wink of sleep for months – and I knew you were all right with the Cartys – you told me in no uncertain terms that you'd rather live in a backstreet in Willesden than in luxury and security with the Adamsons. No, I won't let you make me feel guilty for introducing you to Jake and Mona Adamson – I was doing you a favour – and it's not my fault that you failed to grasp your opportunity. Come along, darling! We've nursed our grievances for long enough. Life's so short – follow my example and take my advice and stop frowning, or you'll get lines on your forehead!'

Eleanor responded indirectly to this monologue: 'Your clothes are pretty.'

Poppy Beck was wearing a pale pink linen overcoat over a frilly pale mauve dress, and long white gloves.

'Why, thank you, precious! You're definitely growing up. I shall return the compliment – and I promise my warnings are meant to be complimentary. In the street outside the swimming baths, when you were standing there in the sun, I could see right through your sweet little rag of a dress – and I do think it's high time you wore a petticoat. The other thing is that you're developing a charming figure, you're beautifully made, made for love, as they say – so you'd better mind out and take care.'

Eleanor had to ask, although she hated herself for being intrigued and excited by the last remark: 'How do you know?'

'What, my pet?'

'The love bit?'

'I just do – it's a matter of proportions – you're like me for better or worse – and it's generally worse. But don't let's go into that side of life. Don't let's be morbid. Tell me your news!'

This imperative was counter-productive: Eleanor had heard it before, recognised it as a signal that her mother was becoming bored, and that nothing she said would be attended to. Silences fell, interspersed with questions which she answered briefly, monosyllabically if possible.

In the teashop Mrs Beck's interrogation took a turn that revived and reinforced Eleanor's hostility.

'Are the Cartys getting you a new music teacher?' she asked.

'I'm not sure.'

'You're not still with that fat frump?'

'Yes.'

'She's no good. You need a higher class of person. I hope that at least Mrs Crusoe keeps you at it?'

'Mrs Cruse.'

'Whatever her name is! Have you been practising your piano, darling?'

'Yes — and doing plays.'

'Plays?'

'Acting them and writing them.'

'Good heavens! What next? What are your plays about?'

'Nothing much.'

'How interesting! I can't supervise the education you should be getting — I have to leave all that to Louisa — but it seems to me you should have the best music teaching, and be made to concentrate on your general studies, instead of wasting your time on amateur theatricals — and it's up to Louisa to make the arrangements, she has lots of money now and absolutely no excuse. Don't you agree?'

'I'm all right, Mother.'

'That remains to be seen. And while we're on the subject of money, Louisa must spend some of mine on buying you more suitable garments. You want to look nice, don't you, sweet?'

'Yes.'

Eleanor was furious with her mother for criticising those who had been kinder and more loyal than she ever had, and for somehow involving Eleanor herself in disloyalty.

And her fury was not allayed when Mrs Beck, having peeped at her wristwatch for the umpteenth time, said in tones of mock alarm: 'Oh dear, my pet, it's frightfully late — have you finished? I'm sorry, I'll have to go — and I know I kept you waiting, but so did you while you were swimming.'

The injustice of incurring any blame for her mother's premature departure reduced her to, and indeed imposed, a seething sort of silence during the drive back to Willesden.

As soon as the car stopped in Summer Drive she kissed her mother even less lovingly than before and fumbled with the door-handle in her haste to get out.

'Oh dear, what's wrong now?' Mrs Beck posed this question pettishly. 'I'm afraid you've got your father's cruel streak,' she concluded, and averting her face from her daughter she ordered Adolphe to drive on.

Eleanor managed not to pay the tribute of tears to the power of her mother to upset her. But, following their encounter, she felt churned up inside, more so than usual, full of regret for what she had said and omitted to say, and especially hurt and unsettled by the other's parting shot. She would demand more information about her father, and could hardly wait to defend him against dastardly slander.

Meanwhile, in her contradictory mood, she vented her displeasure on her dear Auntys, not least because she was able to deduce from their tightlipped references to her mother – 'Was your time with her quite nice, dear? That foreign chauffeur summoned us out into the road to talk to her' – that they had let Mrs Beck ruffle their feathers, too.

Nevertheless, on a morning five days after her mother's visit, when certain internal events and external evidence convinced Eleanor of her imminent demise, she again sought solace in Aunty Lou's arms.

'What is it, child? Tell me, tell me!'

By way of reply Eleanor lifted her skirt.

'No, dear, no, you're not dying, far from it, you're perfectly healthy, I give you my word. But fancy you starting all that so soon! We'll go to the bathroom. Don't cry – you've only become a woman like the rest of us. I'll explain everything to you now.'

Aunty Lou's explanation took Eleanor's mind off her mother at any rate.

The girl was in turn astonished, horrified, fascinated and amused. She broke the news to Flavia, and they soothed their nerves by laughing excitably at the whole nasty business. The fact of life so far as they were concerned was that they could not believe the facts, which were surely beyond the bounds of possibility. How could Mr Simmons have done those things to Mrs Simmons? The same question asked about Polly Cruse or Buzzer Bees was no more

[55]

answerable. On the other hand, Michael Janes' description of the process had apparently not been just a figment of his squalid imagination.

Eleanor's second thoughts were mainly proud. She enjoyed a sense of achievement, and in private looked down on Flavia for being physically less mature although older. She also gained a vague insight into what must have happened between the parents of the members of the multitude, herself included, if as yet she could not comprehend why.

But love preoccupied her increasingly. Her mother's complimentary remark lent personal significance to Aunty Lou's technicalities. Apprehensive thrills ran up and down her spine when she now delved curiously into the romances in the playroom.

On a rainy afternoon in winter she began to read a dog-eared copy of *David Copperfield*. It had an instant and tremendous effect on her. She identified with David, then fell in love with him; but she also fell in love with Steerforth, whose manly charm reminded her of the hero of Fishguard harbour. She felt she was part kittenish Dora and part virtuous Agnes, with pinches of pathetic little Emily and temperamental and tragic Rosa Dartle thrown in; and of course her dependable Peggotty was Aunty Lou. As for David's outcast state, she was so moved by it because it seemed to be her own. Wistfully she wondered whether a fairy godmother would ever stalk into her existence in the guise of a Miss Betsy Trotwood.

The book was formative for two extra reasons.

She could see the difference between it and Aunty Nell's favoured reading matter, and realised that Charles Dickens wrote better than Aurora Macy, more truthfully, more entertainingly. She therefore searched the playroom shelves for other books to read that were good enough to satisfy her and shed some light on life in general and hers in particular.

And then *David Copperfield* modified her attitude to the death in action of her half-brother Vivian.

She was told about it by Aunty Lou, who called her into the parlour one morning soon after Henny-penny had delivered the mail.

'This letter's from your mother, dear,' Aunty Lou said, holding it and regarding Eleanor with worrying seriousness over her reading spectacles.

'What does she want?'

'I don't think you should speak of your mother in that tone of voice – she's in great trouble, poor woman.'

'Oh?'

'Her son Vivian – he was a soldier, you know – he's been killed in the fighting.'

'Has he? Well, I don't know him.'

'Oh Eleanor, it isn't like you to be so unsympathetic.'

'Well – you said I knew him – but I didn't, I wasn't allowed to.'

'Does that matter now? He was your brother, and he volunteered to sacrifice his young life. He must have been a fine boy, and his death's another terrible waste whichever way you look at it.'

At this point in the conversation Eleanor associated Vivian's end with Steerforth's, and suffered a change of heart.

'I am sad, Aunty Lou, really.'

'I'm sure you are, and will be, dear.'

'Is Mother coming down here?'

'She says she's longing to see you, but she's afraid you may still be cross with her. You wouldn't be cross now, would you?'

'No. Tell her I wouldn't, Aunty Lou – or shall I write to her?'

'That would be a kind act.'

A week after Eleanor wrote, Mrs Beck arrived at 14 Summer Drive at teatime. She was beautifully dressed in black, and a taut veil attached to her hat covered her face becomingly. Owing to the veil, she refused the offer of a kiss; and as she held an elegant umbrella in her right hand she could only extend her left for Aunty Lou to shake. Having received the condolences of both Cartys, she was ushered into the parlour and followed by her daughter. The door was then closed behind them.

Mrs Beck, sitting on the settee, began to say something, but had to stop. Her eyes glistened behind her veil, and she cleared her throat.

Eleanor began to cry and impulsively embraced her, exclaiming: 'Oh I'm so sorry for you.'

'Thank you, my pet. But sit down, do! What sweet wet tears!'

A white lace handkerchief in a black-gloved hand fastidiously mopped the veiled cheek.

[57]

'Yes, sit over there, where I can see your darling face. And dry your eyes – the family's cried enough already – Vivian's father's a broken man, and Winnie's been a complete mop. But what's the use? Listen! I've wanted to say something to you specially. I wish I could have brought you and Viv together. I feel I've made so many mistakes. Forgive me, please! Will you ever forgive me?'

'Oh yes, Mother,' Eleanor declared with intense conviction, biting back her sobs.

'You're a generous girl – yes, you are. I'm glad I gave you life and faced up to all the difficulties. At least I was right about that – and your gifts and your strength repay me. I only hope your destiny won't be as up and down as the way you came into the world.'

Aunty Nell knocked on the door, carried in a tray of tea for two with a plate of thin slices of bread and butter, arranged it on an occasional table in front of Mrs Beck, and withdrew.

'Eleanor, be a love and pour me a cup of very weak tea without milk, while I deal with this veil. I won't eat anything.'

'Mother,' Eleanor began to say as she obeyed instructions.

'Yes?'

'What do you mean about the way I came into the world – the ups and downs?'

'Your father was very much in love with me. I was with him, too. It was such a magical crazy time – it was more wonderful and dangerous than you can probably imagine – but you'll sympathise with me soon, I shouldn't wonder. Incidentally, Louisa tells me you've reached the stage at which you've got to be extremely careful in your dealings with the opposite sex, unlike your mother. You do understand me, don't you?'

'Yes,' Eleanor fibbed impatiently. 'But why was it a dangerous time?'

'My dear, if you don't think it's dangerous to bear a child that couldn't be your husband's, you're heading for trouble. I've made you blush, poor precious. You mustn't judge me by the Cartys' standards, or be ashamed of your beginnings. I can't help it that men have always fallen for me – and I can assure you that your father was irresistible.'

'You said he was cruel.'

'All's fair in love – not in war, no, nothing's fair about war. Anyway –

your father expected a lot – he turned our romance into quite a French farce so far as I was concerned – once he hid me behind the curtains in his study for hours while he talked to some people; but then he wanted no more of it. I suppose he got bored with the complications, because he had responsibilities similar to mine – he gave me my marching orders – short and sweet was his idea of love. Did I say he was cruel? He was ruthless, perhaps he had to be in his position, and he certainly understood women, he was conspicuous by his absence when I would have made scenes.'

'Who is he, Mother? Can't I see him?'

'If you turned up on his doorstep he wouldn't thank either of us. He's unaware of your existence.'

Eleanor uttered a small pained cry.

'What's the matter?' her mother inquired dismissively. 'He and I parted before I knew I was pregnant. It was very nice of me, later on, not to try to involve him – and nicer of Charles, my jealous husband, to insist on his never being involved. Charles has supplied every single penny that I've paid the Cartys for you – he says it's the price of keeping me out of trouble – and your father hasn't contributed a sou – not that I blame him. No! But I couldn't possibly foist you on him after all these years – it'd look like revenge, and might add to my matrimonial troubles – and no doubt he'd refuse to believe you were his – and I wouldn't put it past him to murder me. You've inherited your temper from your father – he can be pretty savage.'

'What's the connection between my father and Mr Adamson, Mother?'

'None to my knowledge.'

'But you said they were alike.'

'Did I? Oh yes. Well, you needn't bother your head about that. It's to do with their race. But I've talked too much – I hate raking over the past – and we're supposed to let the dead bury their dead. Tell me – tell me what you want to make of your life.'

Eleanor said: 'I don't know,' shrugging her shoulders. She added: 'I wish I could meet Winifred one day.'

'And I wish you were more aware of the problems you cause me with remarks of that sort. Perhaps I'll be able to arrange a meeting on neutral ground in due course; but I'm not promising anything. Winnie's an innocent young girl – I don't want to shock her by producing you – and I'd much rather she told no tales to her father, my Charles. You don't seem to realise, Eleanor, what I've been through on your account, and how delicately I still have to tread at home. Instead of judging me, and punishing me for not being motherly, it'd be a welcome change if you began to appreciate all I've done for you, and showed some gratitude.'

Mrs Beck's surprising and self-justifying rebuke annoyed Eleanor, and confused her: she was under the impression that she owed gratitude more to the Auntys.

Mrs Beck continued to criticise, since Eleanor must have looked as sullen as she felt: 'Please stop frowning at me! And yes, give me the credit I deserve! Everything would have been so much easier if only you'd played your cards correctly with the Adamsons – I mean meeting Winnie, and for that matter meeting Vivian and Charles and seeing where we live, everything – and your future and your security would have been guaranteed. It's a shame you misinterpreted my motives, and chose to think I was doing you down rather than doing you a favour. I'm afraid certain people bear a heavy responsibility for turning you against me, and ruining your chances for their own financial advantage. However – without crying over spilt milk – as it is – you ought to take my question very seriously – what good are you doing here, and how do you imagine you're going to earn a living? What's happened about your piano teacher?'

Eleanor shrugged her shoulders and muttered: 'Nothing.'

'Well, I give up,' Poppy Beck declaimed, raising her black-gloved hands and her eyes skywards to convey her exasperation. 'Nobody pays the slightest attention to what I want and advise, so I shall leave you to sink or swim in the company of your beloved Auntys. I wouldn't have come all this way to have a row – especially not just now, when all I want is peace.' She stood, shook herself as if to be rid of the discomfiting effects of the visit, and, leaning on her umbrella, extended the side of her face to receive her daughter's kiss. But she had already lowered her veil, and for Eleanor the kiss was a mere scratchy contact of cheeks. 'You see me out of the house, pet,' she added, 'I haven't the heart to meet anyone else.'

Eleanor duly led the way to, and opened, the front door with its stained glass panels.

[60]

Then she remembered Vivian and Steerforth and, overwhelmed by comprehensive unhappiness, volunteered: 'Sorry, Mother.'

Mrs Beck with a pale smile asked: 'Are you?'

Scarcely pausing, she proceeded down the path and through the squeaky garden gate towards Adolphe waiting by her motor.

Some days later Mrs Cruse arrived as usual at 14 Summer Drive. She spoke to the Cartys in the kitchen for a moment before joining her best pupil in the parlour. She put a plump finger to her lips to stop Eleanor practising trills and said in a triumphant tone of voice: 'I've arranged for you to play to Harold Whymper.'

Considerable history lay behind this announcement. Polly Cruse had unbounded admiration for the pianist Harold Whymper as solo performer, chamber music player, accompanist and, above all, teacher. She had attended public master classes he occasionally gave. For several years she had dangled in front of Eleanor's nose the carrot of the outside possibility of a session with him, even a lesson or two.

Yet now Eleanor, instead of clapping her hands or evincing any sign of pleasure, demanded: 'Has my mother been on to you?'

'Your mother?' Polly Cruse was mystified and for a moment crestfallen. 'No. Does your mother know Mr Whymper? I dared to take the bull by the horns and wrote to him about you; and the amazing thing is, although I expect it's typical of his generosity, that he wrote back and offered us an appointment. Can you believe it? I'm so thrilled. We'll have to buckle down to work to prepare a programme worthy of the occasion, won't we?'

Eleanor agreed. She became enthusiastic, hopeful, then mainly apprehensive.

On the afternoon of the day of the appointment a modern motorised taxicab had been ordered to transport her and Mrs Cruse to and from the Whymper address, 25 Abinger Avenue in St John's Wood. She could not enjoy the novelty of the ride: she was too tense to respond to her Auntys' wishes of good luck and waves goodbye, and sat on the edge of the seat in her party dress, silently fuming because her companion had chosen to wear an embarrassing hat with jay's feathers stuck in the band. She owed her extra agitation to sensing that her mother's awkward questions about her future could be answered in the next hour or so.

Responding to Mrs Cruse's knock on the front door of a large ivy-covered house, a middle-aged woman with untidy hair and an apron over her dress opened it and said, smiling frankly: 'I know who you two are. Hullo! I'm Muriel Whymper. Come in – Harold's in the studio and expecting you.'

She led them chattily through a staircase hall and a sitting-room, both in shameless states of disarray, and into a church-like space reeking of tobacco smoke with two grand pianos side by side at the far end.

A man sitting at one of the pianos played a celebratory chord as they entered, stood up, faced his visitors, removed the cigarette from between his lips and greeted them, while his wife withdrew.

He wore an open-necked shirt, a cardigan, baggy corduroy trousers and bedroom slippers. His hair was thin and wispy; but he had a nice-looking face and an easy manner. He suggested they should all take the weight off their feet, indicating a broken-down suite of sofa and armchairs covered in threadbare plush.

Eleanor was so surprised that she had almost forgotten to be agitated. She could not get over what a more sophisticated person would call the bohemianism of the Whympers: that an unmistakable lady like Mrs Whymper should permit herself to be seen in an apron by strangers, that the house was as shabby within as it was imposing without, and that its master – the maestro referred to in tones of hushed respect by Polly Cruse – might have been a tramp. As for the grand pianos, she had never set eyes on one before, let alone a pair – and it occurred to her that with their black lids raised they had a look of monstrous jaws ready to devour her.

Harold Whymper lit another cigarette and, having had some professional talk with Mrs Cruse, turned to Eleanor and observed: 'You're very pretty.'

She blushed and wondered if he might be a bit mad.

He carried on: 'Which is going to make it even more difficult for you to become a pianist. Most lady pianists have arms like coal-heavers.'

She giggled uncertainly.

'How old are you?'

'Thirteen, nearly fourteen.'

'Well then, you've got time to grow into an enormous woman. What about hands? Can I hold your hand, as the boys have probably started to ask you?'

He almost fondled Eleanor's hand in both of his, pressed it in various places and pulled the fingers apart, and finished by jiggling her forearm to gauge the flexibility of her wrist.

'Do you find it hard to relax?'

'I don't know – sometimes.'

'Do you like playing to people?'

'Quite – I don't mind if it goes all right.'

'Same here,' he said. 'Shall I show you my treasures?'

He escorted her on a little tour of the room, pointing out portrait prints of Mozart and Chopin, a bust of Beethoven, a framed signature of Brahms and a bookcase full of music scores. She apologised for her ignorance: he assured her that it would probably be the making of her.

'Now you sit at that piano and I'll sit at this one,' he said. 'Have you ever played a grand? Try it!'

She did so with chords and scales, drawing many amazed and unexpressed comparisons between it and the battered upright at number 14; and, when he called for 'a tune', she launched straight into her Bach Prelude.

In the middle he sprang to his feet, and she stopped.

'What are you doing – or not doing?' he demanded sternly. 'At a concert, if someone in the front row's sick or passes out, the artist takes no notice. I'm only getting myself a smoke. Start again!'

She performed her complete programme, the Bach, the two Chopin and the Mendelssohn pieces, without further interruption, while Harold Whymper strode about in his slippers and perched temporarily on the other piano stool, and Mrs Cruse on the sofa shuffled sheet music in case there should be a lapse of memory.

As Eleanor finished, he clapped and almost shouted: 'Bravo!' – which was the equivalent of 'Hey presto' inasmuch as it wrought, or at least inaugurated, a transformation of her circumstances.

He said she had a touch like an angel's wing and that he had been too excited by her playing to sit still. Instant arrangements were made for her to have a six months' course of weekly lessons at reduced fees. And after the hour and a half of her first lesson she began to see everything in a new light.

Harold, as he wished to be called, managed to indicate the shortcomings of her pianistic technique and taste without destroying her confidence. He did not dismiss the effects of the tuition she had received, but was against whatever he chose to think had been imposed on her natural inclinations. He challenged her assumptions, urged her to break bad habits, and scolded her complacence. He initiated her into mysteries of fingering and phrasing, and gave her insights into the hearts and minds of composers. He set before her a series of musical goals at once idealistic yet accessible by means of hard work.

The minimum of four hours' work a day that he expected her to do, the exercises he wanted her to master, the pieces he told her to learn, the theory to be assimilated, the books to be read – all seemed impossible, beyond her powers, and slave-driving, cruelty to animals, as she tearfully complained at Summer Drive.

Yet the discovery that she was capable of passing such semi-professional tests reassured, disposed her to redouble her efforts, and changed her picture of herself in so far as she had one, and her view of the wide world and her place in it. Soon she would return to 25 Abinger Avenue on Friday afternoons eagerly rather than in dread, although Harold dished out no more extravagant compliments – the terms of his approval now had negative implications: 'Nothing wrong with that ... I can't fault it.'

Strangely, the less he said about her playing the more she valued his comments. Her admiration of her teacher increased week by week, while her liking for the man, down-at-heel as he was, smelling of and stained by tobacco, turned into a sort of love. She got a crush on the whole Whymper family: on Muriel, who made pots in a shed in the garden and sometimes asked her to stay to unhygienic tea after lessons, and on the two grown-up sons of whom she caught rare glimpses, romantically limping Michael, wounded in the war, married and a painter, and the pale and asthmatic aspiring writer Billy. Their particular charm in her eyes was their acceptance of her as a fellow-worker in their field, the immediate comradely welcome they extended to her across all the usual barriers of class, age and convention.

Meanwhile her special desire to be told by Harold she had not done too badly, encouraged her to work ever harder both at her music and the consequential creation or re-creation of her persona. It was as if her fingers on the keyboard summoned a new improved Eleanor from the void. She felt she was becoming something, much cleverer, even somebody, having been nothing and nobody before. She was half-aware of the irony that Harold, who set such store by her ignorance, that is to say by her being open-minded and receptive to his teaching, should have taught her incidentally to be not so ignorant.

She loved him the better for it, she hurried to Abinger Avenue and lingered in his company for as long as he allowed, she glowed at him gratefully for inspiring her to concentrate and to learn, and she gloated over the privilege of the Whymper connection which she had won for herself: thus, for all her cleverness, she overlooked developments elsewhere.

Lou and Nell Carty beside the kitchen range told a different story about their Eleanor and the Whympers. They squirmed verbally on the horns of various dilemmas. They would have liked to rebuke Eleanor for her ungrateful attitude to Mrs Cruse, yet were afraid to seem to be casting aspersions on Harold Whymper.

Kind-hearted Nell said: 'Polly did so much for her and charged so little, and now Eleanor's been persuaded that she was taught all wrong – I've even heard her speak badly of Polly. It isn't fair or very nice.'

But Lou replied with a warning glance over the top of her spectacles: 'We can't interfere – we don't know enough – and we wouldn't want Eleanor to think we're sorry she's with Mr Whymper.'

'She wouldn't be with him if it hadn't been for Polly.'

'All the same, Nell ...'

They were soon worried by the economics of the situation, since Mrs Beck wrote that she could not afford the increased costs of the superior tuition she had wished her daughter to have.

'We'll just pay the difference ourselves,' Lou declared; 'we musn't spoil Eleanor's chances.'

'What happens at the end of the six months, when Mr W. expects his full fee for lessons?'

[65]

'We'll have to choose between paying up and breaking Eleanor's heart.'

Their gladness because the girl was obviously getting on well and enjoying herself became a little less altruistic.

Lou put it in a nutshell one evening: 'These days nothing suits Eleanor here, because Summer Drive isn't Abinger Avenue and we're not called Whymper.'

Nell was more specific: 'Why does she say we should put a whole half pound of butter on the table and let everyone dig into it until it's eaten, like the Whympers, instead of having the fresh pat of butter I make before every meal? She used to be so dainty.'

They were worried by Eleanor's journeys to and from St John's Wood and her determination not to be accompanied; by the form of the friendship between pupil and teacher that she boasted of, and by the extent of her association with her teacher's sons; by her wearing herself out with work, and having no time either for play or for her former playmates; and by her impatient attitude towards life in general as lived at number 14.

'Eleanor says she won't have Fauntleroy in the parlour while she's practising – he disturbs her . . . Eleanor says she can't be fagged to feed Peter any more,' the sisters informed each other regretfully, their reference to the rabbit relating to Peter Rabbit's successor, Peter the Great.

One evening Lou observed: 'Eleanor's growing out of us, that's the fact.'

Nell's answer at once offered comfort and asked for it: 'Well – we know she's got a will of her own. But her heart's in the right place, isn't it? She was playing beautifully today – did you hear her?'

'I did.' Lou sighed. 'We must be grateful for her gift. I hope it'll earn her a living. And we should be used to our young ones leaving the nest by now.'

Almost while her Auntys were coming to these conclusions Eleanor yielded to yet another of the pleas of Flavia Simmons to accompany her on an afternoon walk.

Several times a week for the last three months Flavia had knocked on the door of number 14 and asked for her friend in vain. To start with, Eleanor would explain with hints of self-importance that she could not possibly interrupt her work. As Flavia grew more importunate, the Auntys were instructed to deal with her and turn her away.

[66]

But on the day in question Eleanor ran in response to the doorbell, calling out: 'I'll see to it.'

Flavia, after off-hand greetings had been exchanged, inquired diffidently: 'I don't suppose you'd care to stroll down to the Rec?'

Eleanor's affirmative reply was emphatic.

It surprised both girls, Flavia because she was accustomed to negatives, and Eleanor herself because she had not quite realised how ready she was for a break and a bit of fun. She longed to do something easy for a change, and to be frivolous rather than earnest. She was neither being unfaithful to Harold, nor more faithful than she had lately been to the Cartys and their values. Her youth suddenly and simply rebelled against the strain of her studies.

The Willesden Recreation Ground or so-called Rec consisted of several acres of parkland joined on to playing fields. Ancient trees were dotted about, one of which, a leaning sycamore with a bough that curved nearly to ground level, Eleanor had liked to climb when she was younger. Now, on impulse, perhaps motivated by nostalgia for a liberty she was losing, she straddled the low bough and heaved herself along it and upwards, challenging Flavia to follow suit.

'Oh I can't,' Flavia wailed; 'I can't in my skirt, I'll get my knickers green!'

But soon, in spite of such objections and bouts of enfeebling merriment, they sat facing each other with their legs dangling down on the higher part of the bough near the bole. Eleanor was describing the Whympers: she had to laugh at Flavia saying that it sounded as if Harold was a dirty old man, and Michael and Billy Whymper were nothing to write home about.

Through the summer leaves on the tree Flavia spied a male figure shambling in their direction, and got panicky.

'He musn't find us here — he mustn't see us like this!'

Eleanor said: 'It's too late to escape. If you keep quiet and stay still he may pass by.'

Instead he shambled in his big boots and ragged overalls to a spot immediately beneath them, and leered up at Flavia's heavy reddish bare legs and Eleanor's slender ones. He was unshaven and had teeth missing, and began to say improper things to them in a rustic accent. Eleanor told him to buzz off or she would call a policeman, a threat so empty in the middle of the

Rec that even the girls had to giggle at it. Meanwhile he was drooling on about their legs, and how they were sitting, and what he wanted to do to them and would be doing shortly when he had caught hold of them, and rubbing the front of his trousers and looking peculiar. He then began to jump and reach with great grubby hands for their ankles. They screamed and shrieked at the tops of their voices; a shaggy barking dog bounded towards them over the greensward, pursued by a floppy sort of woman brandishing its lead; the man swore unintelligibly and retreated, and they scrambled down to terra firma and without waiting to be lectured by the woman or bitten by her dog raced home.

For Eleanor, this episode became a laughing matter only in reminiscent sessions with Flavia. She mentioned it to no one else: she would have been embarrassed, the more so because of her mixed feelings. Her memory of the man under the tree still scared her, and she was disgusted, revolted, by his unforgettable speech and actions, but also stirred. In a certain sense she could not get away from him and he achieved his object: he would intrude into her reveries and her dreams.

Through the chink in her attention, as it were, while she thought of something other than measuring up to Harold Whymper's criteria, she arrived at a perception of her changing relations with her Auntys not so different from theirs. She sensed that they had drifted apart, and tried in rather a rush to bridge the gap by talking to them about her work and progress.

Aunty Nell would respond thus: 'Save your breath, my dear, that's far above my head ... So long as you're having a nice time, I'm content ... Besides, there's a lovely piece of fish for your supper in the oven, and needing my attention ...' and Aunty Lou: 'Your Whympers do seem to be a decent family, although I must admit I had my doubts when you started your lessons all alone ... Well, you deserve to succeed, dear ... But please don't work too hard.'

The irreverent contributions of the multitude did not advance the cause of mutual comprehension. Punning on the subject of the surname of Eleanor's teacher irritated her the more because it amused her Auntys. When she nearly lost her temper and then nearly cried over a silly poem by Michael Janes entitled *Whympering in the Wood*, Aunty Nell warned her not to lose her sense of humour.

If they embraced one another unusually often, perhaps they were trying to avert the disintegration of their triangular affections. Eleanor was apt to desert the piano in the parlour in order to seek out Aunty Nell in the kitchen and kiss her shiny hot cheeks. Equally Aunty Nell would celebrate Eleanor's approval of some underdone roast beef by giving her a hug along with a second helping.

Eleanor was now allowed to read late by a bedside light that did not disturb the slumbers of Unity Hart. Often, when her Auntys plodded upstairs, she would suffer an involuntary spasm of annoyance, because of the prospective necessity of having to close her book at an inevitably exciting point in the story, and, more, because she did not, could not, and at number 14 never would have a room of her own. Aunty Lou always changed into her night clothes in the bathroom: she would enter their bedroom in a long-sleeved ankle-length thick cotton nightdress and with her grey hair released from her daytime bun. And Eleanor's good night kisses would be extra loving for unspeakable reasons, to compensate for her unfairness and ingratitude, to hide her frustration, and by way of a protest against Aunty Lou looking older, really careworn and ancient.

Sometimes, after lights out, they talked a little in the dark.

'Aunty Lou, are you awake?'

'Yes, dear. What is it?'

Eleanor would try to tell her about the book by Jane Austen or Sir Walter Scott borrowed from the Whympers which she had been reading, or about the pianistic problem she had succeeded in solving.

But Aunty Lou's reactions were no more than kind, and once she dropped off to sleep in the middle of another dissertation that meant nothing to her.

Eleanor, suspecting it, inquired: 'Aunty Lou?' and again in a whisper: 'Aunty Lou?' – and, relapsing into silence, shed tears as quietly as she could.

She could not bear her Aunty's lack of interest in what interested herself, or the disillusioning limitations of the arbiter of her existence to date. She was saddened by her Aunty's tiredness, and to think that one day she might die.

Where would she be without Aunty Lou to sympathise with and watch over her? She imagined the multitude dispersed and her own confinement in some sort of institution. Her mother was not to be depended on. Aunty Nell would never manage number 14 alone. And she – Eleanor – had total savings of forty-something pounds.

Money, or her lack of it, had begun to alarm her. She had belatedly taken notice of the stuff inasmuch as she realised that no one seemed to have enough of it. She was vaguely aware of the reduction of Harold's fees for six months, and that her Auntys were having to subsidise her lessons. Four of those months had already gone by; therefore, through tears and darkness, she visualised the possibility of neither her Auntys nor Harold being able to finance the furtherance of her musical education.

Everything would come, everything was coming to an end, she decided with a pessimism to match her previous optimism. The futility of life and especially effort made her cry.

She was the more upset to recollect that it was a Thursday evening, and to reflect that owing to her emotional squall and subsequent insomnia she would probably not play so well to Harold tomorrow afternoon as she had hoped to.

The end which Eleanor failed to anticipate was that of the war.

The Armistice raised spirits, including those of a girl who had been engaged in fighting battles in Willesden of greater importance than any others in her egoistic opinion.

And Harold revived her musical enthusiasm by asking her to participate in a concert by his pupils to celebrate peace and no more bloodshed.

He told her: 'You'll be the youngest performer.'

She felt honoured, and honour bound to agree. Her competitive instinct masked her fear of making a fool of herself in comparison with the grown-ups who also studied at Abinger Avenue: she had heard some of them playing expertly, and had been introduced to a few. Moreover, notwithstanding her innocent indifference to the history of the last four war-time years, she liked the idea of paying her tribute to her brother Vivian and the great company of unknown and fallen servicemen.

Nevertheless she resolutely refused to invite anyone but Aunty Lou to the concert: she did not want Mrs Cruse, who knew too much and might be disappointed, and certainly not her mother, who cared too little and was likely to do the disappointing.

For four weeks she put in uncountable hours in the parlour of number 14. She seemed to interrupt her practising only to sleep and eat and, one day, to go to Audrey's to buy a new dress for the occasion. The concert was to start at three o'clock on a Sunday afternoon: Eleanor with Aunty Lou in tow arrived at a quarter to three.

Now, to add to her agitation, she was afraid of having to broadcast her relationship to her companion, whose dowdiness seemed to single her out from all the other people streaming into the Whympers' home. Aunty Lou inquired: should she stay with Eleanor until it was her turn to play – would that be a good idea? Eleanor returned: 'Of course not!' – and, hustling her Aunty through the crowded hall and sitting-room, found her a chair in an inconspicuous position in the studio, as far from the pianos as possible, and left her there.

Back in the sitting-room Harold called out to Eleanor over the heads of guests: 'You're on third, before the interval' – and she quailed inwardly and hated him for always, and so casually, demanding more than she could or thought she could supply.

Muriel Whymper saved at least this part of the day for her by saying: 'Would you like to go into the garden until you have to do your bit?'

She got through the next half hour, pacing about amongst the tussocks of unmown grass and tangled greenery behind the house, and peering in vain through the grimy window of the pottery shed. She tried not to listen to the music or to hear the applause, played and re-played her own pieces by drumming her fingers against her thighs, and wondered why on earth she had striven so hard for the sake of exposing herself to this ordeal.

Yet after receiving Muriel's promised summons, and managing to curtsey to the audience and reach the piano stool, her desire to please, to charm, reinforced training and talent. Although in her chosen programme of three Chopin waltzes she made quite a few mistakes, which she was sure she would never ever live down, she was almost knocked backwards by the clapping of perhaps a hundred hands when she stopped and stood up.

The interval that followed, or most of it, was a blur of congratulations, compliments, handshakes, kisses, of Harold's characteristic and contrary verdict, 'Passable,' and Aunty Lou's diffident signals of encouragement from the back of the crowd.

As the people moved away or returned to seats in the studio, a tall spry bald man in late middle age, obviously a gentleman, wearing a smart pale grey suit and with a monocle on a black ribbon dangling in front of his waistcoat, approached Eleanor decisively, smiling and crinkling the corners of his eyes, and said in a pleasant voice, at once silky and eager: 'May I too sing the praises of your art? How do you do? My name's Sidney Beringer.'

She had noticed him before the concert. He had been smoking a cigarette in a holder remarkable for two reasons: the mouthpiece was yellowish, amber probably, the other end white, and it looked luxurious; and he clenched it between his teeth so that it pointed upwards at a jaunty angle. His cigarette holder, his height and elegant clothes had caught her attention.

She shook his thin warm hand.

He continued with conviction: 'I shall never forget your playing, your sensitivity, and the picture of you at the piano, and I want to ask you a favour. My wife's a fellow-musician, an artist as you are, but her health is not good, she wasn't well enough to come with me today: would you play to her in our house? I know it would give her the greatest pleasure, and it could be your first professional engagement – or should I say another engagement?'

Eleanor was more than willing to comply with the request of this appreciative and courteous stranger.

But Aunty Lou almost barged into their dialogue: 'Good afternoon, sir.'

'Oh? How do you do?' he returned in a surprised voice.

Eleanor, red with resentment, felt the need to make an introduction: 'This is my aunt – well, not my real aunt – I just live with her.'

Aunty Lou volunteered: 'I'm in the place of a parent, sir' – officiously in the opinion of Eleanor, who also hated those obsequious sirs.

'I see. I was asking this young lady if she would consider playing to my wife.'

'I heard, sir. I wonder, sir, what had you in mind?'

'Supposing you brought Eleanor to tea with us in Hyde Park Square tomorrow afternoon – I'd have our car fetch you and take you home – and it could be a professional engagement. The name is Beringer incidentally.'

'Mine's Miss Carty, sir. Thank you, I'm sure. There'd be no need for money to pay. Would you like to play to Mrs Beringer, Eleanor?'

'Yes,' Eleanor replied, smiling up at her admirer.

Mr Beringer exclaimed: 'Capital!' – and producing a diary with a soft blue leather binding and a gold pencil he wrote in it the Summer Drive address.

Then Harold Whymper shooed the three of them back into the studio for the second half of the concert.

Eleanor was displeased, and her dramatic temperament turned displeasure almost into desperation. The degree to which she was shamed and inhibited by Aunty Lou had hit a new high or low. She saw herself dragging Aunty Lou round like a ball and chain for the rest of her life. Why speak so strictly to Mr Beringer? What could he have thought? What would Mrs Beringer think? She could no longer bear to be, or to be presented in public as, the property of such a prim dim person. Class complicated the issue, and loyal affection confused it. In the former context Eleanor was not averse from subconsciously claiming kinship with her mother, therefore the status of gentlewoman: yet socially and for ever, it seemed, she was bracketed with a couple of representatives of an inferior order. At the same time she was too fond of her Auntys, and owed them too much, fully to formulate her adverse criticisms. She just wished Aunty Lou had not spoken like a somewhat insolent servant to Mr Beringer, and she dreaded the conversation and etiquette at the tea party on the morrow.

Music was relegated to the background of these rebellious preoccupations. She could not listen properly to the other pianists; and she suffered from the natural law that caused her to dwell upon what she knew was wrong with her own performance rather than on what others had told her was right. She somehow implicated Aunty Lou in the offence of having failed herself. As for Harold, her unjust and injudicious feelings convinced her that she would never rise in his estimation so long as she was held back and hemmed in by her way of life.

And she was the opposite of mollified on the return journey to Summer Drive, when Aunty Lou tacked the following rebuke on to her expressions of enjoyment of the concert in general and Eleanor's contribution in particular: 'But I didn't like to hear you say you just live with us.'

'Sorry sorry sorry,' Eleanor retorted.

At home her snappiness was attributed to her being exhausted by overwork and to feeling flat because she was no longer the centre of attention. She retired to her bed early: where she at any rate succeeded in escaping further criticism. Unity was already asleep in the bedroom they shared with Aunty Lou, who had not yet come upstairs. Eleanor was as good as alone in every sense, she decided – or as bad. There was nobody in the whole world who understood her, or who was likely to help her out of her predicament. She loved music, but not when it was tainted by materialism. She hated her music when it seemed to beg for alms, yet was paralysed by the prospect of poverty. Her attitude was a muddle: who would clarify matters? Who would clear up the mess of her birth and everything?

The next morning she woke in her black mood, which was becoming less of an exception to her usually sunny temper. She practised without pleasure. She was sure the visit to the Beringers would be spoilt by her inescapable assumption of social responsibility for Aunty Lou, and possibly by further financial talk, revealing how poor she was.

Unexpectedly after lunch it cheered her to be in her party dress again, and, more so, to see a chauffeur-driven silver-coloured car larger and smarter than any of her mother's draw up beside the garden gate of number 14.

She was not as snobbish about money as youth tends to be; but she derived vicarious comfort from her rare brushes with wealth, and it was apparently second nature for her to be handed in and out of limousines like a princess.

Aunty Lou, on the other hand, was unnerved by the car, a Rolls-Royce, its glass partition between front and back seats, the chauffeur in his grey peaked cap and uniform with breeches and leather leggings, and the rug he insisted on spreading over her knees.

She answered tersely, when Eleanor asked about Hyde Park Square: 'It's a fashionable address.'

The car stopped in front of a high terrace house painted shiny white and shaded by great trees in a railed garden. The steps leading to the front door were whitish marble, and the door itself was a liquid-looking black. A grey-haired red-nosed maid wearing a peculiar tiara-like white cap and a pinafore opened it and ushered them into a hall with more marble on the floor. There were garish modern pictures on the walls. The maid was glumly polite and requested them to follow her up the curving stairs covered with thick red carpet held in place by polished brass rods. At the top she threw open one of several dark wood doors and, standing aside, announced: 'Miss Carty and Miss Eleanor Carty, madam!'

They entered an extremely bright spacious room without too much furniture in it. A sofa and some chairs were in the main part, and a grand piano in the smaller part that completed the L-shape.

Mr Beringer stood behind the sofa on which Mrs Beringer lay, propped against cushions, a rug draped over the lower half of her anatomy. She had severe striking features, but a voice even more silky, more harmonious and caressing, than her husband's, and a wonderful warmly welcoming smile with pretty teeth.

She extended both her hands to Eleanor and said: 'Oh my dear, I've been looking forward to this moment ever since my husband came home raving about you.'

Eleanor's excited reaction was to wonder: 'Will she be my Betsy Trotwood, my benefactress?'

1919 ...

But the first half-hour of Eleanor's first visit to 7 Hyde Park Square embarrassed her dreadfully.

Mrs Beringer lay back on her pillows, relaxed yet authoritative, looking extraordinary, her bold high-bridged nose counterbalanced by the delicacy of her lips and the feminine charm of her manner of speaking, her dark eyes glistening and missing nothing, and subjected her visitors to a rigorous and irresistible cross-examination.

'Do tell me what links you two together,' she began.

'I've brought up Eleanor,' Aunty Lou replied cautiously.

'You have the same surname, don't you?'

'Yes, madam.'

'But you're not related?'

'No!' Eleanor cut in.

'You said you were in the place of a parent, isn't that so, Miss Carty?' Mr Beringer recalled.

'Yes, sir. My sister and I have brought her up.'

'How did that come about?' Mrs Beringer pursued.

'I was her mother's monthly nurse, madam.'

'Did her mother not survive?'

'Oh no! I mean yes, she survived, madam.'

'But she has a different name?'

'Yes.'

'What's your mother's name, Eleanor? I wonder if we know her.'

'Mrs Beck.'

'Beck? No – we don't – do we, Sid?'

'I don't think so,' Mr Beringer agreed, shaking his bald head with its well-cut and brushed back trim of greying hair.

'Where does your mother live?'

Eleanor blushed and sought the assistance of Aunty Lou, who said: 'In south London, madam.'

'Not with the father?'

'No, madam.'

'I understand.'

Mrs Beringer pondered for a moment. Everybody waited, as if for some sort of verdict. Mr Beringer smiled encouragingly at Eleanor.

Then Mrs Beringer addressed Aunty Lou and Eleanor in succession with disconcerting force: 'You're to be congratulated on providing such a valuable service ... And you're lucky to have been taught such nice manners.'

She continued by asking Eleanor: 'What do you call Miss Carty?'

'Aunty Lou, and her sister's Aunty Nell.'

'What's your home like?'

'Well – it's a bit full.'

'We look after other children, we always have,' Aunty Lou volunteered.

'How many other children?'

'We have six at present. We can't accommodate more than six, not really, though sometimes we've had to.'

'What ages?'

'Usually right from the start, but from any age, until they're taken away or go to school or grow up.'

'Are they all in the same situation as this young lady?'

'Yes, madam.'

'And suffering on account of it?'

'We hope not ... Yes, sometimes.'

Mrs Beringer turned to Eleanor: 'Are you happy?'

'Yes.'

Mr Beringer remarked: 'That's an awkward question, Myrtle.'

Mrs Beringer laughed; Mr Beringer seemed to laugh because she was laughing; and she to answer him by saying to Eleanor: 'But you owe it to your Aunty Lou to be happy, don't you?'

'Yes, I suppose so.'

'What about school?' Mr Beringer wished to know.

'Eleanor doesn't go to an ordinary school,' Aunty Lou replied with a hint of defiance. 'She's been educated at home. Miss Elmes comes three days a week to teach her and some of the others – Miss Elmes is fully qualified. Besides, Eleanor's been taught her music by Mrs Cruse and now by Mr Whymper, sir.'

Mrs Beringer resumed: 'Can she speak French?'

'You do French lessons, don't you, Eleanor?' Aunty Lou asked for support.

And Mr Beringer posed a third question: 'Parles-tu francais?'

Eleanor replied with a giggle and an apologetic blush: 'No . . . Non, rien,' adding hurriedly under pressure from Aunty Lou's reproachful glance: 'I have done French for ages, but we hardly ever talk it.'

'But that's essential,' Mrs Beringer declared. 'Nobody's educated without a command of the French language spoken and written – and I mean classical French, not waiter's variety. Still, you must have a good ear, and you've time to learn.' She trained her bright black eyes on Aunty Lou again and inquired with reference to Eleanor: 'Do her parents provide for her?'

'I believe her mother does what she can, madam.'

'Is her mother the sole provider?'

'Yes, madam.'

Mr Beringer jumped to a conclusion in his keen way: 'No doubt you have to bridge the gap?'

'Well, sir . . . Some of the other parents are generous.'

'Who pays Harold Whymper?'

'Mostly Mrs Beck, sir, with assistance from my sister and myself. And Mr Whymper hasn't charged his full fee yet.'

'Is it all a struggle?'

'It can be, sir. But Eleanor's like our child, and she's always repaid us for everything we've been able to do for her.'

'Well said, Miss Carty!' he exclaimed, and then: 'I think each of you has reason to be proud of the other.'

The Beringers proceeded to ask questions that Eleanor did not quite understand about Summer Drive, mortgages, outgoings and so on. However, since the subject was clearly financial, she was afraid that it referred to her penurious situation. She longed to continue to please Mr Beringer, and to make a good impression on Mrs Beringer, who was the most formidable person she had ever met – but not in order to be pitied and paid for, not to wring their charitable hearts and rake in their money. Her idea of a Betsy Trotwood was a parental figure more loving and generally supportive than her mother, and more sophisticated than her Auntys.

Mrs Beringer interrupted her pause for thought by suddenly saying: 'Are you going to play for me now?'

Eleanor walked over to the piano, composed herself as best she could, repeated the programme of three Chopin waltzes she had played in the concert at the Whympers', stood up smiling and bowing in acknowledgment of the Beringers' applause, and was surprised and dismayed to see Mrs Beringer in tears.

She was crying rather beautifully, the teardrops welling into her eyes, her lower lip trembling – nothing more – no loss of dignity – and she said: 'Come here, my child.'

Eleanor obeyed her, perching uncertainly on the edge of the seat of the not very comfortable modern armchair she had sat in before.

'You're an artist. Do you know what that means?'

Eleanor was relieved by the positive tone of voice.

Mrs Beringer explained: 'I can pay you no higher compliment. Your music, combined with your youth and beauty, have moved me so. My husband didn't exaggerate – Sid, you were right – art, as usual, changes everything.' She grew less tearful and more excited: 'What an encouragement, the fact that you exist, and to have found you! I want to take you under my wing. I'm a singer – you could accompany me – and Sidney's a writer – we'd be three artists together – what fun!' She turned to Aunty Lou: 'You've nourished a rare and precious creature with outstanding success. I congratulate you again, and still more warmly. But my husband and I have expertise and much experience in the particular field in which Eleanor obviously excels. I wonder if you'd allow us to see her sometimes, and to have a hand in her

[79]

development and her future. We'd like to help, wouldn't we, Sid? We could send our car to fetch her and return her to you. I can assure you that we'd take care of her, and I do believe we'd all gain from an arrangement of that sort.'

Aunty Lou, resistant to tears, suspicious of extravagant compliments, not at ease with long speeches and clever conversation, and torn in different directions by her unwillingness either to sell her dearest charge or to spoil her chances, replied with noticeable reserve: 'You'll have to ask Eleanor, madam, about the visits.'

Mrs Beringer directed the full force of her personality at the girl.

'Will you come and see us, and let us help you realise your talent and thus reach the goal of every true artist?'

'Oh yes, please!'

Eleanor thrilled to the prospect of a dream of hers coming true, and felt the need to compensate for Aunty Lou's ungraciousness.

Mr Beringer commented with a celebratory clap of his long-fingered hands: 'Splendid!'

Mrs Beringer leant forward to emphasise what she had to say to Eleanor: 'You've proved your intelligence again by the decision you've taken. But perhaps only time will tell you how helpful we can be. Meanwhile – listen – I called you lucky to have been so well brought up. Your additional luck, your best luck, is not to be part of a family which would have certain rights and expect certain duties. Make no mistake, you've been born into the situation that other artists struggle for years to achieve and often never do achieve: you stand alone, as you must.'

At this point the maid knocked on the door and entered carrying a folded tablecloth over her forearm and a tiered cake-stand in the other hand, and followed by a younger maid also in uniform bearing a loaded teatray.

The Eleanor who emerged from the Beringers' house was not exactly the Eleanor who had arrived there. The fairy godmother's wand, waved before tea, the spell that had transformed her, consisted of the couple of sentences she was ultimately ordered to listen to by Myrtle Beringer. They as it were turned the logic of her life, by which she and the other children at Summer Drive had lived, to which everyone else seemed to pay lip-service, upside down. It was not her bad luck to be an illegitimate child, it was the exact opposite, according to someone convincingly knowledgeable; and she was not disadvantaged, she had been enjoying an advantage all along, and now was initiated into the secret of it, and need no longer feel sorry for herself. The revelation was two-fold: it revealed not only a new world for Eleanor, but also the magic of its creator.

A week elapsed before the Beringers' Rolls-Royce driven by their chauffeur Mr Stott arrived to transport her on her own from Summer Drive to Hyde Park Square. The picture of her new self, painted in glowing colours by Mrs Beringer, which brushed aside conventional criteria and boosted her confidence, had faded in the interval. Aunty Lou spoke with discouraging wariness of the Beringers' interest in her — 'Let's wait and see if they mean what they say, dear'; Aunty Nell was put out when Eleanor expatiated on the scrumptiousness of their sandwiches and cakes; envy provoked Flavia Simmons to accuse her of loving them because they were rich; and humdrum existence somehow denied the possibility of a few words having the power to effect a great change in anyone's circumstances.

Yet no sooner was she back in the marble-floored hall than she felt the same difference — spiritually reinforced by the atmosphere of high-class calm and concentration. And the Beringers' greetings were not at all disappointing: their delighted smiles and warm embraces were not like those of middle-aged people with much on their minds and better things to do. The attention they focussed upon her was exclusive, and the talk she had alone with Mrs Beringer later on, or with Myrtle as she had been instructed to say, replenished her every resource and again stirred her latent idealism.

She returned to 7 Hyde Park Square to tea once a week throughout that winter. In early summer Myrtle and Sidney removed to a rented house in the country, near the village of Hammerdown in Surrey. But they maintained their influence over Eleanor by means of letters, by sending her books which she had to read and cuttings from newspapers, by inviting her to stay for one glorious weekend, and by French and Italian lessons that they paid for: they also channelled a dress allowance via Aunty Lou for her benefit. In the following winter the visits to Hyde Park Square were resumed, and so it went on.

The three of them had a lack in common: the Beringers had no children just as Eleanor had no parents.

Myrtle sometimes said to Eleanor: 'I think of you as our child ... I can't imagine any real child of ours being closer to our hearts,' while Eleanor honoured both Beringers in filial style, although at the same time regarding them as her best friends.

There may have been another link of an extraneous kind. Myrtle and Sidney were Jews, each descended from a distinguished line of Anglicised Sephardim Jews from Spain, and they were determined that Eleanor was half-Jewish. They based their detective work mainly on intuition, but also on the clues of Eleanor's recollections of racial hints dropped by her mother. They were sure the Adamsons were Jews, and possibly acquaintances of Eleanor's father.

The Beringers were soon in possession of Eleanor's history. They encouraged her to recount it, they seemed never to tire of hearing details of Summer Drive, of her relations with her mother, and of the trials and tribulations of illegitimate children in general. They were horrified by her story of the Adamsons coming to adopt her without warning, almost to kidnap her, and by the part played by Mrs Beck in the transaction. Myrtle said that of course the Adamsons' offer had its attractions, but that it never should have been sprung on a child, especially one who was reasonably content. Sidney could not get over Mrs Beck's neglect of Eleanor, and the cruelty of her unpunctuality and her making and breaking of appointments.

'The point to remember, and the bright side,' Myrtle said, 'is that you're free of her, you don't owe her much, if anything, and you never need to involve yourself with such a second-rate person. How she managed to give birth to you I can't begin to imagine! Please believe me, darling, please take it on trust that the majority of girls have unavoidable difficulties with their mothers even for most of their lives, and usually with their fathers too, for that matter. You're spared more than you've suffered in my estimation.'

The Beringers' notion that her predicament was romantic probably derived from their having been brought up as members of fond and well-heeled families. Eleanor sometimes entertained a fleeting fear that her illegitimacy and poverty rendered her the object of their mere morbid curiosity, a diverting novelty and perhaps copy for a book by Sidney.

[82]

But Sidney would never stoop so low. She had progressed from respect for his age, admiration of his exquisite clothes, and gratitude for his assumption of a fatherly or grandfatherly role and responsibilities, to confidence in his character, realisation that he still had a boyish sense of humour, and the re-creation of her mental image of him in the twin shapes of hero and playmate.

She also thought the world of him because of his books, and as Myrtle did. In the course of an early visit to Hyde Park Square he offered her a little tour of his study on the ground floor. It reached from the front to the back of the building, was two rooms that had been knocked together, a library overlooking the rear garden and a workroom equipped with modern furniture and fittings and having a view into the greenery of the square. The desk and chair were of bleached oak; armchairs were ringed round with convenient tables, ashtrays and reading lights; bookshelves at eye-level lined the walls, having cupboards underneath and a collection of Chinese pots above; and extra interior casement-type windows and a double door excluded noise. Eleanor was impressed by the practical peacefulness of it, and the smartness. She was shown the shelf full of the editions of the works of Sidney Beringer and, on his desk, piles of the manuscript and the typescript of the novel he was writing at present; and was given a signed and leather-bound copy of *The Saving Grace*, the first of his five books so far published.

She read it between that visit and the next, notwithstanding the length and the fashionable stream-of-consciousness method of some of the writing. The story was autobiography disguised as fiction, and dealt with Sidney's marriage to and divorce from a half-crazy girl, and his wretchedness and hopelessness until he met and married Myrtle.

Eleanor thought it a wonderful book. She transposed its characters into the persons she knew, and drew comfort from knowing that the wife of the author had been his saving grace not only because she reciprocated his love, but also because she encouraged him in his forties to write and was the architect of his subsequently successful career. The theme of redemption, of rescue, in literature and in life, in *David Copperfield* as well as *The Saving Grace*, in the Beringers' experience and to some extent in her own, appealed to her strongly; she looked forward to also rescuing, and to being rescued by, some good sad man in the fullness of time.

[83]

She had shown Myrtle her copy of *The Saving Grace* with Sidney's inscription to 'a young fellow-artist', and Myrtle had said: 'It's true.'

The term 'artist' was the ultimate accolade in the discriminatory lingo of the Beringers. It was more often used negatively than positively: so-and-so was damned because he or she was not an artist, had nothing of the artist in his or her make-up, or not enough. They were art, or rather artist, snobs. They could do without dukes, they were not particularly interested in the class system, except in a literary context, and they were too rich to bow down before riches; artists were their aristocrats, almost their gods, and, they claimed not just by inference, their colleagues.

Eleanor was puzzled by their specialised definition of the word. She had thought it meant a painter, then that it described any practitioner of any art, and in her own case was synonymous with 'artiste'. Gradually she realised that for them it summed up a whole range of personal characteristics from creative genius to fine feelings. Their 'artists' did not necessarily have to produce or reproduce works of art; they could be the inspiration of those artists who actually did the job, or artists in the field of life, artists in themselves, sensitive responsive independent uncommon souls with first-rate standards and first-hand ideas. Perhaps, Eleanor had the nerve to wonder, they could simply be people the Beringers liked. Recognition of an 'artist' was an inexact science: in the Beringers' circle, it seemed to be by acclamation mainly by Myrtle, who in turn was acclaimed.

Eleanor's visits always included a stint at the piano. She was asked to play, and, because the Beringers were appreciative and complimentary, and their comments were instructive, she wanted to do so. She would repeat their favourite pieces, try out on them whatever she was learning, and pick her way through sheet music they possessed and put before her. During her third visit, after she had played for about a quarter of an hour, Myrtle offered to sing; rose from the sitting-room sofa, startling Eleanor yet again by the relative shortness of her stature and dumpiness of her figure compared with the size of her head and aquiline features; produced music and made sure it was not too difficult for Eleanor to sight-read; and stood by the piano, poised and infinitely dignified.

The song was Schubert's *An die Musik*. Myrtle's voice was no longer what it must have been in her youth, but she used it with skill and tact. And she so rendered the song that whether or not she could hit the high notes was less important than the sincere and even reverent emotion she communicated. She half-spoke its first words in German, 'Du holde Kunst ...' as if with deep yearning for the days when she was able to pay homage and do more justice to 'music, sweetest of all arts ...'

At the end Eleanor sat entranced, not knowing how to express her admiration and afraid to say something presumptuous. But Myrtle seemed to be content with the tribute of silence, and to have proved the point that she was another artist in music as well as in every other possible way.

Her performance was the first of many shared sessions of music-making. It gave Eleanor an insight into art, its essential laying-bare of hearts, and into the Beringers' almost mystical idea of an artist. They were three of a kind, more than just fellow-workers, and she was thrilled to have been granted entry into their select pigeon-hole.

The last but not the least bond attaching her to Myrtle Beringer and, if at one remove, to Sidney was their mutual interest in love.

Myrtle rested on the sofa because, she said, she had a bad back. She showed to advantage there, pretty rugs spread over the lower half of her anatomy, and her head that might have belonged to an Old Testament prophetess supported by pillows in crisp white linen pillowcases. She cut a somewhat disillusioning figure when she stood up, although she did have a swinging unstoppable sort of walk.

Usually Eleanor spent part of her visits to 7 Hyde Park Square alone with and talking to Myrtle. She would be invited to sit in a chair near the sofa: Myrtle's intimate dialogues with visitors were conducted at close quarters and face to face.

'Tell me what you've been doing – seeing – reading – thinking,' Myrtle would more than likely begin.

The power of her personality, her curiosity, were difficult to withstand.

Sometimes Eleanor revealed her preoccupying fears of the future.

Myrtle brushed them aside thus: 'Your appearance and your talent will take care of you. Never waste time worrying about things that probably won't

[85]

happen.' She was prepared to discuss Eleanor's current problems: that is, she would rap out dogmatic advice, 'Don't do it . . . Forget it . . . Have a shot . . . Why not, what's the harm? . . .' and explore the motives of Eleanor's friends and foes and suggest solutions to their problematical behaviour. But the word love, or any synonym of it, or obliquest pointer in that verbal direction, released her full conversational resources.

She surprised and even shocked Eleanor when she first asked her: 'Are you in love? Who are you in love with?'

Aunty Lou and Aunty Nell steered well clear of the subject. Loving though they were in one sense, they were too familiar with the effects of love in another sense to put ideas, as they might have said, into the heads of its poor little victims. They themselves had done without it and were none the worse, and no doubt wished more people would follow their example. At any rate, at Summer Drive, they maintained, they insisted upon, discretion or indeed prim censorship in all amatory contexts; while facts of life and inevitable physical functions were treated with medical solemnity.

Moreover, for Eleanor, the only alternative to her Auntys' shy-making shyness was secretive sniggering with her contemporaries, Flavia Simmons in particular.

But of course she had been in love repeatedly. She had had transitory feelings of attraction towards her fellows of both sexes and every age almost since infancy. She had hardly ever been out of love: the man at Fishguard Harbour had merely focussed her instincts and impulses, and made her more conscious of them. The recent pattern of her love-life had been positively kaleidoscopic. One day her heart went out to a smiling boy with floppy hair who had bicycled past her in the street; the next day she yearned to be enfolded in the muscular arms of Ken the milkman's successor; then it was Willy Hopkins, although after an hour or two he bored her to distraction as per usual; and then she could think of nothing but the hero or the heroine of some book.

This promiscuity of her affections was as chaste as, for her, it was inexpressible. Her loves were largely spiritual and strictly private.

Therefore, her response to Myrtle's intrusive questions was to blush scarlet and hope to sink through the floor.

Myrtle said: 'I see that I've embarrassed you. How old are you, Eleanor? Fifteen? Well – at your age you should be learning from me, and from anyone who knows anything, the most important of all lessons for a girl. Do you understand? I mean the lesson of how with luck to live happily ever after as a result of loving the right man. Don't make the mistake of thinking every man's as good as Sidney. Don't imagine you could ever be happy without a man to love and be loved by – you're not the type of a spinster or a nun. Don't be English, darling! Innocence may have charm, ignorance is unattractive and bound to get you into trouble. It's high time you realised how pretty and desirable you're going to be, and that very soon you'll be pursued, badgered and bullied by the opposite sex. No, I'm not flattering you. Believe me, your destiny will be a ceaseless struggle to protect your individuality and your talent from men who claim your body and soul. I want you to be prepared, and so far as possible to prepare you. Benefit from my experience, study love with me, read books which are cautionary tales and will teach you how to see through people, actively seek happiness, set about creating your own and therefore others' happiness now, and forgive me giving you such a long lecture!'

Myrtle laughed a little at herself for speaking imperiously as well as at such length, and Eleanor joined in with escapist relief and to hide her excitement at being told that men would deign to notice her.

But Myrtle was not to be denied: she insisted not only on eliciting confidences, also on exchanging them with her young friend.

She shocked Eleanor again and on several other occasions by telling the story of her courtship and almost boasting of the love tempered by time between Sidney and herself: revelations seeming both unlikely and indecent when made by a lady of her seniority.

However, gradually, Eleanor did learn as it were at Myrtle's knee not to be puritanical; and she devised a method of participating in heart-to-heart chats without compromising too much of her privacy. She would put forward a male candidate to be pulled to pieces by criticism, rather as if she were throwing meat to a lion which would otherwise devour her. The virtues of these candidates were, from her point of view, that as a rule she had no romantic interest in them, and, from Myrtle's, that each – presumed to be a suitor – was someone to sink her analytical teeth in protectively.

Myrtle brought artistry to such analyses. She could drag out dissection over days, delving deeper and deeper into character, laying bare qualities and defects.

Eleanor mentioned the fact that Willy Hopkins had always been a bit silly about her, then had to supply details of Willy's age, appearance, parentage so far as she knew it, interests, attainments, aims, ideals, her feelings for him and his for her – from which information the closely reasoned conclusion that they were not meant for each other would be drawn, many significant general laws having been laid down.

The process was fascinating, unlike any form of social intercourse Eleanor had come across or dreamed of. Myrtle turned into a detective of sorts – and Sidney into her deputy – investigating crimes and potential crimes of passion with relentless intelligence, enthusiasm and application. At the same time, all was done delicately and wittily.

And it was not just destructive. Nor was it nihilistic. Myrtle was for ever on the side of true love, and had unshakable faith in the possibility of happiness.

What she militated against were false premises and hopes; masochistic and suicidal conjunctions; the blind alleys of sex appeal; marriages entered into for no good reason and divorces that multiplied mistakes; and especially the folly of women.

She felt a certain solidarity with her fellow-females, and had hosts of woman friends, who, Eleanor discovered, visited her in relays, most of them bearing their troubles like gifts. She would sympathise with sorrow and scold when it was self-imposed, and administer tonic doses of her philosophy: that women were granted by nature superior powers with which to fight the war of the sexes, but were too inclined by feebleness and laziness to yield them up and surrender to men. Instead, they had to believe in themselves – recover that belief – and benefit from their advantages.

She often regaled Eleanor with the exemplary case histories of these friends. A frustrated one was the wife of a man who had expressed his ardour with a single kiss on the cheek before marriage, and had made a travesty of love to her twice in fifteen years of matrimony. Myrtle's comment was: 'She's paying the price of cowardice – she was afraid of being left on the shelf, so she disregarded the evidence and committed herself to a dud.' Another lady was in despair because her husband had left her for his mistress, with whom he had been having a secret affair for five years. Myrtle said: 'She was taken completely by surprise when he walked out on her. But she should and she could have known he was being unfaithful, and then she might have been able to do something about it. Her trouble is that she lacks imagination – she must have been awful to be married to – I don't blame him.'

Eleanor was sometimes confused by the inconsistency of Myrtle's opinions. One friend was at fault for hen-pecking her husband, another for being a doormat for hers to wipe his feet on. Myrtle ruled that women were wrong not to stand up to men and again that they were wrong not to respect men: they had to preserve or win their independence from, while acknowledging and making the best of their dependency upon the stronger sex. Women who decided to do without men were unnatural, conceited, foolhardy, and imposed restrictions on their capacity to develop, she said.

Yet the sole object of the various amatory exercises she recommended was happiness. Eleanor particularly enjoyed the triangular talk she had with the Beringers about David Copperfield's love first of Dora, then of Agnes. Myrtle declared that in reality, rather than in art, Dora the childlike egoist was another 'dud', while Agnes was 'too good to be true', would make David no happier than he had been with Dora, and she would therefore end up as unhappy with him as formerly without him – it was an article of her faith that happiness between lovers was indivisible. When Sidney demurred, laughing and saying that at least Agnes would probably be a satisfactory mother and housewife, Myrtle pointed out that David was becoming a writer and needed a woman able to inspire, understand and promote his work – surely Agnes had none of the essential qualifications of the proper partner of a literary man and creative artist?

Eleanor thought this questioning argument very clever. It killed a small flock of birds with a single stone. It raised a reasonable objection to the matrimonial destiny of David and Agnes; the dogmatism of it was softened by the interrogative form – instead of disagreeing with Sidney it asked him to agree with her; it was flattering both of the artist she was married to and of herself; and it reminded her husband, who might be betraying an incipient sign of sympathy with other women, of her services over the years and his obligations.

The most instructive lesson of the liberal education Eleanor was receiving at 7 Hyde Park Square was observation of the Beringers' relationship. Her mind having broadened sufficiently for her to allow that Myrtle and Sidney in their fifties were not too old for a kind of love, she admired the way their marriage worked or was made to work. She saw enacted before her eyes dramatic definitions of the words that they were always using to describe necessary contributions to happiness, affinity, for instance, the almost supernatural and perhaps pre-determined closeness of two separate individuals.

Their meeting had been miraculous, according to Myrtle.

In her severely white-walled first floor sitting-room, a room seemingly stripped for the interplay of intelligence, she leant on an elbow on the sofa and spoke to the avid listener facing her as follows: 'We were no longer young when we met. My mother had died, and I was still living at home with my father, who was extremely fond of me. My brothers and sisters were all married, but I'd never wished to take any of my chances to wed. I was perfectly content, and having a very nice time. On a summer afternoon I was due to sing at a small reception organised by my father, but caught a cold a few days before it, lost my voice, and only decided I would be able to perform at the last minute. Sidney was a member of my audience. He had been dragged along under protest by his uncle, my father's business associate. The poor fellow was in a bad state, his wife had tried and failed to kill herself after nearly killing him, and he was resolved never again to risk love, let alone matrimony. But when I finished singing he approached me and said with emotion that he would like to, he absolutely must, see and meet me again. I invited him to call on a day a week or so ahead; he departed with his uncle and the rest of the company; and in the evening my father escorted me to the opera. Sidney happened to be sitting in the seat next to mine. He more or less declared himself there and then, I did not reject his advances, and we never looked back – we never have looked back – or at anyone else. So many coincidences – narrow misses – miracles really – were too much for us. We almost failed to attend that reception; we might have been sitting far away from each other in the opera house. And we both acted against our better judgment, and out of character, in deciding at first or second sight to spend the rest of our lives together – each with an unknown quantity – with a stranger: but how were we to resist fate, which had taken matters into its own hands? Anyway, we were right, or fate was — there have been no regrets at leisure, thank goodness. We dutifully cooperated with life, notwithstanding all that had gone before. I adore my husband, more now if possible than when we married, and he tells me the same story, and that he would never have become what he is without my support and encouragement. Darling Eleanor, one day I hope you'll find romance as I did and I have.'

Myrtle was not alone in hoping it. Eleanor thought the Beringers' marriage, the Beringers themselves, their home, their art, their ideas and everything else about them, pretty well perfect. She would have loved to be like them, but was too modest to aim so high. Besides, their age and their wealth rendered them hardly human — more divine than flesh and blood — in her eyes.

Yet she must at least have been infected with a mild version of their critical spirit. She noticed that Myrtle dictated to Sidney under the guise of deferring to him, and that she exercised ultimate control by means of her health or ill health and his concern. He was ever ready to do as she pleased so as to ameliorate the pain in her back.

Again, Eleanor wondered what had happened to Myrtle's abandoned father.

Mr Stott, the Beringers' chauffeur, was a charming man, tall with curling grey hair and heavy-lidded eyes. He had a proud bearing, and spoke unaccented English. There seemed to be mutual respect and affection between him and his employers, although in private Sidney complained of feeling that he should be driving the car and his chauffeur should be sitting in the back behind the glass partition. Myrtle's nickname for Mr Stott was 'the aristo'.

The Beringers' secret nickname for Maud, their parlourmaid who opened the front door and waited at table, was A T, because she had formed the bad habit of ending most of her infrequent pronouncements with the words 'and that'. 'The weather's better today, the rain's held off and that,' she might observe. 'It's tea upstairs with muffins and that,' she would gloomily tell Eleanor who had just arrived at 7 Hyde Park Square. She was a downhearted spinster with a permanently red tip to her nose.

Maud's assistant was her niece Effie, a pretty blond nineteen-year-old, good enough at her work but completely wrapped up in herself and, no doubt, in the young policeman who was courting her. She spoke to the Beringers and their guests only when spoken to, and then with discouraging finality.

The third occasionally visible member of the indoor staff was Myrtle's lady's maid who also valeted Sidney's clothes, Cam by name, which was short for Miss Cameron. She was sixtyish and short, shrivelled, suspicious and sharp-tongued. Her attitude to Eleanor, when they met in the front hall or on the stairs, was hostile. She would pass remarks such as, 'Come again, have you?' and 'That hair of yours needs cutting.' Once, after Eleanor had been playing the piano, Cam said to her tartly: 'Glad you're giving something in return for all you're getting.'

Down in the basement lurked Cook, also called Mrs Selby, although she too was a spinster. Eleanor was neither introduced to, nor caught a glimpse of her for many months; but she rather loved her for her food, which was richer than Aunty Nell's, especially her teatime egg sandwiches made with mayonnaise. One day, as Eleanor was ushered out of the house by Maud, she mentioned the fact that she had never set eyes on Cook and was informed: 'Well, she locks herself in her bedroom every afternoon, leaving us to infuse the tea and that, and she's not to be disturbed on any account till she chooses to see to dinner.'

Annually in mid-May the Beringers moved from town to the country for three months. The house they rented near Hammerdown, Rockery Hill, belonged to friends of theirs who summered in Italy; was an apparently extended bungalow built by some modernistic architect; had beautiful grounds with a lake, and panoramic views; and was fully staffed. Only Cam from Hyde Park Square accompanied her employers, while Mr Stott ferried papers and books and laundry up and down between the two houses.

On a number of afternoons during the Beringers' absence from London, Eleanor by arrangement practised on their grand piano. Mr Stott fetched her from Willesden as usual, and then Maud looked after her. On one such occasion she was finally introduced to Cook, a stout woman with a pasty complexion and a frown, swathed in white apparel.

The trouble with these sessions was familiar; but she suffered from it more because she had no Myrtle and Sidney to hide behind. She did not know what to call or how to treat their servants. She dared not address Maud by her Christian name, she was ignorant of her surname – and what was she meant to call Cook or Mrs or Miss Selby? She had often bitten back the syllable Cam for fear of provoking its owner to bite her head off. At least that trio, plus Mr Stott, called her Eleanor; Effie, not far from being her contemporary, insisted on calling her Miss. She was inhibited by feeling a fraud, that she was less socially respectable than they thought she was, and too shy to ask anyone for guidance, or to tell Effie not to for heaven's sake.

Moreover, should she stop playing the piano for any reason Maud would toil upstairs to the sitting-room to ask her what she wanted, and probably to check that she was doing nothing wrong.

On the other hand the grand piano was better in every way than the upright at Summer Drive, and she was keen to learn to play as well as possible the new pieces which she hoped to perform for the Beringers at Rockery Hill.

She received her invitation in a letter from Sidney when she was beginning to be afraid that he and Myrtle's promises might be broken. By the time Mr Stott arrived at number 14 she was in a dither of excitement: she had had no holiday in new surroundings since that trip to Ireland, and now she longed to be reunited with her best friends. She left London on a Friday afternoon in late July and returned on the following Sunday evening, and every one of her waking minutes in between was pure delight.

She revelled and rejoiced in the kindly weather; the verdant shimmering peace of the countryside, to which she was unaccustomed; the peculiar edifice with its barnlike sitting-room and plate-glass windows opening on to a terrace shaded by a cedar tree; the luxurious white bedroom she had all to herself; the music and the books, the talk of art, the walks, the elegant meals; and the Beringers' welcome, and the unquestionable regret of their goodbyes.

Sidney was the guide and companion of her walks. He was as smart as ever in his paler-coloured suits for country wear and his brown and white shoes, and he showed her round the lake, fixing his monocle in his eye in order to try to identify the waterfowl she pointed out, and leading her farther afield through humming woodland. He did not exactly suggest their expeditions: since Myrtle still could not and perhaps would not take any more exercise than she had to, he would wait — if with some signs of restlessness — for her to make the suggestion. Then he would immediately say: 'What a capital idea! Come along, Eleanor, let's stir our stumps!'

His walking-stick and his panama were reminders of his age. Yet it occurred to Eleanor that, in her company, he was not only boyish, perhaps more like a boy let out of school. They had the sort of fun together which was no doubt the single pleasure not included in his marriage: Myrtle's sense of humour was paradoxically serious. Although Sidney was much amused by his wife's ironical observations, and Myrtle likewise by her husband's perception of the funny side of things, their laughter in unison seemed never to get out of control. There was certainly nothing silly about it; whereas Sidney stirring his stumps in the country air was sillier and sweeter than Eleanor had ever known him. He wanted to play 'I spy', they made up limericks and scratched absurd messages on treetrunks. He challenged her to spell esoteric words, she dared him to follow her down steep banks. And they laughed so much that they had to stop and surrender to it — he defied time by his retention of youth's distinctive ability to be overcome by semi-rational amusement.

Eleanor decided she had never been happier than in those forty-eight hours, nor briefly sadder than when she waved and waved at the Beringers through the windows of their Rolls-Royce which was carrying her back to the noisiness and grubbiness of Willesden, and to exacting work and her feelings of isolation.

But she wrote a thank-you letter pages long, and received consoling replies from each of her beloved benefactors.

Thus communication was maintained until visits to Hyde Park Square could re-commence.

There, the Beringers took to inviting one or more of their friends to listen to Eleanor's music. They were proud of her, and of having discovered her. Myrtle would often ask her to work up the favourite piano-piece of somebody who was coming to tea in a fortnight to hear it; or she would lend Eleanor the sheet-music and want her to prepare the accompaniment of a song she intended to sing to another crony.

To please the Beringers musically was to displease Harold Whymper. Shortly after Eleanor submitted to the musical arbitration of the former, the latter detected a change in her playing and found fault with it.

Harold had passed whimsical and ambiguous remarks about the Beringers as soon as he heard of Eleanor's association with them, for instance: 'You'll have to mind your ps and qs in that circle,' and 'What goes up at Hyde Park Square must come down.' She guessed his hints were critical; but when she asked the challenging question, 'Why did you invite Sidney Beringer to your concert if you don't like him?' he replied, 'Sidney's a fine fellow, and not half good at scribbling, they tell me.' Equally, Harold described Myrtle as 'a hell of a woman and no mistake,' then agreed with Eleanor that she must have been a great singer. 'La Beringer can still knock the stuffing out of a song better than most,' he added.

His slangy contrariness did not mollify her loyalty. She was irritated by his attitude to her new mentors and, particularly, by his dissatisfaction with her work. Recent lessons with him were all stopping and starting and getting nowhere, thanks to his vague interruptions: 'I'm not with you ... What are you saying? ... I'm hard of hearing, remember ... Play up, play up and play the game!' At length she sought and was rather shocked to receive the following partial clarification: 'The Beringers are too keen on performance. What happens or ought to happen in small back rooms doesn't bother them. Technique's the ticket, I say. Scales scale the heights. Your exercises have been missing you.'

His diagnosis was no more acceptable for being correct: Eleanor was aware of skimping her homework for Harold in order to prepare to entertain Myrtle, Sidney and Co. But she now refused consciously to sacrifice sweet compliments galore in Hyde Park Square for hours of tiresome exercises in Willesden and seldom a word of praise in St John's Wood. She was not going to disappoint the Beringers, who said that she played divinely.

One day Myrtle broached the subject of Harold's teaching. Evidently the Beringers had taken over the payment of his fees from the Auntys, and Sidney had just had a scrawled letter from Harold explaining that he needed to raise the preferential rates he had been charging for Eleanor's lessons.

Myrtle delved into her handbag and showed this letter to Eleanor.

'What do you think?' she asked.

'I never knew you were paying – I never meant you to – I don't want you to

– I'm so sorry,' Eleanor stammered out, blushing because of her poverty.

Myrtle dismissed the financial aspect of the matter, but probed painfully into causes and effects: was Harold trying to make a statement about her progress, and what had she learnt and was she learning from his tuition?

'He says I don't do enough scales and things,' Eleanor admitted.

'But that's donkey-work, my dear. Surely he can see and hear you're past that stage?'

'He says nobody's ever past it.'

'Oh – well – in a sense I agree, artists have to go back to basics, we have to keep our feet on the ground. But doesn't he encourage you, doesn't he recognise your achievements? Talent has to be persuaded to develop.'

'I can't ever tell whether or not he's pleased with me. He pulls faces when talent or art are mentioned. Of course he's tremendously expert and everything. He helped me to play much better to begin with. But now he's a bit fed up, or bored, I suppose. And he may be jealous, because I play to you and Sidney. Sometimes he's so hard to understand! You know what he's like, don't you, Myrtle?'

'I used to. People used to bring him along to hear me sing. And I went to a recital he gave long ago. He was a good pianist, and I believe he's an excellent teacher. But I must admit I didn't care for him personally. I'm not attracted to artists who talk slang and pose as the man in the street. Sidney admired him more than I did. Anyway – if money didn't enter into the picture, if you could quite forget the money, how would you respond to Harold's letter? Would you like to go to him less often, say once every three months? After all, you do learn from playing to us, whatever he may say.'

'Oh I do,' Eleanor hastened to assure, in case Myrtle's feelings as well as her own should be hurt. 'And I love your idea about occasional lessons. But I hate costing you so much.'

'Listen, you repay us over and over again. Forget the money. I'll ask Sidney to reply to Harold. There – all done!'

'I don't know how to thank you, Myrtle.'

The consequences of what Eleanor was thanking for were unfortunate in several respects.

She was no longer sufficiently at ease with Harold to concentrate on her three-monthly lessons. She remembered that he had implied disappointment in her, and Myrtle had spoken disparagingly of him. She was conscious of a widening gap between her present musical aspirations and his, and that their relationship was costing an unjustifiable packet. She resented any reminder of her financial dependence, especially one which had threatened to cloud the purity of her friendship with the Beringers; and she blamed her music and was therefore less keen on it. At the back of her mind she had a nasty suspicion that Harold was not altogether wrong, and that the applause of Myrtle and Sidney and their amateurish visitors was indeed unconstructive and enervating. But she could not refuse to oblige, or to devote still more time and energy to accompanying Myrtle's half-spoken re-interpretation of her old songs.

Again, although Eleanor had concluded the conversation above with an expression of her gratitude to Myrtle for various forms of support, retrospectively she was surprised that Myrtle should have shown her Harold's letter without consideration of the damage it would do.

Myrtle now surprised her similarly by suggesting that she should bring her mother to tea at Hyde Park Square.

Eleanor dreaded such an encounter. But Myrtle said it would be interesting, and that she wanted to speak to Mrs Beck about her remarkable daughter, who would soon require assistance to launch herself into adult life. Eleanor, despite being made to feel worse by Myrtle's declared intentions, made the necessary arrangements.

A year and a bit ago she had told her mother that she was seeing the Beringers. Poppy Beck's reaction was: 'But they're frightfully rich people. Well done, darling!' Eleanor was so shocked that she volunteered no further news of her friendship with Myrtle and Sidney, and responded to her mother's venal questioning with reluctance and contempt. Now she braced herself apprehensively to be the interpreter of the different languages her mother and her friends spoke, and not to mind too much if and when Poppy and Myrtle tried on her behalf to extract money from each other.

On the day in question Eleanor was the first to arrive at Hyde Park Square, having been driven down from Willesden by Mr Stott. In the sitting-room with Myrtle, she heard the car and the commotion below, and was startled by the sound of her mother's laughter mingling with that of Maud, who had hardly ever cracked a smile in Eleanor's company. Stranger still, on the landing at the top of the stairs and just outside the sitting-room her mother stopped to exchanged pleasantries with Cam, dour reclusive Cam, who must have engineered the meeting.

Then Mrs Beck made her entrance, bestowing a gracious smile on Maud for opening the door and announcing her. She enfolded her daughter in a scented embrace, and, clasping Myrtle's hand in both of hers, said with a sugary smile that she had been looking forward to this moment for months.

Eleanor blushed and hated her mother for her transparent falseness. But — strangest of all — Myrtle, perspicacity notwithstanding, showed every sign of being charmed, and was certainly amused, by the other's seductive chatter: her plea to be called Poppy, the extravagant thanks for interest in her daughter, the confession that she was green with jealousy both of Beringers who were the love of Eleanor's life and of Eleanor who was privileged to love Beringers, and so on. And Sidney, when he briefly joined the party for tea, far from being put off by Poppy's attitude, the theatrical mixture of modesty and boldness in her glances, the deferential questions — where did he do his marvellous writing, how soon was his next book coming out? — reacted with disappointing enthusiasm in Eleanor's opinion, overdoing his attentiveness, sometimes almost bridling, and joining too readily in the tinkling laughter.

Practical matters were not discussed until Sidney had gone back to his study.

Myrtle began by asking Poppy: 'What are your plans for this young lady?' — indicating Eleanor, who wished she was elsewhere.

Poppy must have prepared her answer. 'Oh I am glad to have this chance of discussing her future with you. I've been waiting and hoping to be able to consult you,' she said. 'What would you like her to do, and when, and how?'

Myrtle countered with a little more caution: 'I'm assuming that she'll need to earn an honest penny?'

'Poor darling, yes, I'm afraid so.'

'And she should stick to her music.'

'Well, yes, since she's been blessed with that great gift.'

'But to earn even a penny from any art can be a long and laborious process.'

'I do believe so – of course, you'd know better than me.'

'She ought to qualify herself to teach music, for instance in a school. At least, then, she wouldn't have to starve while she was pursuing her career as a performer.'

'Oh please don't talk of her starving – it's always been my nightmare. But that idea of yours is brilliant. Eleanor darling, you don't know how lucky we are to have such good advice.'

'She'll have to go to a music college, and have her expenses paid, although she might get a scholarship.'

'If only she could get one!'

'She still would, and will, and really does, require backing for quite a few years, and a personal allowance.'

Poppy was wearing a straw hat with flowers round the brim. She now bent her head either sadly or to hide her eyes behind the brim of her hat, and said: 'I'm very conscious of that. Eleanor always has required, and deserved, more than I've been able to give her. We mustn't complain; but the tragedy for both of us is that I've never had resources of my own. I've had to bring her up on my pin money.'

'Wouldn't her father help?'

'There's been nothing between us since before Eleanor was born. I don't know what's become of him, or where he is – and I wouldn't dare.'

'What about your husband?'

'We lost our son in the war.' Poppy's smile was sad and explanatory. 'My husband thinks kindly of Eleanor. But he and I had two children, a boy and a girl, and he wished to reserve his fortune for his family. Now it's different – and the same – he wants everything to be spent on our daughter Winnie and on introducing her into the best society. I do appreciate his feelings. I can't argue with him – I'm not in a position to. Besides, he's a stubborn man, and generous considering how much of my slender means I've been able to devote to Eleanor's welfare. I'm sorry,' she broke off, hanging her head again and reaching out a beringed hand to clutch Eleanor's forearm, as if to save herself from sinking in a sea of tears; 'I'm so sorry, it upsets me to talk about my precious Vivian, and especially upsetting because I always hoped that when

[99]

Viv was more mature he'd help me take care of his half-sister. Would you excuse me? I'm afraid I'm a cry-baby once I start, and I'd hate to be an embarrassment and make an exhibition of myself.' She raised her head, showing moist eyes, and added: 'Perhaps I should tell you one other thing. My Winnie's growing into a handsome girl, she's greatly admired, she has a success wherever she goes, and she's sensible too. I've no doubt she'll carve out a nice life with scope to pursue her interests, and I just pray that one day the same will apply to my darling little mistake.'

Poppy, on the strength of her half religious and half worldly peroration, rose to take her leave. She sympathised with the spinal condition of Myrtle, who sympathised with her bereavement. She expressed more fulsome thanks, shook hands in a meaningful manner, and asked Eleanor to see her out of the house.

On the stairs she whispered conspiratorially in Eleanor's ear, referring to their hostess: 'What an alarming lady!'

In the hall she kissed her daughter and said aloud for all and probably in particular Sidney in his study to hear: 'Goodbye, darling girl – it warms my heart to think of you having another loving mother here – and such a distinguished man for a kind of father.'

Eleanor re-mounted the stairs sullenly. Her true mother, her untrue mother, had been allowed to get away with something, with lies and shamming, she believed. And another distressing idea occurred to her: Cam had probably broken the habit of her unsociability and spoken to Mrs Beck out of vulgar curiosity, not politely but to gawp at a scarlet woman.

Back in the sitting-room Myrtle reclined against pillows in her brooding judicious pose.

At length she seemed to notice Eleanor and, leaning forward, said in a scoffing cynical tone of voice: 'Well – now I know where you get your looks, if not your brains.'

She continued with conviction: 'I understand what your father must have seen in that woman, and why he never wanted to see her again. You'll probably follow his example when you can. You'll get nothing from her, nothing worthwhile, let alone an extra brass farthing. Her best advice is to marry you off, which would be good for her and could be very bad for you. Ignore it! Don't allow, don't stoop to allow, her inferior ideas to touch you or hurt you. Always remember you're an artist, that's to say solitary, on your own, dependent on yourself in many important contexts, and that you're going to have to create your individual life and happiness.'

Maud knocked on the sitting-room door and announced that Mr Stott was waiting to drive Eleanor home.

In the car Eleanor also came to various conclusions. Myrtle had not really been taken in by Poppy, not got her priorities wrong, not failed her, she reflected. And Myrtle had ended by delivering one of her eloquent and oracular pronouncements, each of which was like a guaranteed programme for existential contentment. She had again impressed and excited her young friend, redeeming herself in those clear eyes.

On the other hand she had contributed nothing practical to the discussion – no solutions more concrete than Poppy's. She resembled, and differed from, Betsy Trotwood in that her beneficence began on the emotional or spiritual heights, and ended there, Eleanor realised. Sidney dwelt in some less rarefied region, and possibly had an empathic conception of the facts of her situation. Yet both Beringers, admirable and beloved as they were, deeply indebted to them as she was, were still not what she believed proper parents could and should be.

They nonetheless continued to change her view-point and views, not least of Summer Drive.

Aunty Lou anticipated events. Returning from her only visit to Hyde Park Square she had reported to her sister: 'Mr and Mrs Beringer are going to suit Eleanor much better than that Harold Whymper – and she'll suit them better, I shouldn't be surprised.'

After some months had passed, late one evening beside the kitchen range, Lou observed with pained stoicism, referring to the smart young lady Eleanor was becoming: 'What did I say?'

Nell replied: 'You were right, you expected it – but it's nature, dear – don't mind it.'

The conduct of Eleanor was the less acceptable because of the transparency of its motivation. She could not help drawing comparisons between Hyde

Park Square and Summer Drive, and showing it. As a rule she could, and did, curb her fiery temper, which had once – for example – frightened Poppy Beck; but she conveyed wordless and withering messages to the effect that she despised almost the whole population of Willesden and objected to the living conditions she had to endure.

Her detachment, the severing of links with her past, the process inaugurated by Harold Whymper who had compelled her to grow up musically and put her music first, gathered momentum under the influence of the Beringers, who raised her intermittently on to a higher, a delightful, plane of existence.

However, if the Beringers were blameworthy for spoiling Willesden for Eleanor, the attitude that enabled Eleanor to grin and bear it, or at any rate bear it, also derived from Myrtle Beringer: to wit, arrogance, the idea that she differed from those she had to associate with daily, and that she was reserved for, just being groomed for, better things.

The weak spot in her defences against the loneliness of Flavia Simmons, the dim devotion of Willy Hopkins, the boredom of Matilda, Jane, Unity and a new little boy with the pretentious first name Tristram, the stupidity of lessons, the primitive downstairs lavatory, her lack of privacy at night and the rest of it, was her love of her Auntys.

She was impatient with them, testy, cross, even scornful, but then she felt sorry and sad.

Her Aunty Lou suffered from the same trouble, and compounded it. She was used to children who had got or thought they had got too big for Summer Drive, she would wish them to flutter somewhere else and give them a push in the desired direction, if possible; but Eleanor was different. She was repeatedly provoked into argumentation, into quarrels over Eleanor's blessed Beringers who had turned her head, and in the inevitable fullness of time into regret, recollection, nostalgia, and reconciliation which was tearful and temporary.

Their relationship was subject to a cruel natural law, according to which the quarrels of two people are made worse in proportion to their fondness for each other. Accordingly their penitent hugs and kisses had a despairing quality, since they were both aware of having chipped away at the abyss with their awfully hard words, that they were likely to do it again, and that soon they would be unable to establish any sort of contact across the gap.

They both attempted to restrain themselves. Their restraint may have increased the tension that burst out at intervals; but it did sanction pale imitations of past concord. Aunty Nell took a different line. Her affections and her nature were either shallower or less controlled, and she disregarded her own advice, she minded Eleanor's attitude, and said so.

She was apt to call Eleanor hoity-toity, la-di-dah, unkind and ungrateful, and to be called silly, ignorant, a philistine, an idiot. She was not at all ashamed to cry. On a number of occasions she was reduced to crying in front of everyone at meal-times at number 14, and once she boo-hooed in the dairy shop in which she had bought Eleanor the wrong ice cream.

She had a knack of sobbing certain unfinished phrases that turned the screw of Eleanor's guilt: 'When I think ... After everything ... You of all people ...' And her sorrow, anybody's sorrow for that matter, but instantly and unfailingly the simplicity and straightforwardness of hers, summoned Eleanor's, causing the truly generous heart of the girl to ache and releasing another of those floods of her tears. They would promise – swear – that they had not meant it, that they loved each other as much as ever, more than ever, and gradually their emotions would subside or appear to, and nothing would be, nothing could be after such scenes, quite the same.

No wonder Eleanor moped and pined for the gilt-edged peace, for the gratifying intellectual atmosphere and the exclusive pursuit of happiness and the beauty of art at the Beringers'.

Sometimes to break free of the vicious circle of her dealings with her Auntys, rebelliously, and notwithstanding the alternative risks, she would escape from number 14 an hour before Mr Stott was due to fetch her, and wait for the car down at the junction of Summer Drive and the High Street.

Growing up had wrought other changes in and for Eleanor. She had begun to be courted by the opposite sex. The men of Willesden of all descriptions, ages, classes, noticed her, eyed her, sued for her favour in their various ways. Workmen digging holes in the road, painters on ladders, pedestrians, bicyclists, drivers of and passengers in vehicles, nearly everyone in trousers noticed her vivid looks, nubile figure, best clothes and music case. Some shouted cheery vulgarities at her. 'Yum-yum, my love ... I'll let you have my kisses for nothing.' They asked her where she was going and if they could accompany her, or, pointing at the music case, if she was ready to play, or, incomprehensibly, what she charged. An older man scolded her with a bit of a leer for standing in the street. Most men smiled at her, and because she evoked their smiles rather than the frowns of the Cartys, because she was grateful for the proof that she could give pleasure rather than pain, because she was relieved to be out of number 14 and excited to be going to number 7, she would smile back.

One afternoon a purple-faced evil-smelling lurching and mumbling man misinterpreted her politeness and seized hold of her with arms as thick and hard as the limbs of a tree. She was terrified, screamed, wriggled free, sprinted home, had to explain matters to Aunty Lou, and received not sympathy but a rebuke reminiscent of that which she had got for stealing pencils, only less effective.

Aunty Lou, having been blissfully ignorant of Eleanor's escapist habits, expressed incredulity, shock, disapproval, anger, deep concern, dark forebodings, general wretchedness, and ordered and implored her never again to parade about in public thoroughfares.

Eleanor promised not to half-heartedly, and interrupted the harangue to say she could hear the Beringers' car and absolutely must not keep Mr Stott waiting.

On this particular afternoon she was due to play to a larger gathering of Myrtle and Sidney's friends. Half an hour after her drubbing from Aunty Lou, an hour and a half after she had felt she would go mad if she spent another moment within the confining walls of 14 Summer Drive, she was being complimented, entertained, teased and metaphorically tickled by distinguished gentlemen in a fine sitting-room in a house with a fashionable address. And not long after that, when she rose from the piano-stool, she was applauded and praised to the skies.

Summer Drive was like an old garment which she shed in the hallway of Hyde Park Square. The company she kept in Willesden would hardly have recognised their Eleanor, who was no longer easy to live with, in the amenable and unassuming nymph of Bayswater, delighting everybody with her music, prettiness and laughter.

She had already struck up special friendships with two members of the

Beringers' circle. They were male, of course, and much older than she was — they were probably in their thirties. Mr Prince, at his request Joe to Eleanor, was a small perfect sort of person. He had perfect little features, hands and feet, wore perfect clothes, behaved perfectly, and spoke in a composed and infinitely fastidious manner. His singular flaw was his hair, which was frizzy and recessive, exposing rather too much forehead. He was in business, had something to do with jewellery; but when Eleanor asked Myrtle where his shop was located, Myrtle smiled and explained that Joe was no common-or-garden shopkeeper, nor did he exactly sell jewels — he 'placed pieces' with discretion now and then, which enabled him to live up to his surname.

Joe Prince's approach to Eleanor was respectful. Initially he startled and intrigued her with the coolness of his tremendous tributes, for example: 'You're already an exceptional musician, because you fully restore to music its power to move people with ears to hear and open minds.' On another occasion he said: 'When you're an inch or two taller, and thinner, and have learned how to present yourself, you could be a great beauty.' He also said with his unflinchingly friendly regard: 'You make me proud of my race.'

His confession that he was Jewish, his assumption that she was, if in part, broke down or at any rate lowered the barrier of the disparity of their ages, so far as she was concerned. Increasingly she liked to feel she was set apart by virtue of the blood of her father in her veins; the idea that she was almost foreign helped her to disengage from her native counterparts at Summer Drive; and she saw herself and Joe, together with the Beringers, as fellow-members of a secret society, of a cultural conspiracy, linked by their breeding.

Besides, he was never — in her euphemistic terminology — funny with her: he did not kiss her wetly, or stare hungrily at her lips or her bosom, or pull her about with a hot hand round her waist or upper arm. Although he was single, he had loved an unhappily married lady for years, Myrtle told Eleanor; and the latter sensed with precocity that his tenderness for her was exactly that of a susceptible man towards a woman he might have cared for, if he had not been involved elsewhere.

Eleanor somehow had a liberating faith in Joe's loyalty to his mistress. She trusted him to embarrass neither herself nor himself — she relied upon his tact. Therefore she was apt to behave more flirtatiously than she otherwise would have dared to do. She sought him out at parties, if he had not sought her, and chattered to him with confidence, while he evinced every sign of being pleased to listen to her and to laugh at her jokes.

At their third meeting he produced his wallet and extracted and handed her his visiting card, cutting through their small talk to say: 'If you should ever need me, write to me at this address.'

'I'll write to you anyway,' she replied, 'if you'll write back.'

'That sounds nice. But . . . You can think of me as your sugar daddy in the background.'

'You're more a boyfriend than a sugar daddy,' she said.

'Maybe,' he laughed non-committally.

The other man she was friendly with was Dawson Douglas, a very different type. He was the Beringers' stockbroker, a moon-faced, red-complexioned gentile, stout, unmarried, sentimental, and an enthusiastic amateur of the arts. He admired her playing, he admired her, and she basked in his admiration; but she was more circumspect in his company than in Joe's.

Dawson asked her if she would like to, if she would be allowed to, accompany him to the theatre, say to a matinée, and he mentioned the successful play *A Bowl of Cherries*.

Eleanor exclaimed: 'Golly!'

She had read about and longed to see *A Bowl of Cherries*. Moreover her involuntary impulse was to please Dawson, not only because he might be called a new conquest. She was amused by his name, she thought and said it was the wrong way round, it should be Douglas Dawson; and they shared jokes about it – he was her 'back-to-front man' and 'Topsy-turvy'. Apart from this nominal bond, Eleanor was touched by his condescension, even his humility, and by an odd facial tic he had: his face relaxed, his slanting eyebrows levelled, his scalp seemed to loosen and his ears to move, whenever he received a positive response to his tentative speeches.

He had framed his invitation to the theatre thus: 'Look – I suppose I should keep quiet – I'll probably get the rough side of Sidney's tongue for thinking of such a thing, let alone saying it – but you'd be doing me a great favour, and it would be so frightfully nice, if you could come to the play with me one day . . .' etcetera.

Eleanor took the evidence that her monosyllabic answer relieved the tension of his countenance as a compliment: he was showing her that she had cheered him up.

But she kept her head to the extent of adding that she would have to consult Myrtle and Sidney.

Myrtle was outraged: 'I won't have you going to the theatre alone with a man – I won't have you ruining your reputation before you're even seventeen – in the next few years you have a particular obligation to be above and beyond reproach.'

Sidney was as critical of Dawson as Dawson had expected him to be: 'Stupid fool! It's unforgivable behaviour. At his advanced age he should know better than to ask you anywhere – he's nearly old enough to be your father. Who does he think you are? I just hope he's more responsible in dealing with our financial affairs.'

The Beringers undertook to convey a polite rejection of the offer to Dawson.

Eleanor swallowed her disappointment at not seeing *A Bowl of Cherries*, and considered the matter closed.

Yet a week or so later at Hyde Park Square she was on the receiving end of a couple of cautionary lectures.

Sidney said to her after she had played the piano to both Beringers, and while Myrtle was out of the sitting-room: 'My darling, by now you've proved you have a precious gift for music. I can't tell whether you play better or worse than you did when I first heard you at Harold Whymper's. But I can tell you that men, many men, will soon be doing their level best to distract you, and get you to switch your attention from music to themselves. Do you follow me, darling girl? Believe me anyway. The process has started already – some men wanting you to do things that would be bad for you. I feel bound to warn you about the precariousness of art. I must love you because I feel so protective! Art may be the strongest man-made force in the world, and the fount of religion, politics, progress; at the same time it's fragile and elusive. It can be easily lost by civilisations and by people. Try not to lose your art – guard it from men for as long as you can and as well as you can! Be careful! There – I won't go on – but you're such a good kind girl that sometimes I can hardly bear to think of the harm you may let your lovers do to you.'

On the same afternoon Myrtle, alone with Eleanor, carried on from where Sidney had left off: 'Can I talk to you seriously? You know how fond we are of you, and we believe you're fond of us. But we're concerned in case our mutual fondness should mislead you. You see, your life to date, although deprived in one sense, has been unusually sheltered in another. You had no direct experience of the married state until you met us. You'd had no relationship to speak of with a grown man. Innocence, trustfulness – they're attractive qualities; but perilously so in a world in which you're supposed to eat or be eaten. Sidneys don't grow on trees, I assure you, and he'd presumably say the same of me. As for our marriage, it's one in many more than a million, and partly because our luck extends to having interests in common and the wherewithal to pay for our pleasure: even affinity can starve to death, sad to say. You'll make mistakes – who doesn't? But don't make them because of us. Don't expect every love you're offered and you reciprocate to be like Sidney's and mine, as equal and fulfilling. For that matter, don't expect your new friendships to have the character, which is unique in my opinion, of ours. Above all, don't hurry. That's what my advice boils down to, dearest. Let men wait for your love, if you can. And if you can't, and disillusionment and disappointment get their teeth into you, never lose faith in life and in the existence of happiness and your ability to find it.'

The Beringers' words of wisdom were counter-productive: perhaps the words were unwise.

Their convictions that men were about to queue up to pay court to Eleanor, to be jealous of her music, to possess her and be possessive, to subject her to unimaginable trials and wrestle with her for her very soul, merely added to the excitement of the potential victim.

In July the Beringers departed for Rockery Hill, and Eleanor would watch out for Henry Menny, her Henny-penny the postman of yore, meet him in the garden or the street, seize any letter addressed to her in Myrtle or Sidney's handwriting and scan it for an invitation to stay. No mention of such a visit was made for weeks.

The summer weather was bad, either wet or steamily grey. Eleanor, in her correspondence with Myrtle and Sidney, commiserated with them for not having the glorious sunshine which she had so much enjoyed last year. Her only dependable treat was to be driven to and from Hyde Park Square once a week by Mr Stott, and to spend a few hours tinkling on the grand piano in the refined luxury of the empty sitting-room. If Maud was in a good mood she might bring up a tray of tea and biscuits – Cook did not bake cakes for the likes of Eleanor: who, incidentally, never dared ask for refreshment. Her concentration was fitful, her attention to her music wandered – there was no prospect of her playing it to sympathetic people. One early evening Mr Stott inquired if she would care to drive the long way home, and took her on an interesting tour through Regent's Park. The interest for her was threefold, and hardly topographical: she liked to be looked at in the Rolls-Royce, she felt grand – she was poor enough not to suffer from social guilt; she very much liked to establish ocular contact with masculine strangers, to play eye-games, and especially to play them in remote localities with young men she was unlikely ever to see again; and she was pleased to delay her return to 14 Summer Drive.

She could settle to nothing in the environment of her childhood. She resented the pressures exerted upon her – in effect, to remain a child: the early nights, the edicts of the Auntys. She read books upstairs. She disregarded Aunty Lou's pleas and flung out of the house to go for long solitary walks. She was simultaneously low and high – the accompaniment of her depression was her uplifting, pounding sense of being poised on the threshold of real life with its new opportunities and gratifications.

She had a lesson with Harold Whymper which went as badly as she had feared.

At the end of it he said: 'You may be going off the boil. Worry not – give the keyboard a rest. Write to me when you next feel musical, and we'll take it from there.'

Her negative reaction was to hope he would not report the poorness of her playing to the Beringers or Aunty Lou.

August in Willesden seemed to get less and less tolerable.

But just as Eleanor was beginning to wonder if she should now look forward to Myrtle and Sidney's return to Hyde Park Square she received a letter from Sidney inviting her to stay the weekend at Rockery Hill, where they had decided to remain until mid-September.

Mr Stott drove her down on the Friday afternoon. The weather had relented: it was sunny and still. She loved the extended bungalow, the landscape gilded by autumn, her white quiet room, and above all the Beringers, who kept on praising her looks — she loved everything more than ever. Her spirits soared, as a result of which, and with a little assistance from Sidney, she had an uncontrollable fit of giggling at nothing at teatime. She was nonetheless able to perform on the piano without incurring too much criticism, and she pleased Myrtle by accompanying the singing of her songs for most of the rest of the evening.

They went to bed early. Eleanor could not sleep. She gazed out of her bedroom window at the dusk and the harvest moon, then in bed was loth to lose consciousness and waste a moment of the joys of smooth cool linen sheets and pillows of preternatural softness. At length she dropped off to a lullaby of ducks' quacking and the hooting of owls.

She had not drawn her curtains and was woken by the first light. Through her open window, nature seemed to puff sharp pure air in her face. She rose, looked out of her window again, and saw a layer of white mist blanketing the lake and weaving amongst the trees in the woods beyond. There were rabbits on the edge of the sloping lawn, a big rabbit like Peter, a smaller one and several exuberant madcap babies, racing and leaping. She wanted to play with them; and now a ray of sunlight shot upwards through the mist as if to beckon her. The paving stones of the terrace were only a few feet below her windowsill, and she climbed and clambered out and on to them, and ran towards the rabbits, which scuttled into and disappeared in the longer grass. The chill dew on her bare feet caused her to shudder; but her nightdress had impeded her running, and on a further impulse she discarded it, shuddering and shivering more violently in her nakedness, although she was the opposite of cold. In spite of being in full view of the house she never looked back: she did not care if she was seen — it was another sort of excitement to think that she might be seen. She ran, she capered in baby rabbit style, down the incline into the silvery dampness of the mist and, scattering and putting to flight the waterfowl on the shore of the lake, began to dance about, assuming poses meant to be graceful, and kicking up her legs with abandon. Her exertions made her hotter, so she lay on the dewy grass and rolled over and over and rubbed herself ecstatically with dew until she lay panting and spent.

The sun had half-risen, and was dispersing the mist. Eleanor, overcome with sudden self-consciousness, hid behind shrubs and bushes as she stalked her nightdress, which she then held in front of her for the final dash to the sanctuary of her bedroom. A couple of hours later she was called by Cam, who did not look at her any more severely than usual, and snapped that breakfast would be served on the dot of eight.

Eleanor spent the rest of that idyllic morning on the terrace, reading and talking to Myrtle. After lunch Sidney proposed a drive in his new car, an American open tourer he had bought in addition to the Rolls-Royce. At three o'clock Mr Stott brought it round with the hood stowed; Myrtle sat in the front passenger seat, Sidney and Eleanor in the backseat; and they progressed through shadow-dappled sunny lanes and main roads on which the car could show its paces.

The faster rush of air, meeting the windscreen, as it were bounced over the heads of Myrtle and Mr Stott and hit the pair behind them slap in the face. Sidney, trying to say something, opened his mouth which filled with air and ballooned out funnily. Eleanor opened her mouth wide on purpose, achieved the same effect and amused Sidney. She stood up to get more air in her mouth, he caught hold of her to stop her falling, and they ended up in each other's arms sitting on the lid of the boot with their feet on the backseat and convulsed with laughter.

Myrtle turned round and told them it was dangerous. Sidney did his trick with the air for her benefit; but she must have thought it silly, and was probably too worried to join in the fun.

Sidney was undeterred. They drove through a village, and he screwed his monocle into his eye and blew out his cheeks at the astonished populace. In a town he pulled long noses at rear views of policemen, and he smiled and waved at strangers and greeted them like long-lost friends, bellowing through cupped hands: 'Hullo, old bean! . . . Fancy seeing you after all these years, dear lady!' At a pompous-looking gent he shouted: 'Don't forget we're expecting you for dinner tonight!' In between these sallies he giggled at as well as with Eleanor, who was laughing so much that she cried.

The best joke was that she called him 'Siggy' by mistake. It kept them in fits all the way home. They were 'Siggy' and 'Eggy' to each other, gasping declarations of love — 'Oh I do love you, Siggy . . .' 'And I love you, Eggy' — holding hands, embracing, and vainly attempting to maintain straight faces.

When the car stopped at Rockery Hill Myrtle stumped indoors without waiting, as if ashamed of them or annoyed, and retired to her bedroom to rest.

Sidney said he had work to do in the room he used for writing, and Eleanor repaired to the terrace to read.

The Beringers rejoined their guest at teatime. Sidney quickly drank his cup of tea and went back to work. Myrtle reclined on a long garden chair with her feet up, facing down the slope to the lake and the vista beyond, but perhaps not really seeing it. Her eyes were fixed and her countenance was in its immobile cogitative mode.

Eventually she stirred herself and broke the silence, turning to Eleanor with a smile.

'I'm sorry, I was thinking,' she explained. 'I was trying to decide whether or not to tell you something.'

'Oh do, Myrtle.'

'I wouldn't want to raise hopes which might be dashed.'

'You're making me more curious, Myrtle.'

'Curiosity . . . Oh dear! Oh well!' She hesitated uncharacteristically before sharing her secret: 'A certain young man of our acquaintance is taking an interest in you.'

Eleanor blushed and asked: 'Do I know him?'

'No.'

'But he knows me?'

'No.'

'How then . . .?'

'He's heard about you. He's seen a photograph of you.'

'Who is he?'

'A terrible ladykiller, I'm afraid. Almost every woman he meets seems to fall in love with him — he has such charm. But I can't approve of his cavalier ways.'

'Why is he interested in me?'

'That's a fishy sort of question. But I suppose it needs to be answered. He's interested for the usual reasons, because you look pretty in the photo I showed him, the one of you sunbathing when you were staying here last year. He only pretends it's your music he's after. I've been doing my best to keep you out of his reach.'

'Who is he, Myrtle?'

'David Ashken.'

'The violinist?'

'Yes.'

'But he's famous!'

'He's very talented. He's an artist, the virile exuberant type. And he belongs to my race and no doubt yours. You would have much in common. Apart from anything else, he says he's madly in love with you already, and I don't expect you'd be able to stop yourself falling in love with him. My concern is that you wouldn't be equal to him at your age. He's quite a lot older than you and has had so much experience.'

'How old is he, Myrtle?'

'Twenty-eight or twenty-nine.'

'That's not too old.'

'From some points of view, his experience might be good for you, I agree. I'm apprehensive nonetheless.'

'Please don't be – I can take care of myself.'

'Can you, my dear?'

'Of course!'

'Do you want to meet David? He's dying to meet you. I could invite him to hear you play when we get back to London.'

'Yes. What's he like?'

'He has beautiful brown eyes. He has the authority of success. He's extremely well-to-do, he earns a lot of money.'

'He sounds nice.'

'Don't expect niceness. He expects to be spoilt. He isn't dull at any rate. Shall I invite him to Hyde Park Square, Eleanor?'

'All right.'

1922 . . .

ELEANOR CARTY met David Ashken on a Saturday afternoon in late September at 7 Hyde Park Square.

She was nearly seventeen. She was almost out of her mind with excitement: anticipation, apprehension, hope and despair had done their worst since her visit to Rockery Hill. She saw, she received a blurred impression of, a stocky dark man with black curls on his forehead like a bull. The hand she shook was unexpectedly small, also hot and pudgy, yet strong.

Myrtle, having introduced them, asked her to play. There were other visitors present — it was a gathering of ten or twelve people, including Dawson Douglas. She had practised and practised her pieces with new-found enthusiasm. Now, she thought she got through them quite well, if mechanically. And she received applause. But David Ashken did not congratulate her or speak to her or even glance at her: he conversed throughout tea with a couple of smart animated unknown old women aged thirty-five or so. Eleanor was stuck with Dawson, looking as if he was going to cry because of her inattentiveness.

Myrtle came to the rescue. That is to say she called out above the conversational hubbub: 'David, you ought to talk to your fellow-musician.' A temporary silence ensued. Eleanor rather wished she were dead. But David did swagger across with his hands in his pockets and addressed her thus: 'I'm obeying orders.'

She was speechless. He laughed or sniggered as if to apologise for his ungallant greeting. Dawson melted into the background – Eleanor was edging towards the sofa on which Myrtle lay.

David said: 'I know about you. Myrtle's told me. Your story's romantic, and you've got the face to go with it. What are you doing after this bun-fight?'

'No ... Nothing ... Driving back to where I live,' she stammered.

'Where's that?'

'It's Willesden.'

'Willesden? I've never heard of it. Is it in London? Is it in England?'

A giggle escaped her, and at last she ventured to raise her eyes for a second.

David exclaimed: 'Those eyes of yours are something! You're better than your photograph. As long as you know where Willesden is, I'll drive you there later on.'

'Oh no, Mr Stott's taking me soon.'

'Who's Mr Stott? I'm jealous of Mr Stott.'

'He's Sidney's chauffeur,' she giggled again.

He turned towards Myrtle and, ignoring the guests bidding her goodbye, grumbled: 'Your Eleanor likes Mr Stott better than me.'

Explanations, and Eleanor's shyly mumbled denials, followed.

Myrtle spoke to David, brushing aside the minor matter of transportation: 'She can't be late home – her people are expecting her,' and changing the subject: 'I want you two to play some chamber music here. You could both come to lunch and practise one afternoon.'

'What – the Kreutzer Sonata?'

Myrtle laughed out loud, a rare occurrence, but the joke was completely lost on Eleanor.

Then Myrtle suggested: 'Why not keep her company in our car?'

'Clever Myrtle,' David commented and turned back to Eleanor and said: 'Strange to relate, I'm on my way to Willesden too. I'll be coming with you.'

'But your car ... How will you get back?'

'Thanks to Mr Stott.'

'Are you ...?'

'Coming for the ride? Yes.'

'It's very far ...'

'Well – don't give me cause to complain about the distance. Are you ready?'

'What's the time?'

'Time to go. I can't stand parties.'

Eleanor mentioned goodbyes.

His gesture of impatience alarmed her.

He muttered: 'I'll be in the hall.'

They parted briefly.

She then ran down the stairs with breathless haste, although whether her breathlessness was due to joy or terror she did not know. She had never dreamed that anyone like David could exist, a man so superior and sophisticated, so difficult to please, understand and talk to.

His black looks were impenetrable and thrilling. The power of his personality overwhelmed her. She climbed into the Rolls-Royce rather as if it had been a tumbril.

'Myrtle's an old matchmaker,' he said. 'Do you mind?'

'No,' she replied uncomprehendingly and at random.

He gazed out of the window for a minute or two. Their conversation was punctuated by his silences.

'Are you happy?' he asked.

'Yes.'

'Happy, healthy and fancy-free.' She was nonplussed by this statement. He made it into a question: 'Are you fancy-free?'

She blushed and laughed: she could not tell him the truth.

'I'm not good for women,' he confessed gloomily.

'Oh – I should think you are.'

'Would you? Thank you. But you're too young. Don't ever say you weren't warned.'

Silence fell.

Eleanor was ashamed to be tongue-tied and to feel almost paralytic.

'Do you love Mr S. desperately?'

She had to laugh even as she shushed him. The glass partition between the front and back seats of the car was raised; but Mr Stott still might overhear and put two and two together.

'Will you love him till you die, or he does?'

[116]

'No,' she scolded.

'Wouldn't you be sitting beside him if I was out of the way? Apologies for wrecking a passionate friendship.'

'No, no!'

'Don't take any notice of me.'

'No,' she lied. 'I won't.'

They had already driven along Connaught Street and were proceeding up Edgware Road.

Eleanor forced herself not to miss her opportunity to say something: 'Do you play chamber music sometimes?'

'I'm busy these days.'

'Oh yes, I know you are – and I'm not good enough to play with you, I know.'

'That's not what I meant.'

'Did you hear me . . .?'

'I did.' He paused before yielding to her attendant attitude. 'I'm not a critic, thank God. I wouldn't judge colleagues if I could – I wouldn't if it were possible to pass judgments on art. My criticism boils down to a question: what's music to you?'

She hesitated, he continued.

'Music's my life. It's me – I'm nothing apart from music, music and love – but they're really the same thing. That's why I'm no good at parties or friendly relations.'

She wished she had been able to give him such an answer. His sentiments applied to herself, they were another bond between them, she felt; and they touched as well as impressing her.

She inquired humbly: 'Why did you say the Kreutzer Sonata?'

'It's a story by Tolstoy,' he almost snapped in reply, 'about jealousy.'

Maida Vale merged with Kilburn, and he inquired: 'You're Jewish, aren't you?'

'Myrtle thinks so. My father was Jewish probably.'

'I'm a Jew by birth, not by religion. Jewishness is a help in music at any rate. Have you no idea who your father was?'

Eleanor winced, blushing, as he touched the sensitive spot of her illegitimacy, and said with regret: 'Myrtle's told you everything about me.'

'Not everything, not more than she must have told you about me. What does it matter? Fathers can love daughters too much.'

'I've got a mother.'

'And she neglects you. Jewish mothers do the opposite. Who are these people of yours in Willesden?'

'Oh – my nurse and her sister – no one.'

Eleanor blushed a deeper red for another reason, because of denying her Auntys.

In Brondesbury David broke the oppressive silence to say: 'How are we to respond to Myrtle's invitation?'

Eleanor in her confusion was at a loss.

'To lunch, to lunch,' he jogged her memory.

'Oh – whatever you think.'

'I'm off to Scotland by the night train for a week of concerts, then on to Dublin.'

'When? When do you go?' she asked in an involuntarily tragic tone.

He laughed at her for the first time – a surprisingly indulgent laugh – and replied: 'This evening.'

'I'll leave the lunch and everything to you,' she said with more control over her voice.

'Okay. Can you sight-read, supposing we decided to play together?'

'Yes, if the music's not too difficult.'

'Don't bank on it, don't look so eager! I'm promising nothing – no commitment. I hope I haven't made a mistake already. Better forget this drive – understand?'

'Yes.'

Soon afterwards Mr Stott swung the car into Summer Drive.

'I live here,' Eleanor said defensively, seeing through David's eyes the meanness of the street.

'Good God, I never would have guessed!'

'What?'

'That you and your playing came out of a place like this.'

She stole a glance at him to check that he was paying her a compliment; but

[118]

his face was averted, and she could be sure of nothing except that he had glossy crinkly black hair.

The car stopped.

'Goodbye,' she said.

He disappointed her by echoing at once, 'Goodbye,' without turning towards her.

She opened the door and began to get out.

'Can I reach you through Myrtle?' he asked. 'Or what's your address?'

'Fourteen Summer Drive, Willesden.'

'Summer Drive's nice — so was what we've had, although our summer's a bit late this year.'

'Yes.' She managed to giggle. She was encouraged to look at him at last, straight into his long-lidded slightly protruding brown eyes, at his wide mouth with a row of little even teeth only visible as he smiled, at his chubby or heavy countenance, red cheeks, brownish complexion and the curls on his forehead. He was obviously pleased with his play on words, and now exchanged his grumpy sulky expression for a boyish self-satisfied one. She added in a spirit of recklessness, gambling with her destiny, staking herself to win the game: 'I'm not as young as all that.'

'No.' His smile faded. His negative indicated agreement. His gaze rested on her and he repeated in a strange thicker voice: 'No.'

She stepped on to the pavement. Mr Stott was holding open the door of the car for her. David shouted at him, laughing: 'Home, James!' Mr Stott shut the door in an affronted manner, and bade her good afternoon with extra dignity. Eleanor waved uncertainly at David, who was staring ahead and ignoring her. She loved him madly, abjectly, despite her fleeting wish that he had been more polite to her chauffeur friend.

Or was it the world, was it life and living, that had gone mad?

Eleanor walked on air, or crawled in utter despondency beneath the surface of the earth. She shed tears over the beauty of existence in Willesden, or closed her eyes so as not to have to see the ugliness of her surroundings. Time was either lead or mercury. She as it were sleep-walked through her days, and woke in her dreams of David. Her thoughts ran on the tramlines of the two syllables of his first name. She was oblivious of her Aunty Lou and Aunty Nell and fellow inmates of number 14; she looked down on them or up, but always as if from another planet. She hardly ate — she feasted on the food of love, and played every sadly romantic piece she knew over and over again on the piano in the parlour. Henny-penny became her torturer, because he brought her no letter from David. Her waist grew smaller, her eyes — when they were open — larger and brighter, and at night she clasped to her bosom the make-believe of her pillow and whispered to it: 'I adore you.'

A week after meeting David at Hyde Park Square she returned there in accordance with custom.

Myrtle was alone in the sitting-room, resting on the sofa as usual, and she cried or crowed, smiling and gesticulating with vicarious delight: 'I knew he wouldn't be able to resist you!'

Eleanor longed to believe her, but replied mournfully: 'No — I can't resist him.'

Myrtle was doubly delighted: 'That's perfect, that makes it mutual.'

Moreover, in spite of recently advising against just such a headlong rush into love, she was prepared to dispel Eleanor's doubts by reasoned argument.

'He asked you to spend the evening with him, he agreed to drive miles in order not to be parted from you — of course, and naturally, he found you irresistible,' she pointed out.

Eleanor bewailed her youth, which David had objected to.

Myrtle laughed and explained: 'Men say girls are too young only when they're tempted to get involved.'

'But he hasn't got involved, he hasn't written to me.'

'Patience, I say, although I'm well aware that every lover abominates the word. He wanted your address, which is enough to be going on with.'

'I'm afraid I love him much more than he loves me or ever will.'

'As a rule women love their lovers before their lovers love them. You'll have lots of time to break hearts, perhaps including his.'

'What am I to do, Myrtle?'

'Nothing — and absolutely nothing without my consent and approval. I feel like a dragon of a mother-in-law in the making. I'm not handing you over on the cheap.'

Sidney interrupted his writing to join them for a cup of tea.

Myrtle told him: 'Eleanor has her first serious follower.'

'Oh?'

'It's David Ashken.'

'Oh —' he frowned '— is that a good idea?'

'We'll see,' she said.

The Beringers had plans of their own to discuss.

Then Sidney, having drunk his tea, turned to Eleanor and demanded: 'What about you — do you like David?'

She said she did and was annoyed with herself for blushing: she was embarrassed by the suspicion that she had disappointed Sidney.

'Well — he's a talented man, he's gone from prodigy to virtuoso in next to no time. But you don't play the violin as he does without being odd. I'd have to qualify my admiration. And I wouldn't have thought he was the one for you, whatever you may be for him.'

Myrtle weighed in by asking with her delicate steely smile: 'Are you trying to put Eleanor off, Sid?'

'No . . . But she needs to be cautious.'

'I promise to see that she is. Now don't worry — you carry on with your work.'

He asked Eleanor almost wistfully: 'No music today?'

Myrtle explained: 'She's got other things on her mind.'

He seemed to want to say something more. He stood there almost scowling, but decided against it and left the room rather hurriedly.

Myrtle was right: Eleanor longed only for answers to her innumerable pent-up queries — was David in love with another woman, had he been in love often, what was he really like, who were his parents, where did he live, would he ever look at her, and so on.

She left Hyde Park Square in a dreamily happier mood. At least she had a confidante and an ally in Myrtle, who sympathised with and entered into her feelings reassuringly.

But a whole second week dragged by without a sign of life from David.

She again kept her appointment with Mr Stott and again ascended the stairs to the first-floor sitting-room wondering how on earth she had got through the intervening days since she had descended them.

Myrtle was laughing, half-clapping her hands, waving a white card in the air and saying: 'I've got a treat for you!'

The card was issued by a music academy, and would admit two to the Wigmore Hall for a fund-raising concert performed by some ex-students. Eleanor's attention was drawn to the list of participating artists on the back of the card, especially to the last, David Ashken. The concert was scheduled to begin at three o'clock on that very afternoon.

'I'm taking you,' Myrtle announced.

'Isn't Sidney going?'

'He's otherwise engaged.'

'But we'll be late for it.'

'Our seats are reserved. We'll get there in good time.'

'I'm not dressed properly.'

'Your clothes are charming.'

'And you don't like outings and public places, I know.'

'I've said my say. We leave in half an hour. What fun!'

'Oh Myrtle!'

At the Wigmore Hall, in a pause between items, as applause subsided, Myrtle in hat and fox fur strode up an aisle with Eleanor in tow, and they were shown into seats in the front row.

A flautist and a pianist, both female, appeared on the stage and played vigorously.

Myrtle remarked in too loud a voice: 'David must be next.'

Eleanor was afraid that not only Myrtle, but the thumping of her heart, would disturb the proceedings. To be sitting so close to the stage gave another bewildering spin to her mixed feelings. It was a slight relief to her to clap her shaking hands, although she had not listened to a note of the music.

David emerged from the door on the right of the stage, carrying his violin and bow. He wore a dark suit, which somehow matched his countenance. He inclined his head unsmilingly to acknowledge more clapping, hesitated, cleared his throat and declared: 'I shall play . . .' and caught sight of Myrtle and Eleanor.

He did not exactly smile at Eleanor, but his whole face lightened, his mood obviously changed, and he must have changed his mind too, for he began again in a happier manner: 'I shall play the Chaconne from Bach's Partita in D minor,' as if to suit the improved circumstances of the occasion and to dedicate his performance of the piece to the girl in the front row.

How different was her reaction to this music!

Now every unexpected inevitable flamboyant note seemed to run her through like a sword.

And the artist's confidence, mastery, passionate self-absorption or selfless service of the composer, and swaying body and sweat that stuck his black curls to his forehead, stirred deep dormant forces in her being.

He finished and collected himself, then stared at her so hard that she had to look away, before he bowed repeatedly to the audience, and was eventually permitted to leave the stage.

Myrtle said to Eleanor: 'He's yours.' She laughed and added: 'Come and congratulate him.'

Eleanor protested in a weak voice: 'I can't.'

But Myrtle was already leading the way towards the door into the backstage area.

They were almost the first of the many members of the audience heading for the artist's room. Ahead of them was an elderly couple, a florid woman and a man with markedly Jewish features, both of whom embraced David, uttering congratulatory noises that sounded like lamentations. He hustled them aside, smiled at and kissed Myrtle, and, paying no attention to her compliments, greeted Eleanor.

His mobile face assumed a serious or even a hard expression, he took her outstretched hand in his, in both of his, and made the following statement, unintelligible although she understood it, in a voice at once reproachful, glad, throbbing with emotion and exclusive of the social niceties: 'That's it, you know. I've been trying not to contact you. But you've done it.'

He did not wait for her response: he must have felt obliged to introduce the elderly couple, his parents.

Eleanor vaguely registered the fact that his mother eyed her with displeasure. Her vagueness was partly due to hearing David say in an undertone to

Myrtle referring to herself: 'When can I see her again?'

Myrtle replied: 'Well – you remember my invitation – you could play something together in my house.'

'But I'm doing concerts in the west country for a fortnight, leaving tomorrow,' he muttered plaintively.

'What about a day or two after you get back?'

A date was agreed.

Then he smiled and said: 'We'll play Beethoven's Spring Sonata. It fits the bill for both performers in one way and another, doesn't it?'

He turned to Eleanor.

'We'll make beautiful music. Meanwhile I'll depend on absence to do its trick. Think of me.'

He attended to the next people in the queue of his admirers.

Myrtle exchanged nods goodbye with Mr and Mrs Ashken; and in the car driving back to Hyde Park Square she expatiated on the subject of the conquest by Eleanor, still the merest chit of a teenage girl, of David who was a mature genius and a catch by any standards.

Eleanor could only think of saying in reply: 'How can I get a copy of the Spring Sonata?'

Myrtle undertook to have one sent to her.

Sixteen days passed by, despite Eleanor's firm conviction that they never would. She dreamed through them, and for that matter through the nights, although she did not sleep much.

David, when she met him again, cruelly confirmed her scepticism in respect of Myrtle's optimistic forecasts. For a giddy hour or two at the Wigmore Hall and afterwards Eleanor herself had believed that her love was reciprocated. But absence, even while it reinforced her feelings, had only cast doubt on the strength of his: how could Myrtle possibly be right, how could he with his talent and career and position and wealth love a little nobody from nowhere? And at lunch at Hyde Park Square he duly treated her as she had dreaded and perhaps deserved: that is to say he confined his greeting to an off-hand hullo, avoided her dog-like regard, talked exclusively to the Beringers and ate heartily whereas she could eat nothing.

After coffee in the sitting-room Myrtle left them alone together to rehearse the Spring Sonata, taking Sidney with her. Eleanor was relieved not to be on the receiving end of Sidney's concerned and compassionate glances; but she, and David humiliatingly even more so, had tried in vain to persuade Myrtle to stay and listen.

He went down to the hall to fetch his fiddle, she composed herself as best she could on the piano stool. They started and they stopped. He stopped her three more times with increasingly rough injunctions: 'Wrong . . . Play the music . . . Listen to what I'm doing, use your ears . . . Don't be so nervous!'

Then she stopped of her own volition and cried up at him: 'Why are you nasty to me?'

He retorted as if engaged in some violent quarrel: 'Why do you think? You've upset everything, my life, my work. I can't get you out of my head – you're too seductive, damn you!'

She smiled at him slowly, but he did not notice. He was striding about, apologising for his outburst.

'Sorry – I've told you to take no notice – this is hopeless – come on, come on!'

They resumed where they had left off. Eleanor played much better, and David interrupted her only to repeat passages that he had not got right. During one such pause he asked her if she had ever before played a sonata, and when she replied in the negative he seemed to express approval: 'Okay.' Myrtle rejoined them at four o'clock, and the guests trooped in soon afterwards.

The performance was a success.

Social obligations kept Eleanor and David apart until the customary signal from Maud informed her that Mr Stott was waiting to drive her home. Having said goodbye to the Beringers, she approached and told David she was going.

He groaned: 'Oh no! Oh don't!'

Then he commanded her: 'Wait for me downstairs!'

A few minutes later he joined her in the hall, where Maud stood by the door to usher her out.

She extended her hand and said: 'Thank you for playing with me.'

He uttered a brief barking laugh at the double meaning, she saw the joke and also laughed; but he was not really amused, he looked bad-tempered, and he took her hand and dug the fingers of his other hand into her forearm and said in a grinding sort of voice: 'I don't know what to do about you.'

Her reply was inconsequential: 'You played wonderfully,' as indeed was his: 'I can't come with you to Willesden.' He stared at her uncertainly, squeezing and hurting her arm, said, 'Goodbye – don't forget,' and abruptly turned his back on her and re-mounted the stairs.

Why was she a trifle more confident, or less prone to deep depression, in the next fortnight? Perhaps because she heard from Myrtle that David, as she had suspected and hoped, had professional engagements in the provinces; or perhaps simply because she was obeying his orders to think of him and not to forget – forget, for instance, that he could not get her out of his head.

She still met Henny-penny on the doorstep of number 14 or at the garden gate early every morning: which was just as well, considering that on the first day of November, her birthday month, she bustled down the stairs before anybody else and found a missive on the tiled floor of the hall. It was an unstamped envelope with 'Eleanor' scrawled on it; must have been delivered by hand; would have created difficulties for her if it had been seen or heard of by the Auntys; especially since it contained this compromising message on a scrap of paper: 'Be at the end of the street at three tomorrow, D.'

By devious means, and notwithstanding her awareness of the trouble she might be getting into, she did as she was told. He was half an hour late; but she dared not reproach him after climbing into his big car.

'How are you?' he asked without much interest, driving on.

She had a more urgent question for him: 'Where are we going?'

'Who cares?'

'I haven't got long – not more than thirty minutes – please!'

'How stupid!'

She blushed and wished she was old.

As if telepathically he asked her: 'How old are you?'

'Nearly seventeen.'

'What does nearly mean?'

'I'm seventeen on the twelfth of this month.'

'That's strange.' She had no idea what was strange about it. He complained: 'Why do you have to be such a baby?'

'I'm not,' she contradicted him more flirtatiously than crossly.

'No,' he agreed in his thicker voice, braking and parking the car in an unknown street.

'Where are we?' she demanded repetitively.

'Stop worrying.'

'But you will get me back to Summer Drive, won't you?'

'Come here.'

She was alarmed by events, by the dusk closing in, by that voice of his seemingly thickened by emotion, by his impractical imperative in the cramped circumstances, and by his reaching across, dragging her towards him and kissing her face.

She had imagined their kisses would be gentler. She had looked forward to giving him her first serious heartfelt kiss. But he was surely bruising her, and biting, and, when it came to kissing her lips, trying to do something that shocked her, and from which she recoiled, although she had been excited to read and to be told by Flavia Simmons and others that it was a common amorous practice.

He drew back and muttered: 'You've got a lot to learn.'

She felt flustered and inadequate, that she was failing him, and continuing to do so because his hand behind her head kept on tweaking her hair and distracting her attention from what he was saying.

'But you're not a baby in every way, that's the problem, or maybe that's the solution. I'm going to foreign climes the week after your birthday. There aren't many days left in which to settle matters between us. What do you say to that?'

'I'm sorry, I don't understand.'

'Don't you? Don't you, Eleanor Carty? Don't you, Miss Innocent: you want me to grovel and lick your little boots, do you?'

'No!'

'Okay – I will.' His voice thickened again and he tweaked her hair harder between sentences. 'Myrtle worked me up about you before we met. But she didn't need to, no! You created havoc all on your own. I haven't time for a girl like you. Even this evening I haven't time to do you wrong – that's why you can stop fussing. I'm in demand, everybody wants me to play everywhere, I'm on the treadmill, I've no time and very little energy to spare, and the last thing I want is to have to drag you round after me. But I'm going to Australia for six months. And ripe peaches aren't left hanging on the tree – some man picks them. I'm not asking you to wait for me, because you think you will but you won't. Nor can I lose you – do you understand now? More to the point, do you understand me?'

The surging emotion he conveyed was like a wave overwhelming her.

'I'd do anything for you,' she averred weakly.

'Is that a promise?'

'Please,' she almost squeaked with pain while attempting to remove the hand that was pulling her hair.

'Marry me then.'

She was instantly immobilised; her heart seemed not to beat; yet the street scene, the smoking chimneys against the indigo sky, the pools of light under the gas lamps, impressed itself indelibly on her memory.

'Marry me, come to Australia with me, love me only – I'll make you love me.'

She was speechless – amazement, gratitude, amenability choked her – now her heart was in her mouth and she began to shed the accumulated tears – because her past, her whole life, had been redeemed by this beloved person who wanted her for her very own sake – who was prepared to marry her and care for her in sickness and in health without being pressurised by obligation or payment – who was the best man and the most brilliant artist in the world, yet had stooped to pick her out of the gutter and honour her with his name and fame – therefore, and as it were, each tear washed away another of the congenital and chronic ills of her spirit, which she had borne bravely and grown half-accustomed to – and in a recuperative passion of thanks she threw her arms around David, she threw herself on his mercy, crying: 'Oh yes! Oh yes!'

The wedding was to take place in the Registry Office in Golders Green on the eighteenth of November, in the morning of that day on which the married pair were setting sail for Australia. David and his family were not religious Jews, and Eleanor had no formal religion, whence the civil ceremony; and Golders Green was where the senior Ashkens lived and David had a flat in a purpose-built block. The so-called wedding breakfast would be a lunch in the home of Aaron and Naomi Ashken.

Between accepting the proposal and sealing it legally Eleanor met David only once more: he was otherwise travelling round the country and giving performances. A consequence was that she had both to break the news of her engagement and explain away his absence.

Late in the evening of the day she became engaged she summoned her courage and crept downstairs in her dressing-gown to tell her Auntys. It was awful: she could not have borne it if she had been less excited. Aunty Nell accused her of slyness and goodness knows what else, Aunty Lou buried her face in her hands. Eleanor stood before them like a criminal and was asked over and over again: what on earth did she think she was doing, were the Beringers behind this madness, where was this David-person, why had he not sought their permission or their blessing, or at least come to see them and tried to justify or explain his running off with a girl, a child, who was in no way ready for matrimony?

The next morning, to escape their inquisition and reproaches, she took public transport and walked to Hyde Park Square, arriving there at eleven o'clock. She was eventually escorted by Maud and by Cam to the bedroom where Myrtle, lying in a vast bed, expressed opinions diametrically opposed to the Auntys'.

Eleanor deserved congratulations because, according to Myrtle's analysis, she had won a prize many women had competed for; would gain a name of her own, and become respectable; would have financial security, leisure and scope for the development of her talents; and was a step or several steps ahead of her contemporaries. Furthermore, since she was going to have such a lot to do between now and her wedding and the long voyage out to Australia, she was lucky that David would not be hindering her.

Myrtle then demanded and enjoyed a full account of what she called the whirlwind romance, and, typically switching from spirituality to materialism, went into the monetary side of things. She discovered that Eleanor had no more than thirty-odd pounds of savings, and wrote out a cheque for a hundred to pay for a wedding dress and a trousseau of sorts. She said she had guessed that David would be blissfully ignorant of his fiancée's shortage of cash, and promised to mention the matter when she wrote to congratulate him.

The only fly in the ointment of Eleanor's visit was Myrtle's refusal to let her see Sidney. He was writing, she said, and hated to be interrupted without warning. She herself would pass on the information, and persuade him that all was for the best: from which statement Eleanor deduced that Sidney might be against the marriage.

However, as if to balance the books, the young idea at Summer Drive was that she was making a pretty clever move. Even faithful Willy Hopkins, while bemoaning his future loneliness, mumbled that he did not blame her and, confusedly, that he envied her. He meant he wished he could get away from number 14 and from the implications of being there – and he spoke for most of the other children, present and past, happy enough though they were and had been in the institution run by their Auntys.

Flavia Simmons, too, was pleased to hear of Eleanor's engagement. She looked forward to satisfying her lubricious curiosity by means of her friend's marriage.

'What has he done to you so far?' she asked, and, having accused Eleanor of being secretive and selfish, she continued: 'At any rate swear you'll write and tell me every detail?'

In the middle of the third night after the crime was committed, as Eleanor's agreement to marry David was obviously seen by the Auntys, she was woken by sniffles, and the following conversation, whispered in order not to disturb Unity, took place.

'Aunty Lou?'

'Yes, dear.'

'I'm sorry I've made you sad.'

'No, dear, it's the other way round.'

'But I do love David, and he loves me so.'

'Well – I realise you wouldn't want to stay with us any more. If you weren't going with David, you'd be flying off to do something somewhere. I'm not blaming you – just so long as you're happy.'

'I am! Will you come to my wedding, Aunty?'

'Thank you, dear. It was the shock that upset us – the shock of you marrying at your tender age, and our having to say goodbye to you.'

'But it won't be goodbye.'

'There never was another like you, Eleanor, or will be.'

'Oh Aunty Lou!'

'Now it's my turn to apologise. I didn't mean to make you cry as well. But we'll be happy for you from now on. Go back to sleep, child.'

A couple of days or nights later Eleanor was taken by David to have dinner with his parents.

In Summer Drive at the appointed hour he honked the horn of his car and she ran out and got into it: neither of them could face the introductions to everyone – he had written in a note that he would be too nervous. Perhaps his nervousness accounted for the fact that in the car he had no embrace for her or term of endearment: he did say she looked nice and he had better not mess up her hair, then spoke of nothing but finding and often losing the way.

His home was more opulent and less cosy than any house she knew – all brocade, suites of sofas and armchairs, carpet like quicksand, and gilt cutlery on the marble dining-room table.

Mrs Ashken greeted her by shouting at David: 'She is beautiful, I will allow.' Mr Ashken was more welcoming and quieter. He put a glass of champagne in her hand, which in due course she decided was worse than medicine to swallow.

Her discomfiture was completed ten minutes after her arrival. Mrs Ashken wanted to know if she had anybody in mind to witness the wedding. Eleanor looked pleadingly at David, who would not meet her eyes, and mentioned Aunty Lou.

'Who's she?' Mrs Ashken demanded with raucous scorn.

David was talking to his father. Eleanor had no alternative but to speak for herself. She jerked out that Aunty Lou was the person she had always lived with.

Mrs Ashken must have been in possession of the history of her prospective daughter-in-law, for she commented knowingly, if with snobbish disappointment: 'Oh yes ... Well ...' then asked or rather challenged: 'But what about your mother?'

'My mother wouldn't be interested,' Eleanor said.

'You can't expect me to believe that,' Mrs Ashken retorted.

'My mother doesn't know I'm engaged. She doesn't know or care what happens to me. She never has. And I've already asked Aunty Lou to be at my wedding, and she's agreed to come.'

Eleanor's speech or agitated manner of speaking it clearly evoked irritation rather than sympathy, no doubt because construed as further evidence that she was unfitted to be the consort of Naomi Ashken's very own ewe lamb.

'You're missing the point, my dear,' she was informed curtly and with patronising force. 'I've nothing special against your aunt. But whatever you think of your poor mother she should be at your wedding, and witness it too, provided mothers are eligible. That's the natural thing, it's only right – and I hope you and I aren't going to get into silly disagreements so early on.'

David now, belatedly, intervened.

Red in the face, looking angry and ugly, he rounded on his mother and accused her: 'I've heard you bullying my girl. I've been waiting for you to try it on. You stop it, Ma – or else!'

Mrs Ashken shrugged off his reproof, somehow wriggling her heavy shoulders and laughing unrepentantly. At this convenient moment a maid in uniform announced dinner, and they adjourned to the dining-room.

Eleanor found it difficult to eat the rich food, let alone drink the wine. She responded to Mr Ashken's occasional kindly queries with miserable monosyllables, and felt still more inadequate when she had to answer the single new question fired at her by Mrs Ashken – could she cook? – in the negative.

Meanwhile David and his mother argued or, by Eleanor's standards, quarrelled almost non-stop and exclusively: he ignored his fiancée. They were meant to be planning the wedding reception and deciding which of their relations and friends to invite or not to invite. He objected to her every suggestion, they called each other names, obstinate, bossy, impractical, half-baked, and in between bolted first and second helpings, and their voices grew louder and louder.

In the middle of the pudding course David jumped to his feet, said to his father, 'Sorry, Pa – I'm sick of this!' and to Eleanor furiously, 'Get up – we're going!' And circling the marble table he seized her by the hand and dragged her out of the dining-room and the house to a chorus of vain parental reprimands and pleas.

As the front door slammed behind them Eleanor began to cry.

'Oh God, what's the matter with you?' he demanded, squeezing her hand hard and shaking it.

'You don't love me any more!'

'Oh shut up! I can't help it if my stupid mother thinks you're wrong for me. Why do you imagine I've been in a state all evening? I knew there'd be a row. Well, I tried to protect you – what have you got to complain about? Don't make everything still more difficult.'

'I'm sorry,' she sobbed.

'You won't have to see my people for months, or ever again. I don't care! One of your jobs is going to be to protect me from them. To hell with families! I want to show you my flat.'

'Oh – but I ought to get home – where is it?'

'Eleanor Carty – lesson one – do as you're told.'

He walked so quickly for three or four minutes, pulling her along, that she had to break into an intermittent run. They mounted illuminated steps, entered the hall of a modern block and a flat on the ground floor, where David did not switch on the lights. Instead, he embraced her roughly, manhandled her, covering her face with wet kisses, moaning and frightening her with his unexpected and indeed alien ardour.

'Oh please, no, no,' she kept on begging him.

At last he desisted, he paused to ask, as if emerging from a fit or an anaesthetic: 'What?'

'I must get home.'

'You little fool,' he said.

But he let her go. He turned on a light, glanced at her, gripped her forearm and swivelled her round to study her face, and exclaimed: 'You're looking awful.'

She wrenched herself away from him, crying again with a hand hiding her eyes.

'How ridiculous!' he half-laughed. 'You cry because I am marrying you, my mother cries because I'm not marrying somebody else. Oh well, cheer up, I'll take you home – I never did like a snack anyway.'

He refused to show her his flat: 'It's a pigsty – I'm selling it – we'll find something better when we get back from Australia.' In the car he was calmer and more communicative.

He said: 'Don't worry about this evening – my ma's always driven me crazy, but we can't do without each other. You'd better mobilise yours. I've concerts all over the place right up to the day we marry and set sail – my agent's organising tickets and so on. You'll see me next in the Registry Office – we'll be together from then on. Are you better?'

'Yes.'

He stopped his car at a distance from 14 Summer Drive and put his arm round her shoulders in the dark.

'We're both artists, so anything can happen and probably will – you do realise that, don't you?'

'Yes, David.'

'Here – buy yourself some clothes.'

He had taken an envelope out of the inside pocket of his jacket, and he tossed it on to her lap.

'What is it?'

'What do you think? Cash! I've got pots – don't you dare refuse!'

'Oh David!'

'And here's a trinket for you.'

Another envelope landed on her lap: it contained a small square hard item.

'Keep it for after I've gone – don't thank me – don't lose heart – good night.'

She hugged him, and he allowed himself to be kissed.

'You do love me, don't you?' she pleaded.

'You wait and see,' he replied.

She got out of the car, waved as he turned it and drove off, stuffed one envelope into her pocket, extracted the jeweller's box from the other, lifted the lid and exposed a diamond ring that sparkled in the gaslight. She put the ring on her matrimonial finger and admired it, not minding that it was a size too big. Still in the nocturnal street she opened her bag, produced a comb for her hair, then a powder compact: she wiped her cheeks and powdered them carefully. At last she squared her shoulders, walked with brisk footsteps along the pavement and knocked on the familiar door inset with stained glass.

[134]

Both her Auntys, who had been sitting in the kitchen, stood before her. One of their questions was: 'Did you have a nice time?' By way of answer she held out her beringed hand.

But that night, each of her remaining nights before the wedding, those final nights in the first floor bedroom she shared with Aunty Lou and Unity, were disturbed by spells of wakefulness positively schizophrenic.

She had become the heroine of a true romance, a latter-day Cinderella about to marry her prince of music. She suddenly and as never before had prospects, and would have an enviable future and role in life. She had a diamond ring on her finger, an envelope in her bag containing two hundred pounds, and looked forward to a prolonged honeymoon and sea voyage to faraway places, and then probably to being the lady of a house and a home with a better address than Willesden. Gratitude fanned the consuming flames of first love. She loved David the more for his unaccountability, his inaccessibility, for what she was pleased to think was his manliness.

Yet, alternatively, she saw black cloud instead of silver lining. She could not get to sleep for fear, or was woken as if by an electric shock of despondence. Her excitement seemed to drain away and her heart to sink: she had remembered David's strangeness, the difficulty of talking to him, the strain of his company, the violence of his advances, the shortness of his temper, and his horrid hostile mother. She did not know him really, let alone understand him, and could not cope with him: what had she let herself in for? She shuddered to think of the nuptials, which, she acknowledged in her present realistic mood, were unlikely to consist of sentimental exchanges and a gradual initiation into the rites of love: his 'Wait and see' was more threat than promise. Perhaps the people who considered she was too young were not just jealous and past it.

In the daytime Eleanor unified these contradictory views of her situation by means of activity, mainly shopping.

But then she attempted to do as David had told her in respect of her mother.

At last she had the confidence to demand to know where the Becks lived, and Aunty Lou decided she had no more reasons to withhold the information. Therefore, one morning, partly because letters would take too long, partly in a new spirit of self-assertion, also to satisfy accumulated curiosity, Eleanor called at the smartly painted stucco terrace house in Marshall Street in Chelsea.

She rang the doorbell. Nobody came to the door. Her courage turned into cowardice. Her desire for revenge was superseded by a stronger urge to run away. Only pride, combined with recognition of weakness of her knees, kept her on the doorstep.

The door opened a few inches and a girl peeped through the gap and snapped: 'Yes?'

Eleanor was taken aback, she had not heard a sound from within the house, and the girl's upper class voice was so unfriendly.

'Is Mrs Beck in?' she managed to inquire.

'No.'

'I'm Eleanor,' she said.

'Eleanor who?'

'Are you Winnie?'

'Yes. Why? Who are you?'

'We're half-sisters.'

'Good heavens!'

Winnie loosed the security chain and opened the door wider, but stood there forbiddingly, blocking entry. She was a statuesque cool blonde with outsize blue eyes under the tipped brim of a hat.

'I'm afraid nobody's in,' she continued. 'And I'm going out – I was dressing when the bell rang.' Eleanor noticed that Winnie was not wearing shoes, whence the silence of her approach to the front door. 'But it's nice to meet you,' Winnie drawled without conviction. 'What do you want?'

'I'm getting married.'

'Goodness! How old are you?'

'I'll be seventeen next week.'

'Well, I'm twenty-three, and I'm not going to miss all the fun for ages yet. When's the wedding?'

Eleanor supplied the date, the hour and the location of the Registry Office, and asked Winnie to ask their mother to be there. She gave David's name and, when Winnie showed neither respect nor interest, boasted that he was the most famous young classical violinist.

[136]

'I suppose I ought to congratulate you and wish you happiness,' Winnie vouchsafed. 'Sorry I'm in a rush. I'll tell Mother this evening.' She hesitated and added with a mixture of complacence, slyness and a pinch of Poppy Beck's charm: 'We're lucky to be pretty, aren't we, in our different ways?'

Eleanor agreed and said goodbye as the door shut her out.

This episode corroborated her gloomiest views of life in general and her forthcoming marriage in particular, while the idea of the fun Winnie was having and intended to have for ages lodged like a dagger dangerously close to her heart.

On that same day, by arrangement, she progressed via various shops to 7 Hyde Park Square, arriving there about three-thirty. When she was in the hall, having been admitted as usual by Maud, Sidney emerged from his study and called her in.

He greeted and embraced her as if to say farewell instead of hullo, and led her to one of the two chairs in front of his desk, then sat facing her in the other.

'Darling girl, tell me about your financial situation,' he said, fixing his monocle in his eye and regarding her with businesslike concern.

He repeated his question in a simplified form: 'Have you any money in the world?'

'Oh yes,' she replied, listing Myrtle's contribution, David's two hundred pounds in cash for clothes, and her own few pounds in a Post Office Savings Account.

'Is that all?'

She nodded and he frowned.

'Has a marriage settlement been mentioned?'

'No.'

'Or provision for your future, or for emergencies?'

'No.'

He reached across and took her hands in his and spoke earnestly: 'I believe David's parents are well-to-do, and David must have made money, so I hope and believe that you as his wife and next of kin would always have some security. My worries refer to if you should find yourself on your own, say in a foreign country. I haven't objected to your marriage – I wouldn't or won't, because such objections are pointless. You're marrying your David – it's

[137]

nothing to do with anyone else. You have my best wishes, of course. But I love you very much – yes, we both love you – and we want to give you a present of a little more money – on certain conditions, just in case. I'm putting five hundred pounds into an account in my name at my bank, which can become yours whenever you need it and wherever you are simply by writing to the bank manager. It'll be your nest egg, your reserve fund, your secret store to fall back on. Here's the bank manager's card with name and address – don't lose it – though you could contact him through Myrtle or myself, if the worst came to the worst. Be happy, my darling. Now, at any rate, you should be safe.'

Eleanor cried, and there were more protracted hugs before she resumed her progress to the first floor sitting-room; where she believed she again succeeded in concealing the fact that she was crying not only gratefully, but also because – at least according to Sidney – the five hundred pounds represented an equivalent number of doubts about her chances of living ever after, let alone happily, with her husband-to-be. Indeed, the gift and his reasons for giving it implied that he expected her to come to grief soon, even in Australia, and thus lent weight to her own frightened prognostications.

Luckily or unluckily for Eleanor, Myrtle for once differed from Sidney in this context, and stood by her differences. Her enthusiasm for the marital project, surprising as it was, never wavered, her assurance reassured and her mounting excitement was infectious. By coming down on the side of optimism she as it were helped to balance the books of Eleanor's divided imagination.

Two more of the remaining few days of Eleanor's juvenile spinsterhood passed by, and a letter from her mother had a similar effect. Far from reproaching her daughter for invading her privacy, it was unusually loving, and its underlined congratulations and good wishes were compensatory.

The last lap of the rush to the Registry Office, if not the altar, was merciful inasmuch as Eleanor was too busy and tired to contemplate her fate.

She had to interrupt her packing twice over to celebrate her birthday, once at lunch at Summer Drive and again at a Hyde Park Square tea party.

On the twelfth of November Flavia Simmons' combined birthday and wedding present was a brooch of gilded letters of the alphabet spelling *Bon Vovage*; Willy Hopkins' was a folding leather purse containing a scrap of paper on which he had written, 'You should of waited for me'; other members of the multitude had clubbed together to provide articles of clothing; and the Auntys produced a whole hundred pounds.

'Oh no,' Eleanor protested after opening the slim rectangular parcel they had wrapped in paper decorated with notes of music.

Aunty Lou explained why they had decided against household goods and jewellery: 'Where would you put pots and pans in the meanwhile? And things do get lost and stolen on a journey.'

'But it's too much. I can't accept so much of your precious money, which you need.'

'Think of rainy days, dear.'

'It doesn't rain in Australia.'

The three of them laughed tearfully: although the Auntys seemed to share Sidney Beringer's lack of faith in Eleanor's future, the state of their finances as a result of their unselfishness worried her more than their expectation of her own impoverishment.

She added: 'I know you can't afford it.'

'We can for somebody,' declared Aunty Nell, her cheeks burning bright.

Later, Aunty Nell cooked Eleanor's favourite lunch of rare roast beef and crisp roast potatoes, followed by birthday cake, having agreed not to be disappointed by the overwrought girl's lack of appetite.

Then Mr Stott arrived, and at Hyde Park Square more presents were given and received: Sidney's real gold pin and a fond embrace, an antique brooch and more offers of help from Joe Prince, and a little painted wooden box in the shape of a bleeding heart from Dawson Douglas, whose especially tense and tragic facial expression was soon relieved by Eleanor's grateful kiss.

Harold Whymper was there and passed one remark, the effect of which was delayed, like a sort of bomb.

He said: 'Well, what did I tell you? You've got the opposite sex to contend with, as well as music. Still, art's the better for the difficulties it overcomes.'

Eleanor kissed him too, uncomprehendingly.

Two days before the wedding she received a letter from her fiancé. It ran: 'With love, Impatiently, D.'

She scarcely slept that night or the next. She could not stop trying to remember what she had forgotten.

Her wedding day dawned. In the back of the Beringers' car with her Auntys, on the road to Golders Green, three overdue thoughts, a trio of simple questions she had omitted to ask herself and now could not answer satisfactorily, caused her almost to faint or be ill. They were: what am I soon going to do, can I get out of doing it, what will become of me after it's done? She clung to Aunty Lou and gripped the hand of Aunty Nell until she squeaked.

Poppy Beck, wearing a competitively pretty lavender-coloured outfit and waiting for her daughter by the door of the Registry Office, settled the matter: Eleanor would not stoop to show her mother that she was very much afraid she might be making a mistake, and anyway her mother immediately stepped forward and snapped a string of small pearls round her neck as if to chain her to her fate.

The rest was a blur: the dark appearance of David, who did not smile at her; signing her new name; being driven back to the Ashkens' house by David's father; the formal kisses, the introductions and handshakes, the food, wine, crowd, noise, laughter and play-acting of the reception; changing her clothes; goodbyes; and being driven to Tilbury, once more by David's father, with whom she had to attempt to converse while David read through telegrams and letters piled on his violin case balanced on his knees, speechlessly thrusting some in her direction for her to look at.

Her husband spoke to her really for the first time as they followed their luggage up the gangplank of the *Bristol Maid*, bound for Australia.

He said: 'I wouldn't want to go through all that again in a hurry.'

Her reply, 'No,' must have sounded heartfelt, for he put his arm round her waist and added with a quite comforting smile: 'My poor little girl . . . But now we've a chance to recover and have a nice time.'

Her agreement was nervous.

They were shown into their double-bedded cabin and left alone.

He approached and commanded her thickly: 'Take off your clothes.'

She could not believe her ears. She was alarmed by his unseeing stare. She stepped backwards.

He reached out, caught her by the neckline of her dress, tugged at it, ripped it and likewise her underwear, saying or growling repeatedly: 'I'll teach you lesson one.'

After astonishment and fear came pain, injury, revulsion, coercion, anger, anger mostly against herself, shortlived hopes of reconciliation, more fear, and so on over and over again.

She had known nothing of men. She had known so few so slightly: only dear old Buzzer Bees, Henny-penny the postman, two or three other Willesden characters, and Harold Whymper, Joe Prince, Dawson Douglas and Sidney Beringer. David Ashken's differences from these good kind affectionate people were exactly what had appealed to her romantic imagination. Admittedly, unwisely, she had taken up Myrtle's challenges to catch David's wandering eye; but then her eye had been caught by his quality of untamed elusiveness – she had attributed to him the irresistible appeal of her mythical father.

The sexual side of her marriage was as far as possible from being mythical or romantic. It was all violence, and, for her, blood and tears. Excitement and pleasure did not enter into her defeats and the transitory relief of his victories.

She fled him, sought refuge in bathrooms and lavatories, hid from him in solitude or in the most public recreation areas of the ship; but, at least to begin with, duty and loyalty compelled her to maintain appearances and eventually forced her back to the so-called honeymoon cabin. She fought and lost battle after battle there by day as well as at night, and was left to staunch the wounds, one wound in particular, that he inflicted on her. When she showed him the latest wad of cotton wool and the bandages which she was going to have to throw through the port-hole, he modified his behaviour to the extent of expressing his feelings in ways that either pained her more or made her physically sick.

She dreaded, she was haunted by, that thickening of his voice, the meaning of which had become all too clear to her, and by his sightless impersonal surging and exigent expression. She learned, amongst many lessons, that his amorous appetite stopped at nothing – almost nothing – for a meal, though it had once resisted a snack.

Were other husbands so potent, demanding, selfish, cruel, she wondered.

[141]

Did every wife suffer as she was suffering? Why had no one warned her? Why had she not read a true romance that told the truth?

David was nearly thirty years old. He had the authority of age and of masculinity on his side, while her awe of him and her inexperience were not conducive to the correction of the errors of his experience. The only words he spoke and wanted her to speak as he exercised his rights were dirty ones; and his responses to the objections she dared to voice, such as 'No . . . Please don't . . . I can't . . . You're hurting me,' were 'Shut up!' or 'You'll love it soon enough,' or 'A lot of women would pay for what you're getting,' or simpler angrier curses.

The geographical positions of the ship were like stations along the way of a form of martyrdom. For instance, at Gibraltar she ventured to inform her husband that she felt she ought to consult the ship's doctor about her bleeding. David told her she was fussing, it was natural and temporary, and he did not mind whether or not she bled a bit, and anyway he was not having a tuppenny-hapenny quack meddling in his marriage. And he made it still more difficult for her to seek medical attention by pointing out the doctor in question, Doctor Cousins, who was discouragingly boyish-looking, and listing all possible improper things that he would probably do to her in the course of the gynaecological examination.

Not just sex, carnal, verbal, relentless, also David's work, writing innumerable letters, learning music and practising, interrupted their purely social intercourse. When he was not too close he was too remote: even at meals Eleanor could sometimes get no more than grunts out of him. He consumed vast quantities of the richest food, which with luck had a mellowing effect. Then he might describe the miseries of his prodigious childhood and being dragged through it by his ambitious mother, or expatiate upon the psychology of audiences – 'Don't expect applause for ending on a quiet note . . . Ugly soloists get nowhere.' He said that an artist could hope to be fully appreciated by two percent of his audience, and quoted the wry witticism of some Jewish maestro: 'They clap even when it's good.' He was clever, and liked to assume the pedagogic role and teach her lessons less controversial than number one.

In these intervals of peace or armistice between them she could see why she had believed she loved him. He could re-cast his spell, interest her, and regain a measure of her admiration. His artistic conscientiousness and conscience impressed, and she half-appreciated that she was no more than the safety valve of the pressurised dedication to his career. The root cause of her difficulties was his having neither the time nor the inclination to be bothered with, or distracted by, her feelings and her thoughts. He was particularly bored by any sign that she was capable of mental activity, and so snubbed and squashed her that she took care not to speak her mind. His exclusive wants seemed to be to make free with her physically, and to be able to count on her mute subservience. The singular chink in his armour-plated egoism was music: contradictorily, he wanted her to think well of his musicianship.

She wished – what changes of his heart and her circumstances did she not wish for? – but often she wished that they could talk together more, however one-sidedly. In places less perilous from her point of view than their cabin, she had a vague hope of solving their problems and saving the day with words. But David, whose fame may have preceded him, who advertised it with his practising, was soon the cynosure of the other passengers. Eleanor came in for some reflected glory, and the Ashkens were seldom left alone together in the dining-room or on deck for long enough to have any worthwhile private conversation.

By the time they reached Naples the temperature had gone up as if in relation to Eleanor's spirits going down.

In the farther end of the Mediterranean there was a three-day storm, during which she was unable to look at food. She was already very short of sleep, and more debilitated than she knew by nearly starving and by her continuous hemorrhage.

The night after the storm was beautiful, moonlit with huge stars in a velvety navy-blue sky, hot and languorous. The *Bristol Maid* was sailing parallel to the coast of North Africa, and heady foreign scents mingled with the ozone. David, having had to neglect his violin because of the recent rolling of the ship, now took it to an upper deck and partly practised, partly performed in the open air for a couple of hours. The passengers joined Eleanor to listen to him, and clapped and cheered when he gave them the chance.

The picturesque scene, the plangent music had their effect on his wife. Her raw nerves were soothed. Panic and escapism were transmuted into a yearning for reconciliation. Could David not be persuaded to love her properly, and let her love him?

When the impromptu concert ended she struggled out of her deckchair and fainted. Dr Cousins was summoned, and, since he could not immediately revive her, ordered her to be carried on a stretcher to the sickbay.

She found herself in a narrow bed in a white cabin attended by a nurse in uniform half an hour later.

She had been undressed and was wearing a strange nightgown. Her secret, therefore, had been discovered, and her injuries treated. Nursie, as she asked to be called, a middle-aged cheery person who reminded Eleanor of Aunty Nell, pieced the whole story together from the patient's reluctant answers to her questions. In the light of this information Dr Cousins, overruling David's objections, kept Eleanor in his care until her wounds healed, her bruises disappeared, and she had regained her strength.

Her situation changed twice in the course of her sojourn in the sanctuary of the sickbay, and while the *Bristol Maid* steamed through the Suez Canal and the Gulf of Suez.

On her second evening in bed David visited her, was unsympathetic and impatient, gave the impression that he suspected her of malingering, used violence in trying to make love to her, was interrupted by Nursie, scolded and shooed out of the room. Afterwards Eleanor cried for hours, not as she had before, because of the matrimonial shock and the immediate pain, but for her lost innocence and freedom, because of her folly, because her present was so unpleasant and her future looked worse. She seemed to cry the last of her illusions out of her system, perhaps because it was safe to, she had Nursie to protect her, and to hold her hand and wipe her scalding tear-stained cheeks with a cool cloth.

The other, and consequential, change occurred in the intemperate zone of the Red Sea.

When David came to collect her from the sickbay she asked him as winningly as she could to sit down for a minute.

'Sit down where?' he replied grumpily. 'Let's get out of this place.' His hatred of the atmosphere of illness had been his excuse for not spending time by her bedside.

'I must talk to you. Please,' she insisted.

He slumped on the single hard chair in the room and began to exercise and massage the fingers of his left hand.

She had braced herself to air her grievances in a positive manner, and plead for a little tenderness. But, standing in front of him, she quailed before his obvious signs of boredom and irritation, his dark regard, heavy-lidded eyes and the sweaty black curls on his forehead.

'It's about our marriage,' she said weakly.

'There's nothing wrong with our marriage. It'll get better when you give it a chance.'

'It shouldn't have made me ill.'

'Are you accusing me of something?'

'No – of course not – but couldn't you be more loving?'

'I thought my love was your problem. Personally, I've had enough of your nonsense. Come on,' and he caught hold of her by the wrist and tugged her out past Nursie and along passages and up and down companionways and back to their cabin, where history repeated itself.

Yet Eleanor, having at least challenged the principle of wifely submissiveness, and translated her dumb physical resistance into moral and vocal terms, was now able by means of another word or two, or a look or shrug of her shoulders, to convey the message 'I'm not willing, I'm not happy,' and thus emphasise her point that indeed there was something wrong with the marriage, namely her husband.

Christmas added another sickness to her catalogue of complaints: homesickness. And David loved her in his unremedial fashion throughout the length of the Arabian Sea and into the Indian Ocean. The novelty of the new year was that he began to tell her so almost defensively, if in the savage accents of passion: 'See how I care for you ... Doesn't this say it all?'

But Eleanor's body expressed disagreement, and lack of reciprocation, by again shedding blood, and contracting other female ailments, and interposing the sweet security of the sickbay between herself and her lover.

The turning-point was located in the Bay of Bengal, and was unexpectedly nothing to do with sex.

David had been practising one evening, and a sign of the times was that

Eleanor, instead of listening with exclusive concentration and some pride, was moved to think again of her own music. When he finished they dined, and over dinner at their table for two she mentioned her longing to resume her piano-playing.

He commented: 'Why bother?'

She asked him what he meant.

'Why work if you don't have to? I can earn enough money for two, and one musician in a family is probably one too many.'

'You're very encouraging.'

'Well, you'll never make it as a soloist, being so highly-strung. I suppose you could accompany me.'

'Thank you,' she said.

She was hurt, injured in another and even more sensitive spot, and angered by his arrogant and insulting dismissal of what she believed to be her talent, and of her years of application. His materialistic attitude to art, her art in particular, showed the extent of the gulf between them: his cynicism and her idealism were antagonistic, and never would unite or should have been united. She brooded and grew angrier.

At about ten-thirty they returned to their cabin, he made advances to her, which she rejected, there was a tussle, she lost her temper as she had never quite lost it with him, her eyes flashing fire kept him momentarily at bay, she forbade him ever to touch her again, opened the door and ran away.

She spent the whole of that night on deck, hiding and wondering what would become of her.

In the morning she sought and found Nursie, who exclaimed at the sight of her: 'You do look bad.'

'I am bad,' she replied, 'I've slept out, I've left my husband.'

She duly received more medical treatment and permission to stay in the sickbay. Although David was informed of her whereabouts, he did not visit her until the *Bristol Maid* docked at Singapore.

The most reasonable reason he advanced for kissing and making up was that she was ruining his reputation.

She resisted the temptation to retort that he had ruined her life.

She remained in the sickbay for the last leg of the voyage from Singapore to

Sydney, thanks to Nursie and Dr Cousins, who stretched points in consideration of her plight. That David did not agitate for the return of his wife was probably and partly due to his working harder than ever to prepare for his Australian concert tour: his dedication to his art was almost neurotically obsessive, despite his tough talking to the effect that he only played the violin for money. However, he did ask her to dine with him for the last week of the voyage and she consented to.

At these meetings he was in turn patronisingly reproachful – 'What on earth do you think you're doing?'; testy – 'You little idiot!'; threatening – 'I may sue you legally for the restitution of my rights'; and nostalgic – 'It was fun while it lasted.' His preoccupation was such that on the whole he seemed not to care how and where she was passing her time, or what her plans might be. The valedictory note entered in after the following terse exchange.

He said: 'My tour's going to be rough stuff, rushing round all over the shop – are you up to it?'

'I'm afraid not. I want to go home.'

'That'll be the end of us, you know.'

'Yes.'

'Love'll get better for you. You'll get better at it. What about trying again?'

'No! The trouble's not just that side of love. I must go home and be myself.'

'What do you propose to use for cash?'

'I've cash of my own.'

'Well, it's your lookout, isn't it?'

'Certainly.'

Neither of them apologised: one would not dare, the other would not stoop, to show weakness. There were no loud rows – their quarrels had always been wrestling rather than shouting matches. David's rueful comments were: 'Women think of nothing but personal relations, which I've no time for . . . I was crazy to marry you – the last thing I needed was to be responsible for a nervy musical under-age virgin . . . Everything's your fault for being so seductive . . . Am I being crazier still to let you go?'

The night before the *Bristol Maid* was due to arrive in Sydney he gave her a ticket for the voyage back to England on the same ship.

'Thank you, but I can't accept it,' she said.

[147]

'Don't be babyish, don't look a gift-horse in the mouth – you're getting nothing else.'

'All right, if you'll accept my engagement ring.'

He made an angry gesture of refusal, and she felt she had better let the matter rest.

After dinner that evening he bade her goodbye.

'Won't I see you in the morning?' she asked.

'That depends. The ship docks early, and there's a reception committee coming on board for a working breakfast and to take me to a rehearsal.'

'Oh – well – I see.'

'By the way, if you want your stuff from our cabin you'll have to collect it now or never.'

She hesitated. Pragmatism and prudence urged her in the direction of the sickbay. But David was capable of chucking her worldly goods through a port-hole. Besides, to part with him for ever distrustfully, casually, was difficult. On an impulse of former love and gratitude she gave in, and therefore paid the price, the last instalment of it, she hoped, of being married to her husband.

A few weeks elapsed, she was halfway home, and as if by remote control David dashed that hope with typical physical force. She contracted appendicitis, which, possibly caused and certainly complicated by her pregnancy, developed into peritonitis.

Dr Cousins, Tim Cousins, protested that he lacked the surgical facilities and the skill to operate, although maybe he had simply grown too fond of her to do so and risk her life. At Colombo in Ceylon she was carried on a stretcher from the sickbay into the local hospital, where Tim and Nursie had to abandon her and rejoin the *Bristol Maid* before it sailed on.

At first she was glad not to be dead. Then, as the effects of the operation, of fever and delirium wore off, she was glad to be nowhere near and no longer under the influence of David Ashken. And how infinitely glad she was not to have his ultimate threat of motherhood hanging over her, although she had special reasons to sympathise with the unwanted baby!

The worries came next. They crowded in, shouldering the gladness aside.

[148]

She was in a private room with a balcony in a fine clean hospital on a hillside overlooking Colombo and with views of the sea: how was it all to be paid for? She put the question to her Ceylonese nurses and doctors, who eventually, for the sake of her health, summoned the hospital treasurer to her bedside. She was shown a contractual undertaking to pay the expenses she might incur signed by Timothy Cousins.

'Oh no,' she exclaimed, touched, yet still more agitated because one worry had been replaced by another, that she was in imminent danger of becoming embroiled with Tim.

She told the treasurer how much money she had in the world, not counting Sidney Beringer's nest-egg: would it be enough to pay for everything? Could it be sent out to Ceylon? And would her ticket be transferable to another ship, and valid as soon as she was fit to use it?

Positive answers seemed only to make space for new questions. Unless she had recourse to Sidney's five hundred pounds, she was not going to have a penny to bless herself with when she arrived in England: where and how was she to live?

It was like stepping on a nest of wasps, her reactions to this last query.

She drew the line, mentally, at throwing herself on the mercy of her Auntys: she would have to swallow her pride, admit she had been wrong and they right, seek their pardon for deserting her husband when they had scarcely come round to pardoning her for marrying him, explain that she wanted a divorce, of which, generally speaking, they disapproved, defend herself by dragging their innocence through the mire of her sexual experience, and tell them she was broke, she had spent their money, and sue for their further support, their charity. No, shame on the one hand, and love of her Auntys on the other, would not allow her to do it, to deface her image in her own eyes and in theirs, and impose upon their generous hearts.

The Beringers for similar reasons, although they could afford to be generous, were even less approachable, whence Eleanor's determination not to have revealing recourse to the five hundred pounds in their bank in London.

She had been regarded as a success by Myrtle and Sidney, successful at overcoming the handicap of her birth and upbringing, a successful artist in her own small way, and so on: what would they make of her failure? Their

[149]

friendship had been based upon respect — at least respect — that was mutual: surely Myrtle, who had commended and been so excited by her marriage, would despise her for discarding husband and security in a matter of weeks. She was no longer the girl carrying all before her whom the Beringers wished to live happily ever after, and was loth to introduce them to the homeless and hopeless pauper she had become, and thus yank their relations out of shape, and possibly lose their invaluable love.

Moreover Myrtle was not the sort of person one asked for favours. Sidney might be — but he would follow Myrtle's lead. Although the latter had undoubtedly been Eleanor's benefactor, her benefactions were nothing if not voluntary, her own idea and her pleasure. True, Sidney had discovered the girl who charmed eyes and ears in Harold Whymper's studio; yet he subjected their future association, and indeed every other dealing with her, to the arbitration of his wife.

No — again no — Eleanor could not beg directly from Myrtle or indirectly from her via Sidney — she would not make that extra mistake. They had done, and would no doubt share her opinion that they had done, enough for her. She simply could not bear to seem to be taking advantage of their interest, or to suffer their censure and rejection in any form.

But how, in that case, how was she to re-establish the conditions in which she would be prepared to meet everyone that mattered? Where not only to sleep and eat in the meanwhile, but to catch up musically?

Despairing necessity summoned the image of a certain smart stucco house in Chelsea, where her mother's luckier daughter padded about in stockinged feet and had fun that would be missed by marrying.

But no sooner had Eleanor turned in her imagination to her mother than a home truth struck her. Poppy Beck had given her a prize, those pearls, and written her a lovely loving letter for a change — why? — because Eleanor was transferring the responsibility for herself from her mother to her husband, and, in a short sharp nutshell, Poppy was getting rid of her once and for all.

She — Eleanor — would be wanted in Marshall Street even less than in Hyde Park Square.

Her connection of the addresses, as if she were putting two and two together, was productive of a nastier deduction, or at any rate an additional and thoroughly nasty suspicion.

For Myrtle Beringer, the Myrtle she almost worshipped, had been even more in favour of her marrying David than her mother was, had virtually made the match, as David once remarked, and had then been exclusively keen on it bearing the fruit of a wedding ring, notwithstanding awareness of the drawbacks for the bride, the child-bride, who would be and indeed became the plaything of a brutal satyr almost twice her age.

And Eleanor was convinced that Myrtle would not have acted irrationally or without cause. Lying on a sort of day-bed on the balcony of her hospital room with nothing to do except think and try to recuperate, two memories oddly linked by time came back to her, of her last weekend at Rockery Hill with the Beringers and in particular a country drive, during which she had called Sidney Siggy and he had called her Eggy, and the two of them had plighted their love for each other and had such fun, followed by her talk with Myrtle, who put the idea of David into her head.

Was the talk the consequence of the drive? Had Myrtle been annoyed by Eleanor carrying on like that with Sidney, or vice versa, and had she deliberately set out to distract the romantic attention of the temptress from her susceptible spouse? It was incredible, ridiculous, Eleanor thought, that Myrtle should have been jealous of her; and disloyal to dally with the base notion that she had been sacrificed on the altar of Myrtle's selfishness.

Yet further cogitation tended to be confirmatory.

There were stifling Asian nights when Eleanor could neither sleep nor forgive Myrtle for so misunderstanding her feelings for Sidney, so mistrusting her, and, in an almost literal sense, for throwing her punitively and callously to the wolf of David. She felt her love of Myrtle had been betrayed, and, in view of Myrtle's presumably similar feelings, that they would never be able to meet again. In the smallest blackest hours she hated Myrtle, whose beneficence had deteriorated into meanness, who had raised her higher only to drop her more shatteringly even than her hateful mother had, and was now robbing her of the recollections of the friendship she valued most, of the precious little she had been left with.

Some dawn shed a belated ray of light on her situation. For she realised she was not alone in having erred: Myrtle was also to blame for the error.

Complicity would facilitate reunion. Eleanor's guilt and shame inhibited less because she considered they should be shared. Her blame of Myrtle was modified, or, rather, could be modified by reparation.

After all, who else owed her anything, and had the necessary resources, the house-room, and a mind open and broad enough to listen comprehensively to her account of the tribulations of her introduction to love?

The decision she reached more emotionally than logically was to brush aside impediments, not least the untruthful postcards she had written, and despatch a telegram to Beringer, 7 Hyde Park Square, which ran: 'Have been very ill stop Can I stay with you stop Would notify time of arrival.'

An increasingly anxious week crept by before she received this reply: 'So sorry stop Yes come here stop Love.'

The sender was Sidney, which Eleanor took to be a bad sign.

In due course, considering her youth and robust constitution, she was sufficiently recovered to travel, she boarded a sister ship of the *Bristol Maid* called the *Bristolian*, and continued her round trip towards Tilbury.

She was depressed, lonely, still pretty feeble, and extremely apprehensive. One night through her port-hole, right in the middle of it, framed by it, she saw three stars, a trio of stars in line, like diamonds on a brooch. They twinkled brightly and winked at her, and she could not help smiling back at them. She fancied they were her friends, her guardians, and that while they shone on her not too much could go wrong.

At Tilbury, by arrangement, she was met by Mr Stott and driven to Hyde Park Square. Maud opened the front door, her nose judicially red. Either Sidney was not in his study or did not emerge from it.

Maud preceded her up the stairs and ushered her into the sitting-room and announced: 'Mrs Ashken.'

Myrtle, reclining on the sofa, reached out her arms in a gesture of welcome, and Eleanor ran and flung herself into them.

When they had both finished embracing and crying, Myrtle said: 'I sensed you were in trouble. It wasn't only your health, was it? I guessed what you were in for at your wedding, and have reproached myself ever since for not objecting to such a misalliance. Sidney was right – I should have listened to him. But

Sidney and I also had confidence in your ability to work out your own salvation. And here you are! You've escaped, your ordeal's over, temporarily or permanently, as you wish. I expect you feel and have felt rotten in every way. But you'll soon be strong again, and you've stolen another march on your contemporaries. Think of it — aged seventeen you've been loved by a man who's extraordinary, you've loved him too, and for good reasons you've had the strength to leave him — you've acquired an enviable wealth of experience. And you'll learn from it, you have the intelligence to profit from it, and you'll use it to enrich your art. I won't pity you. In my opinion, you're the luckiest girl alive.'

1928 ...

JOE PRINCE wrote: 'Very dear Eleanor, You are a better correspondent than I am, you answer my letters by return, and then I let weeks pass before I answer yours. I'm horrified to check the date on your delightful epistle from Pittsburgh, Pennsylvania, written not weeks but nearly three months ago. So sorry for what my father would have called my "tardiness". However, thanks to it, I now have news that may interest you.

'You were well eleven weeks ago, and things weren't going too badly for you – I hope your situation is the same today. As you know, I regretted your flight to America after the breakdown of your marriage to David Ashken. I thought that with the help of your old friends, and of the new friendships you were and always will be bound to form, you could have reorganised your life and made a career in music here.

'Far be it from me to heap more coals of fire on your pretty head, but I must admit I was especially saddened by your decision, your being forced by circumstances to decide, to express your talent on the stage rather than the concert platform.

'I've no doubt you're a good actress, or are in the process of becoming one. People like yourself usually have the ability, and often the desire, to shine in an art or arts other than their own. Perhaps their modesty and sensitivity to public opinion undermine their faith in the value of their first and foremost vocation.

'What is beyond question is that you've survived bravely and resourcefully in the USA, and hung on to that most precious of all possessions, integrity.

[154]

Your uncomplaining stoicism, your cheerfulness and high spirits, your untainted idealism and the development of your critical and discriminatory faculties and stubborn refusal to be impressed by anything second-rate, even though communicated to me only by post in these last six years, have all deepened my admiration for you. I can imagine the forces and pressures ranged against you – the idea of a sweet girl of seventeen arriving in a strange rough country and having to earn a living there still makes me shudder.

'Agreed, the above is not my news, nor for that matter new – I've always paid you compliments, haven't I?

'And I'll pay you another before I get down to brass tacks: when I do finally write to you, it's my pleasure to ramble on and, in a sense, stretch out my time in your company.

'Anyway, forgive me for boring you, and please read and inwardly digest the following.

'I have recently had two strokes of luck. One in business, the other in my private life. The latter means that I shall be residing, and not just at weekends, in my country house, which the lady I love is finally in a position to share with me, and that in consequence my flat in Westminster requires a tenant. It's in Smith Square, contains a goodish piano, and has two bedrooms.

'My secondary luck is a windfall of money. To cut a long story short, would you consider five thousand pounds of it a fair price for luring you back to London to keep my flat warm for me?

'Yes, I have an ulterior motive. Although unwilling to interfere with your American arrangements, theatrical and otherwise, I would dearly love to help you to play the piano again. But, I repeat, I don't want to knock down what you've built up over there, or to bribe you to do any single thing you'd rather not do. If you were to turn down the offer of the flat, you could have the consolation prize of the money.

'I promise you there are no strings attached, and I believe that you know me well enough to trust me.

'I trust you neither to raise conventional objections to accepting my gift, nor, of course, to discuss it with anybody.

'Please take your time. I shall not expect an answer about the flat for the next few months, or need one. As to the future, I suppose that if I were to find myself

[155]

in financial difficulties I might have to realise all my assets. But I can't envisage such a disagreeable eventuality.

'Don't thank me too much, dear Eleanor. I've always had a tender feeling for you, I've hated to think of your struggle to keep body and soul together, and my favourite hobby and pastime is to protect those I care for, so I'm really being more selfish than generous.

'With love, Joe.'

Eleanor re-read her letter in New York's Central Park: it was a sunny and mild autumn morning, and in those un-permissive days a solitary desirable female could safely cry over correspondence on a park bench.

The two main causes of her tears were gratitude for obvious reasons, and disappointment. She had been so excited on first reading Joe's letter, she had been on the point of rushing to wire him a telegram of acceptance, but second thoughts were raising obstacle after obstacle in the path of her return to her homeland, her musical as well as native homeland.

How could she pack her bags and go? Her life was never simple – was life for anyone? Although she was out of work for the moment, she was due to start rehearsals of the tour of Edgar Truehand's successful play *Tea for Three* in a fortnight. She could not let Edgar down, or spurn the chance he was giving her, or turn her back on her painful progress through the theatrical ranks and now the possibility of stardom, or cut her professional and social connections probably for ever, or throw away six years of hardship and effort as if they were worthless. She could not do it – she dared not.

She dared neither abandon her new life, nor reconstitute her old one. She recoiled guiltily from even thinking of Willesden. Otherwise in England, apart from Joe Prince, Dawson Douglas and the Beringers, who remembered her? And she knew that Joe would wish not to seem to be forcing his attentions on her, that she would seldom see him, that she ought not to see too much of Dawson, and that it might be difficult to see Myrtle and Sidney frequently.

There was also Flavia Simmons, who was acting on the English stage. Three years ago Flavia had somehow got hold of the review of a play in which Eleanor was appearing, had noticed her name, written her a long boastful letter and sent it to the theatre in Chicago. Eleanor refrained from replying. She was sorry not to write back to silly old Flavia. She would quite like to see her again.

[156]

But she had noticed that the address on Flavia's letter was the Simmons family home in Summer Drive, and she was afraid that whatever she wrote would be retailed to number 14. She could not have that. She wondered if she would ever run the similar risk inherent in a reunion with Flavia.

The fact staring her in the face was loneliness in London equal to that which she had gradually alleviated, if not overcome, in America.

Besides, she shied away from the listed piano in Joe's flat. She had scarcely touched a piano for six years – she would not count odd days and hours at the keyboard – and was afraid to find out that she was no longer able to play, had lost the knack or the art or the talent which Joe and others carried on about.

Music was more like her home than her homeland, another home, her spiritual home, also neglected, where she might never again be welcome; or perhaps like a lover she had betrayed, who would not forgive her for having done so. To vary the latter simile: she had broken music's hold over her with the greatest difficulty, and was reluctant to negate the effort and sue for reconciliation. She feared that if she were to embrace music once more, it would be for better or worse and until death supervened. And that 'worse', for her, was insupportable: she could not bear to make yet another – and such a vital – mistake.

Therefore, in view of these prospective obstacles and pitfalls, Eleanor on the park bench resolved tearfully to return to dear Joe not a spontaneous yes but a qualified no.

She could not help thinking longingly of the five thousand pounds; yet, in spite of Joe's imaginative reference to the cash as a consolation prize, she felt it would not be fair to accept the less meaningful part of his magnanimity.

In bad moods, in harder than usual times, she blamed Myrtle Beringer for her sojourn in America, or her exile.

But she was too truthful not to acknowledge, on reflection, that everything had been her own fault.

Everything, in her mental vocabulary, was the chain of events, or misfortunes, beginning with Myrtle's insidious linkage of her destiny with David Ashken's. She should not have listened to Myrtle at Rockery Hill, or believed that David did, would or could love her as she wished to be loved. She should not have been so optimistic, gullible, foolhardy, or married anyone at her age, let alone David, or maybe, after the divorce, opted for emigration and privation in order not to have to share a continent with her dangerous ex-husband.

Of course, getting to the root of the matter, she should not have been born out of wedlock, the daughter of a goose, of an unprincipled woman of pleasure, who played fast and loose with her sense of security and provided her with no knowledge of the world and the wild men prowling it.

Six years ago, having gone to Australia and come back to the first-floor sitting-room of 7 Hyde Park Square, where Myrtle made the astonishing statement that the errant and wretched bride had done the right thing and was lucky, Eleanor had cried with relief and the far-fetched hope that her troubles were almost over.

An hour or so later Sidney returned home, mounted the stairs calling her name, burst into the sitting-room and embraced her closely and breathlessly.

Eleanor stayed with the Beringers for four months. She recovered her appetite for food, re-established her pattern of sleep, grew calm enough to read and lose herself in books, and, yielding to requests and the pressures of obligation, performed on the piano and tried to practise.

Her admiration of Myrtle deepened. She could not get over Myrtle's unexpected, unconventional, even original in the context of the morality of the period, restorative and uplifting first response to her predicament. One of the Beringers' definitions of genius — attempting to define it was an evergreen topic of their serial conversations — was that it changed the view of life of lesser mortals, and their idea of physical, material and spiritual geography: Eleanor could provide evidence of the genius of Myrtle according to that criterion.

More simply, she loved Myrtle better, and better still for believing that she was loved likewise.

They discussed David Ashken endlessly. Myrtle differentiated between interpretative and creative genius, and thought the former could be a kind of innate and untutored facility of the nerves and muscles, citing as examples child prodigies of music often fizzling out as soon as they knew what they had been doing, and certain famous opera singers who had never mastered musical notation. David belonged in such a category, she opined, he was a natural with a one-track mind, clearly more egocentric than she had ever imagined, interested in nothing outside his art except the satisfaction of his grosser appetites, and totally lacking general culture and existential refinement. Naturally, she said, men of that stamp attracted women, they provoked women to try to tame them, and introduced exceptionally powerful elements of excitement, risk, competition, and possibilities of gratification into the sexual equation; but they were a menace not only because they were incapable of empathy and fidelity, nor because they exclusively used and abused, and in truth hated women, but also because they made other decent sympathetic men look insipid.

She – Myrtle – repeated her apologies for having favoured the mismatch of David and Eleanor. She was apt to convey them additionally by means of an excusatory gesture, indicative of some justification of her actions, which she expected Eleanor to comprehend and condone. In her subtle way she forged a new link in their friendship by treating Eleanor's marriage as her initiation into adult membership of the conspiracy, the freemasonry, of the female sex.

Myrtle was far from being a feminist, she was horrified by the minority of women who wanted to be like men, and compromised the traditional privileges of every woman in order to gain for themselves a few of the trappings of worldly power; but, believing that the majority of women were fulfilled, and thus enabled to develop, by means of loving and being loved by the men of their choice, by inspiring, by helping to realise the particularly masculine gift of vision, and by softening the hearts of their consorts, she joined forces with womankind inasmuch as she was ever ready to serve the real romantic interests of her sisters, and to call upon them to serve her own.

Eleanor was not slow to see the point of that conspiratorial gesture. For one thing it derived from the last part of Myrtle's feminine philosophy, described above; for another, Sidney militated against obtuseness.

On the very first day of her stay with the Beringers, Sidney's enthusiastic greeting had embarrassed her.

If jealousy was one of the motives of Myrtle's matchmaking, by means of which she had seemed to be rid of her young rival, she must have hated to see her husband rushing to clasp Eleanor in his arms – and to think of the unspecified number of days and nights that Eleanor had been invited to spend under the roof of her marital home.

Eleanor loved Sidney, she reciprocated his love in filial measure. But he could have been her grandfather, he was the object of her great respect; and in the days of her spinsterhood, according to her consciousness and conscience, their relationship was pure as driven snow.

Unfortunately the suspicion of Myrtle's ambivalence towards herself dredged up memories that might corroborate it. Eleanor now, knowing men better than she had done, recalled glances which in retrospect were not grandfatherly and hugs a trifle too prolonged.

In the sitting-room of Hyde Park Square, when Sidney charged upstairs calling her name, she could not help blushing. She wished Sidney would be more discreet, then immediately wished she had not acknowledged his indiscretion – to that extent she was dealing doubly with his wife. She caught an enlightening and shocking glimpse of their triangular situation past, present and future as if through Myrtle's eyes.

It was a nasty fly in the ointment of her homecoming.

However, thanks to her prudence at any rate, to Sidney's gentlemanly behaviour and possible unawareness of the occasional truancy of his matrimonial feelings, and of course to Myrtle showing nothing but confidence, they began to co-habit without mishap.

Eleanor managed not to be much alone with Sidney, although Myrtle would urge them to walk and talk together. She profited from the example of Myrtle, who used her health or ill-health to control the attention of her husband, or, in common parlance, as a weapon in the war of the sexes: so Eleanor pleaded indisposition in order to evade Sidney unhurtfully. She regretted the strains introduced into an association that had been beautified by its freedom from them, and was intermittently sorry that her charms were troublesome. On the other hand she was pleased to be steering clear of disloyalty, and repaying debt by meeting the claims of solidarity with the woman who was her hostess and guiding light.

In the third week of her visit the Beringers gave one of their tea parties, and all the men in the room, not only Joe Prince and Dawson Douglas, made a noticeable fuss of Eleanor.

A few days later Myrtle spoke to her young friend of marriage and married happiness.

'I'm sure you're not yet ready to take stock or make plans, and you can be sure I wouldn't wish to push you in any direction, but,' she said, 'I do have high hopes of you, higher than ever, not the least of which is that you'll benefit from my experience. Marriage needn't be like yours was. For a woman, escape from bullying is imperative, and independence is very well. You've had the courage not to sink into a slough of misery, and you're prepared to pay the price of loneliness and insecurity. Nevertheless, sooner or later you'll yearn to swap liberty for love, you'll fall seriously in love with one of the innumerable men who are going to love you, and you'll want to marry him as much as he'll want to marry you. I find the theory of love that doesn't want to marry the beloved, or to bind the beloved to it by every available means, incredible – I don't believe that sort of love is love. Anyway, I count my blessings daily, and would like to re-count them for your edification. Sidney's given me, apart from little things such as his heart and soul, the chance to become myself, or whatever I am. I know it, and I know how good a husband of Sidney's quality would be to and for you. His kindness and sensitivity have been my joy, and he's taken such care not to show me the other side of the medal, his susceptibility. He's hardly looked to right or left for all the years we've been married, or caused me more than a momentary anxiety. Faithfulness, being true to each other, is an absolute pre-condition of happiness in love or marriage, and has to be volunteered, insisted upon, fought for, guaranteed: jealousy equals defeat, a terrible waste of time and energy, damnation. When Sidney and I became engaged, he said he would have to go and see and tell his first wife that he was about to marry again. I begged him not to, I was afraid he'd weaken and be stolen from me, I warned him to choose between the two of us once and for ever – and I've always been willing to force similar issues. A woman mustn't make it easy for the man she loves to betray her. You're so pretty and lovable, my darling, it may be years before you'll have to worry about the preferences of any lover of yours; but the day will dawn when you too will have to decide whether or not to take the natural, essential and pardonable steps to protect everything you've helped to create, that paradoxically strong and weak structure, where you've learned to live and hope to die, what could be called your heart's home, which is liable to sustain damage from an unchecked whisper or a sigh. There, that's all. Do you think you understand?'

Eleanor understood better when in the course of another conversation, after a jolly evening of playing duets on the piano with Sidney, Myrtle asked her: 'Isn't David Ashken going to hunt you high and low on his return from Australia? Shouldn't you be getting legal advice and a divorce? And would it be a good idea for you to be somewhere else when David's here, perhaps abroad for a bit?'

Then Myrtle whisked Sidney away to Rockery Hill rather earlier than usual for the summer.

Eleanor remained at Hyde Park Square. She was alone in effect, notwithstanding the presence somewhere in the house of Maud and Cook. She ate from trays of food which were deposited in the dining-room, often by unseen hands, and was reluctant to go out because she would have to ring the front door bell to get in again.

Her own devices that she was left with were bi-weekly ordeals in the offices of the Beringers' solicitor, who was compiling a cruelty case for divorce from the intimate details of her marriage; occasional lunches with Dawson, and one with Joe; books and music; a variety of anxieties, which mounted steadily; and indecision.

She could not decide to contact her mother, although she felt she should. She was painfully torn in respect of her Auntys: she longed for them, but not to have to tell them truths that would mortify her and they would hate to hear — she could not face their first words, which were bound to be hard, or their pitying afterthoughts, or accept any more of their charity. And for how much longer could she impose upon the Beringers, more especially since their trio seemed to have become a triangle, the eternal sort? And where on earth was she to decamp to, and how was she to earn her livelihood?

All she apparently could do was to ask herself these unsettling questions while the passage of time and her inaction were bringing David nearer, and turning him into a vengeful ogre in her imagination, who was about to find, catch and re-possess her.

Books were more help than music. She had not minded accompanying

Myrtle's spoken version of her songs, as she always had done. But playing the piano to please the Beringers had been no pleasure, she was too out of practice to play encouragingly well, and the necessary hours of concentrated work in Myrtle's sitting room which was above Sidney's study would not have been a polite possibility even if she had had the inclination. What particularly disinclined her was David's opinion that she was not cut out to be a successful professional pianist.

In the Beringers' absence she was at liberty to play the piano nonstop. Yet it was as if David, and to a lesser extent Harold Whymper, who had prophesied accurately that her good looks would be bad for her music, had put a curse on her. Their two critical pronouncements ousted hundreds of compliments from her memory. She could no longer see the use of practising. Her musical aspirations were or would be futile. She shunned the very sight of the piano, preferring to read stories with happy endings in her bedroom.

And since music had been her one and only skill, for performing which somebody somewhere might have paid her something, without it her fears of becoming homeless and hungry were exacerbated.

She wrote to Myrtle, who did not reply. Perhaps her letter was so resolutely cheerful that Myrtle decided no comfortable words of hers were required for the moment.

But the moment became hours and empty days. Three and a half weeks passed, and Eleanor wrote again to say she was concerned to have heard nothing from Rockery Hill. She hoped there was nothing wrong, that she had done nothing wrong.

An invitation to stay arrived by return. Embarrassingly, like the telegram she received in Colombo, it was signed by Sidney. He did not refer to her letters to Myrtle; nor did Myrtle's postscript, which merely stated, 'Much looking forward to your visit.'

Eleanor arrived at about four thirty on an afternoon in early June, having been driven down by Mr Stott. She was again greeted with undiplomatic warmth by Sidney; but Myrtle gave every sign of being almost equally pleased to see her. The talk over tea on the terrace was animated; then Sidney withdrew to work in his study.

Myrtle, lying back in her long garden chair with a rug over her knees, asked

Eleanor, who sat beside her gazing across the wooded landscape: 'Tell me, darling, how have you really been?'

Eleanor had rehearsed her reply: 'I musn't grumble. How could I, when you've been so good to me and taken me in and let me live in Hyde Park Square? I simply don't know how to thank you, Myrtle. But – really – well – I can't say I haven't been worried.'

'Have you reached any conclusions?'

'No. That may be what's worried me.'

'How open-minded are you prepared to be? Are you prepared to consider a somewhat extreme suggestion of mine, and judge it on its merits?'

'Absolutely.'

'I've been thinking of America.'

'America!'

'Don't be alarmed. The first and obvious question is: what ties and prospects do you have in this country? Have you been in touch with your mother or your people in Willesden?'

'No – I couldn't somehow.'

'Is there anyone you wouldn't be able temporarily to leave behind? I know about you and us, and how sorry we'd be to say goodbye to you for a year or two. But the fact is your life can't and won't revolve round ours – it didn't, for instance, when David came along – we never were or will be more than your friends. Is there anyone else?'

'No, no one.'

'You're not half-wanting to wait for David?'

'Good gracious no – I dread him – he's nearly my worst worry! But how would I manage by myself in America?'

'I've got a cousin in New York – Ernest Moss and his wife Ruth would provide bed and board – they're Jewish, they'd keep an eye on you. And I'd be happy to support you until you found your feet. Listen – these arrangements are hypothetical – the question is whether you'd like me to contact Ernest – and the stage beyond that, provided Ernest returns satisfactory information, will be your yes or no.'

'I'd be more afraid than ever in America, Myrtle.'

'Would you, poor darling? In that case you shan't go. But may I just put

[164]

forward some pros of going, despite your irresistible con? You would escape David. You could forget your past trials, and start afresh. In America, the circumstances of your birth and upbringing would not count, would not inhibit you or hold you back socially, and you'd be able to find your level amongst your peers, that is in the true aristocracy of Stendhal's "happy few" – artists and cultured discriminating people – who are apt to be unhappy in fact – but that's beside the point. No – I don't exaggerate – I mean what I say – and I love you for succeeding as a human being and for becoming a fine woman – and suggest America because I believe your accomplishments would be recognised and rewarded sooner where merit takes precedence over prejudice. But please, please, do nothing for me or for my sake. Your life is your own, and you're in the enviable situation, however lonely and alarming, of being free to live it as you wish.'

Eleanor's unspoken response to the above was: 'Oh Myrtle – you're doing it again – how could you?'

And instead of weighing the American scheme in the scales of reason, she wondered how on earth she could wriggle out of it, feeling cornered and frantic.

Myrtle, by 'suggesting' America as she had 'suggested' David, far from removing Eleanor's worries had brought them to a head, and added new ones, for instance that she was the opposite of free, she was at Myrtle's mercy notwithstanding duplicitous assurances to the contrary, and that she would emigrate as she had married, because not she but Myrtle wished it: for to refuse, to rebel, might well displease, lead to the cancellation of sympathetic interest and support, cast her into the outer darkness of penury.

During the next two days Eleanor quailed before her every prospect, and her other main feelings were resentful and hurt. Myrtle was banishing her in spite of her efforts to cause no trouble, efforts even extending to the possible sacrifice of her friendship with Sidney.

The third day of her visit was beautiful, especially the windless golden early evening. At six-thirty-ish Eleanor was reading in her bedroom, having complained of a headache and extricated herself from Myrtle's company, when Sidney knocked on her door and asked if she was up to a short walk: 'It might do you good – look at the weather – and I've been seeing too little of you.' She had to accede to this request: to have said no would have been churlish. Her inexorable sense of guilt as she and Sidney swung downhill towards the lake and the woods in full view of Myrtle made her sadder and angrier.

They chatted inconsequentially until, in a green glade barred with shafts of sunlight, Sidney halted, raised his monocle, regarded her through it and said: 'You're not happy, are you, dear girl?'

Against her will she began to cry.

Sidney enfolded her in his arms, which merely multiplied her sorrows, and she struggled away and stood alone, as if with the bars of sunlight between them.

He protested: 'Why are you like that – distant with me – please say?'

She shook her bowed head, hands covering her face.

He insisted: 'Why, Eleanor – I know you've had a bad time – but why now, since you've been at Rockery Hill?'

'I can't tell you,' she sobbed.

'You know how fond I am of you, I get fonder and fonder ...'

She interrupted him: 'Myrtle wants me to go to America.'

After a pause he asked in a crisper crosser voice than she had ever heard him use: 'Since when?'

Eleanor, frightened, pulled herself together and explained pacifically: 'She only suggested it the night I arrived.'

'I know all about Myrtle's suggestions,' he commented. 'You're against this one, I gather?' He must have taken it for granted that she was, for he continued: 'America's a long way off – if you go there I won't see you for months or years or ever again – no, I probably won't – and I've hardly been allowed to see you since you got back from Australia. Myrtle's a wonderful woman, but she can be very misleading, as I believe you've reason to agree. Follow your own star, dearest, that's my best advice. You have my permission to stay with us for as long as you please. Now, here's my handkerchief. I'll take you home.'

As they retraced their steps Eleanor said at various stages: 'I'm so sorry ... It's not Myrtle's fault ... I don't mean to be distant with you,' and received ominously curt replies.

She excused herself, because she said she looked such a fright, from entering the bungalow via the terrace on which she would have to confront Myrtle. Instead she reached her bedroom from a back door, applied cold water to her burning eyes and cheeks, overheard Sidney haranguing his wife, and collapsed on her bed in a longer and more fatalistic bout of crying. Eventually she was able to write a note to Myrtle and Sidney to say her headache was worse and she hoped they would forgive her for not keeping them company at dinner – she would try to remedy it with sleep. But she did not sleep, and in the small hours of the next June morning she stole out of her bedroom and slipped another note under the door of the Beringers' room.

It ran: 'I've decided I would like to go to America, if your cousins would put up with me for a bit. Thank you so much for thinking of it. From your loving Eleanor.'

She did not regret her decision, having taken it, for she again basked in the full approval of Myrtle, whose excited and helpful attitude to the American adventure could be infectious. She turned her face against fear, was determinedly enthusiastic, and able to convince Sidney that she was in charge of her destiny. Both Beringers gave her money and letters of introduction, and they booked her passage on a Dutch ship, the *Willem*. On the day before her departure, when everything was fixed, and she was almost sure she was out of the danger of David, a letter arrived at Hyde Park Square addressed to her, marked Please Forward and Urgent, and in her Aunty Nell's writing.

Eleanor opened it against her will with shaking hands. It told her that Aunty Lou was mortally ill and would probably be no more by the time she received the letter in Australia or wherever she was. It complained sweetly of having no address to write to except the Beringers', of having not had a word of news from Eleanor since her marriage, and expressed hopes that she was well and happy. It said Aunty Lou had heart trouble and had been sad not to see Eleanor once more.

The recipient of this letter did nothing about it, except agonise. The combination of guilt, grief, new fears of missing the boat in many senses, and the realistic counsel of the Beringers, from whom she could not conceal her dilemma, immobilised her. She minded her last-minute business and packed her bags. The next day she duly waved goodbye to Sidney and Mr Stott from the deck of the *Willem*.

On board she wrote page after sorrowing page of explanation, excuses, recollections, gratitude and condolence to Aunty Nell. In time in New York she received a reply that neither judged nor condemned her, and contained the half-consoling information that Aunty Lou had actually died on the very day on which Aunty Nell had posted her original letter. In other words, Eleanor would not have seen Aunty Lou alive even if she had set everything else aside and rushed to Summer Drive on her last day in England.

Of course she could and should have written to her Auntys long before that, and not been too proud, and too reluctant to reveal the inglorious truth, to see them and love them in the four months of kicking her heels at Hyde Park Square. But the shock of her first personal and remorseful experience of mortality was to some extent delayed, or, put another way, postponed, while she fought battles on other fronts.

She was beset by new impressions, not to mention the opposite sex: on the *Willem*, although she luckily shared a cabin with three other women, she was not protected from strange men by a husband, the ship's doctor or the state of her health, as on the *Bristol Maid*.

In New York she was met by Ruth Moss, who greeted her by saying with dismay: 'Good grief, Myrtle never told me you were this pretty.'

Ruth was a fleshy sixty-year-old with brightly dyed red hair, her husband Ernest was a successful businessman, about the same age but better preserved, and rather too pleased to make the acquaintance of their lodger.

Within hours of taking up residence in the Mosses' smart apartment, Eleanor, having learned her lesson, and not forgetting Ruth's reaction to her appearance, realised that she would have to move out as soon as possible if she was not to be the cause of more matrimonial strife.

The next day she kept the appointment made for her by the Mosses with their friend Jacob Levy, a theatrical and concert agent and impresario. He differed from the professional stereotype, was elderly, gentle and polite, ushered her into the elegant room where he worked, and after a quarter of an hour of pleasant conversation asked if she would like to play something on the piano. She had steeled herself to be as tough as she had expected him to be, had been disarmed by his kindness, felt suddenly exposed and nervous, and gave a disastrous performance. He stopped her apologies with gestures of his hands, and offered her the following advice. On the negative side he said that as a musician she was clearly out of practice, and that she was likely to find it difficult – because time cost money, and pianos to play on and studios to play them in were also expensive – to raise her art in the foreseeable future to the requisite commercial standard. In the meanwhile, moreover, she would be wasting the asset of her good looks. His positive alternative took the form of two queries: had she had any experience of, and had she any objection to, work in the theatre or in films? She remembered theatricals at Summer Drive, and acting the fool with Flavia Simmons, and in a wild way answered yes and no. In that case, he said, he had a tiny idea at the back of his mind and would see if he could convert it into money in her bank account.

Jake Levy's idea was not as tiny as all that: it turned out to be the stout figure of Edgar Truehand. He invited Eleanor to have lunch with himself and the corpulent, flamboyant, fashionable and English-born septuagenarian play-wright. She pleased Mr Truehand not least by having no idea who or how important he was, and by being no nicer to him when informed that he had three plays running on Broadway, and two already on tour and another about to go into rehearsal. They shared their nostalgia for London, she impressed him with her knowledgeable fondness for the works of Charles Dickens, and he amused her with his elegiac reminiscences of English puddings.

In short, they became friends; he allowed her to audition for the part of the debutante in his play of that name; she toured in it and intermittently in other Truehand plays throughout her years in America; and thus solved the problems of which roof to sleep under and where her next meal was coming from.

Edgar was sprightly for his age. He had never married, yet liked women, and cleverly kept his relations with Eleanor between the bounds of platonic flirtatiousness and paternalistic pride and indulgence. He was quick to realise she was not one of nature's actresses, and took care not to try her on the stage too highly. But he was right to expect theatregoers to approve of her beauty, grace and charm, as he did.

He boasted that he attended a performance of his plays on tour every week, which meant that he had to be driven hundreds of thousands of miles a year in his yellow Rolls-Royce. He called the car names, for instance 'home sweet home', his 'little bit of England', his 'lucky charm' and 'the gold-digger', because it took so much of his money to keep in good repair. He told Eleanor the story of it changing his luck some years back, when he had apparently had a succession of theatrical flops and was on his uppers. He had an appointment with a rich man who might finance one more of his plays, so he spent his last few dollars on hiring the yellow Rolls and a uniformed chauffeur to drive him to the house of the potential angel. The latter deduced from these signs of wealth that there must be more money in Truehand plays than he had imagined, and immediately signed on the dotted line. No doubt the powerful presence of his visitor also influenced the rich man to part with his savings.

Anyway the investment was rewarding for all concerned, and enabled Edgar to purchase the Rolls, employ the chauffeur, and live the life of a genuine millionaire thereafter.

He had a prawn-pink complexion, a circlet of grey hairs round the bald dome of his head, a countenance at once soft and sharp, jowly and quadruple-chinned with pointed nose and duellist's eyes, and a comfortable corporation. He wore loud check suits, carnations or orchids in their buttonholes, smoked cigarettes through a long holder, and walked with a stick, usually a shooting-stick on which he could take the weight off his legs. His laughter was eupeptic, his wit publicly cynical and potentially cutting, and he inspired considerable terror in the thespian community.

He never frightened Eleanor. He soon knew enough of her autobiographical details to admire her courage. He considered courage was the answer to the riddle of existence, and, comparing his arrival in America with hers, confessed with unwonted modesty that he might not have dared to do what she had done if he had been a tasty female morsel entering a world of hungry men. He certainly would not have dared to step straight on a stage without training or experience, he said: he had earned his daily bread in Grub Street, as a journalistic hack, before he begged and borrowed the money to mount his own first play.

He bracketed himself with Eleanor in other contexts.

'I'm too intelligent to have been a tiptop actor, and the same applies to you,' he said. 'The best actors don't have brains, and they shouldn't have morals or principles either. The very best ones are a type of prostitute, mindless slaves of playwright and producer, soliciting the favours of the public, prepared to supply every demand, and blessed with an exclusive genius for adaptability. God save us from clever actors with opinions, who have ruined many a good show! God save us from cleverness for that matter! What I think intelligent is, after all, after all the regrets and doubts and hesitation, being the master of your fate, or, as in your case, if you'll pardon the expression, the mistress. I've made my own career, I've taken responsibility for myself, and you seem to me to be doing likewise.'

He was against pretentiousness, and had arranged for the word 'Craftsman' to be carved on his gravestone. His plays were light comedies: 'Farce is too serious a business, and tragedy is coals to Newcastle so far as most members of any audience are concerned. The more weight I've put on, the lighter my comedies have become.' He would mock actors who altered or attempted to improve upon the productions of his plays: 'Surely you can't imagine you're funnier than me? If you presume to know better, do please go away and write and produce your own smash-hit and be as successful as yours truly.'

He spent a few hours weekly with Eleanor during tours, he would engage her for lunch or give her a night's stay in a luxurious local hotel, and he saw her more often and sometimes took her to the theatre in New York in between the touring.

Although their relations were impersonal, outwardly at any rate, and notwithstanding his parade of egotism, he interested himself in a manner that was almost underhanded in her well-being. For instance at their first or second meeting, when he heard she was living with Ruth and Ernest Moss, he let drop a hint of the excellence of a cheap hostelry for actors called Woods Rooms; and on her applying for accommodation to Mrs Woods, the proprietor, she received a specially warm welcome because Mr Edgar Truehand had written a note of commendation. Again in the early days, Edgar having heard an account of her marriage and drawn the correct conclusion that she was averse to certain masculine attentions at present, he somehow made clear to her fellow-actors that she was his property, potential vandals and thieves of which would be prosecuted. At the same time he singled her out for no embarrassing favouritism in front of everybody at rehearsals, often waiting until they were alone together to coach her through some scene. Above all, he gradually convinced her that he had no selfish axe to grind, and she could rely on him not to tamper with the terms of their friendship.

Her indebtedness concerned her.

She would ask outright: 'Edgar, the list of things I owe you for is getting longer and longer – how can I ever thank you?'

But he replied: 'I'm richly rewarded by your smiles, my dear.'

'No – seriously!'

And he would add, shaking his chins at her: 'To be able to help the people one's fond of is the last fulfilment for a gentleman of my age.'

So she always took care to smile and sparkle at him and to be cheerful and agreeable.

But Eleanor's cheerfulness throughout her protracted visit to America, her ready and nearly rollicking laughter, her stoicism, amounted to a triumph of the will. She as it were guarded her private life with her good humour. She allowed no one into the home of her soul in which she wept and trembled.

She recalled an aphorism of Myrtle's: 'The true artist is afraid of everything,' and derived ironical satisfaction from measurement of the truth of her artistry according to that yardstick. She looked back with overdue terror at the narrowness of the squeaks of her short adult existence. She might not have liberated herself from David, she might have been saddled with his baby, she might have died in Colombo, and starved in the USA but for Edgar Truehand.

Her capacity for fear sometimes seemed to be mainly retrospective. Her hopes were like a blind eye which she turned on risk and peril; while disappointment could be compared to a telescope or a magnifying glass that enlarged or brought forward the foolhardiness of her doings. How could she have imagined that aged seventeen she would be able to cope with a moody violinist and sex-maniac of thirty? Why had she never thought of the menace of motherhood? And her American adventure, retrospectively, made her blood run cold.

Her stage-fright accumulated; her terror of being tracked down by David did not diminish. She collected her mail from the Post Office near Woods Rooms with breathless nervousness in case he had written to her. Legal divorce was not much of a relief: she knew he would take no notice of it if he wanted her again. She used to study the pages of newspapers advertising concerts in which he might have been, but thankfully was not yet, playing.

The programmes of those concerts, and the names of beloved composers, pricked her conscience. She had not done right by music, which was exacting its revenge. Admittedly she had access to the piano in Edgar's apartment in New York, and practised on it whenever she was in town and he was out. But her former skill eluded her. She suffered from feeling she had killed the thing she perhaps loved best in the world and certainly yearned for, the sweetest of all arts, its solace and solutions. More humbly and personally on the same morbid lines, she fancied she had indeed buried her talent and would never disinter it.

She was uneasy not only for art's sake when Edgar referred to the prostitution of acting. His metaphor raised the ghosts of sex that haunted her. She was afraid of men in general, or, rather, reminded to be afraid of them by their eye-contacts that always went further than hers, and their amorous overtures, whispers, touches, threats. Her instincts and her affectionate nature were inhibited by her recollections of sexual catastrophe, although she was also unnerved by accusations of frigidity and lesbianism. She even had reservations about women after a night of sharing a bedroom with another young actress on tour who had seemed to be a friend. As for the future — the futility stretching ahead and the bleakness of her prospects — she censored the very thought of it.

A consolation was correspondence. She exchanged letters with Aunty Nell, with Joe Prince annually, with Sidney Beringer and often with Myrtle. Maybe Myrtle had sacrificed her twice over, more or less married her to David and despatched her to America, in order to keep her well away from Sidney; and undoubtedly Myrtle had not scrupled to place her in situations more hazardous than any she herself — cosseted from birth, an heiress enriched by marriage, who ventured nothing and nowhere — had been exposed to. But Eleanor forgave although she did not quite forget, she acknowledged the extenuating circumstances of Myrtle's conduct from a woman's point of view, and, simply, she surrendered to her needful love of Myrtle. And the latter compensated for whatever she had and had not done to and for Eleanor by means of her long letters which arrived without fail and had unfailing tonic effects. Her selective news interested, her reflections fascinated, and her compliments raised spirits. One fact, repeated and emphasised, made a great difference: in almost every letter she drew attention to Eleanor's age, for instance to her being no more than twenty in her third year in America, and so on. Whether or not for reasons of her own, Myrtle reassured by persuading her dearest girl that she could afford to spend time in America since she still had the best part of her life before her.

Consoling, too, was the trio of stars which shone in the clearer skies of Eleanor's American nights, and seemingly assured her, as they had ever since she made their acquaintance, that they were her guardians and her guarantee that nothing irreparably bad was going to befall her.

Four years passed, then five.

And she received Joe Prince's offer of a home in England and the money to live in it.

On reflection, suspiciously, in spite of Joe's claim that the idea of his benefaction was his own, Eleanor wondered if his letter could be connected with one of hers to Myrtle of a few weeks ago, written in a particularly depressive vein after another of her semi-love affairs had come to nought; and she wished with a spasm of irritation that Myrtle would mind her own business for a change.

Joe's generosity, which might be called princely, had reduced her to tears on the park bench. If Myrtle was behind it, she would also be grateful to Myrtle.

The trouble was that she was as apprehensive about returning to England as she had been about leaving. Would she act or have a shot at playing the piano? Would she be safe from David?

She had actually been feeling the opposite of depressed when she opened Joe's letter, and after reading it she contradicted her six years of homesick reactions by remembering how many reasons she had to stay put in America.

She wrote at once to thank Joe; but she clutched at the straw he had held out, adding that she would follow his advice and think carefully before severing all her American links; and in her heart of hearts she was sorry to exchange her previous customary emotional state for a new maelstrom of mixed feelings.

Coincidentally, what made matters worse for her was meeting Virginia Heims at a party thrown by Edgar Truehand while she pondered Joe's letter, and receiving a second extraordinary offer.

At this party Eleanor consented under pressure from Edgar to play something on the piano, as a result of which she was approached by a good-looking, well-dressed, enthusiastic and somewhat soulful young woman. They talked, they found out they were exactly the same age, both having birthdays on November the twelfth, and Eleanor, having revealed she was an actress, was told that she was wasting her time on the stage, that she must devote herself to music, and could do so right away in a rent-free cottage in Santa Barbara in California. Her self-styled twin and aspiring sponsor happened to be the multi-millionairess Virginia Heims, who declared with disarming impetuosity that she liked Eleanor and admired her playing very very much, and that in the grounds of her house in Santa Barbara she had this empty cottage which was Eleanor's for the practice of her art for the asking.

The bewilderment of the next ten undecided days was sharply arrested by the hand of fate, or, more precisely, by the unexpected amanuensis of fate.

A scrawl of a letter reached her. It stated that Aunty Nell was going downhill fast and was signed, 'Willy (Hopkins)'.

Eleanor resolved as she read it that she would not give death the chance to weigh her down with a second millstone of contrition. She went to see and explain her situation and say sorry to Edgar. She sent telegrams to 14 Summer Drive, to the Beringers and to Joe Prince. She spoke on the telephone to Ernest and Ruth Moss, Jake Levy and her few friends. She wrote a note to Virginia Heims, and caught the next boat home.

Mr Stott met her at Southampton and drove her straight to Willesden in the Beringers' Rolls. At number 14 the remains of the garden gate sagged open and dirty scraps of paper were hooked on the thorns of the woody rose bushes bordering the crazy paving of the path. Eleanor knocked, then banged on the door with stained glass panels, fearing she was too late, had once again missed her opportunity, and Aunty Nell was dead and buried. The windows of the parlour on the right and the playroom on the left, and the lace curtains within, were filthy, and she wondered if the house had already been sold. She felt sadly desperate, and was on the point of running along to Flavia Simmons' old home in hopes of getting help there, when she heard dragging footsteps on the tiled floor of the hallway.

Tears started into her eyes at the sight of Aunty Nell, and she was additionally distressed by Aunty Nell's failure to recognise her.

'It's me – Eleanor – I'm Eleanor,' she repeated as she almost forcibly embraced the shrunken and blanched figure.

'Oh my dearie,' Aunty Nell quavered. 'I was expecting you. But it's nearly seven years, you know. What a beautiful lady you've become! Come into the warm now. You're not here to put me in an institution, are you?'

'No,' Eleanor cried with sympathy, 'never!'

She helped Aunty Nell along the passage and into the kitchen, which was more or less unchanged, except for the dirty crockery on the table. Aunty Nell slumped onto the cushions on the seat of her Windsor chair beside the range, which looked as if it might be out. Her uncharacteristic white head nodded forward sleepily.

Eleanor knelt to rouse her or indeed recall her to life.

She was suddenly asked: 'How's our dear Eleanor?'

'Oh Aunty Nell ... How are you? And can you be comfortable in that hard chair? And who's looking after you, and where are your children?'

'You're still a great one for questions, dearie. Give the fire a poke, and we'll boil the kettle, won't we?'

Eleanor did as she was told, made tea, found a few biscuits in the familiar biscuit tin, and woke Aunty Nell who had again drifted off to sleep.

'That's better,' Aunty Nell said. 'You sit across in Lou's chair. All our children are gone, all except Willy – I couldn't do with them after Lou died – but Willy's kept me company and been such a good boy to me. You and Willy were our best children, Eleanor.'

'Oh no, Aunty Nell, I can't forgive myself for not coming to see Aunty Lou and you before I left for America.'

'None of our children had easy beginnings. You had your way to make. We never thought of being put first. And we guessed long ago that you'd be troubled by men. Are you happy, Eleanor?'

'Yes,' Eleanor lied through her tears.

Aunty Nell fell asleep again for a minute or two, woke and exclaimed: 'I'm happy too — I'll die happy because you've been here — thank you for that.'

'I'm not leaving you.'

'Oh but you can't stay in this house, it's not fit for you, and I'm not able to cook any more. Willy gets me a bite to eat in the morning, and brings something home for me when he finishes work. But I'm not hungry. You go to your fine friends, please, dear.'

'You're my friend. I want to cook for you and try to make you a bit more comfortable.'

'You never were a cook. You just knew how you liked your roast beef. That's the difference — you were above us.'

'Won't you let me stay, Aunty Nell?'

'I'd be embarrassed, dear. You owe us nothing, that's what we always said. We counted ourselves lucky to have our children for as long as they were with us — and you were such a loving bright girl. There there now! Very well, stay and see Willy — he'll be back at six. He's still sweet on you, Eleanor. He wouldn't do, I know, though he would keep you safe and not bother you.'

While Aunty Nell slept or relapsed into a sort of coma, Eleanor slipped out of the house, entrusted Mr Stott with messages for the Beringers who were expecting her to stay until she could move into Joe Prince's flat, requested Mr Stott to return to Summer Drive at six-fifteen to ferry her down to Hyde Park Square, waved him goodbye and resumed her vigil in the kitchen.

It was a penance. She was more afraid that Aunty Nell would die before her very eyes than she had been afraid Aunty Nell was dead. She had so wanted to see and be seen, but could scarcely bear what she saw. The physical evidence of human frailty horrified her, she felt herself being torn asunder by squeamishness and compassion, and mourned the complete reversal of Aunty Nell's former position and her own.

Masochistically, in between Aunty Nell's intervals of fading lucidity, Eleanor peeped into the dusty parlour where she had slaved at the piano to no avail, and into the playroom in which she had prematurely had to fight for her life — or so it had seemed — against her own mother and the Adamsons. The dirt everywhere in a house which had been spotless was horrid. She tiptoed upstairs and into the bedroom where Aunty Lou had scolded her for stealing pencils, and in which, later on, inaccurately named little Unity Hart was

[177]

parked. The curtains were closed, and no light switched on. How impatiently she had yearned for her transfer from the middle-sized bed of the three, vaguely visible, into David Ashken's – how stupid she had been!

Where was Aunty Nell sleeping now? Surely not in her old bedroom on the top floor: how did she get there, did Willy carry her up the stairs, and make the bed, and attend to her nocturnal needs? Or did Aunty Nell sit out nights in her chair beside the kitchen range?

Eleanor was repelled by the squalor of such speculations, or, rather, propelled downstairs and back to the kitchen. She was loth to probe into the sinister privacy of old age, and at the same time ashamed to recoil from its pathos.

Aunty Nell woke and mumbled incomprehensibly; and Eleanor fled to the local shops, bought tins of soup, returned, opened a tin, heated the soup and served it in a cup to her Aunty, who shamed her again by thanking her for her kindness.

'But I hope you didn't come all the way from America to be with me.'

Then, after another comatose pause, Aunty Nell said: 'This house is for you and Willy. Lou wanted it split between you two, and so do I. I've done my will to say so.'

Eleanor cried. She cried the more because Aunty Nell did not remain conscious long enough to be thanked in her turn, she neither expected nor required thanks, and never had. She cried because of yet another upsetting comparison, between the selflessness of her Auntys, and the satisfaction they had apparently extracted from denying nature in order to raise other women's children, and her – Eleanor's – dissatisfaction with her lot, although she had men queueing up for her love, and some talent and some prospects and her youth.

As she dried her eyes Willy Hopkins arrived. He was like an overgrown version of his younger self, four-square, fresh-faced, tongue-tied but soft-voiced, and with a slow winning smile. He was a manual worker of sorts, a roofer's mate, and wore dungarees and boots.

Eleanor brushed aside his bashfulness, spoke to him repressively, said she was grateful for his letter, and asked him what was to be done about their Aunty.

He interrupted her talk of hospital and proper rest in bed by putting a finger to his lips and gesturing with his thumb towards the parlour. She stood by the parlour window, keeping an eye on the road, while he, standing in the doorway, explained that Aunty Nell was not hard of hearing, and had a fit if doctors or hospitals were mentioned, although she had pretty much refused to take care of herself since she was poorly; but, he added, blushing on account of his ulterior motives, things might get better now Eleanor was back.

'Aunty Nell won't,' Eleanor replied. 'She's dying, Willy. And I'm not staying here, she doesn't want me to, and anyway I can't, other people are expecting me, and a car's coming to fetch me any minute. Sorry! I'll give you my address and telephone number, and I'll pay another visit as soon as I can. Will you be all right?' He looked crestfallen, and perhaps surprised by her heartlessness, so she supplied excuses: 'I only stepped off the boat a few hours ago, I need time to get organised. You can reach me in an emergency.' Through the window she was pleased to see the Rolls-Royce. 'Here's my car now.'

'That's a pity,' Willy said.

She edged past him, and in the kitchen kissed the insensible head of Aunty Nell, and saying a brisk goodbye to Willy swept out of the house.

She hated herself for her tough attitude, for abandoning her Aunty and leaving Willy to cope; but her sympathies had been superseded, and her confused responses unified by the instinct of survival. She had become aware of — as it were — currents and undercurrents carrying her towards rapids and whirlpools where she would drown. In down-to-earth terms, she could not and would not nurse her nurse, or enter into a relationship with any oafish manual worker, however long she might have known him and however good he might be, she would not become anybody's drudge, nor revert to the sub-class in which her upbringing had placed her — she would protect her hard-won social advancement at all costs. It was not snobbery, nothing so frivolous as snobbery, but the mortally serious business of commanding respect and preserving life-saving hope — or, put the other way round, of eluding certain poverty and refusing to sink into a common nothingness of hearts and minds.

She was putting as much distance as possible between her clean cultivated travelled self and death, death of one sort in the care of a man with mucky hands, and was spurred on by the threat of another sort of death uncared for, alone and incognito, in hospital or the workhouse, in one of those institutions for destitute old people which her Auntys used to describe with horror, and she had visited in recurrent nightmares.

She arrived at Hyde Park Square in a distressed state, and felt that she failed to rise to the occasion. Myrtle and Sidney were overjoyed to see her after six years, and heaped praises on her improved looks; but her joy was checked by their equally changed appearances — they were now in their later sixties and might have been silvered by frost. This extra evidence of the ill-effects of time reduced her to more tears, but she accounted for them by telling the story of her experience at Summer Drive. Immediately dinner was done, she pleaded exhaustion and retired to her room.

First thing the next morning she was summoned to the telephone and informed by Willy Hopkins that their Aunty Nell was dead.

A few days later she attended the funeral. The only youngish mourner, apart from Willy and herself, was an unknown down-at-heel man of thirty-five or so. The rest of the minute congregation consisted of three or four strangers, a superannuated Miss Elmes who had tutored the children of number 14, and a mustachioed ancient, Buzzer Bees.

It was a miserable day, though dry, and in the draughty graveyard after the interment Eleanor and Willy, having said hullo and goodbye to an anecdotal Miss Elmes and a maudlin Buzzer, chatted for a few minutes.

'Where was everyone?' Eleanor asked. 'Why didn't Donald and Michael and Matilda and Jane and the rest show up?'

'Well, Donald's in India. He would have been here if he could. The rest dropped out years back. They couldn't wait to forget they'd been at Summer Drive. They don't want no one to know they were illegitimate. They wouldn't show their faces at a public do for our Auntys for toffee.'

'Who was the man looking like a tramp?'

'He was one of us before our time. He did call on Aunty Nell not too long ago. I think he came to beg for money. So he hadn't a lot to lose today. I can't remember his name.'

'Talking of money, Willy, who's paying for the funeral?'

'Well, the price could come out of number 14, which belongs to us two. I expect you'll be wanting to sell the house, won't you, Eleanor?' She gestured

[180]

indecisively. 'Or you and me could live there,' Willy pursued with phlegmatic romanticism. 'It could be a snug place.'

'Good gracious no, never, not ever!' she exclaimed in an unarguable tone of voice.

On a valedictory impulse she put a comforting hand on Willy's thick shoulder and said: 'But you must stay in the house for as long as you like. If you decide to sell, deduct the cost of the funeral; if not, let me know what I owe you for my half-share. I've got money, and don't need any more at present.'

'Oh, I'll sell now.'

'Where will you live?'

'In lodgings.'

'I'm sorry, Willy.'

'Not your fault, never was.'

'What about your parents? Have they ever shown any interest in what happens to you?'

'No. They've not known me and I don't know them. The money for keeping me at number 14 came from solicitors. And that stopped when I was seventeen. Aunty Nell let me stay put and pay my own way. Never mind! Will you be all right, Eleanor?'

'My mother's useless. I've no idea who my father was or is. A friend's lending me a nice flat to live in for as long as I'm in this country. I'll write and tell you my address.'

'Won't I see you again?'

'Number 14 makes me sad.'

'I could call on you.'

'Dear Willy! Good luck anyway. Goodbye.'

But it was not only the reminiscent bricks and mortar of number 14 that made Eleanor especially sad nowadays. Sidney Beringer was slower on the uptake and stiffer in the joints. In his elegant suits, with his monocle and courtly manners, he seemed old-fashioned as well as looking and acting unlike the energetic and quick-witted man she had known. He had published nothing and perhaps not written much for years, and was more doting than loving where she was concerned; while she was inclined to feel either sorry for or annoyed with him for not being quite what he had been.

Age, in Myrtle's case, had added to the distinction of her appearance and the force of her opinions. Yet here too Eleanor was conscious of a new unbridgeable gulf. They were still close when they spoke of books, music, love – at least Eleanor had no fault to find with Myrtle's sympathetic comprehension of her wifely sufferings, and was again moved by her idealistic and practical analyses of true love. But why did, how could, Myrtle hint reproachfully that she should have played the piano, instead of acting, in America? What did Myrtle think she would have eaten to enable her to play exclusively, and where laid her head to sleep at night after playing? Myrtle, sheltered by and from birth, who had not married until she found a husband ready and able to continue to shelter her, knew nothing, except theoretically, of being a poor girl, let alone of being a poor pretty one in a strange country, or for that matter of having been conceived on the wrong side of the blanket, and an unwanted half-orphaned child without a penny-worth of security; and in the context her contempt for compromise, whether ignorant or arrogant, was insensitive, jarring, and destructive of Eleanor's confidence in her wisdom.

For these reasons, Hyde Park Square had turned out not to be the promised land of Eleanor's exiled imagination. For the first time, and almost as soon as the front door of number 7 was opened by grim old Maud and she stepped inside, she felt cooped up there, and no longer content to worship uncritically at the feet of her host and hostess.

She had therefore contacted Joe Prince without delay, and received an invitation to dine with him and discuss and possibly view his flat that would be hers.

Two days after Aunty Nell's funeral, between seven and eight in the evening, she prepared for this engagement. She was in her bedroom at the Beringers', had bathed, put on her best black dress and was sitting at the dressing-table and making up her face. She wanted to please and to be a credit to Joe in the smart restaurant where he had said he was taking her, and her reflection in the mirror assured her she would do so. She had been looking forward to seeing Joe and regaining some independence even if by becoming dependent on him. But a snatch of American slang crossed her mind, and she dropped the lipstick she was using on the glass top of the dressing-table and wondered how she was going to get through the next few hours.

The slangy phrase was: what the hell?

Hurrying back to England as she had, to catch a glimpse of Aunty Nell and to shrink from all Aunty Nell represented, was nothing but an exercise in futility. She had neither cause nor much inclination to live in London: that plan was also futile. And the same applied to her life in America, her succeeding not to starve, and to her marriage and everything else. She was a straw in the wind or a piece of flotsam, and, without her talent, such as it was or had been, worthless.

What the hell, she asked herself, meaning what did it matter where or in fact whether or not she lived. Who really cared?

She heard the doorbell ring.

With an effort she put the finishing touches to her appearance, and in the first floor sitting-room summoned smiles and a warm greeting for Joe, who was chatting to Myrtle and Sidney.

In due course Joe escorted Eleanor downstairs and helped her into his chauffeur-driven car and joined her on the backseat.

'Darling Joe,' she said, sure that the term of endearment would not be misunderstood and gratitude would not get her into trouble, 'darling Joe, I'm overwhelmed by your generosity.'

He replied: 'You deserve a little luck, my dear – and it's my luck to be able to do these things.' It was some relief to her that Joe had not changed physically since she saw him last. He was the same small gentleman who was gentle with a big heart in a big car, eternally middle-aged, resembling a dignified Jewish sparrow.

'Oh Joe,' she sighed, 'setting aside your kindness, I haven't been feeling lucky just lately.'

He gestured sympathetically, but was too polite to ask why. As she did not volunteer further information, he remarked: 'I was hoping to introduce you to my lady-friend this evening. Unfortunately she's been detained in the country – she sent you apologies and good wishes. The consequence is that we shall be three, if you know what I mean, and three's supposed not to be company. I'm sorry, I'd invited someone else to join us, and considering his frame of mind I didn't like to put him off – he lost his wife some six months ago, poor fellow. But I promise you he won't parade his grief, he's charming in his

[183]

private life as well as professionally. No doubt you know his name, Leslie Vaughan.'

She loved him at first sight, or almost. Maybe she loved or was ready to love him before they met, because news of his remarkable interpretations of the classic stage roles had reached her in America, and she had read with admiration accounts of his insistence on long rehearsal periods and his unyielding perfectionism.

He was waiting in the restaurant when they arrived, sitting at Joe's table for three, and he stood up and greeted them with a grace which, if practised, was an example of the high art that conceals art. He was in fact Joe's age, fifty-five years old, but looked much younger, more like thirty-five. He was nearly six feet tall, slim in an athletic way, and had thick iron-grey hair with a wave in it, a browny-pink complexion, very blue eyes, and his frank smile showed a nice array of white teeth. He was not only a handsome man; his expression was attractively eager and questing, or, in a word, youthful.

She loved his modest self-confidence, his open regard, so unlike her David's antagonistic scowl, his firm yet caressing handshake, his unassuming masculinity which took nothing for granted, and his easy strong voice, and manners of talking, laughing, eating, drinking, smoking cigarettes, moving his supple artist's hands.

The month was now December. The weather for Eleanor, both meteorological and personal, had been overcast. Metaphorically, even in a stuffy indoors restaurant, the skies seemed to clear because she had made the acquaintance of Leslie Vaughan: it was just like the corniest popular song.

Yet her feelings were surely as original as they were exciting. They might have been silken strands spun out of the depths of her being with which she was lassoing him and drawing the two of them together in a sort of cocoon. Her feelings were totally different from the crushes of girlhood, from her initial grateful bedazzlement by David's interest, and from strictly sentimental and transient flirtations in America; they were whole-hearted, and like a rush of un-pent emotion flooding in his direction.

[184]

Moreover she knew, as women are supposed to but she never had known before, her intuition assured her beyond the shadow of doubt, that she would give herself to him, she was prepared to and it would happen some day; and, in a further flash of prophecy and unwonted certainty, that he would be equally generous.

The tone of the lively conversation at dinner was set by her rising spirits, although Joe and Leslie actually made most of it. At some point Leslie was prevailed upon to talk shop, that is to discuss a projected production of *La Dame aux Camélias* by Dumas Fils: he had been pencilled in as Armand's father, who for the sake of conventional morality forces the dying courtesan of the title to renounce her love of his son.

'It's not much of a part, and unpleasant to boot, and I'm not keen. And the play's nothing to write home about. Have you seen it? Have you acted it?' he asked Eleanor, and when she shook her head he continued: 'The play must have been bad to start with. Then Sarah Bernhardt got hold of it and inserted a lot of semi-literate show-off speeches. The result's a morbid mess in my opinion. On the other hand it's one of those works of art, not necessarily the best art, which capture the imagination of succeeding generations: ignora-muses can trot out their names, the Venus de Milo, Mona Lisa, Madame Bovary, Jorrocks and Scrooge. *La dame aux camélias* – well, she's responsible for oceans of tears, and she's inspired an opera, *La Traviata*, and I suppose you can't deny she's another of the heroines of art and romance.'

They adjourned after dinner to the flat in Smith Square, Westminster, belonging to Joe, who presented her with the keys.

She thought and said it was wonderful; and she would move in tomorrow, she said, and in a week or ten days throw a house-warming party and play Joe's piano for everybody – he had to promise to be there, she insisted, hugging him – 'Please, Joe, one more favour!'

She turned to Leslie Vaughan: 'Will you come to my party?'

'I'd like to very much,' he replied.

Half an hour later, alone with Joe in his car driving back to Hyde Park Square, she elicited the following information: that Leslie had apparently been faithful to his late wife, although much in demand by other ladies; that, to the best of Joe's knowledge, he had formed no new attachment since becoming a widower; and that he lived in a large house in Mayfair, the address of which was 10 Green Street.

The car stopped.

She thanked Joe yet again, and not least for introducing her to Leslie.

'Oh – yes – he's a fine serious person,' Joe commented. 'Incidentally, he shares his house with his daughter Patricia and her husband and their three or four children.'

Eleanor did not care, she hardly noticed, that the man she loved was a grandfather.

She duly moved into Joe's flat and, having issued a few more invitations to her party, worked overtime at the piano to restore her playing to a presentable level.

The small company of her friends assembled round about nine o'clock, minus Leslie Vaughan, who arrived late, listened to the music and left early. But Eleanor was not put out by his elusiveness: she realised he was running away from her.

Besides, as if in spite of himself, his goodbye was like a sort of greeting.

He held her hand in his for longer than was necessary – or was she holding his hand? – and said with enthusiasm: 'There are lots of fairly beautiful actresses but not many beautiful pianists. Unselfishly I have to agree with our friend Joe that you belong to music, not to the stage.'

As soon as Leslie had gone, and her mental processes were again in working order, she wondered how, or rather, considering her fatalistic mood, when she would see him again.

The Beringers, Joe, the Whympers and finally Dawson Douglas took their leave.

In the doorway Dawson furrowed his brow and slanted his eyebrows and remarked that he supposed she would not want to accompany him to a charity do, a fancy dress dinner-dance a few days before Christmas.

'Oh Dawson,' she replied in reluctant accents.

'It's for a charity for actors, Eleanor, it's a bit up your street, and Leslie Vaughan's promised to come.'

'All right, I'd love to,' she declared contrarily, marvelling at the resourcefulness of whoever made matches in heaven, and laughing with

[186]

pleasure which, disingenuously, she attributed to Dawson's funny trick of relaxing his facial muscles.

He asked, after saying well done and how sporting of her: 'What shall we go as?'

'That's my secret. You'll have to wait and see,' she laughed.

A long week passed.

Dawson, shyly wearing the costume of Harlequin, rang her doorbell at eight-thirty on the evening of the dance.

When she opened the door he so far forgot his diffidence as to exclaim: 'I say, Eleanor, you've gone to town and no mistake!'

He asked who she was meant to be in her bare-shouldered long dress decorated with white flowers which were also entwined in her shiny dark brown hair.

'La dame aux camélias,' she replied.

The location of the dance was a theatre converted for the occasion. Dinner was doled out from buffets in foyers and bars, and eaten picnic-style in the circle seats and the boxes, while the band played onstage and the stalls area was cleared for dancing.

Dawson met friends of his by arrangement, they introduced one another, collected food and drink, and packed into a box on the lowest of several rising tiers.

Eleanor spotted Leslie at once, and her heart seemed to turn a somersault. She not only loved him, she also loved every novel and authenticating manifestation of her love. She was aware of another sensation, choking and almost tearful, as if caused by her heart in her throat.

He was dressed in white, a white suit with an Edwardian-style jacket and a dark red carnation in the buttonhole.

But he did not see her. There was a horrible moment when she suspected that he saw and by accident or by design did not recognise her. Then she lost sight of him. And time was ticking by, and she danced and grew tired of dancing with Dawson and the other men, and her brain was being addled by small talk, her jaw ached from smiling falsely, and her mobile heart sank and sank. When the lights dimmed romantically, she excused herself and hid her disappointment in the cloakroom. It was getting on for midnight, and she resolved to ask Dawson to take her home.

She returned to the box, which at that moment was empty. She moved towards the front of it, and Leslie was standing on the dance-floor just below and looking up at her.

'Hullo,' he said.

'Hullo.'

'Will you dance with me?'

'Yes.'

He met her by a swing-door into the stalls.

'I know who you are,' he said.

'Yes.'

'It's lovely.'

'Thank you. Who are you?'

'The man who broke the bank at Monte Carlo.'

She slipped into his arms. She had the feeling that the two of them might have been dove-tailed, although they did not dance close to start with. Their occasional snatches of speech were like verbal shorthand: voices, eyes and physical contact decoded and expanded their exchanges.

'Are you alone?' she asked.

'Yes, at last.'

'I saw you earlier.'

Perhaps he had indeed seen her when she feared he had, for he explained: 'I wasn't free to be with you until now. But you're not alone?'

She replied with the ruthlessness of love: 'That doesn't matter,' sparing a quarter of a pang of sympathy for Dawson.

Later on Leslie asked her if Dawson had brought her to the dance: 'I wondered if he would and hoped he would.'

'He told me you'd be here,' Eleanor returned.

'Is that why you wore the camellias?'

'Of course.'

'They're lovely, like you.'

'Falser than me,' she said.

The lights dimmed, the music was slow, and he gently and with her full consent drew her closer.

'Should you dance with someone else?' he asked.

'No. Should you?'

'No. Are you tired?'

'No. Are you?'

'No.'

Then they confessed in turn: he said, 'I talked to Joe about you,' and she said, 'So did I about you.'

Somewhat enigmatically he went further: 'I think I must have known you in a former existence.'

'Yes,' she commented, believing she understood him, and that her sense of understanding everything he did and everything he was derived from similar foreknowledge.

They danced in a rhythmic silence contradictorily full of other forms of communication.

Dawson intruded into their paradoxical privacy in the crowd of dancers.

'Oh there you are!' he said to Eleanor, and, after respectfully greeting her partner, continued: 'I've been looking for you – but it's so dark in here one can't see one's hand in front of one's face – the point is I was wondering if you were ready to leave – I've agreed to drop a few other people home.'

Leslie removed his hand round her waist, as if yielding to Dawson's prior claims, and Eleanor asked: 'What's the time?'

Dawson justified himself by saying: 'Well, it's two o'clock.'

'Really?' She could hardly believe it – the precious minutes spent in Leslie's arms had gone too fast. 'Would you mind very much if I stayed on, Dawson?'

'No – but I must leave because I've promised these other people – and who'll take you home?'

She raised her eyes to Leslie's.

'Would you?'

'I'd be honoured.'

Dawson said: 'Oh – good – in that case – yes!'

Eleanor thanked him and kissed his furrowed countenance, he departed, and she and Leslie re-clasped each other with relief and conspiratorial smiles.

But the interruption had changed the mood of their meeting; they were already involved in advance in the next act of their drama.

[189]

After a little more dancing she pulled away from him and inquired: 'Shall we go now?'

She collected her wrap from the box, and he his long blue overcoat from wherever he had left it, and they met again quite shyly in the bright light by the erstwhile box office, and emerged into the lovers' element of night, and held hands as they walked through the crisp winter darkness to his car.

He drove to Smith Square, parked and said: 'I feel a bit guilty.'

'Oh no – why?'

'About Dawson and things.'

'What things?'

'You've been so incredibly sweet to me, and you're so young and have so much to offer.'

'You offer more.'

'I'm afraid not.'

'You musn't argue with me. Please!'

'No, but ...'

'No buts!'

He laughed more tensely than usual, and resumed: 'I don't want to take advantage of you, as they say. You've turned my world of grief etcetera on its head. You've given me back happiness and hope. What can I give you? It doesn't seem fair.'

'Come in with me.'

'My daughter's much older than you are.'

'Oh, that! You're wrong to think me so conventional. How could I be conventional with my background? And a splendid artist like you can't be conventional either. I've looked and looked for you for so long in vain.'

'My darling girl ... I don't want to disappoint you or hurt you.'

'Same here.'

'It's folly.'

'How do you know?'

'Eleanor ...'

'Wouldn't you like to come in?'

'Yes.'

*

Eleanor between the ages of sixteen and twenty-three had been in receipt of countless declarations of love and propositions, and even of a good few proposals of marriage. When she was acting in plays in the USA, male members of her audiences would wait for her at stage-doors, or sometimes force their way into her dressing-rooms, or write her notes or messages on bunches of flowers, or pursue her to her lodgings and pour out their hearts or confess their baser desires.

And despite her inhibitions and choosiness, and notwithstanding the protection of Edgar Truehand, she had repeatedly had to extricate herself from minor involvements with theatrical colleagues.

In other words she had much romantic experience with which to compare Leslie's attitude in the first abbreviated period of their relations. He never told her he loved her, he promised nothing, he was hesitant and he hung back. Yet she ended by behaving out of character, more like the spider with its parlour than the fly. She was kinder to him than she had been to men who had courted her assiduously, sworn they would love her for ever, and offered her gratuities and diamonds and their names and the moon itself if she would look with favour on their suit.

The spell Leslie cast over her, and vice versa, which changed minds and moods, and caused her virtually to seduce him without embarrassment and him to be seduced against his better if belated judgment, would probably have been called in Myrtle's language of love an affinity. It was inexplicable, beyond definition or analysis, instant, overwhelming. A minute or two after they had met words were to all intents and purposes superfluous between them. And in Joe's flat their communion justified every risk they were running on the strength of so slight an acquaintanceship.

During some interval or pause for breath during those early morning embraces she glanced through the net curtains across the bedroom window at the church in the centre of Smith Square and the still dark sky above. Slanting up there was her line of three stars, to which she inwardly addressed the tentatively rhetorical question: 'Am I happy?'

The blessings she could now count were this luxurious flat; more money in the bank than ever before; friends ready to sponsor her on both sides of the Atlantic; and Leslie, who had exorcised the spectre of her former husband.

She was blessed again to have been able to attract the man of her choice and to have had her feelings for him reciprocated. And the consummation of their love had been showered with the blessed stardust of a million differences from the marital so-called rights which she had rebelled against.

For the irrational reasons of love, she had suspended her horror of sex as soon as she set eyes on Leslie. She had not only forgotten to remember and be put off by the prospect, but yearned for every possible union of themselves and their destinies. He rewarded her confidence in him with patience, tenderness and passion.

At a hint from dawn he left her premises. He said there would be high strikes in his home if he missed his breakfast. But he returned later in the day, and so it went on over the Christmas period and into the first months of the next year.

On Christmas Day itself he had family engagements until teatime, then hurried back to Eleanor bearing turkey and mince pies for their supper. He never took her out to restaurants or public places: he explained that he preferred to keep the orchestra pit between himself and his fans, and that, since he was so recently bereaved, he could and should not be seen gadding about with the prettiest of girls. He also said that it might not be good for Eleanor to be visibly associated with an old fogey; but she mocked and scolded him for his reference to their respective ages.

They were reunited with relief in Joe's flat, and made love, and ate things when they felt like it, and talked the hours away, and she would play the piano for him and he would read to her, and in dry inviting weather they would walk through miles of night with her hand in the pocket of his blue overcoat, sometimes in remote quarters of London, the Isle of Dogs for instance, and eventually repair to their paradise in Westminster, and make more love, and part like faery creatures for the hours of daylight with protests on her side and regrets on his.

She seemed to need hardly any sleep. Her life had become too exciting and beautiful to be wasted in insensibility, and her body flourished along with her soul as never before. Newness was the order of these days for her, and Leslie promised her that he had never known anything like their loving or anybody so lovable as herself.

She looked up to but was not afraid of him. She was grateful but not beholden to him. They met each other halfway, on the equal terms of each being able to give the other exactly what was wanted: their love was that optimum kind which is not far removed from enlightened self-interest.

And it was educational, as true love has to be. It pooled information and to some extent experience, and enabled each to see through the other's eyes.

Whereas Eleanor had not dared to think about the man she had married, what he was really like, what he had done, was doing and would do, and how he would do it, the exact opposite applied to her lover. She was engrossed in every aspect of Leslie's existence, as he was in hers. She told him of Summer Drive, her Auntys, Peter Rabbit and Peter the Great, her careless mother and the Beringers, and she absorbed her pangs of envy and jealousy in order to obtain accounts of his middle-class upbringing with a doting mother and dependable father, and of his contented marriage to untheatrical stay-at-home Barbie, and his daily doings with their only child Patsy, Patsy's banker husband Geoff, and his grandchildren Anna and Keith.

She took Leslie to Hyde Park Square where, although he was alarmed by Myrtle's intellectualism, he nonetheless managed to bowl both Beringers over. Myrtle later confessed that she loved him too, and Sidney said he was even better off the stage than on it.

Then Myrtle and Eleanor, putting their analytical heads together, as it were dissected him into three parts. There was the polished social Leslie, the worldly image of a successful actor; lurking underneath was the seeker after affection and approval, agelessly responsive, amenable to the point of malleability, and capable of spontaneity and laughter at absurdities; and at base, perhaps taking up most of his being, was the artist, the Leslie that Joe had called serious, a reserved and almost secretive dreamer with first-hand views and stubbornly strong principles.

Eleanor was impressed by part one of Leslie; by part two she was continually surprised, delighted, amused, honoured – she was honoured to be told that better late than never she had introduced high romance into his life; while she revered and was intrigued by, and played the piano for, and picked up any crumbs of wisdom that fell from the table of part three.

The biggest compliment Leslie paid her playing was to say it was 'right'.

He was an appreciative audience, he trusted her artistic judgment on the whole; but he derided fulsome praise and fuss, he considered flowery epithets and intense discussions pretentious, and that pretentiousness was good for nothing. Like Harold Whymper, he used slangy language to bring high-falutin talk down to earth. He would practise and perform miniature demonstrations of his art for her edification as well as his own, just as she did of hers. He must have spoken the last sentence of *Love's Labours Lost*, Don Armado's 'You, that way: we, this way,' fifty times, trying to get it 'right' and to his satisfaction: he said it was 'the best exit in the business'. However, notwithstanding his earthiness, he remarked mysteriously that the secret of the creation of worthwhile 'work' was 'balance'.

He had not gone into that production of *La Dame aux Camélias*, which, in typical theatrical fashion, had 'folded' somewhere out in the provinces. Eleanor had never seen him act on the stage, and often wished aloud that he would accept one of the many offers he told her he was receiving. But his response to such urging was either to shake his head, regarding her with a slightly sorrowful expression, as if sad she was missing the point, or renew the type of warning he had first issued before they committed themselves to their love affair. He said: 'But I'm always working – every moment of every day,' and: 'You don't know how single-minded I can be,' and: 'You won't love me when I start acting and can't do anything else.'

She denied the latter statement, and turned the others into a joke. When he was temporarily silent or solemn she would beg him to set his work aside. And he would comply to the extent of smiling at and kissing her again.

She was convinced after two months of exclusive joy that they could not and would not cause each other alternative emotions: they were best friends, when all was said about love.

She did not pause to concentrate on the future until her mother came to tea.

On an optimistic impulse she had written Poppy Beck a note inviting her round to Joe's flat. The visit began well: middle age and grey hairs, and possibly the pleasure of beholding her beautiful daughter's improved situation, seemed to have a good effect on Poppy. Eleanor was complimented on her flat, clothes, career on the stage, independence; and treated to humorous reminiscences of painful episodes in the past, for instance her stout refusal to be adopted by the Adamsons.

Then Poppy boasted of Winnie's conquests of men, armies of men, and said: 'At least both my daughters have inherited something useful from me.'

Preening herself, and refusing to be restrained by Eleanor's embarrassment, she pursued: 'No, darling, you can't get away from it – aren't you installed so comfortably here because of your charms which I'm a little bit responsible for?'

Eleanor tried to explain the nature of her arrangements with Joe Prince.

'My sweet girl,' Poppy scoffed, 'don't tell me your blue eyes have no influence with the kind gentleman. Anyway, you wouldn't be looking so well if you didn't have a loving friend, whoever he may be.'

Eleanor's reluctance to deny this charge amounted to an affirmative.

'I hope he's nicer to you, he must be nicer to you, than your beastly husband.'

Eleanor felt bound to say: 'He is,' but resisted the temptation to remind her mother of how pleased she had been to hand over her bastard to David.

'Is he going to marry you, sweetie? That's the acid test.'

Eleanor shrugged off the question. It was irrelevant. But she could not forget it; and then realised that Leslie had been and was decidedly vague about future plans.

One evening he presented himself at her front door in dinner jacket and black tie. He apologised for having to go later on to a theatrical awards ceremony and reception at a grand hotel. She helped to remove his blue overcoat, out of a pocket of which fell the gilt-edged white card inviting Mr Leslie Vaughan and Partner.

'Who's your partner?' she inquired.

He replied, obviously put out, that he had been going to take his daughter Patsy, who had cried off at the last minute.

'Take me,' Eleanor said.

Although, after a short argument, he agreed to, he was not himself at supper, neither relaxed nor entertaining, and he communicated varying degrees of anguish while she changed, on the way to the hotel, throughout the sociabilities, especially when he had to introduce Eleanor to people, and driving back to Smith Square.

When the car stopped, and they should have been hurrying up to her flat to make love, she burst into tears and said: 'You're ashamed of me.'

Almost crying too, he attempted to rebut the charge.

'But you are, you've never taken me anywhere, you must hate to be seen with me in public, and you've wrecked our evening, and I can't bear it, and won't be kept in a cage for anyone.'

Explanations followed, they lasted till morning, and predictably satisfied neither party, and sullied their joy in each other, or at any rate destroyed her complacence.

His argument, in a nutshell, referred to the disparity of their ages; he was more than thirty years older than she was, therefore, mainly for her sake, he was not prepared to put their love on any sort of permanent or public footing.

Hers was that he was breaking her heart.

He said: 'What do you think it's been doing to my heart, knowing I was loving you in borrowed time? I'm so sorry for you as well as for me, I shouldn't have let it happen, but how could I resist you? I realised I was too old in one way, I felt I was too old in another, too old to turn down the chance you were offering me to be happy again, happier than I ever have been. Forgive me for wanting to be and having been so happy! And believe that it's my truest love which refuses to expose you to the malice of the world and throw you into a whole sea of troubles! When you're thirty I'll be an old age pensioner. Meanwhile you'd be patronised by my family, and called a gerontophile, and I'd be accused of baby-snatching and mistaken for your father. Then other men would volunteer to provide you with fun and games, and I couldn't compete, I'd be past it. No! You understand everything – understand why and how I've protected and prolonged our love in this idyllic desert island in Westminster!'

She disagreed: 'I'm old enough to take my own decisions. I've had to stand up to the world for as long as I can remember. I thought you understood, that I'd found someone to love and understand me, but I seem to have been wrong. What do you, what did you, expect me to do? You're robbing me of my chance to be happy, you and your cowardly attitude to public opinion, because I won't kowtow to it, and I can't sit here for the rest of my life, rot here waiting for you to pay me a visit. You've made our relations conditional and temporary, and hardly worth going on with, since I'm not accepting your conditions. Why couldn't you — at least — have left things as they were, and allowed the future to take care of itself? Why couldn't you simply be proud of me, to show me off and be seen with me, as I am or I was proud of you? Your intentions may be good, but I see why they say the road to hell is paved with them.'

Finally, miserably, they drew together; and the act of love, obeying its natural laws, aggravated the moods they brought to its performance, turning sweets into bitterness.

Leslie departed in the dawn and returned to Eleanor a few hours later ashen-faced and in an even shakier state.

He confessed that he was starting rehearsals of *Othello* in a couple of days, he had just received notification that the schedule was being advanced. Moreover he had signed on dotted lines and could not break his contract and his word.

'Why should you?' she asked.

The young producer had novel ideas, he replied; the play would be rehearsed for six weeks in the barn of a farmhouse in Yorkshire; and the cast was to work in isolation there, cut off from contact with life as normally lived.

'So now I'm not to see you for six weeks?'

He hung his head.

'Oh go away, go, go, go!'

'I love you, Eleanor.'

'I hate you,' she cried.

Eleanor cried nonstop for one week, and for most of the next three. She ran the hackneyed gamut of emotions of people in her situation; rage against him, rage against herself, remorse, penitence, willingness to forgive and forget, vain longings to swap on any terms what was for what had been, surprise and disappointment that he did not come crawling back to her, more rage because he ignored her, general wretchedness, and so on. She rushed to respond to doorbell and telephone; but it was always the milkman, always the wrong voice. She dared to ring Leslie's house in Green Street: a man told her that his father-in-law was not available for the time being. She stooped to write Leslie an angrily pleading note, but had the residual sense not to post it. She ached for him. She had fulfilled her mother's prophecy, she had discovered she was made for love, and was loveless. She shunned the piano, and cried on the keyboard when she tried to play. She was too restless to read. She had every blessing except one, and not having that one was like a curse. She was reduced to wishing she was dead, and weighed the pros and cons of killing herself.

Myrtle came into her own in these circumstances. She might have been the heroine of another book called, like Sidney's, *The Saving Grace*, written by Eleanor. Her availability at all hours of the day and even of the night, thanks to the telephone, was Eleanor's lifeline. She listened, commiserated, salvaged Eleanor's sinking confidence, put forward reasons for living. She cried with Eleanor, yet was bracing and strengthening.

Sidney too was involved in the turn of events, if in a different way. When Eleanor paid her first visit to Hyde Park Square after Leslie deserted her, she was summoned into Sidney's study on the ground floor and almost excessively sympathised with, kissed, hugged and patted. Her distress distressed him greatly, and reinforced his view, common to ageing artists in particular, that all was far from right with the world, that men were mad and cruel, that selfishness was in the ascendant, and that the beauty in every form which he had worshipped and worked to create was a butterfly for breaking on the vandals' wheel.

His fulminations, although they grated on Eleanor's contrary susceptibilities, had a positive effect. The harder Sidney was on her truant lover, the softer her heart. She recollected that Leslie had claimed and probably believed that he was sacrificing himself for her sake.

Perhaps her qualification of blame was a recuperative signal. But she was rendered uneasy by Sidney's partisan espousal of her cause and other attentions, for instance his letters packed with effusive compliments and depressing predictions, and a couple of unannounced calls at the flat in Smith Square. Her gratitude was shot through with more nostalgia for the innocuous comradeship of their good old days.

A month after her catastrophe she received Leslie's last words on their subject.

On a sheet of paper without an address he had scribbled: 'I'll never get over you. That's why I'm playing Othello. Please don't see my performance. Still convinced you'll be better without me. Good luck – you deserve it – I've used up mine.'

She restrained herself from writing back: she was afraid that in his absence letters posted to Green Street would be opened by his daughter.

Joe Prince persuaded her to have lunch with him, and, when he said he had heard of her troubles from the Beringers and she cried over the first course, he remarked with his quiet certitude: 'Leslie's right – he's been very brave.'

Joe also said that he was not going to apologise for having introduced her to Leslie, because one day she would be glad to have been the close friend of such a superior man.

Over the coffee she asked: 'What am I to do, Joe?'

'Wait for life to tell you,' he advised.

Life's messenger turned out to be Virginia Heims, or rather a telegram from her.

Eleanor had written to Virginia from England to thank her for the offer of accommodation on her Californian property, and a peculiar correspondence ensued. Virginia answered that letter by means of a long chatty telegram which must have cost a regrettable sum of money. Eleanor wrote again, feeling obliged to respond to various questions, and another telegram arrived. Then Eleanor wrote about Leslie and loving him, and soon, too soon, was writing that she – they – it had come to grief.

Virginia's next telegram was imperiously to the point, and ran: 'Your home away from it all awaits you in Santa Barbara stop wire travel plans stop.'

Eleanor discussed the idea with Myrtle.

'Should I go?'

Myrtle's verdict was largely conveyed by means of one of her woman-to-woman looks, explanatory and apologetic.

'I'll mind being without you more than I can say, I'll miss you so much,' she replied. 'And poor Sidney, he'll miss you dreadfully, he's taken a turn for the better since you've been in England, and the combination of your departure and his advancing years will be bound to have a bad effect on him. All the same I think you ought to seize this interesting new opportunity. Your commitment won't be final or inescapable; at your age you do still have time to explore and add to your growing store of experience; in California you won't be troubled by scenes and souvenirs of the past; you won't have to avoid Leslie, or be afraid that you can't avoid him – or David, for that matter; and this Virginia does seem to appreciate you and your playing, she's in a position to help you with your career in music, as you'll undoubtedly help her with your intelligence and culture. Besides, I wouldn't want you to see my darling Sidney growing old and even less like himself. Why not sample the arrangement?'

Eleanor understood that Myrtle was once again rationalising her possessiveness and asserting, by the removal of her friend and rival, her exclusive rights to her husband's affections.

She could not and would not cross Myrtle, who as always had talked encouraging sense.

She rang up Joe and explained things and said: 'I feel I can't clear out of your flat and pocket the money you gave me to live in it.'

'What you definitely can't do is give the money back to me,' he laughed, 'so long as you promise to try to pursue your musical studies in America.'

She bought tickets, wired Virginia, packed and bade goodbyes of different degrees of difficulty to Joe, Dawson, her mother, Myrtle and Sidney, and the staff at Hyde Park Square.

Her goodbye to Sidney was the worst.

She found him in his study, expecting her, wearing one of his lovely pale grey flannel suits, a white shirt, a bowtie and the ribbon of his monocle round his neck; but he was slumped in the visitor's chair on the wrong side of his desk.

He struggled to his feet, courteously smiling, although his lower lip trembled, and took her two hands in his and said: 'This is temporary, isn't it, my dear?'

She hoped so.

Next, he seemed to abandon pretence as he asked her: 'Shall I ever see you again?'

'Of course,' she assured him, but could not stop the tears welling into her eyes.

He embraced her, comforted her, and they both sat down on the day-bed under his shelves of books.

[200]

He squeezed her hand and said in a voice that quavered: 'I know I'm not the best writer — no, don't interrupt — but I've loved the best women, Myrtle and yourself. How many old men have even half that satisfaction?'

'Oh Sidney!'

'If I were the right age, and had not met Myrtle, I would have courted you.'

'Oh thank you.'

'I won't prolong the agony. Remember, you represent a rare species, and you're a vulnerable creature, notwithstanding your youth and vitality. For everyone's sakes, tread carefully now. Are you all right for money?'

'Yes, thank you.'

'Apply to me if you're ever short. Was Myrtle in favour of America?'

'Sort of.'

'Myrtle's devoted to you, but her counsel isn't always objective. Will you remember?'

'Yes.'

'You've made me as happy as you possibly could, dearest Eleanor.'

'And you ...' she choked.

They hugged each other crying, then she fled.

In the flat in Smith Square, the evening before she exited from the scene of her great love for Leslie, she received a telephone call from Willy Hopkins, whom she had warned by letter that she was leaving the country.

He told her Summer Drive was sold and he would be sending half the money to her Californian address. He was vacating the place shortly.

'Well, goodbye, Willy,' she finished up.

'Eleanor,' he said, 'I'd marry you. I always would have, since we were kids, and I'd be pleased to any day.'

She returned: 'My life might be a lot easier if I could. It certainly would have been if I had. Sorry, Willy. Sorry!'

1932 . . .

THE so-called Heims Residence in Santa Barbara had every amenity that money could buy: an elegant Spanish-style exterior, many rooms crammed with valuable pictures and furniture, a numerous resident staff, and, from its windows and terraces, vistas of rolling lawns and the forest trees that screened it from prying eyes and cameras. There were tennis courts, a swimming pool, garages full of cars, almost a village of staff quarters, a high wall surrounding the property, and entrance gates opened and closed by gatekeepers who lived in a pair of lodges; and about two hundred yards from the main house but partially hidden in greenery, beside a stretch of water bordered by weeping willows, stood Pond Cottage, an extensive bungalow with wide verandah, a large white-painted sitting-room with red-tiled floor and white curtains containing a white grand piano, and two bedrooms having their own bathrooms and closets, a kitchen complex, staff quarters etcetera.

The estate was one of several created by Virginia's father, and inherited by his only child. Eddy Heims had been a second generation American, the son of an immigrant from Estonia, had made a fortune in oil, buried his first barren wife and married another in his later seventies, sired his daughter at the age of seventy-nine and died the following year.

Virginia's mother had neglected her, as had Eleanor's. Marie-Lou Heims, widowed and incredibly wealthy, was courted by crooks and wed the worst of the lot, who did her in with drink and drugs and made off with the available Heims money he had not already stolen.

The childhood of the orphan was ruled by lawyers and security guards. Being so rich seemed to have been as bad for her as illegitimacy was for Eleanor, and in one way worse, since her favourite nursemaids, governesses and tutors were often replaced in case they had formed links with kidnappers. For that same reason, and no doubt to keep the various Heims houses aired, Virginia and her entourage were repeatedly uprooted and removed from one to another.

Aged seventeen she came into millions of dollars, at twenty-one she got more, and at twenty-five the rest. Now, in her twenty-eighth year, she had married and divorced three husbands for a price. In the temporary absence of a fourth, she had time for Eleanor, and was pleased to please and be friends with her.

Eleanor was bowled over by Pond Cottage, and by the fat black smiling maid Dolly who lived there and cleaned it and was going to cook and look after her.

'It's too beautiful for me,' she told Virginia, and then: 'I'll have to pay you rent.'

Virginia laughed and replied: 'That might be expensive, and would mean to me approximately what a postage stamp means to you.'

When Eleanor attempted to insist, Virginia cut her short: 'Pond Cottage has been empty for ages – being so close I can't let just anybody have it – but it's yours for your music and for as long as you like – only don't talk about money – I'm bored to death by money.'

Half a dozen times in the next few months Eleanor dined at The Residence alone with Virginia, who once or twice condescended to come to meals at Pond Cottage, or partake of picnics in picturesque spots in the grounds, also telephoned a lot, and quite often walked across and into the white sitting-room without advance warning.

Eleanor had no objection to becoming Virginia's companion, or, not to put too fine a point on it, another member, if a superior one, of her staff. She never forgot to be grateful and soon had additional reasons for gratitude, she grew fond of Virginia, was touched by her generosity and friendly overtures, relieved to discover her friendship was not at all perverse, fascinated to find out what happened in regions rich beyond the dreams of avarice, and paradoxically pitied her.

Although the experience of their respective twenty-seven years of age had been so different, they met on the common ground of feminine sympathy and their romantic aspirations. Mutual admiration came into it, too: Virginia loved Eleanor's playing, and marvelled at her capacity for survival, for having as it were surfaced in such good shape after originating in the lower depths, while Eleanor admired the other's prettiness, her neat features and blond colouring, her dress sense, and her attempt to control her empire and not to yield to the temptations of excess and indiscipline.

Virginia's occupation was that which is imposed by bank balances such as hers: she worked at giving away her money. She had secretaries, accountants, trustees, committees doing nothing but organise the distribution of her largesse. She, or they, received a mailbag full of appeals for help daily; yet in too many cases she herself apparently had to decide whether or not to be helpful. Her privacy was invaded and her peace shattered by people wanting a word with her.

She was responsive to art, and dabbled in writing poetry. She had a sense of humour, American-style, but life for her was not a comedy, and she would beg Eleanor to play the saddest and soupiest pieces. She had some taste but not much discrimination: she was struck by the confident judiciousness Eleanor brought to matters artistic, and by her ability to supply chapter and verse, to draw comparisons and enunciate principles, in support of her judgments.

Virginia's hope, which sprang through the eternity of three marriages and innumerable flirtations, was to be swept up by a tall dark horseman riding out of nowhere and carried on his saddlebow over the horizon and into a future of uninterrupted and irresponsible sweet talk: her ideals might have been made in nearby Hollywood.

Eleanor could see with ominous clarity that Virginia was not winning her war with mammon. The poor heiress, weakened by her own uncertain character, simply had too many dollars ranged against her. She wanted to be loved, to be and to do good, yet was unable to detect or resist a bad cause, or, in personal terms, a sponger, thief, confidence trickster, fortune hunter: owing to the crudity of her amorous fantasies, she was attracted by men desirous of rather than daunted by her riches. Searching for fun, and to get away from her far-flung employees who pestered or robbed her — probably both — she was inclined to rush around the country and the world: thus the disease of persons in her position gained an ever firmer hold — she was more and more spoilt for and by choice. Her only refuge from the complexities of her existence was ill-health, by means of which a bevy of doctors unable to cure her were enriched.

Eleanor's heart sometimes went out to Virginia as to a person in unstoppable decline. Alone together, dining on the moonlit terrace of The Residence, or wherever the latter's picture-postcard mentality pleased, they discussed their lives and loves. Virginia repeatedly said that Eleanor was the one friend who asked her for nothing and was therefore trustworthy, while Eleanor on her side had no secrets to hide from her latest patron.

Yet here again money intruded: their soft voices were half-drowned by the chink of gold.

Virginia revealed that her first husband had had 'her virginity and one point two', and her second had left her 'with a torch to carry worth one point five' — the figures referred to millions of money, and the torch she carried to her unabated weakness for the man who had relieved her of the larger sum. As for her third husband, he had been a 'cheapie'.

Despite her fanciful notions of love, she said: 'My accountants tell me I can afford another ever-loving.'

Her response to the story of Eleanor's marriage to David Ashken was to scold her for failing to get 'a hell of a lot' of alimony out of him. And she consoled Eleanor for having lost Leslie by saying: 'Look on the bright side, he didn't bleed you white.'

She was aware of the danger of money gaining the upper hand, but dismissed the obvious solution to that problem: 'Why should I pauperise myself? What would I be without my cash behind me? Daddy would haunt me if I gave the whole harvest of his labour to a dogs' home. No — never! The root of all evil is not money but the love of it. Well, I hate it. Hating it's going to save my bacon.'

It was wishful thinking that she would be saved, and not true that she hated money. In between spending time with Eleanor and travelling, Virginia threw parties — 'thrashes', she called them. There would be twenty-plus for supper night after night at The Residence, and a reception of sorts for two hundred or more every fortnight or so. Eleanor was usually invited, and introduced to the company as the 'twin sister' of the hostess, and commanded to play to the smaller gatherings. She could not help noticing that Virginia was more excited by a rich guest of honour of either sex than she was even by some reputed Casanova from Hollywood. Her own detachment would be assailed with statistics: 'He's got twenty tons of gold bricks and has to hire the US Army to transfer them from the vaults of one bank to another ... Her jewellery's worth twice as much as the crown jewels of England.' Virginia in fact if not in theory felt more at ease with her peers of fortune, and tried to justify her preference, and simultaneously fish for approval of herself, by persuading her poorer friends that wealth merited their interest and respect at the very least.

As a rule at her thrashes she behaved badly. At the end of them, when sufficient wine had been consumed, she would begin really to enjoy herself – that is, to flirt with any available male. These nocturnal activities redoubled the complications of her days: men came back for more and made trouble when denied it, jealous wives threatened to cite, sue or murder her, newspaper columnists dished the dirt, money passed as usual, hangovers were aggravated by shame, and she felt crushed by the gilt-edged burden of her destiny and retired hurt and to bed.

Then Eleanor would be summoned to Virginia's grandiose bedroom, in which, through the gloom of shutters and blinds excluding daylight, the cheeks glistening with tears and the down-turned mouth of her friend cowering in the draped four-poster became visible. A hot damp hand would reach out for her to hold, and she would have to take issue with repetitive confessions of failure as a daughter, wife and woman, as a landlady, as a philanthropist, and dole out the requisite contradictions.

Perhaps Virginia was mortified in due course to have humbled herself thus. Of all the pills she had recourse to, perhaps one specially hard to swallow was the proven absurdity that she who had everything had had to beg from Eleanor who had nothing. Regrettably she had revealed not only that she was incapable of coping with her enviable life, but also the terror of top people, her panicky attitude to illness and to death, which cannot be bought off.

Perhaps, again, Eleanor incurred displeasure by steering clear of Virginia's more exuberant social impulses. She excused herself from participation in the larger and wilder parties, she drank water, was positively puritanical with men, and always wanting to go to bed early and alone. Virginia was apt to accuse her of being Miss Perfect; and although once upon a time she had insisted on Eleanor practising and raised objections when she did not hear the piano through the open windows of their respective dwellings, now she definitely invaded Pond Cottage in order to interrupt work which she chose to regard as reproaching her idleness.

Whatever had gone wrong between them was not too serious, and righted itself predictably.

Virginia fell in love. She was no longer capricious, tricky, sorry for herself, less friendly. Her beloved was an Argentinian polo-player with an odd combination of names, Emilio Macmurdo. He was a noted ladies' man, actually more possessed by ladies than possessing them, a handsome idiot, although with both his black eyes fixed firmly on the main chance.

Virginia told Eleanor: 'Emilio's a dear, a dear boy, I mean an expensive one who'll cost me dear, but a bargain from some points of view, anyway from mine.'

Suddenly she was planning to accompany Emilio to South America, India, England, and probably to invest in her fourth marriage.

'What will happen to The Residence?' Eleanor inquired.

'The usual thing – mothballed.'

'I'll remove myself from Pond Cottage.'

'Please don't, I'm relying on you to hold the fort, it's yours to use until further notice, or not to use, if it comes to that.'

'You are and have been so extra kind to me.'

'Well – you've seen me through a bad patch – and how can I thank you for all that lovely music?'

Virginia's thanks, or maybe her peace offering, took a typically material form. She overcame Eleanor's scruples in respect of gifts by having a load of her dresses and other wearable garments delivered to Pond Cottage – Eleanor was requested to dispose of whatever was not wanted. And at a last party she introduced Wilbur Bryant.

*

Six months separated Eleanor's farewell to Leslie Vaughan and her goodbye for the foreseeable future to Virginia Heims.

She had recovered so far as was possible from the first parting when the second occurred. New surroundings and distractions, combined with her renewed dedication to the sweetest art, had gradually alleviated the pains of love rejected and missed.

But she had also become aware of a law governing relationships such as hers with Virginia: to wit, that the association of a person with limited means and a person with unlimited means, however kind and well-intentioned the latter person may be, is going to cost the poorer person more money than he or she can afford.

Eleanor found herself augmenting the wages of Dolly, and that she was expected to tip other members of Virginia's staff, lodge-keepers, chauffeurs, gardeners and swimming pool attendants, for essential services rendered. She had paid to have things mended. She had bought smarter clothes than she would have needed in humbler circumstances, she had had her hair done more often, and so on. Entertaining Virginia in the style she was accustomed to upset the economic apple-cart.

As a result Joe Prince's lump sum was spent and her share of the Summer Drive proceeds not what it had been. Admittedly Virginia had relieved her of the anxiety of having to vacate Pond Cottage and rent alternative accommodation. Yet it could be that Virginia's charitable act was once more unintentionally backhanded, for Eleanor had an inkling that lodgings elsewhere would make her money go further.

She was not averse to turning an honest penny. While she pondered the ever more pressing problem of how to earn her living, Edgar Truehand came to call on her in his yellow Rolls. They had corresponded, and he was seizing the opportunity afforded by a business trip to Hollywood to see her again and to speak his piece about her return to the east coast and her career on the stage.

'But I can't think of anything except my music,' she explained, to which he retorted: 'Does music taste good? Is it nourishing?'

Edgar was right and wrong. Music would not feed her body, any more than the theatre would feed her soul.

She did not know what to do, and was poised uncomfortably on the horns of her dilemma, when she shook the hand of a prosperous-looking fair-haired middle-aged man with good teeth and not much else in his appearance to recommend him: Wilbur Bryant.

She had just played the piano for Virginia and her guests, including Wilbur, another pianist, a fairly successful pro, who congratulated her with ungrudging warmth.

Somebody said: 'You two should play together,' and Wilbur queried: 'Why not?' and Eleanor volunteered: 'I'd like that' – and so the duo of Bryant and Carty was launched, and in due course won the favour of the public.

There was never a breath of romance between them. Wilbur had a wife as dull as himself and several dull children. He was more a technician than an artist, but proficient, reliable, no fool and a good businessman. He was perspicacious enough to see that he would do better professionally as more or less the accompanist of a beautiful young woman who could make music like an angel; and he excelled at marketing their services.

He was clever with Eleanor, too, or perhaps he was just as nice to her as he could not help being. He was exceptionally generous with praise, steady under fire from her nervousness, philosophical about minor faults and failings, resistant to adverse criticism, and he reassured her with his optimistic commonsense. More importantly, with his age and authority he was like Harold Whymper and Edgar Truehand in exerting the paternal form of influence and control she and her artistic self required.

Bryant and Carty began by performing once every couple of months; they both had to learn the musical repertory for two pianos, and perfect it by practice. Then they were playing once each month, then once a fortnight, and after that as often as they could and as travel arrangements permitted. The work was demanding and quite satisfying, although Eleanor still hankered after becoming a solo turn; and the money it earned was timely.

She was almost too busy to be sad. She wrote cheerful letters to Myrtle, who responded for Sidney as well as herself: apparently he had not been too well. She also kept up a leisurely correspondence with Joe and Dawson.

In the December after her flight from England she received from Myrtle a description of Leslie Vaughan's Othello. The production had been a success and tickets hard to get, but Myrtle had finally obtained one for a matinee. She admitted to Eleanor that she had never seen the play better done, and that in her opinion Leslie deserved his plaudits. In the early scenes he had conveyed his love for Desdemona with such engaging modesty, as if he could hardly believe that it was reciprocated, with so much gratitude and a yearning sort of pathos, and then his jealousy was terrifying and his appreciation of his folly at the end tragic. The strangest thing, or at any rate a shock for Myrtle, was that the young actress playing his wife bore a slight external resemblance to the woman in real life he was obviously still in love with.

What shocked Eleanor, when she read this letter, was that the passionate girl who had once worshipped Leslie seemed to have died in her. Not long ago she would have run the gamut of feelings over the account of his re-enactment of their love affair on the stage, and his theatrical reaction to the supposed infidelity he himself had almost forced upon her. But she – Leslie's Eleanor – had lived in a different country, city, era; and the tenant of Virginia Heims' cottage in sunny Santa Barbara, USA, and the possibly better half of Bryant and Carty, had neither the ability nor the time to emote for the same reasons or in the same way, if at all.

Did her detachment signify the death of the heart before she was thirty, she wondered. Her appearances on concert platforms dispensing the aphrodisiacal charms of music had lengthened the queue of her suitors; but with difficulty, and thanks to Wilbur's protection and the security gates and guards at The Residence, she had kept them at bay. She had crept into her shell with relief. Yet now she began to worry that she would never again emerge. Was she already spent? Where was the happiness that she had so far only glimpsed momentarily, in passing, as it passed her by? She felt alternately hollow and leaden inside, and an absurd question was apt to jump out on her and prey upon her mind: not when was she going to come back to life, but when was she going to start to live.

As she searched her soul, or for her soul, her friend Virginia, after a year of love in South American fashion, returned to The Residence without her Emilio, who had earned sufficient Heims money in the relevant period to acquire a ranch in Argentina and a virginal bride.

The friends were pleased to see each other again, although Eleanor was soon inundated with invitations to waste time at thrashes at The Residence, and Virginia complained of Eleanor's preoccupation with her new career and accused her not so much of playing the piano as playing hard to get.

One afternoon Virginia, no doubt by way of a protest against Eleanor's exclusive and prolonged sessions of practice, brought across to Pond Cottage and introduced a Dr Hal Bremner and his wife Cissie.

She excused herself for interrupting by saying pettishly: 'None of your black looks, please, Miss Carty, because we're putting a spoke in your musical wheel! These people have news for you worth listening to. Besides, Dr Hal's my gynaecologist, and you never know when he may be needed.'

Virginia with a mischievous glance at Eleanor then departed.

The Bremners' news was to ask Eleanor to play at a reception at their house for a fee four times as big as the one she had received for the two-piano concert at which they had seen and heard her.

She accepted the offer not merely for the money. Hal Bremner was the Friar Tuck type, in his early forties, stoutly strong, red-cheeked and red-lipped, agreeably grinning and exuding bedside manner. Eleanor was not sure about his black eyes that lingered, but could not quite resist his compliments and knowledgeable contributions to the discussion of the programme of the forthcoming recital. Cissie Bremner was older, maybe fifty-four, and a fading beauty. However, notwithstanding her unnaturally blond hair and jarring scarlet lipstick and nail-varnish, she had refined, sympathetic and wistful charm. Eleanor took to her at once, and since the musical reception seemed to be her idea, endorsed and financed by her husband, was delighted to oblige her and simultaneously to have the chance to perform without Wilbur.

Cissie was even more complimentary than Hal – the three of them were immediately on first name terms. And Cissie was more subtle. Whereas he said to Eleanor, 'You must be the one musician in the world who's as beautiful as the music played ... I swear I'll never allow my image of you playing the piano to be desecrated by some ugly horny-handed old thumper,' she said sighing, 'Oh Eleanor, how I wish I were you!'

The Bremners explained that their home was two hours' drive from Santa Barbara, and that their chauffeur would fetch Eleanor at about six o'clock in the evening of the reception, which would start at nine and might not finish until the next morning.

Cissie therefore invited Eleanor to stay the night: 'You'll probably be playing between ten and eleven, and we couldn't bear you to leave without giving our friends a chance to meet and talk to you – which will make it late for our chauffeur to drive you home. Please stay! We'd be so honoured, Eleanor.'

Hal added: 'Staying's part of the deal.'

Eleanor again accepted, and under pressure she took Hal's payment in advance by fat cheque.

In the next few days she refrained from mentioning her engagement to Virginia, who thought she liked art but had no patience with the processes of creating it. Anyway, Virginia forgot the Bremners, she had too many other matters on her mind, and she was travelling somewhere for a week before their reception and a week afterwards.

Eleanor duly arrived at The Bremner Place, so-called, a lonely estate in the hills; was greeted with kisses by Cissie and Hal and shown round the palatial house; tried the grand piano; was escorted to the guest suite in a detached bungalow; changed her clothes; performed and was much applauded, and mingled with the crowd until it finally dispersed.

The time was one-thirty in the morning, and Cissie, having run out of superlatives to apply to Eleanor's contribution to the proceedings, said to her: 'You must be quite exhausted, although you look fresher than any daisy – how do you do it, how could you do it to me? – I know I'm drooping visibly – what about bed? – and would you forgive me if I disappeared and left it to Hal to see you across to the guest house?'

They kissed good night.

Then Eleanor assured Hal that she could find the way on her own.

But he insisted on accompanying her, and out of doors, on the ill-lit path from the terrace to the guest house, he took her hand and tucked her arm under his. And when she tried to stop to say good night to him, instead of letting her go he opened the door with his free hand, almost bundled her through it, laughing, and followed her and shut the door and did not turn on the light.

'What on earth do you think you're doing, Hal?' she asked, laughing too but trembling.

'Relax, keep calm,' he said in that thicker voice she recognised. 'I've been crazy for you ever since I set eyes on you.'

'Don't be so silly. And please let go. Where's the light switch?'

'Where indeed? Listen, why not talk this thing over like sensible adult people?'

'There's nothing to talk over. Don't be ridiculous!'

'I'd say you were the one being ridiculous. You should know the score at your age. Come on.'

He locked the door and pulled her towards the bedroom in the dark.

'Hal, for heaven's sake, are you drunk or something? Let go or I'll scream the place down.'

'Scream away – who'll hear, honey?'

'Cissie will – I'm not keeping any secrets from Cissie – take your hands off, Hal! – I swear I'll show you up – don't do that, don't!'

They were now in her dark bedroom, and Hal, struggling with her, sat down on the double bed dragging her onto his lap.

'Listen, little girl,' he said, 'who do you think's playing Cupid? I've a very obliging wife. She makes sure I get what I want even if she's no longer able to give it to me. Go ahead and call her on the telephone if you like – she'll help me to hold you down.'

Eleanor lost her temper with him, but her nails were kept short for playing the piano, and he was so much the stronger. He laughed as she tired herself out; and the tussle, combined with his obscene, gynaecological and boastful promises, obviously increased his excitement. Her dress was torn, her feelings too were hurt by his telling her he had paid her all that money more for sex than for music and she damn well should have known it, she was also terrified of straining a wrist or dislocating a finger, and at last she could fight no more.

He left her at four-thirty. She cried, bathed, packed, and at five-thirty used the telephone to ask Dolly at Pond Cottage to come and rescue her in a taxi without delay. She then stole out of the guest house and escaped down the drive and waited behind some bushes by the entrance to The Bremner Place until the taxi arrived and she collapsed in Dolly's arms. She directed the taxi to her doctor's house, and after receiving certain medical attentions she retired to bed at home.

No lasting physical damage was done, but psychologically she was stricken. She cancelled concerts with Wilbur, and berated herself for having trusted Hal Bremner, and raged inwardly against Cissie, another woman, who had posed as her friend, and deliberately and cruelly betrayed her. Cissie resembled her mother, or had turned out to be on her mother's side; and, when all was said, Myrtle was another member of the conspiracy to complicate her existence and even wreck it.

Hal Bremner had defiled the act of love into which Leslie Vaughan initiated her, but he was a mere beast, a grinning Hallowe'en mask of a man, and beneath her contempt. Her furious disillusionment was reserved for the woman behind him, and those other female figures in the background who had also played her false.

In her imagination she could visualise the expression that Cissie's countenance would assume if they were ever to meet again, apologetic yet justifying her conduct thus: 'I couldn't help it, I love Hal and want to hang on to him, and at my age one has to compromise – you may blame me now, because you're the top dog or top bitch, but you'll grow old, you'll understand one day, you'll be just as unscrupulous for love's sake, you wait, as I shall to be forgiven – after all we're women, we're born knowing we have to fight for our own with every weapon that comes to hand, we know ourselves and therefore one another, don't we? – and frankly, my dear, what's the fuss about?'

Eleanor had seen that expression on female faces before, and come up against those unspoken arguments.

And her memories of such casuistry, and of attempts to cover a multitude of sins and crimes with appeals to feminine solidarity, were refreshed by Virginia.

The part of the conversation that exacerbated Eleanor's bad feelings, when Virginia returned to The Residence and heard she was not well and eventually visited her in Pond Cottage, ran as follows.

Virginia inquired as she wandered restlessly round the white sitting-room: 'What's wrong with you anyway?'

Eleanor discreetly, and because she realised her friend did not like other people being ill, replied: 'Oh, nothing much – I'm better now.'

'By the way, did you play for the Bremners?'

'Yes.'

'Was that okay?'

'Yes.'

'Hal wasn't a fate worse than death?'

'Is that his reputation?'

Virginia shrugged.

Eleanor said: 'You might have warned me.'

And Virginia looked at her as if to convey the same hard message: 'I'm not responsible for you – haven't you learned the lesson that it's every woman for herself?'

From this exchange Eleanor deduced that she would have to leave Pond Cottage as soon as she could.

Virginia was by accident or design an accessory of Hal Bremner, she had exposed Eleanor to his criminal interest while pretending to do her a favour, and had shown she could not care less about the consequences. Whether or not she had sexual as well as medical and social connections with Hal was beside the point, which was her generally incurable and destructive frivolity. Her money was mostly to blame, and Eleanor pitied her for that: because there was virtually nothing it could not buy, it reduced the value and the importance of virtually everything. Whence the shrug of her shoulders in response to the probability that her friend, her dearest twin, had indeed suffered and was suffering as half-expected to.

Well, Eleanor would take Virginia's implied advice and save herself from sinking by association into the same trivialising quicksands. That it would be difficult for her to reject Pond Cottage, both in relation to her landlady and economically, and that she had neglected to set aside cash against such an eventuality, showed how far she had already sunk without really noticing.

She would do as all the women who had messed up her life had done, and be selfish. She rebelled against her own gullibility and amenability, and resolved to turn over a new leaf of scepticism and egoism. She would somehow establish her freedom as an artist, and her independence – and she wished always to emulate the courage of her childish refusal to be adopted by the Adamsons.

But what she would not do was to think of Summer Drive or of her Auntys, who had been the exceptions that proved the rule of the almost evil influence of her female arbiters, and the memory of whose unalloyed benevolence would weaken her will to be different.

Little by little the rage of recognising the part women had played in her unhappy story centred itself on Myrtle Beringer. Perhaps, as she had loved Myrtle, so she resented and even hated her. She might have recovered from the injustice of her mother if only Myrtle, for jealous and possessive reasons, had not pushed her into the arms of David Ashken. She might have done better if Myrtle had not exiled her for the same reasons to America, and twice over. She had had to earn her living by hook or by crook in a new country, thanks to Myrtle, who had never had to earn hers. At least she would never have been assaulted by Hal Bremner, but for Myrtle.

While Eleanor planned her move out of Pond Cottage, and began to skimp and hoard her fees for concerts, she could not bring herself to answer Myrtle's letters. She would have liked to write to Sidney, but drew the line at causing more of the dissension that had landed her where she was sorry to be. She hardened her heart against Myrtle's epistolary pleas for news and for assurances that she was neither ill nor in trouble.

After four months she was punished for her attitude and for acting out of character.

She received this tiny note from Myrtle: 'Sidney's dead, and the best of me has died with him.'

And she made another mistake.

Her remorse, her grief, her sense of the loss of her most loved and trusted and oldest friend – her wretchedness was interrupted by the arrival of Dawson Douglas, her faithful old Topsy-turvy. He was in California on business, and had been directed to Eleanor's address and to discover how Eleanor fared by Myrtle.

She cried terribly on his shoulder. He comforted her, crinkling his brow and slanting his eyebrows. Then he declared his love for her, that he had loved her for years and years, that he wanted to devote his life to taking care of her, and begged her to marry him.

She answered in the affirmative.

*

Their marriage lasted for two nights and one day. It had been a counsel of despair, and proved hopeless in every respect. Dawson loved Eleanor enough to agree to their immediate divorce after thirty-six hours of it. She was sorry, sorry to have wrecked their friendship, sorry for everything or sorrier.

She wrote to Myrtle, who, writing back by return, dismissed her guilty feelings, her regrets and apologies. Myrtle's friendship had always been distinguished by its undemanding nature, and she saw nothing wrong in Eleanor's previous epistolary neglect, and denied that Sidney had ever been disappointed by her conduct.

Characteristically, again, Myrtle did not dwell upon Sidney's decline and the circumstances of his death; and she neither boasted about their matrimonial successes nor bemoaned her widowhood. Instead, she expressed relief that Eleanor was alive and well, and sympathy in respect of the Dawson business.

'You were not wrong to marry again, nobody's ever wrong to be ready to experiment, and you're quite right to extricate yourself from an untenable position without delay and before it's too late,' Myrtle wrote. 'Dawson's lucky to have been your husband, however briefly. I hope he also realises that, as he's not a sadist, he's lucky to be spared the ordeal of making you repent at leisure and turn against him. Now,' she continued perspicaciously, 'you must put the whole episode behind you, together with the mood that led you to imagine Dawson was worthy to be your partner. You must renew your natural idealism, and remember always to have faith in life. I can vouch for the facts that miracles do occur and happiness does exist.'

Virginia Heims had no such comfort to offer. Death was her most taboo of subjects, and she resented Eleanor's mourning for Sidney, one of those best beloved Beringers of whom she was vaguely jealous or anyway sick of hearing.

Moreover she turned the screw of Eleanor's embarrassment over her change of wifely mind, if not of heart, which was never involved. Virginia treated the marriage to Dawson as a joke, cast unfair aspersions on the husband behind his back but in public, and was delighted to the extent of crowing competitively because Eleanor's second marital adventure had lasted even less long than any of hers.

Their relations had become so tangled that the knot had to be cut somehow, Eleanor realised. She ached to escape from Virginia and her Residence and

Pond Cottage and the stifling effects of glut and obligation and cloudless skies and weather without surprises.

But how could she suddenly switch from thanking to accusing Virginia?

How could she fasten on her benefactor's frail wrists that chain of events, like handcuffs instead of jewelled bangles, beginning with Virginia's either spiteful or careless complicity in the crime of Hal Bremner, a consequence of which was Eleanor's impulse to hit back at all the women who had hurt her, especially Myrtle, although her chosen weapon of silence might do and doubtless had done most damage to Myrtle's better half and her own darling and dying Sidney?

More practically speaking, where was she to go, and how to survive?

The temporary answer to these impossible questions was the monosyllable: work. At the piano she felt she would have been and perhaps was pleasing Sidney. There, beauty rectified error, and healed the wounds of the heart, and supported Myrtle's claim that life in spite of its tragedies and tears was always worth living. Music, with help from Wilbur Bryant, also promised to rescue her financially from her present situation.

She practised and performed duets with Wilbur, and corresponded with Myrtle. The difficulties between herself and Myrtle had been laid to rest with Sidney, and now the loving letters from Hyde Park Square were additionally pleasing in that they contained wishes to welcome her home before too long.

Of course Virginia was bored by the unsociable activities of her resident friend and entertainer, and grumbled and interrupted them. Eleanor for the sake of peace and politeness had to attend numerous thrashes, at one of which she met Sean Duncan.

Sean was a young Scotsman, one of the horde of tourists who, armed with introductions, beat a path to Virginia's various doors. Far from being the stereotyped Scot with red beard and rough manners, he was exquisite, an exception to the aristocratic rule in that he looked like an aristocrat — his father was a lord, according to Virginia. Unfortunately the good impression created by his tall and slim elegance was negated by his insolence.

When Eleanor had responded to his interrogation, explaining who she was, why she was in America, where she lived and so on, he annoyed her by asking: 'Are you Miss Heims' paid companion?' – and by laughing at her denial and walking away from her.

A day or two later Eleanor mentioned Sean and his bad manners to Virginia: 'Who does he think he is?'

Virginia replied: 'He thinks he's going to be god's gift to some poor little rich American girl, I guess. He's short of money, they tell me – his father's only a bad baron living on porridge in the wilds of Scotland.'

A week passed, and Eleanor and Wilbur gave a recital in an obscure Methodist church hall in Los Angeles. After it, Sean Duncan queued up in the artist's room to offer his congratulations.

'I was impressed by your playing of the *Marche Caractéristique*,' he said; and she was impressed in her turn by his knowledge of the title of that piece for four hands by Schubert, which had been an encore neither announced verbally nor listed in the programme.

She was also surprised and gratified that he had bothered to come to her concert, and to be treated with more respect.

At the end of their snatch of conversation he asked relatively humbly: 'Would you ever have dinner with me?'

She replied: 'You can reach me through the private telephone exchange at the Heims Residence.'

He rang the next day, by which time she was sorry to have made herself even telephonically available. She was not drawn to him, and she was afraid of stepping on Virginia's toes.

The persistence with which he pinned her down to a date to dine with him, and his odd mixture of pleading and bullying, put her off still more; and, although she was relieved at least to have ascertained that Virginia had no romantic interest in Sean, she dreaded the involvement of an evening in his company.

It was not too bad. The restaurant he took her to was not so expensive as to compromise, and they talked about music, and he told her virtually the story of his life, which spared her the perennial mortification of having to tell him the story of hers. On the other hand it was not too good. When she refused to go on to a night-club with him, he was instantly and alarmingly petulant. And driving her back to Pond Cottage he flung at her that she was probably in love with somebody else, which she said with equal warmth was none of his business.

He was obviously a contradictory character, or, in Eleanor's more downright opinion, a bit mad. He claimed descent from the Duncan King of Scotland murdered in Shakespeare's *Macbeth*, yet almost simultaneously confessed to having an awful inferiority complex, of being broke, jobless, unloved and lacking confidence. He was at once haughty and cringing. He said his father Lord Duncan of Duncansby was unkind, his mother was only interested in her successive husbands, and that his parents divorced when he was five years old and his holidays from school were spent either miserably in northernmost Scotland or miserably in the sunnier climes which spawned his stepfathers. He cursed his bad luck without consideration of the worse luck of his interlocutor. He was keen on music, he had listened to and learned a lot, and he admired Eleanor's playing; but he objected to her wishing to get to bed early in order to practise effectively the next morning. He was self-centred to a nearly laughable degree, and selfish to boot. Nevertheless, escorting Eleanor into and out of his car he held her hand more like a child than a man: it was as if he were delivering himself into her keeping, or perhaps forcing her to assume a certain responsibility for his uneasy being. As for his reference to love, it was simply cheeky, though again childish, the frustrated outburst beyond the control of a spoilt and overgrown child.

Eleanor resolved not to be, or to feel, threatened by Sean – she would see him no more.

But he had different ideas, and began to sue for her attention, buzz round her, lay siege to her, make a thorough nuisance of himself.

Eleanor was bored, irritated, and above all taken aback by his obduracy. He was four years younger than she was, and looked younger still, nowhere near twenty-six; initially she had thought of him as another impertinent youth, and believed she could brush aside his presumptuous flirting. She discovered she was wrong, and that she felt defeated rather than amused or charmed by his capacity to do and say unexpected things, and get round her resistance to meeting him.

She did not know how to deal with what she had reason to call his grim whimsy. He rang her up, interrupting her work and intruding into her privacy, but before she could protest he would giggle over some titbit of gossip, or want a list of the dates of her concerts, or pass on an item of musicological scholarship, or ask her advice about a job he was applying for or the state of his digestion or, in sudden accents of desperate exasperation, the direction of his life. Provided such communications remained innocuous from her personal point of view, she was bewildered but relieved: she would try to be patient and polite and respond to his unrestrained cries for help, then more than likely would be upset by his interrupting her to demand why did she loathe him, what was the matter with her, who was the man or the woman she loved. And although he was impervious to gentle rebukes and laughed at snubs, if she attacked him too strongly his capitulation was immediate and worse for her than his belligerence.

Once she was driven to say to him on the telephone: 'Leave me alone, I'm fed up with you!' – whereupon she heard a sort of strangulated sob as he rang off; persuaded herself that he would punish her by committing suicide or something; tried for hours to reach him telephonically; and when she at last did so, was enraged by his airy dismissal of the whole affair and his mockery of her concern.

She was nonetheless careful thereafter not to reduce him to the point at which she feared his instability; and of course she loved him no better for imposing upon her, without the shadow of a right, this constraint.

She was also inhibited by his attendance at her concerts. His admiration notwithstanding, he did nothing much but pick holes in her performance. One evening he sat in an empty row of seats near the dais in the concert hall and ostentatiously took notes while Eleanor and Wilbur played. Later, in the artists' room, she reproached him for doing it: 'You're as bad as the critics.' He retorted: 'Well – you weren't good tonight.' After another concert he nagged her for hitting a single wrong note, and she ended by begging him not to come and hear her in future. He said: 'You shouldn't perform in public if you don't want an audience.' Inevitably he then complicated the issue by telling her she was or could be a very fine musician, and that he was merely trying to point out her few rectifiable failings; and complicated it further by being rude to Wilbur, who nicknamed him the Gilded Mosquito.

Meanwhile he found, as Eleanor lost, an ally in Virginia. He may not have taken Virginia's fancy, but he shone at her thrashes, he showed to more advantage in a crowd than in a twosome, she liked his ornamental appearance and his banter, and invited him to The Residence when Eleanor considered herself duty bound to be there. He would then embarrass the latter in different ways: either by following her about like a dog or a husband, or by ignoring her and carrying on nohow with some other woman, or by announcing loudly that she was hard-hearted and beastly to him, or by giving offence to a fellow-guest or a servant. And Virginia sided with him to the extent, for instance, of saying to Eleanor: 'Couldn't you give the poor guy a quarter of a break? After all, it's not too much of a pain to be loved.'

Sean cannot have been quite as poor as Virginia believed: perhaps she was comparing his resources with hers. He was living in a hotel, not hunting for a job seriously, seemed to be always socially available, and joined daytime tennis and pool parties at The Residence. One afternoon Eleanor walked across to the swimming pool according to her custom, ran into or nearly and more accurately swam into Sean, and then noticed that he was even contradictory in a physical sense: his heavy arms and legs did not match his delicate extremities and the refinement of his facial contours.

On another day he displayed the range of his contrariness. Eleanor decided she must entertain Virginia once more and invited her and her house-guests to lunch at Pond Cottage. She duly received a message that seven unnamed people would be coming from The Residence: which was just about the number she had expected. She planned to give them a barbecue picnic under the trees and beside the pond, as on previous successful occasions.

The group that Virginia brought included two US senators with wives, an inevitable financial adviser, and Sean, who entered smirking, as if pleased with himself for having sneaked through Eleanor's defences, also to challenge her to throw him out. The hostess was disconcerted by his presence, and seethed inwardly over his trick of taking advantage of her good manners, and over further proof of Virginia's treachery.

Eleanor and Dolly between them had lit the barbecue, and Eleanor was to cook the food which Dolly had prepared. As soon as she began, having settled her other guests with drinks on prearranged deckchairs and rugs, Sean harassed her with questions, advice and criticism, and when she told him to go away he laughed at her and called her hopeless.

More disasters followed in quick succession. A sudden wild wind got up, causing the barbecue charcoal to flare and singe Eleanor's hand, and scatter sparks and ash in all directions. The food was spoilt, the blue hair of one of the Senators' wives caught fire, Pond Cottage was too full of choking smoke to be a refuge, and Virginia led a general retreat to The Residence.

Then Eleanor realised her hand might be burned badly enough to impair its pianistic movements, and fear took precedence over other emotions. She sought out Dolly in the kitchen of the Cottage and had the burn attended to, and in her sitting-room, where the smoke had dispersed, discovered Sean Duncan lounging on the white sofa.

'What are you doing here?' she demanded.

'Are you all right?' he asked.

'Of course I'm all right. Of course I'm not all right,' she replied, bursting into one of her passions of crying.

Obviously startled and dismayed, he rose to his feet and paced about the room, saying: 'Oh God, I suppose it's my fault – what have I done now? – oh do stop – this is too awful – no luncheon party's worth crying for – do stop, for pity's sake!'

At length she was able to tell him: 'You understand nothing, nothing – I may not be able to play the piano and earn my living – why are you so dense? – and everything was horrible before I asked those idiots to lunch – not Virginia, I don't mean Virginia's an idiot – and you bully me nonstop – and why are you here? – I thought I'd got rid of you – please go – I never want to see you again!'

He said: 'I came back to cope with the barbecue.'

'Oh.'

'Everybody thought your house was going to be burned down with you in it.'

'Oh.'

'You're not fair to me.'

'What's happened to the barbecue?'

'I kicked it into the pond. It was red hot. The gardeners can fish it out. I was trying to save your life.'

'Oh, sorry – but why bother? – because it's no good – you know nothing about me – anyway I'm leaving soon – and I need a handkerchief.'

She delivered this last inconsequential speech from the chair on which she had sat down to cry. As she half-stood, he came across, knelt down beside her, produced his own handkerchief and clumsily attempted to wipe her eyes.

'No,' she said crossly, 'let me do it.'

He looked somewhat squashed, but replied with a touch of dignity: 'You shouldn't curse me for being nice.'

His rebuke summoned her tears, more tears, and she buried her face in his handkerchief while he continued: 'It's a pity you hate me. I care for you more than for any of the girls I've met in America, and I could care more if you were kinder. You say I don't know you. What I do know is that you've had a difficult chequered past, and I've been biting my tongue ever since we met in order not to vex you with awkward questions. I have respected your privacy in fact, however much you may think I've invaded it. And you say you're leaving here. So am I, my father's cracking the whip: can't we be friends for the present? I'm not really a bully. You're so frightfully sensitive that you mistake my teasing for bullying. There there,' he said in a patronising tone, patting the top of her head. 'You have got lovely hair, I must admit. Are you better? Shall I go now?'

'Please.'

'May I come and collect my handkerchief some time?'

She hesitated, sighed and said yes.

Later in the day Virginia rang Eleanor.

They both regretted the fiasco of the lunch, Virginia asked after the burned hand, which was better, and Eleanor ventured to say: 'I wish you'd warned me you were bringing Sean.'

Virginia, either because she did not like to be reproached, or to give as good as she got, or from more considered motives, countered: 'If I had, you would have asked me not to bring him. And I believe you're making a mistake, you shouldn't write him off. There's more to him than meets your eye, he's not just a glamour-boy, he wouldn't pursue you if he was fortune-hunting, and he's always badgering me to get him together with you.'

'Well – I can't think why.'

'For the usual reasons, my dear.'

'Well – all I can say is that I don't love his idea of love.'

Yet as a result of this exchange with Virginia and the preceding scene with Sean himself, Eleanor, when he telephoned the next morning, invited him with a good grace to call in at Pond Cottage.

He arrived at six o'clock. His handkerchief had been washed and ironed, and she returned it with thanks and offered him a drink.

He sank down on the sofa in his lounging fashion and said to her, while she mixed him a martini with gin that was no longer legally prohibited: 'I've had another letter from my father threatening blue murder if I don't pack up and go home immediately. What should I do?'

'Don't ask me.'

She was standing by the table with the bottles and jug of ice on it, and her back was turned to him.

'No, seriously, you're the very person I should ask. Do you want me to stay here in California or disappear?'

She had to laugh at so leading a question, and at his far-fetched notion that she would answer it.

'I do wish you didn't laugh at me – okay, I'll ask you something else – will you marry me?'

She stopped stirring the mixture in the jug.

He added: 'I don't mean at once – and I know you're too clever and talented and beautiful for me – but I would try to appreciate you – could you? Will you?'

She was dumbfounded: they were strangers, she had never talked to him intimately, never vouchsafed him even an encouraging look, never lent credence to the claim of third parties that he loved her, and never imagined loving him.

She swivelled round.

He was still lying back in the sofa, not regarding her fondly, desirously, intently or anxiously.

'Are you teasing me again?'

He averted his head, but not before she saw that his lower lip was trembling.

*

Eleanor had never before seen a man really cry, let alone reduced one to crying. She had thought men did not cry like women, except in books. And she wished she had been allowed to retain her illusions.

But she had to console Sean. She felt guilty for having somehow hurt him so badly that he shed tears. Besides, although his proposal struck her as both silly and alarming, she did feel — she felt she had to feel — grateful for it.

She took hold of the hand with which he was covering his eyes and gave it a comforting squeeze; then he pulled her down on to her knees, and she had to yield her shoulder for him to cry on; then he hugged her and she was too polite not to hug back; and a few one-sided kisses followed. As soon as possible, when he had more or less pulled himself together, she suggested a restorative stroll in the grounds of The Residence, she insisted upon it, and later she cooked eggs and bacon for their supper, after which she packed him off protesting to his hotel.

The pleasures of solitude were shortlived. Sean had been as good or as bad as his word, he had proved his seriousness by harping on the matrimonial theme throughout the evening, and an hour after leaving her he telephoned to resume the pressing of his suit. She silenced him by demanding time in which to ponder his offer in peace; but soon realised that this last show of her strength, because of the reference to pondering, weakened her position.

Not in a very peaceful mood she attempted to dismiss the whole episode. It was absurd: he was younger in years and much younger in experience than she was, what they might live on was a big question-mark, she was not convinced that he loved her, he himself admitted the plain truth that he was ignorant of the opposite sex, and she certainly did not love him. His courtship was another whim, she must be a schoolboyish craze for him, no more; and her recent marriage to and divorce from Dawson Douglas scarcely encouraged a repeat performance.

Two facts emerged on the other side of the argument, and stubbornly refused to go away. Since Sean was not mentally deficient, he must have been aware that he would be regarded as eminently marriageable by hundreds of well-bred well-heeled girls; yet he had picked her — Eleanor — to be his wife despite her lack of material advantages. Secondly, she was afraid she would not be able to keep him at arm's length.

As usual, when in doubt, she wrote to Myrtle.

The good blown towards Eleanor by the ill wind of Sidney's death, and the curtailment of jealousy and injustice, was that she and Myrtle were drawing ever closer by post. Eleanor now committed all she knew of Sean to paper, and requested advice.

Meanwhile, after an intermission of a couple of days, Sean decided unilaterally that Eleanor's time to ponder was up. He renewed his persuasive efforts, and she braced herself to withstand them.

She permitted him to return to Pond Cottage where she could quietly ask why he thought he wanted to marry her.

His answer was reasonable and touching in a depressing sort of way.

He listed her more obvious advantages, then said: 'I don't feel shy with you, your courage makes me brave, and to marry you would be an achievement for a change — you're so remarkable that people would be impressed by your husband — and with you behind me I might succeed at something.'

She suggested that his modesty was false, especially as it was combined with what often looked and sounded like arrogance.

And she inquired: 'Are you fishing for compliments? Are you vain? Oh dear! You've told me what you hope to gain from marrying me, but not one word of my gain on a personal level from marrying you.'

He hummed and hawed and eventually replied: 'You could depend on me.'

In short, he acquitted himself better than she had expected throughout her examination. But between this meeting and their next she realised that she must not subject his feelings, whatever they were, to a type of horse-trading, it was vulgar and unfair, and the more so because she had no intention of marrying the man. She therefore invited him in again to break the news that would place her surely and safely beyond his reach.

She told him she was illegitimate.

He said he had thought as much after discussing her origins with Virginia.

'You mean you proposed to me in spite of it?'

'Yes.'

'Well – you shouldn't have, you can't marry me, I won't let you.'

'What's the difference? Lots of girls don't have fathers, they lost them in the war, or through illness or divorce. I don't see that it matters.'

'Oh but it does, it would in your walk of life, it'd shame me and be a millstone for you – what would your father say, what would you put in those books of reference, how would you explain to your smart friends that I've no pedigree?'

'Why should I explain?' he retorted, unmoved. 'You don't explain, you haven't even to Virginia, who merely put two and two together as I did – no mention of your parents, no family. We could easily cook up a convincing story. I promise to keep your secret. You needn't worry about any of that.'

He impressed her thus with his unconventional order of priorities: by putting love, or at least loyalty, before the shibboleths of society.

As a result she indicated her willingness, if only out of generalised approval and gratitude, to answer the questions about her childhood and youth which he had refrained from asking before. But although he could be curious to the point of inquisitiveness, for instance delving deep into the painful details of her relations with her mother, she was aware not so much of his sympathy as of the difficulty of holding his attention. His whimsicality, and knack of going off at a conversational tangent, worried her. There was definitely no potential marriage of minds between them. And her heart sank under the burden of knowing that she would have to try again to wriggle out of his toils.

During his next visit she pleaded the gap between their ages: which got her nowhere. He was clearly in favour of having a senior partner on whom he could rely and, she suspected, lay blame in times of trouble.

Then she spoke of her previous marriages, the aberration of the second one, which did not incline her towards a third, and the unforgettable horrors of the first, including her illness, her peritonitis and aborted pregnancy, which might have ruined her chances of bearing another child.

He said he would risk it: after all, barrenness could never be insured against, and accidents were always happening to children born and unborn. He did not want to marry her exclusively to breed, and he was not dead set on lengthening the line of the Duncan dynasty. And what about third time lucky, he asked.

Finally, defensively, she broached the subject of music and her dedication to it.

'I love music too,' he returned; 'you can't deny that we have music at least in common.'

She had to try to combine diplomacy and accuracy: 'I know you love it. The difference between us is that it's such a large part of my life. I'm afraid you'd be unpleasantly surprised by the duties that art imposes on artists, and the various obligations artists impose on themselves and others.'

'You could play the piano to your heart's content. I very much like your playing.'

'I know you do, and thank you,' she said. 'But what I'm talking about are the hours of uninterrupted and constructive work one has to put in, which can't be done between too many social engagements and holidays, or after too much fun or too many late hours, or for that matter too much housework and drudgery. It's like being an athlete and keeping in training, permanently in training; and it wouldn't suit a husband hoping for a useful sociable partner.'

He laughed at her and commented: 'Poor little you, condemned to lead such a ghastly existence!'

'I don't want to make your existence equally ghastly, as you call it, because of my vocation.'

He shrugged his shoulders and threw out: 'Fiddlesticks – I'd let you do as you please.'

'I bet,' she said satirically as she failed once more to convince him that she would be a bad and reluctant wife.

She had now run out of reasons proving that his proposal was a mistake, and still not emphatically said no; and the difficulties of saying it had multiplied.

What had emerged from this testing period was that for all his self-centredness he had some intentions and some capability to protect her, and that she was bound by reciprocal honour, and by her nature, to be no less protective. She had to take ever more care not to make him cry. She hesitated to deny him the demonstrations of affection he claimed, which kept him quiet. He would probably ignore her definite matrimonial negative; but in the meanwhile she could not bring herself to inflict it on him.

[229]

At the same time, although she accepted a degree of responsibility for his welfare, and was getting used to and a little fonder of him, she was against matrimony and indeed their further involvement. He had said she could depend on him; yes, she reflected, to make even more of a mess of her life. Yet she was not too fearful of the outcome of their unromantic negotiations. She counted on Myrtle's reply to her letter either to deliver her from the evil of Sean, or to give her the strength to deliver herself; and she prepared him for rejection and ejection into outer darkness by speaking of Myrtle and her wisdom, her wise advice which she – Eleanor – always followed.

The letter that at last arrived ran as follows: 'I think you should marry your suitor, and so does clever Joe Prince. Sorry to be abrupt – I'm cutting corners to give you my views with minimum delay. Your situation may have changed; but I have studied the evidence you supplied, discussed all with Joe, and we are agreed that you are unlikely to do better than to become the Honourable Mrs Sean Duncan, and ultimately Lady D. Moreover I'm certain my darling Sidney – our darling Sidney – would be of the same mind. Here are a few hasty whys and wherefores: S. must be discriminating and charmingly unworldly – he chose you rather than Virginia Heims or any of the wealthy women of the Heims circle; S. has enough intelligence to know that he needs you to prop him up, and enough feeling to cry over the prospect of not winning you; his being younger than you would probably suit your agelessness, and his innocence would enable you to mould him to your own satisfaction; his good looks would be a credit to you, and his name your passport into the society of people with sufficient leisure to acquire refined tastes, who would recognise your superiority and your art. Joe's researches have shown that the Duncan family is far from bankrupt, and he and I are fully agreed that it's high time you had no more money worries. As Sean's wife you would have security and position, the hugely advantageous position in practical terms of a married woman, and you would at last gain the status and find the social level to which your native distinction entitles you. I beg you not to be too critical of his peccadillos. We women are designed to be adaptable. Remember, marriages of convenience have often turned out to be the happiest. I rely on your good sense. But I cannot help being excited. Lovingly ever, Myrtle.'

On the morning Eleanor received, read and re-read this letter she was unable to settle to her normal stint of work, and was therefore more welcoming than usual when Virginia intruded through the open french window into the white sitting-room.

Virginia said: 'I didn't hear your music and wondered if all was well. As a rule I'm lured here by your siren song.'

Eleanor replied: 'I'm not sure how well I am,' and handed over Myrtle's letter after eliciting Virginia's promise to keep it to herself.

She paced the floor while Virginia perused, then burst out in agitated accents: 'It never crossed my mind that Myrtle would be so dogmatic.'

'Any good friend of yours would have to tell you more or less the same thing,' Virginia said.

'But I'm not in love with Sean – I made that clear to Myrtle.'

'Oh – love! Falling in love's so easy, and out of it for that matter. Whether or not you're in love is just a minor detail.'

'I can't marry him all the same, I can't understand him and he doesn't begin to understand me or even try to. Honestly he's not as sensitive or as gentle as you may imagine, judging by his looks.'

'I'm still expecting a happy ending in the last reel.'

'I wish I was.'

'Eleanor, forgive me for saying that I think you take Sean far too seriously. He's provocative, he's the naughty little boy who likes to puncture the balloons at the party, and he's apt to get a bit above himself. He probably picked you out because you don't slap him down. But that's what's required. You shouldn't let him worry you.'

'I feel he hasn't picked me out so much as picked on me.'

'He means better than you give him credit for, and he's offering you quite a lot.'

'You too!' said Eleanor.

Virginia returned: 'Sorry, darling. But frankly what's the alternative?'

For the next two days Eleanor managed to keep Sean out of Pond Cottage, and deliberated indecisively. Then his plaintive telephone calls numbed her scruples and she agreed to a meeting.

She asked him to what she hoped would be a harmless cup of tea.

He arrived and inquired: 'What's the verdict of the oracle?' referring thus to Myrtle and her advice.

Eleanor accused him of having spoken to Virginia, or, by implication, Virginia of having spoken to him.

'Oh,' he said, 'so the oracle has pronounced, and you've discussed her pronouncement with Virginia, who'll tell me the truth.'

Eleanor could have bitten her tongue. She thought angrily: that's why I can't marry you, because you catch me out, because you take a delight in pouncing on my errors and scratching at sore spots, and you degrade my motives.

Aloud she retorted: 'I'll tell you the truth myself, as I always have, but not yet. And if you go and bully Virginia to divulge my secrets, I'll finish with you immediately.'

His schoolboy's witticism at her expense, 'Keep your hair on,' neither mollified her nor contributed much to the resolution of her dilemma.

For another two days she dodged Sean by motoring with Wilbur Bryant up north to Monterey, where they played to the students of a music school and afterwards stayed the night with one of the teachers.

In the car on the way home Eleanor broke a long silence by saying what was uppermost in her mind: 'The Gilded Mosquito wants me to marry him.'

'You have my sympathy,' said Wilbur. 'Or should you have my congratulations and apologies?'

'That's just what I don't know.'

'Is he giving you no peace?'

'His father wants him back in Scotland, and Sean wants me in tow.'

'What does that mean, a draughty castle in the rain?'

'I suppose so – and no more Bryant and Carty.'

'Bryant ought to be okay – I'm getting more solo work nowadays – don't fret about Bryant – it's probably time for me to plough my lonely furrow.'

'Would you rather perform on your own?'

'I'm not saying that – Bryant and Carty have been a good thing which you can't have too much of – but you do as you please, Eleanor.'

'Thank you,' she said, adding under her breath and speaking almost to herself: 'What pleases me is the problem.'

One other conversation with an outsider exerted an influence on Eleanor.

In the morning after her return to Pond Cottage she discovered Dolly crying in the kitchen.

On being asked what was wrong, Dolly answered: 'They say Miss Heims is planning to sell The Residence, she's planning to sell up in Santa Barbara altogether.'

'That can't be true, Dolly. Miss Heims would have told me.'

'I reckon Miss Heims wouldn't tell you till it was all fixed, she wouldn't like to worry you, Miss.'

'What makes you think it's going to happen?'

'Those finance folk have been talking more than they should.'

'If there is any truth in the rumour, I know Miss Heims will take care of every single member of her staff. I'm sure she'd look after you wonderfully well. And I'd do all I could to help you, Dolly − I always would.'

'I believe you, Miss. But I've been crying for you too. Where would you go? Where would you find a beautiful big piano to play on?'

'I've had to fend for myself before, and I would again.'

'You need a nice husband, Miss, you do, and will more than ever when you ain't got Dolly.'

They had to laugh together, and Eleanor observed: 'Nice husbands don't grow on trees.'

'Those are true words, Miss. But Mr Duncan, he's your sort, Miss, he's not like Mr Douglas Dawson or Mr Dawson Douglas, he could be in films. Why don't you marry Mr Duncan, beg pardon for saying so? He's a gentleman.'

'Is he, Dolly? Well − you never know.'

Meanwhile Sean had returned to the charge impatiently.

Eleanor arrived at half a decision: she could not keep him dangling, and being tugged in different directions by his father and his feelings for herself, for very much longer.

She had agreed to dine with him. After dinner, when he drove her back to Pond Cottage, he implored her to allow him to come in. She granted that wish and, later, impulsively and perhaps to complete her researches, his other wishes or whims − she granted all, as the saying goes, barring agreement to let him make an honest woman of her.

Then in the small dark hours, lying alone at last in her bed, too strained to sleep, also kept awake by a sense of finality, she reviewed her situation.

She knew for certain that she would never be in love with Sean: Virginia, saying that she would be or could be, under-estimated her romanticism and over-estimated the appeal of her lover. Therefore she did not want to, nor should she, marry him. Not doing so might mean the end of Pond Cottage for her, homelessness, and, considering the attitude of Wilbur, of Bryant's ambition to sever his connection with Carty, unemployment. She saw farther into the future than Dolly: the probability was that she would not only have to live without a piano, but have to renounce music altogether in the shorter or longer term. Yet she had done it before, and she thought that, although she was no longer in her wide-eyed youth, she had adequate reserves of courage and could somehow do it again. Edgar Truehand would help her to get a job on the stage maybe. She would maintain her proud independence by becoming a shop assistant or a waitress. Or could she hire a piano, get engagements, teach music? Of course she would be ignoring the counsel she had received, flouting the doctrines of self-protection, enlightened self-interest, commonsense and so on. But an individualist and artist such as she was, whether or not she was able to practise her art, must never pay too much attention to the opinions of other people, and she had repeatedly landed in the soup through following her darling Myrtle's directives.

On the other hand now, after the events of the night, and in her heart of hearts, she was becoming convinced that she could not escape. A few hours ago she had had reason to dismiss Sean, she could have banished him from her bed and her life there and then. But his wretchedness had won her sympathy, and his dependence her patience and assistance. She did not have the heart to be as selfish towards him as he was towards her.

Besides, his determination to succeed sapped her will. Where would he not pursue her to? She could not run away from Pond Cottage, or hide from Virginia or from Myrtle, with whose assistance he would track her down. He was as inescapable as fate, and her fate at that, more than likely.

At this point in her cogitations a revolutionary idea struck her. She remembered the question put to her by some would-be seducer, by Hal Bremner in fact: who or what was she saving herself for? She had known the answer to that question, although she might not have been able to put it into words; a combination of the man who had borne her in his arms aboard the Irish ferry, David Copperfield, Sidney Beringer and Leslie Vaughan. He – her ideal – would be utterly devoted to her and faithful, and as sensitive as she was, an artist who would compensate for everything and make her happy for a change and ever after. But none of her lovers had been like that, not even Leslie, she had never found her perfect love in all her years of looking, and it could be that she was wrong, time seemed to prove her wrong, and she had been saving herself for a will-o'-the-wisp, a myth, and more precisely a fallacy of egotism. For she had yearned to be given happiness without any formal commitment on her part to give it. She knew, realistically and not arrogantly, that she was blessed with the knack of making others feel good, or better, women as well as men. Her natural cheerfulness was communicative, her compassion and generosity were involuntary, and her beauty was a benefaction of a kind. Still, she had never expected or prepared herself to transfer a proportion of her potential happiness to the man who loved her, or to renounce any of her aspirations in order to preserve his soul or his sanity. Had that been her error, which she had been granted an opportunity – in the form of Sean Duncan – to rectify? The meaning of his declaration that he would go mad or cut his throat if she abandoned him might be not intolerable blackmail, but her chance to deny her misleading ego, to savour the novel sweets of altruism, and gain the great satisfaction of preventing a catastrophe which would otherwise weigh on her conscience. The material advantages of marrying Sean had not swayed her, and she had tried not to submit to the urgings of third parties. However, to be his salvation might be hers, or at any rate an honourable new response to the Hal Bremners of past and future.

Thus Eleanor rationalised her conquest or his, and regarded it as a victory.

Eight months later in London, at four-forty-five in the encroaching dusk of a wintry Saturday afternoon in November, Eleanor and Sean Duncan were going to tea with Myrtle Beringer.

Outside 7 Hyde Park Square Sean parked his car, got out, crossed the pavement, mounted the front steps in his loose-limbed gangling manner and rang the doorbell without waiting for his wife.

She, having checked her make-up once more, emerged from the car and joined him.

The two of them, standing in their dark overcoats on the top step, did not converse.

Maud opened the door, and at the back of the hall old Cam and even Cook completed a sort of welcoming committee. Maud's nose was bright red and her unaccustomed smile trembled, and Eleanor embraced her not least to stop herself crying and causing her mascara to melt; then she hurried to hug the other two. There were professions of the pleasure of seeing one another again after so long; in the exclamatory confusion Eleanor was called by her Christian name with and without the prefix Miss, also, amidst apologies, laughter and congratulations, Madam; and introductions to Sean were effected, and a belated wedding present of a bouquet of flowers was produced and thanked for.

The three aged ladies, all looking to Eleanor as if they had been sprinkled with icing sugar, were obviously charmed by her husband's handsome appearance and lingering handshakes.

Although Eleanor was loth to cut short his enthusiastic reception, and to seem to be doing so, she felt bound to say to him as she continued to stand with one foot on the stairway: 'I'll go ahead – Myrtle will be wondering what's become of us.'

She hurried up the stairs and into the sitting-room and the outstretched arms of her friend, who, reassuringly, reclined as usual on her sofa and was not changed too much.

They had not met since Eleanor returned from America, and for getting on for three years before that. Myrtle had been widowed in the interval, and Eleanor married, divorced and re-married. The joys of reunion put their tribulations to flight, and would have been more relievedly tearful if Myrtle had not wished to look her best for Sean.

'Where is he?' she asked. 'I'm dying to make his acquaintance.'

'He'll be coming up in a minute. He was chatting to Maud and Co,' Eleanor answered.

'Oh,' Myrtle said in a disappointed tone.

It was not much – smiles resumed their sway – but Eleanor realised she had not been diplomatic, that her answer should have been that Sean was equally keen to make the acquaintance of his hostess – and she kicked herself for having forgotten to tell another loyal lie in his interests – and the incident for all its pettiness added to the strain of having to assume social responsibility for him on this particular afternoon.

He now sauntered into the sitting-room, and after greetings had been exchanged sat in one of the armchairs arranged in a semi-circle facing Myrtle – Eleanor was already seated.

To account for his previous absence he announced: 'I got embroiled with your servants.'

Myrtle's corrective reply was delivered with a winning smile: 'It's strange for me to hear you refer to them as servants. They've been my friends for ever and a day. Anyway,' she proceeded, 'I must say, if you'll forgive me for not having time at my advanced age to beat about the bush, you're quite as good-looking as I was led to expect.'

'Oh,' he laughed, bridling somewhat, 'spare my blushes, please!'

'No – I refuse to spare you just yet – because you've managed to win the hand of one of the most remarkable women of her generation – which is a great achievement. You do know how remarkable, how exceptional, your Eleanor is, don't you?'

'That'd be telling, wouldn't it?' he parried, turning and then directing Myrtle's attention towards his embarrassed wife: 'There, look what you've done, you've gone and made her blush too.'

Myrtle, barely acknowledging his pleasantry, continued to address him: 'I respect you for persuading Eleanor, who has such discernment and sees through everybody, that you qualify to be her lawful wedded husband – and I almost love you for loving her. You've been very clever, you've been very lucky – and the rest is up to you, for I know she'll be a fine dear wife. Naturally you have my best wishes – and it may be a good sign that, sitting together as you are now, you do seem to be well matched in terms of beauty – I'll have to reserve my final judgment about brains.' She laughed a little and concluded: 'I've said my say – thank you for listening to me. Eleanor's a combination of my daughter, sister and best friend, and I entreat you to cherish her as she deserves. Last but not least, your child, which she carries so discreetly that

[237]

I can't notice it – your child's something else for you to be proud of.'

'What a speech,' he commented. 'What an act to follow!'

Myrtle either did not comprehend or did not appreciate his jargon, and sank into silence.

Eleanor came to the rescue, saying how lovely it was to be back in her home from home, and asking Myrtle how she was.

'I thought I was well, but I'm all the better for seeing you. How you are is very much more important.'

'I haven't had any problems because of the baby, not yet at any rate.'

Myrtle said to Sean: 'That's another stroke of luck for you, having a healthy wife.'

'Yes,' he agreed languidly; 'she's as strong as an ox.'

Myrtle asked Eleanor: 'And are you settled in London?'

'Not organised – settled but nowhere near straight – we've only been living in the house for a fortnight.'

Sean interrupted with one of his tangential queries: 'Am I allowed to call you Myrtle?'

'Of course.'

'In that case, Myrtle, may I ask what ails you, and why, according to Eleanor, you lie on that sofa day in and day out?'

His insolent inquisitiveness, amounting to rudeness, made Eleanor squirm; but Myrtle explained levelly that she had a spinal injury and was forced by it to rest.

'You can sit in a chair, though, I mean you're able to?'

'Certainly.'

'Wouldn't the right sort of chair be more restful for you than having to twist to one side and lean your weight on your elbow?'

'No, I don't find it so.'

'Well, my father had a bad back, and what I mainly wanted to tell you was that he consulted an excellent man in Harley Street – I've forgotten his name, but I'll get hold of it – who could put you on your feet again, I'm sure.'

Eleanor now intervened, scolding and pretending to laugh: 'For heaven's sake, Sean, do stop bossing about!'

Myrtle, more crushingly, reasoned with him as if he had been an ignorant boy: 'If you should ever injure yourself – and I hope you don't – you'll discover that one has to cope as best one can. As for excellent men in Harley Street, I've consulted enough to last me a lifetime.'

'Oh – sorry – I was only trying to help,' Sean said, and Maud entered the room with a teatray.

While tea and sandwiches were consumed, Eleanor supplied details of the wedding, the grand reception given by Virginia Heims in her Residence, which was immediately afterwards put up for sale, the honeymoon journey by land and sea to the far north of Scotland, and the newly-weds' sojourn of six months or so with Sean's father at Duncansby House. Sean in less controversial mood volunteered more of the story by explaining that they had been stranded in the back of beyond because his stingy father would not provide any cash until legal and tax matters were settled and reams of documents signed and sealed – the end results of which tedious process were not to be sneezed at, however, since they entitled him to most of the family property, including the mansion in Holland Park, where he and Eleanor had been living in style since they came south two weeks ago.

Eleanor added with either a touch of wifely pride or to show her husband in a better light than he had shown himself: 'Sean worked so hard in Scotland, he slaved away not only for his father and with the lawyers, but applying for a job in London, writing letters and telephoning and badgering people. And he's got just the one he hoped for – he's been earning our daily bread for a week – that's why he couldn't come to tea on any day except this Saturday, his afternoon off.'

Then Sean answered Myrtle's inquiry by saying he was employed in the head office of Bradlock and Joseph, the Anglo-American travel agency, which work would entail quite a bit of globe-trotting.

'Will you like that?' she asked.

'Oh yes. Wouldn't you?'

'I'm not very good at moving my body round the world. I prefer talking and reading.'

Eleanor was amused by this typically eccentric statement, but Sean shrugged his shoulders dismissively.

In a challenging tone of voice he announced: 'I've invited Eleanor's mother to lunch tomorrow.'

'Oh,' Myrtle said. 'You haven't met her yet?'

'No.'

'I wonder what you'll make of her.'

'She's written me delightful letters. I think she sounds quite delightful. You know her, I suppose?'

'Slightly.'

'Does that mean you're as down on her as her daughter is?'

Eleanor edged in: 'It's silly to say I'm down on her. Nobody's down on her.'

But Myrtle took over: 'To tell you the truth, I feel I've better things to think about than Mrs Beck. More to the point, have you found a good cook who'll help you to entertain?'

'Not yet. Eleanor can rustle up something to eat for lunch tomorrow. I'm all too aware that she hates cooking; but she jolly well should be able to produce a bite for her own mother to eat.'

'Her own mother didn't cook for her, and wouldn't have in any circumstances.'

'That's all water under the bridge. And I don't believe in that eye for an eye business. Eleanor's at liberty to loathe her mother, but I refuse to have my mother-in-law treated like dirt.'

'Do stop, Sean!'

Eleanor repeated her previous plea with disciplinary crispness and a flash of her eyes at her husband, who now sniggered and whined ambiguously: 'It just seems inconsiderate to me.'

Myrtle said: 'Yes, I would agree,' fairly obviously transposing his criticism of Eleanor into her criticism of himself.

'Shall I play the piano?' Eleanor suggested in a loud voice, rather as if she were distracting quarrelsome children.

But here again there was trouble. Music or the prospect of it failed to soothe. While Myrtle was saying she had pined to see Eleanor at her piano and to hear Eleanor's inimitable playing, Sean asked: 'Which pieces are you intending to subject us to?' And on being told he hung his head in a gesture of intense boredom, accused the pianist of never learning anything new and of having a pathetically small repertoire, and put this request to Myrtle: 'Would you mind if I looked at your pictures – I can't sit through another performance of Eleanor's old chestnuts?'

Then disruptively, not content with wandering round the room and even moving furniture in order to peer at the pictures on the walls, he winced and drew in his breath when Eleanor played an occasional wrong note, and voiced his disagreement with her interpretation of certain passages.

After five minutes of it she gave up, and, exchanging a meaningful glance with Myrtle, said: 'Some other time ...'

Sean exploited the turn of events teasingly: 'What's the matter, my pet, has your memory let you down, or are you punishing me or sulking? Poor Myrtle! I must apologise on behalf of my wife for giving you such a measly show. And Myrtle, talking of time, you'll also have to forgive me – I hope you were warned that I've a cocktail party to go to – and if I don't rush I shall be late for it. What about these teacups? Shall I carry them downstairs?'

'Thank you, no, it's not necessary.'

'But don't you want to save your friends trouble?'

'No – I believe my friends would prefer my visitors to mind their own business.'

Myrtle laughed in order to soften her snub, and Eleanor's laughter, pitched between exasperation and sympathy, seemed to convey the message: 'Well – you've been asking for it – that'll teach you.'

Sean, looking crestfallen momentarily, said: 'Oh – I see.' He bent down to kiss Eleanor goodbye, and she presented her cheek to be kissed, but he insisted on kissing her lips at some length. When he had finished he grumbled at her: 'I do think you're beastly not to be coming with me to this do. You'll be much missed, and I'll be asked by everybody where you are and what you're up to, and you could and would have helped me a lot.' He turned to Myrtle. 'Goodbye – I get a feeling of not having given satisfaction here – don't worry, I'm getting used to it since marrying your pernickety friend – but please persuade her not to henpeck me for doing badly – and thanks for the tea and for your advice about minding my business.'

He departed, leaving the sitting-room door open.

[241]

The two women sat in shocked silence for a minute.

Eleanor went to close the door and Myrtle asked her: 'Should you be accompanying him to this party?'

'Certainly not – it's in some South American embassy – I'd know no one and no one would notice whether or not I'm there – and Sean would desert me as soon as we set foot in the place – and I'd be too miserable to be helpful – no – he loves to flutter round any lit candle – it's one of the differences between us.'

'But I hope your remaining with me won't cause you difficulty at home.'

'Well – I've looked forward to being with you for so long that I'm quite prepared to pay the price of difficulties – still, there won't be any, I promise – Sean lives for the moment.'

'I'm glad – I could never tell you how glad I am to see my dearest girl.'

'Nor could I tell you how glad I am.'

A pause ensued, a silence, during which Eleanor and Myrtle communi⁄cated and perhaps shared their thoughts by means of their eyes.

Eventually Eleanor said: 'I'm mortified.'

'And I'm afraid I made matters worse by being sharp,' Myrtle confessed.

'He was impossible – he's jealous of you – impossible and irrepressible – but he showed you his absolutely worst side.'

Eleanor did not add that Sean was upset to have received no wedding present from Myrtle, and that he resented having to spend a weekend in town to be introduced to her when he might have been staying with representatives of high society in a rich country house. His deliberately boorish behaviour at Hyde Park Square, and his invitation to Poppy Beck, were his forms of revenge upon the agent of his discontent, who put Myrtle first.

Eleanor resumed: 'But we haven't talked about Sidney – and I've thought of him so much, so often, especially downstairs in the hall outside his study – you will talk to me about him, won't you, when you feel you can and you wish to?'

'Yes, my dear, thank you – one day soon – but only to you. Meanwhile I'm afraid of something else – that I gave you bad advice.'

'Oh no, Myrtle – you weren't alone in advising me to marry Sean – everybody advised it – and rightly, no doubt – I can't and mustn't complain – think of what he's done for me – I've got in⁄laws and relations and a circle of acquaintances with titles and pots of money, and a marriage settlement and a great big house and I'm loved and envied.'

'Will you be able to settle for it, I wonder.'

'Three marriages are enough — besides, in many respects, it is third time lucky for me — I'm not wriggling out of this one — if Sean should ever want to get rid of me, that would be a different matter — but he won't.'

'I hope he doesn't bully you.'

'Oh he tries to — he accuses me of nagging because I tell him he nags — he's like a schoolboy whose best repartee is "Same to you" — but in fact, behind all that insolence and bravado, he has no confidence and not too much power to do damage.'

'You mustn't under-estimate the strength of the weak.'

'No indeed — he never tires of exerting that strength in order to gain some sort of ascendancy over me — being his wife often seems like being his adversary — yet at the end of the day I can more or less control him — and will for as long as I'm emotionally independent.'

'And your health holds out.'

'Yes. If I were to weaken, he'd trample on me. Darling Myrtle, you're the only person in the whole world to whom I can tell the truth. And what a luxury it is, not having to trim or be tactful! But the truth is that Sean's better than his behaviour today and than I've made out. He's unconventional as well as conventional, he didn't have to marry a nobody; he won't let his snobbish father and friends turn their noses up at me; he nags everybody to be as efficient as he is, he'll probably do well in his work; he doesn't bother me in the way that David Ashken did, on the contrary, or bore me in Dawson's way; and he has charitable intentions, and is particularly nice to strangers. His intelligence is quick if not deep — and who am I to say that he's undiscriminating and lacks judgment? Best of all, he allows me and I believe will allow me a certain amount of freedom within my gilded cage.'

'I don't think he and I will ever get on.'

'No. I dreaded bringing him here because I knew it. He doesn't begin to be an artist. Although he says he loves music, and is more cultivated musically than me, he has no comprehension of the poetry or power of the musical or any other art. No — you two are oil and water — and I won't mix you up again.'

'I was so keen to meet him, I insisted on meeting him, I'm sorry.'

'Don't be – I would have had to introduce him to you sooner or later – and now you've seen for yourself, and will understand and help me to solve the problems he poses. But remember, what you've seen is no more than one aspect of my destiny.'

'Are you unhappy, Eleanor?'

'Considering how I've already held forth, darling Myrtle, you may not have been quite as wise as usual to ask me that question.'

'Tell me nonetheless.'

'In these last months in Scotland I've had less to do, I've been under less pressure to work and earn money, than ever before in my life. Sean was busy with his father, he left me alone, I could stop and think for a change. To say I repented at leisure wouldn't be accurate, because for once I didn't marry in haste; but – putting the truth before loyalty – and please remember I'm speaking personally and then forget what I'm saying – I found I had everything that doesn't matter, and almost nothing that does. You see, I finally married Sean more for his sake than mine, because he persuaded me or I persuaded myself that he would be a lost cause without my support. Of course I also hoped, or imagined, that he'd develop, or, as I think you suggested, that I'd mould him, into the sort of person whose wife I wanted to be, someone I could love, or at any rate talk to. Yes – well – I tumbled into a booby trap, perhaps waiting to catch women like me especially, reserved for soft hearts and soft heads, for optimism or recklessness, and, I regret to say, for the vanity of imagining one's indispensable. People, adult people, remain pretty much the same, they don't develop and actually can't be moulded, unless or until they fall in love, or, maybe, they're fallen in love with; and how many are capable of loving like that, or worthy of being loved? I discovered that I wasn't and never would be able to love Sean so as to make him different or to make any difference, and that he only loves me enough to lean on me in every sense, not to learn from or alter for. I mustn't grumble – I've no excuse for getting into this latest scrape – and I'm not even depressed any more – because I do believe mistakes are meant to teach one something – and goodness knows I've been wrong so often that I ought to be a scholar by now! My answer's no, darling Myrtle, a long-winded negative – I'm neither unhappy nor happy; but I hope I

[244]

have hung on to my integrity, and can hang on to it in future by not compromising and not telling or living lies; and I still count on having my portion of happiness, or on getting my chance to have it, on taking my chance and thus perhaps becoming a better, more useful person.'

'Could your baby be that chance?'

'I don't know. Sidney once said to me that never knowing is a reason for staying alive. He said the trouble with suicides is that they're know-alls – they think they know that life has nothing else to offer them. He was so clever and constructive! Not to be having a baby would have been an extra worry in my situation, and not to have had a baby, and a boy at that, will be worse. If all goes well, it – or rather he – may make me exclusively happy. But I'm not in principle maternal. The love I have to give isn't or is no longer blind. We'll both have to see, my child and I. No – the chance I'd seize, although I mean to stand by Sean as he's stood by me, is the one that everybody's supposed to get once, and every single lonely person's waiting for.'

'What would Sean have to say about sharing you?'

'He'd be relieved. But I'm not planning to commit adultery. I'm merely aware of not being immune from love. Marriage hasn't stopped me searching for my other half, who would complete me, and compensate for the difficulties men have caused me from my father onwards. In America and then in Scotland I was needlessly afraid of the death of the heart.'

'A heart like yours doesn't die until, perhaps, it ceases to beat. And I can tell you now that my similar fears were premature, my heart hasn't died after all, even though it belongs to Sidney, who's dead at least and possibly at most in a medical sense.'

'Oh Myrtle, how can I thank you for having faith in me and in life? Your faith reinforces mine. I don't want to hurt Sean or be selfish or behave badly or commit any crime. Such awful things have happened and are happening nowadays, I mean wars and cruel political things – and people are being persecuted, the people of our race yet again – and there's probably worse to follow. I don't want to add by one iota to the horrors or the suffering, or to seem to be ignoring them by dreaming of art and love. But it would be wrong for me to pretend to be what I'm not, and two wrongs certainly wouldn't be right. May I be egoistic for a moment more? I regret nothing, I'm not entitled to, but,

[245]

objectively speaking, I can say to you that my life to date would no doubt have been simpler if I'd had a father, and no interest in music, and a plainer face. As it is or was, the consequences have been too many misunderstood men who misunderstood me, and too little music, and less money, and the inflexibility, the resistance to settling for any old job, for instance, which a vocation does impose. Everything seemed to come between me and my music, men got in the way of it by accident or usually on purpose, then music's reproached me for my silence as they've reproached me for my songs, and I've been left feeling guilty for not having served my talent better. Three months ago I decided I couldn't go on. Don't look anxious and sad, darling – you don't need to. For a few days only I was so ashamed of the muddles I've made and the waste of my life, whatever that amounts to – I was unbearably ashamed, and so appalled to think of the years ahead, the years and years of the mixture as before – that I longed to bury my head and put a stop to the repetitions of my history. Don't cry, Myrtle – the story doesn't end there – it begins – because I reversed my decision, I passed that turning-point and realised how much I had not known and didn't know, and became pregnant, and here I am. Phoenixes are stale buns – but my past did look to me like ashes and my future ditto – forgive the mixed metaphors. What happened, thanks to something not happening – and not happening thanks to something else, to three stars always shining in the sky, though that's another story – was more than recovering sanity and vitality and getting my confidence back, more than growing up and all the other hackneyed descriptions – it was a sort of conversion to your religion of believing in miracles. Being Sean's wife and going to be the mother of his child are really sub-plots – which is not to say, which is very far from saying, I promise you, that I don't care for one and won't care for the other. Yet the end of my autobiography, and its main theme and message, is that I shall play the piano for better or worse, by hook or by crook, in spite of Sean and notwithstanding motherhood, and that I believe in the possibility of the miracle of meeting my Sidney, of loving and being loved by a man without reserve or reservations, and in our happiness.'